Dee Williams was born and brought up in Rotherhithe in East London where her father worked as a stevedore in Surrey Docks. Dee left school at fourteen, met her husband at sixteen and was married at twenty. After living abroad for some years, Dee and her husband moved to Hampshire, close to the rest of her family. She is the author of ten previous hugely popular sagas set in Rotherhithe.

Also by Dee Williams

Carrie of Culver Road
Polly of Penn's Place
Annie of Albert Mews
Hannah of Hope Street
Sally of Sefton Grove
Ellie of Elmleigh Square
Maggie's Market
Katie's Kitchen
Wishes and Tears
Sorrows and Smiles

Forgive
and
Forget

Dee Williams

headline

First published in 2001
by HEADLINE BOOK PUBLISHING

First published in paperback in 2001
by HEADLINE BOOK PUBLISHING

10 9 8 7 6 5 4

ISBN 0 7472 6450 3

Typeset by Letterpart Ltd
Reigate, Surrey

Printed and bound in Great Britain by
Clays Ltd, St Ives plc.

HEADLINE BOOK PUBLISHING
A division of Hodder Headline
338 Euston Road
London NW1 3BH

www.headline.co.uk
www.hodderheadline.com

This is for Sue, with a big thank you for the wonderful cake she made us last year.

Chapter 1

Ruth Bentley sat staring into space. She shuddered. Although it was the end of June and the weather was warm, air-raid shelters always felt damp and smelt musty.

Her mind skittered about as she sat in the underground shelter close to the church with the vicar, her sister, Joyce, and her brother-in-law, Frank. She was miserable and tired. She wanted to shut out the present and the past – and what about the future? Alan, who was God only knew where, and her girls, miles away, did they have one? Her mother didn't, not now. Ruth raised her eyes. If there was a God above why couldn't He let them bury her mother in peace? And please, please take care of my family, they *must* have a future, after they had endured so much . . .

'It's all got to end one day,' said Joyce nervously. 'Especially now they've landed in France.'

At twenty-five Joyce was seven years younger than Ruth. Their parents had had no other children. They were so different in ways and looks. Joyce had a neat little black hat sitting on her bleached hair. A spotted veil covered her immaculately made-up face, but tears had made her mascara run like dirty streaks down her cheeks. She was slim

1

and always looked well dressed. Today she was wearing a smart black two-piece. Ruth, who was also slim, looked down at the clothes she was wearing. They weren't her own. Her friend Lucy had lent her the black skirt, white blouse and black hat. All Ruth possessed was her underwear, a pair of black trousers, the short-sleeved jumper and the serviceable shoes she wore to work. Everything else, including her new high heels, had been destroyed, gone for ever. Although people had been kind, she felt so dowdy and unhappy and, even with her sister near, so alone.

Ruth looked about her at this sad little scene. What did Joyce really know about what she had been through? Joyce had been evacuated, away from it all, sheltered in a lovely house in the country since the early days of the war. She hadn't lost her home yet again.

Sitting opposite Ruth, on the hard wooden slatted seats that ran all along the shelter walls, Joyce jiggled Bobbie, her year-old baby son, up and down while making soothing noises in his ears.

He smiled at his auntie and put out his arms. Ruth leaned forward and took the small chubby hand. The dimples in the back of his hand reminded her of when her own daughters were babies. Her thoughts went to their warm, sweet smell after a bath, and how she used to nuzzle her head into them to savour it. She choked back a sob. All the photos she'd had of them when they were babies had gone. Her wedding photos too. She wanted to put her head back, but knew the sides of the shelter were cold and damp. She closed her eyes and tried to remember Alan's smiling, handsome face. She knew from his letters he was abroad. At the cinema she eagerly watched the newsreels, hoping that one day she would get a glimpse of him. She was suddenly aware the conversation had been continuing around her.

'Now we've got 'em running, it won't be long 'fore it's all over,' said Frank.

Everybody had been elated when they heard about the D-Day landings, but that hadn't stopped Hitler sending over more bombers and now there was this new menace: V1s.

Ruth looked at her brother-in-law who was sitting next to Joyce. He gave her a slight nod and a wink and her nerves went taut instantly. She wanted to scream at him. Somehow he'd managed to stay out of the thick of the war. He said he was exempt because of his ears, but as far as Ruth could see there wasn't much wrong with him. True, he was an ARP warden – in charge of his post, in fact – but he should be fighting like her Alan. They had had some bombing round Sutton where Frank and Joyce lived, but nothing like they'd had here in London. Ruth knew he had been in London when they wanted help during the heavy raids, but she was never quite sure if it was to help others or himself. Buying and selling had been his business before the war, and it didn't look like he had stopped.

She didn't really dislike Frank, he was good to Joyce and the children and was great fun at parties, but she wanted everyone to go and fight the Germans and help to get this damn war over.

The vicar gave Ruth a slight smile. He looked tired. Like most people she met, he had that pale sallow look from spending so much time in air-raid shelters.

Then Ruth became angry with herself. She knew she

shouldn't be hard on her sister; after all, Joyce had lost her mother too, but she was angry, so very angry, with the war, Hitler and everybody who had helped kill her mother and put her father in hospital. Every day since she left the clothes shop where she had been employed and had joined the Civil Defence she had tried to harden herself against some of the horrible things she had seen. Old couples who had died in each other's arms. Crying children, who had been clinging to their dead mothers, whom she had to drag away. Although these had upset her, nothing affected her as much as the sight of her mum and dad lying in the overcrowded hospital. She knew by just looking at her mother's terrible injuries that she wouldn't last the night. Ruth had sat holding her hand till the end.

She was suddenly brought back to the present by a quick intake of breath from everybody. A silence fell over the small gathering as they strained their ears. Ruth knew the difference between the sound of the engines of the German and British planes. But it was a new menace that had taken their mother, their home and everything they had. It had even interrupted the service at the graveside. She wanted to yell out: Go away. Leave us alone. Slowly a tear trickled down her cheek. She wanted to run away. She wanted to leave all this death and destruction that had been going on round her day after day and year after year.

In the air-raid shelter, along with Joyce, Frank, their baby and the vicar, were two old men, the grave-diggers. They sat nonchalantly puffing away on their hand-rolled cigarettes. Ruth knew by their lack of expression that they had been through this scenario many times before.

All eyes were raised to the roof of the shelter when they

heard the sputtering engine right above them. Ruth gave up a silent prayer and hoped it would pass over. In many ways it was wicked to pray for someone else to be killed, but she'd had enough of death.

The engine cut out and they threw themselves to the ground. Ruth began mentally to count slowly. It was a habit people had got into. The number you reached before the explosion was supposed to tell you how many miles away the bomb had fallen.

Joyce began crying; her scarlet lips trembled as she held her baby close. Frank nervously wiped his forehead with a white handkerchief. It was spotless. Ruth surmised that, with Joyce away, his mother had been doing his washing. She couldn't see him standing over a scrubbing board. Her own mother had never really taken to Frank. She always reckoned he had shifty eyes and was only mutt and jeff when it suited him. Amid all this drama, Ruth wanted to smile. Who knows, perhaps her mother had been right. Why did these strange thoughts always come into your mind in a crisis?

The explosion was a short distance away, but the shock waves still made the ground heave. They sat back up and brushed themselves down because of the fall of dust that always accompanied a falling bomb, or, in this case, a doodlebug.

'I'm frightened,' said Joyce.

'I know,' said Frank, putting his arm round Joyce's shaking shoulders.

Ruth took off her borrowed hat and pushed her short dark curly hair back from her face. This was a familiar scene. She had lived with this for four years.

'Don't worry, love,' said Frank, patting his wife's hand. 'You'll soon be back with Alice.'

'Frank!' Joyce's face was full of fear. 'What if anything happens to us? She'll have no one.' She began sobbing, making Bobbie cry.

'Nothing's going to happen to us, and you'll be back home as soon as we can get away.'

Alice was their four-year-old daughter and Joyce had left her with Mrs Cotton, the woman she and the children had been billeted with. Joyce's kids were under the age of five and the government said they were to be moved from the danger zone. Ruth wasn't sure if Sutton had been considered a danger zone, but, somehow, Joyce had managed to get herself evacuated after Alice was born. Mr and Mrs Cotton were farmers near a small village in Sussex. They had a very large house and Joyce had a nice self-contained flat there.

If only Ruth could get away. But how could she with their injured father in hospital? And her job. What about her girls, though, if anything happened to her? They were safe in Wales, but how would they know if . . . Ruth let her tears fall.

'This is going to upset the girls, and Alan, losing Mum and your home again,' said Joyce, as if reading her thoughts. 'How will he and Shirley and Kay find out where you live now?'

'I don't know about Alan. I've not heard from him for a while.' Ruth gave them a faint smile. 'But that's the way it goes, then I get a few letters all together. But he's never been much of a letter-writer.'

'You still reckon he's in Italy?' asked Frank.

Ruth nodded.

'Been pretty bad over there.'

Joyce nudged her husband.

Frank looked embarrassed. 'But don't worry. Alan's a survivor.'

'I have written to him and the girls. I've told the post office to send my letters to Lucy; she's going to let me stay there till I get something sorted.'

'The girls are going to miss Mum.'

'I don't know. They haven't seen her for years. They lead very different lives now.'

'You ought to try and get to see them,' said Frank.

'I'd like to. It's been a long while, nearly a year. I expect they've grown.'

'Well, at least you know they are being looked after all right,' said Joyce. 'You hear terrible stories about what's happened to some evacuees.'

'Do they ever ask to come back?' Frank asked.

'No, not now. When they came home during the so-called silent war it was all right, but after that night of the big blitz on the docks, they couldn't wait to get away. Nor could I wait to get them on that train again.'

'That was a terrible night,' said Frank.

'The first of many,' said Ruth. 'At least I wasn't here when they tried to set London alight.'

'December 1940, just after Christmas as well. All those incendiaries. That was a bloody awful night.' Frank, realizing what he had said, quickly looked across at the vicar. But he had his eyes closed and appeared to be nodding off.

'Ruth, if there's anything I can do to help . . .'

'I'll let you know, Joyce. That bag of clothes and those

7

blankets will do fine to start with.'

'Good job we're still the same size. I've put a pair of nylons in the bag. As soon as you get sorted I'll let you have some cooking utensils. You know you could always go and stay with Frank at our house. There's plenty of room.'

'Thanks. But Sutton's a fair way from here and, what with all the diversions, and the buses and trains all over the place after a raid, I wouldn't be able to get to see Dad so much. 'Sides, I've still got to go to work every day.'

'I'm glad they let me in to see him,' said Joyce.

'I think the strict rules about visiting times have had to go by the board. We have to go in when we can.'

'But he was lying so still – it was terrible.' Joyce dabbed at her eyes, making more dark smudges round her eyes. 'D'you think he'll get better?' she asked her sister.

'I don't know. He might feel better when his leg, or I should say the stump, starts to heal, but I wouldn't like to say. It's early days yet. I'm worried about what other damage he's got. His breathing's terrible, and I don't know how he'll feel when he finds out about Mum.'

'Will they send him out of London?' asked Frank.

'I don't know,' said Ruth. 'We'll have to wait and see.'

As the sound of the all clear filled the shelter Ruth could almost hear everybody breathing a sigh of relief. The two old men shuffled to their feet.

'Shall we proceed?' said the vicar.

The sorry group made their way across the graveyard.

Ruth looked down at her mother's coffin. She was aware of the vicar's voice droning on, but she wasn't paying attention. She wanted her girls by her side. She wanted Alan. She wanted to lie in his arms. She wanted him making love to her. She wanted to feel like a woman again.

Joyce nudged her arm and put some wet sticky earth in her hand. Joyce threw hers on to her mother's coffin and Ruth did the same.

The vicar shook her hand. 'God bless you and good luck, my dear.'

'Thanks.' She raised her eyes to heaven. She needed all the luck and blessings He could send her.

'Come on Ruth,' said Joyce. 'Let's be off.'

Ruth let Frank take her arm and lead her out of the cemetery.

'We'll pop into that pub on the corner for a nice drop of whisky. It'll do us all good.'

'What about me and Bobbie?' asked Joyce as she tripped across the damp grass in her black suede high heels.

'I don't reckon the landlord will mind us taking him in – probably be glad of the custom, that's if he's got any drink in the place. Mind you, it might be watered down. With all these shortages it wouldn't be the first pub not to have any beer.'

Although it was warm Ruth couldn't help shivering.

'It's probably delayed shock,' said Frank.

'You'd think I'd be used to it be now, wouldn't you?'

'I don't think we'll ever get used to it,' said Frank. 'Come on, let's get a drink inside us.'

Ruth would have happily settled for a cup of tea, but she was so weary that she just let Frank take charge.

The landlord didn't mind Joyce bringing Bobbie inside, as they were the only ones in the pub. Frank ordered three whiskies. The landlord shook his head and looked about him.

'Er, I'm sorry, but we don't have any whisky.'

'Look, mate, we've just come from across the road; these two have just buried their mother.' Frank pointed to Ruth and Joyce who were sitting close by. 'Surely you can find them a small one?' He put a ten-shilling note on the counter.

The landlord moved away from behind the bar and returned almost at once with a bottle held down low. 'Can't let anyone see it. Usually save it for me regulars, but with the way things are going I won't have any left soon.'

'What, whisky?'

'No, regulars.'

'Pour yourself one, mate.'

The landlord smiled. 'Thanks a lot.'

Frank put the three glasses on the table. 'Get this down quick. Reckon I can get him to part with another.'

'This is enough for me,' said Ruth. 'I'm on duty tonight.'

'Surely you can stay at home for one night?' said Joyce.

'What home? Oh, Lucy's all right, but sitting in the shelter with her and her mum ain't the best place to be. 'Sides, I feel I'm doing something worthwhile when I'm on duty.'

'Now promise me you'll come down as soon as you get a couple of days off.' But without waiting for a reply Joyce looked nervously at her watch. 'I don't like to be a killjoy, but I'd like to get away as soon as we can, Frank.'

'Certainly, love. Are you sure you won't come with us, Ruth?'

She shook her head.

'Can we give you a lift back to Lucy's?'

'Thanks, Frank, that'll be a help. Gawd only knows what

the buses are like, or where they finish up. Some times the diversions take them miles off their routes.'

Outside the pub Frank held the door of his car open.

'How do you still manage to get petrol for your private use?' asked Ruth.

He touched the side of his nose. 'It don't pay to ask questions like that. Remember, careless talk costs lives, or in my case it could cost a heavy fine or even prison.' He laughed. 'I do get an allowance, remember.'

Joyce sat next to him in the front passenger seat with Bobbie on her lap. 'I keep telling him, that's where he'll finish up, in prison. All this wheeling and dealing he does.'

'You can't grumble. You've always got nice clothes and the odd pair of nylons, when I can get hold of 'em. And living on the farm, you get more than enough to eat. I can tell you, things have really improved since the Yanks came over. They're good blokes and, well, we've all got to do our bit to make them feel at home. Now don't you go worrying your pretty little head about me. I can spot trouble a mile off.' He looked over his shoulder. 'Don't forget, Ruth, I can get hold of most things, so just drop me a line if there's anything you're short of.'

'Thanks, Frank, but at this moment I'm short of everything till I can find somewhere to live. Mind you, that shouldn't be too difficult with all the empty houses. It's just finding one that's habitable. I'm waiting for the nine pounds they hand out to help you get started again.'

'Nine quid? Blimey, is that all?' said Frank.

'It's all we got the last time. Good job Dad was handy and could make it liveable. And we got clothes from the WVS.'

'I can get hold of plenty of second-hand furniture, so let me know what you want.'

'I'll do that.'

'I do feel awful,' said Joyce. 'You've got nothing and I've got it all.'

'Make the most of it, Joyce. We never know what's round the corner.'

'That's true,' her sister replied sadly.

Chapter 2

Ruth pushed open the front door to her friend's house and called out Lucy's name. They had long since given up locking doors, as most nights front doors were blown open and the locks broken. 'Anybody home?' she faltered.

There was always that hesitation when you walked in, especially if there had been a raid. Lucy was a clippie on the buses and should be home as her shift finished at two, but since Ruth didn't know where the doodlebug had landed, she couldn't stop the familiar feeling of apprehension, that dread, stealing over her.

Lucy had been Ruth's friend since the beginning of the war. They had met in an air-raid shelter. Lucy's husband Charlie had just gone into the navy and she needed someone to talk to. As Ruth was also alone she was glad of her company; when they were able, they went to the pictures and the occasional dance together. Lucy and Charlie hadn't been married very long before he was called up and they didn't have any children. Lucy lived with her widowed mother a few streets away from where Ruth and her parents had lived before they had been bombed out the first time. Ruth had moved in with her parents when Alan was called up and the girls evacuated. There didn't seem any point in keeping two homes going then. Now they had been made homeless again; they said the bombs follow you.

It was Lucy's mum who, the following day, had been standing in a queue and had heard the news about Ruth's parents being badly injured, and her being made homeless for the second time. News travelled very fast. As soon as Mrs Graham had told her, Lucy went to the Warden's post and asked Ruth to move in with her and her mother.

'I'm here, in the kitchen,' called Lucy.

Relieved at the cheerful sound of her friend's voice, Ruth stood for a moment or two before walking down the passage, letting her eyes get accustomed to her gloomy surroundings. Although it was still early afternoon and the sun shining, the windows had lost their glass again and were boarded up with any old bit of wood or lino that could be scrounged from a bomb site, and so no light could get in. She moved into the kitchen where a bare bulb hung on its brown flex from the centre of the ceiling; the glass shade had been shattered long since. The back door was open, letting in a meagre amount of light.

'Well, how did it go?' Lucy's hands were covered with flour.

Ruth took off her friend's hat and, after patting her hair into place, carefully placed the hat on a chair. Pulling another from under the table, she sat down. 'As well as any funeral goes, I suppose.'

'Sorry, that was a silly question to ask, but you know what I mean. Did that doodlebug drop anywhere near you?'

Ruth shook her head. 'No, but we had to sit in the shelter with the vicar.'

'So you had to mind your Ps and Qs then?' said Lucy with a slight smile.

Ruth nodded.

'Was Joyce looking all glamorous as usual?'

'She looked very nice. I felt such a mess beside her.'

'Thanks. That was my skirt and blouse and hat you was wearing, remember.'

'I know. I'm sorry, I didn't mean . . .'

'Only kidding. I thought you looked very nice. The kettle's just boiled so I'll just wipe me hands . . .'

'I'll see to the tea. What are you doing?'

Lucy grinned. She was a short, well-built young woman in her early twenties. Ruth had had to put a pin in the waistband of Lucy's skirt to keep it up as she was thinner. Lucy's dark hair had been tucked into a scarf that formed a fat sausage-like roll round her head. Her dark eyes flashed with excitement. 'You're never gonner believe this, but Mum managed to get half a rabbit, so I thought I'd make a pie.'

'Half a rabbit?' exclaimed Ruth, opening her eyes wide. 'Half of a real rabbit?' Rabbit was off the ration and a rare treat.

Lucy nodded. 'Mum was queuing up at the butcher's, someone said he was gonner have some sausages. You know what it's like, two women can stand outside a shop having a natter and before you know it, there's a queue formed behind them.'

Ruth smiled. 'Done that meself.'

'It seems this bloke came up on a bike of all things and when he took about half a dozen rabbits out of his bag, well. Mum reckons he was lucky to get into the shop without being attacked. She said most of the women went berserk and tried to drag him and his rabbits off the bike. The butcher had to come out and wave his cleaver at 'em. Talk about never a dull moment!' She laughed.

Ruth made the tea and put the pot on the table. 'We'll certainly have a few things to tell our kids in years to come.' She sat down and began pouring out the tea. 'Joyce wants me to go down with her when I get some time off.'

'Well, why don't you? It'll do you good to get a decent night's sleep – and in a bed an' all. Now, that's got to be something – a real luxury. I'd love to get in a bed and pull the blankets up round me face.' She grinned. 'And it'd be a bloody sight better if I had Charlie next to me.'

'I know. I wish I had Alan sharing me bed, I'd risk all the dangers of staying in the house.'

Lucy sighed. 'So would I. I do miss my Charlie.'

'And what about having a lovely bath with lots and lots of hot water in front of a roaring fire with the towels warming on the fire-guard.' Ruth raked her fingers through her hair. 'This feels dirty and greasy.'

Lucy had a dreamy look on her face. 'And then, with just a towel wrapped round me, I'll jump into bed with Charlie.'

'You can have Charlie, I'll have my Alan.'

They both laughed.

'Perhaps one day,' said Ruth.

'God, I hope so. I don't know how those people can do, you know, it, down the underground with everyone listening.'

'I suppose it must get the better of you.'

Lucy still looked all dreamy. 'Yer, I suppose it must.'

'I wouldn't like to sleep down there. The *smell*. All

unwashed bodies and wintergreen ointment,' said Ruth, wrinkling her nose.

'I know. D'you remember that night we was coming back from up West? The stink? They reckon that some old dear had upset the bucket.'

Ruth smiled. 'I thought they was gonner lynch her, poor old girl. She looked scared stiff.'

'Yer, but they've got it sorted out now. It's much better organized, and you have to have tickets to get a place in some of the stations. It's more like home for some of them. Sometimes they have some right old knees-ups and some good turns.'

'I'd rather sit in the theatre.'

'So would I.'

'By the way, where's your mum?'

'Gone along to see Mrs Plater. She worries about her being all on her own now her Richard's in the army.'

'It's a shame when the only son goes,' said Ruth.

'That's all the poor old dear had,' said Lucy sadly. 'If anything happens to him I don't reckon she'd be long after. Idolizes him, she does. It's a good thing that so far, touch wood, she hasn't been bombed out. I dunno how she'd get on.'

'Like the rest of us,' said Ruth. 'But it's bloody hard.'

'I can remember when Dad went. It was hard for Mum. Good job I was working.'

Ruth had been told all about how Lucy's dad had been killed in the docks two years before the war. He fell off a barge and drowned. The docks had been one of the main industries round this way before the big blitz in 1940. Ruth's dad had worked there till then. Ruth shuddered. If only he hadn't been home that night with his rotten cough. But he would have still lost his wife. *What will he do now without her? And what about when he realizes he's lost the lower half of his leg?* She sat with her elbows on the table holding her cup with both hands, and stared into space, fear once again filling her mind. So many lives had been shattered. *What will I do if anything happens to Alan? And what about my girls if anything happens to me?*

Ruth closed her eyes and tried to picture them. They must have grown since she last saw them. Shirley, with her dark hair pulled back into thick plaits. Her round, laughing face and warm inquisitive brown eyes, always looking and taking in all that was around her. She had a caring nature, and even at twelve she was the sensible one; she could keep Kay in order, but for how long?

Kay was blonde, tall for her age, and flighty; although she was fourteen months younger than Shirley, she was taller and slimmer than her sister. Her long legs seemed to go on for ever; she was very pretty with large blue eyes that could melt any heart. Ruth worried that with her bubbly outgoing personality, she would be a handful when she got a bit older.

How many times had people who knew Ruth and Joyce commented on how it looked like history repeating itself? Ruth had been the dark-haired, brown-eyed sensible one, while Joyce was the blue-eyed, flighty blonde.

Thank goodness they had been lucky enough to be billeted with Mrs Davies and her daughter. They were nice people.

Ruth thought about when they were tiny. Shirley had

been a good, quiet baby, so when Kay came along they really knew they had her, with her yelling and always wanting to be the centre of attention. Alan was wonderful with the girls. He loved them dearly. When Ruth first met Alan she had been in the cinema queue with Joyce, who, as usual, had done all the talking. But Ruth managed to sit next to him. She found he was shy, but he did ask her out and within a year they'd married. She sighed: 1930, that seemed so long ago.

'Ruth. Wake up. I asked you what time you are on duty?'

'Sorry, I was miles away.'

'So I could see.'

'I'm on the eight till six shift, that's of course if it ain't a bad night and I stay on. I hate it when you've been helping to dig someone out and then, just as you're almost there, they make you go because your shift's over.'

'But you don't always go, do you?'

Ruth shook her head.

'They're only trying to help. If you've been at it all night, you're exhausted. Sometimes a fresh crew will be stronger and more alert.'

'I know, but we still all resent it. I'll be going to see Dad before I go on duty.'

'You still haven't told him about your mum, then?'

'Didn't see the point till he was able to take it in.'

'No, s'pose not.'

'He don't even know he's lost a leg. Since the op he just drifts in and out of consciousness.'

'Bloody shame.'

Ruth didn't answer.

Lucy continued to roll out the pastry, then she put it on

top of the pie and held the dish up. 'I can't wait to get me teeth into this.'

'It'll be a nice change.'

Lucy placed the pie on the oven shelf. Straightening up she said, 'Be lovely if we could have some really nice exotic veg with it. Mum got some carrots.'

'They're supposed to be good for you. Help you see in the blackout.'

'They'll have us believing anything they tell us.'

'I wonder when this will all end?'

'Dunno.' Lucy sat at the table next to Ruth. 'I hope this'll be last one we see.'

'So do I. I feel so sorry for our mums and dads. They've had two wars to put up with, and the depression.'

'I know. Makes you wonder how they manage to carry on.'

'Lucy, if anything happens to me . . .'

'Now don't you go start talking daft.'

Ruth looked down at her hands. 'At night when I'm driving round picking up casualties, I don't have time to worry about meself, but when we get back to the depot, I can almost hear myself praying.' She looked up again. 'And you know that ain't me. But you will tell the girls, and Joyce, won't you?'

'Do you honestly have to ask?'

Ruth shook her head and a tear ran down her face. 'I'm so tired.'

'I'm not surprised. You been on duty all night and at your mother's funeral this morning. Look, why don't you go and have a little lie down? I'll call you when the pie's ready.'

'Thanks. I think I will. Luce, you don't happen to have a button, do you? Only the nob on my suspender's broken and I ain't got a farthing to put in it.'

'Christ, you ain't that hard up, are you?'

'No. I've only got ha'pennies and pennies.'

'That's all right then. Mum's button box is over here.' Lucy went and took it from the cupboard next to the fireplace. 'It was an old tea caddy.'

Ruth studied the faded pictures on the side and lid. After years of handling they had almost worn off. She tipped the contents on to a sheet of newspaper and began sorting through them. Tears began to run down her face again and she sniffed.

'What is it?' asked Lucy. 'What's wrong?'

'I just realized I ain't got a button box now. Like you, I had me mum's. It was blown away like everything else. All the years it took her to fill it with interesting buttons, hooks and eyes and press studs, and the bits of trim that was cut off favourite frocks. Me and Joyce used to play for hours, stacking the buttons up, putting them in colours.' Ruth gently ran her fingers over these gems. 'Have you got any favourites in this lot?'

'I love those glass ones. If you hold them up to the light, they sparkle. They came off a dance frock me mum had before she got married.'

Ruth held the button up to the light. 'They are very pretty.'

'Never had the heart to put them on anything I made. Didn't seem right somehow.'

'I bet she would like you to use them.'

'I might, one day.'

Ruth picked out a button and put the rest back into the box. 'Thanks. I'll just go and have a lie down now.'

'I'll call you later.'

Ruth woke with a start and sat up.

'All right then, gel? Been dreaming?' Mrs Graham, Lucy's mother, was standing over her. She was a round woman with an equally round happy face. Her dark hair, now sprinkled with grey, was cut short to her ears and pulled back with a hair clip. She had honest brown eyes that were full of concern and she was always kind and helpful.

'No. I think I was too tired to dream.'

'Sorry I had to wake you. You was really gone then. That pie's ready. Can't wait to get me choppers into it.'

'It smells good.' Ruth followed Mrs Graham as she shuffled out of the front room, where Ruth had a bed.

'Let's hope it's as good as it smells,' she said over her shoulder. 'That half of rabbit wasn't very big, so I hope the poor thing didn't die of old age.'

Ruth laughed. Mrs Graham was such a cheerful old lady, who never let anything, or anyone get her down. It was easy to see where Lucy got her personality – as well as her looks – from.

Ruth looked at the kitchen table. The three plates appeared to be loaded with steaming food.

'This is more like a feast,' said Ruth.

'Let's hope it ain't the last supper.'

'Mum! What a thing to say.'

'Sorry, gel, I didn't mean . . . Well, you know what I mean, we ain't gonner get another rabbit for a while, and after all it's his last supper, ain't it?'

22

Despite the swift cover-up, Ruth knew that Mrs Graham had just been telling the truth. People knew that every meal could be their last, and every night, the end.

'Well, I reckon we should have a little snifter with this banquet,' said Mrs Graham, opening the black bag on the floor next to her. Wherever she went, the bag never left her side. It contained her insurance policies, a small piece of jewellery, photos of her late husband and Lucy's wedding, as well as a small bottle of whisky.

Everybody had a policy bag like Mrs Graham's, which was always thrown into the air-raid shelter first. Ruth always left her bag at home when she was on duty. She had lost all her photos and personal belongings when the house was bombed.

'We can't drink that, that's for emergencies,' said Lucy.

'Emergencies, and treats, and I reckon this is a treat. 'Sides, we can water it down well.'

'I hope I'll be in a fit state to drive tonight if we get called out.'

'Why's that, gel? You're only getting the one.'

'I know, but I had one at lunchtime. I reckon that's what made me sleep so well.'

'Well, that little forty winks didn't hurt you,' said Mrs Graham, pouring a small drop of whisky into three glasses.

'Look, you two, stop mucking about and sit down otherwise this dinner will be stone cold,' said Lucy.

'Course it won't. Here's to all our good health and a long life.' Mrs Graham raised her glass.

'A long life,' said Lucy and Ruth together.

That's all anybody could wish for these days.

Chapter 3

Joyce held her son close and let her thoughts drift as they sped through the open countryside. It had been a sad, long and worrying day. Frank had collected her early that morning before Alice was even awake. Thank goodness she had Mrs Cotton around to look after her daughter. Even so, Joyce had only gone to London for the day.

It had been a while since she had been to Rotherhithe and, as Frank drove her to see her father, she couldn't believe how much damage had been done. It was as if a giant's hand had smashed down, destroying everything in its path.

Streets she had known as a child had disappeared. She tried hard to remember what was there before. Shops and pubs had gone; she couldn't recognize many roads; and there were lots of places they couldn't get to because of damage and diversions. The strain of it all was evident on the faces of people they drove past.

There hadn't been time for her to drop by the house she and Frank rented in Sutton. It was almost a year since she had seen it. What did it look like? Did Frank do any cleaning? Joyce knew that as his parents lived close by, his

mother would be looking after him most of the time. That
was when he wasn't working, or with her and the children.
He had told her they hadn't had too many bombs round
them, so there wasn't any damage. But with these doodlebugs, how long would it stay standing? Somehow she
couldn't get very concerned about it; she really didn't feel it
was her home any longer. She should feel guilty about that
when her sister had lost her home yet again.

Joyce had never really felt at ease in Sutton; she preferred
London where she had grown up with its bright lights and
wonderful shops. But Frank, who was ten years older than
her, had insisted when they got married that they rent a
house there. Both his parents were still alive and lived in
that area. At the beginning she had been happy enough
working in a large department store, but a year later when
she found she was pregnant with Alice, and the bombing
began, she knew for her baby's sake she had to get away.
Frank worshipped Alice and when his son came along he
told Joyce his happiness was complete.

Joyce glanced at him. She loved him. He was tall and
good looking, with his mop of dark hair and lovely dark
eyes. He could dance well and was good company – both
men and women found him so. And he never seemed to be
short of money. She smiled when she remembered how she
had met him at a dance. He had made her feel so special
and, much to her parents' disapproval, had swept her off
her feet. Her mother knew that Joyce was a dreamer and
always drooled over film stars: she worried that Joyce had
fallen for Frank's sophistication, rather than the man himself. Nor did Mrs Harris approve of the fact that Frank
didn't have a proper job. But Joyce adored the way Frank

made her feel: very grown up, and accepted immediately when Frank asked her to marry him. Her parents, however, refused to give their permission as she was under twenty-one. Frank promptly threatened to take her to Gretna Green, which Joyce thought was very romantic. When her mother and father heard that, they gave in and Joyce and Frank were married with all the trimmings.

Did she want to go back to Sutton when this was all over? Joyce mused. Much to her surprise and despite being a Londoner at heart, she had found she loved the country. Her children looked so healthy, out in the open air all day. This morning she could see that the children still in London looked pale and scruffy, and skinny and underfed. What sort of parents would let their children stay there with all that danger?

Her thoughts went to her mother. If only she had seen her before she died, been able to talk to her, hold her and tell her she loved her. But everybody takes parents for granted. They're always there when you need them. Now she was gone. How dare this bloody man kill her mother and maim her father? How could Ruth bear to stay in London with all that death and destruction going on around her every day? What if anything happened to her? Joyce knew she would look after her sister's girls if . . .

She tried to dismiss all these morbid thoughts from her mind, but she couldn't.

It had upset Joyce to see her father lying in the hospital bed, so pale and still. He looked lost, small and vulnerable. He didn't even open his eyes all the while Joyce sat there; when it was time for her to leave she gently kissed his cheek, but he didn't make any movement. The nurse said he was heavily sedated. How would he manage without Mum? They had been married for so long. And without his leg? He was always such an active man, this would devastate him. She let a tear gently slide down her cheek. Now she didn't have a mum.

'You all right, love?' asked Frank, gently patting her knee and interrupting her thoughts.

'Not too bad,' she sniffed. 'Young Bobbie's nodded off.'

'It's been a long day for him. You should have let Mrs Cotton look after him.'

'I couldn't do that. I couldn't leave him. What if he got upset or something?'

'You worry too much about that boy.'

'No I don't.' Joyce was on the defensive. 'No more than I worry about Alice.' But deep down Joyce knew that Bobbie was her favourite. He was the boy she had always wanted.

At last they reached the village and the house came in sight. As they turned into the tree-lined drive, Joyce felt a pang of relief: she was home, even though it was only one living room; the bedroom they had to share with the children. But the kitchen Mrs Cotton let her have was a dream. It had been part of the old dairy, it was light and airy and looked out on to the garden and the green fields beyond, and she loved it.

She knew Frank couldn't wait to get back to Sutton, or London. Was it because of his work? Joyce had never really known what he did for a living, yet she never went short of money. 'Why can't he tell us about these little so-called deals he's always supposed to be doing? Too bloody smart to be a rag-and-bone man.' Joyce could hear her mother's words ringing in her ears. Even after they had married, Mrs

Harris had never trusted him. She glanced up at the sky and whispered under her breath. 'Well, you'll never know now, Mum.'

Frank was very generous. He told her he was in the business of buying and selling anything that he could make a profit on, but she didn't know what. Nor did she care. He was always very smartly turned out and he was never in trouble with the police and he adored her and the children.

As he turned the key in the large ornate front door and pushed it open, Alice, their four-year-old daughter, came running up to them.

'Daddy. Daddy,' she called.

'Shh,' said Joyce. 'You'll wake Bobbie.' Her son gave a little whimper.

Alice's little pink mouth turned down.

'How are you, darling?' said Frank, lifting her off the ground and kissing her cheek. 'Have you been a good girl?'

She nodded her head vigorously. 'You didn't come and see me this morning.'

'You were still fast asleep.'

'Are you going to stay with us a long time?'

'Just till tomorrow.'

'That's good. I can show you some flowers me and Mrs Cotton picked for Mummy today. Come on.'

Frank was led away by his daughter.

'Has she been all right?' Joyce asked Mrs Cotton who had come to the door behind Alice. She was plump in a nice way and looked just like the farmers' wives you saw in children's picture books.

Mrs Cotton's shining, rosy cheeks curved with her

beaming smile. 'She's no trouble. It's been a pleasure having her around. How did it go?'

'Not too bad. There was an air raid and we had to wait for the all clear before we could bury Mum.'

Mrs Cotton put her hand to her mouth. 'My dear, I'm so sorry. Did you get a chance to see your father?'

'Just for a short while. He didn't wake up. Oh, Mrs Cotton, when's it all going to end?' Suddenly Joyce slumped into a chair in the vast hall and began to cry.

'I was a bit disappointed you didn't get time to go home,' said Frank that night when the children were asleep.

'I didn't want to stay up there too long, not with the raids an' all. Besides, I couldn't leave Alice for too long.' Joyce was bending down and peering into the dressing-table mirror as she removed her make-up. 'Frank, I'm worried about Ruth. And I expect young Kay and Shirley are going to be upset about Mum. They were very fond of her.'

'Poor kids, stuck in Wales.'

'Ruth was saying the woman and her daughter who they live with are very nice. They give the girls lots of treats.'

'That's as maybe, but it's a long way away. What if anything happens to Ruth?'

'That did run through my mind, but we mustn't talk like that.'

'Well, let's face it, girl, she is in the thick of it all.'

'I know and it worries me to death. I don't think I can stand much more of this.'

'Come here.' Frank put his arms round her slender waist and kissed the back of her neck.

'I'm glad you're not too far away,' whispered Joyce.

'I wish we had our own room and could romp about on the bed and not have to worry about waking them.' He nodded towards the bed on the far side of the room where the two children slept.

Joyce settled into his arms. 'So do I. I'm so lucky to have you around.'

'Well, you will all the time they don't start calling up us poor old bods with only one good ear.'

'Ruth was saying she couldn't understand why you haven't been called up to do war work?'

'I do my bit. Blimey, sometimes we're in the thick of it. And I reckon we do a sight more than some of those blokes in the forces, especially those who sit at a desk pen-pushing all day.' Frank's voice rose slightly.

'Shh,' said Joyce.

'Sorry, love. But don't you go worrying your pretty little head about things like that. I'm a warden and somebody's got to look after people. Remember, careless talk costs lives. Now, let's stop talking, shall we?' He kissed her tenderly at first, then with the passion that Joyce had come to expect from him.

'What you got there?' Kay asked Shirley when she walked into the bedroom the girls shared.

'A letter.'

'Let me see,' said Kay, snatching the paper her sister was holding. 'Who's it from?'

'Mum.'

'Why are you crying? Hey – it's got a different address.'

'Mum's been bombed out again and Gran's dead and Grandad's lost his leg,' Shirley said bluntly. She looked at her sister, waiting for a silly remark like: That was careless of him, but even Kay with her quick answers was subdued. Shirley wiped her tears with the back of her hand.

'That's awful,' said Kay softly. 'Poor Mum and Grandad. Where's she living now?'

'She's staying with her friend Lucy till she gets something. Why won't she go and stay with Auntie Joyce in the country? I wish she would get away from all those bombs. I wish this bloody war was over.'

'Shirl.' Kay quickly glanced at the closed bedroom door. 'Stop swearing. What if Mrs Davies hears you?'

'I don't care. Oh Kay, when are we going to be a family again?'

'I don't know. Poor Mum.' Kay held her sister close and they cried together.

'I don't want Mum to die as well,' sobbed Shirley.

'She won't,' said Kay, rocking her sister back and forth.

'She will if she stays in London.'

'Don't say things like that. Where will we live when the war's over?' asked Kay.

Shirley shrugged.

'How will Dad know where to find Mum?'

'I expect the army will tell him.'

'Shirl! What if both our mum and dad get . . . We'll be orphans.' Kay began to cry harder. 'I don't want to be an orphan.'

'Nor do I.' Shirley wiped her eyes. 'We mustn't think like this. Come on, let's go and tell Mrs Davies what's happened.'

Kay put out her hand and stopped her sister. 'I want to go back home.'

'So do I. But we can't. We don't have a home, remember. Besides, Mum wouldn't let us.'

'We could go on our own. Mum would be ever so pleased to see us.'

'Would she?'

'I think so.'

'Well, I don't think she would.'

'I reckon it could be very exciting. D'you remember that night when they bombed the docks?'

'Yes I do. I don't suppose I'll ever forget it. Mum couldn't wait to get us back here, out of harm's way. I wouldn't want to be there now, not with all these bombs.'

'I don't know.'

'I was frightened, and I remember you cried and was scared stiff as well.'

'It's different now. We was a lot younger then.'

'Oh yes. You're all of eleven and I'm twelve, really grown up.'

'You'll be thirteen this November, and next year you'll be leaving school and going to work. Will you get a job here in Wales?'

'I shouldn't think so. 'Sides, we might be home by then.'

'Well, if you go, then so shall I. But I still think we should go now.'

'We can't.'

'It could be exciting, going back.'

'Sometimes, Kay Bentley, you talk a right load of rubbish.'

'Well, I think we should go and see our mum.'

'And how could we pay the train fare?'

'We've got some money.'

'Not that much. Anyway, I thought you liked living here?'

'I do. But I want to be with Mum. I want to see her.'

'So do I, but we can't. She wouldn't be very pleased about us going to London on our own. It's a long way away, so stop talking stupid.'

'When we first came here we were on our own.'

'We came with the school.'

'I'm going to find out how much it will cost. I mean it. I want to be with Mum,' said Kay defiantly.

'We don't know where she lives.'

'We've got an address, so we can ask someone.'

'No, we can't go, Mum would be livid. I'll write and ask her to come here to live,' said Shirley, trying to make her sister see sense.

'Can't see her doing that. She wouldn't leave Grandad, would she?'

'I don't know. But I can ask.'

Kay sat on the bed. 'It would be nice to see Auntie Joyce and her babies.'

Shirley sat next to her. 'We've only had that one picture of her little Alice and Bobbie.' She nodded towards the dressing table where the photographs of their family were displayed. There was one of their mum and dad, gran and grandad; it had been taken by a beach photographer when they all went to Southend for the day. Shirley remembered Kay getting really cross because they were playing in the sea and so missed out on being in the picture. There was a picture of their handsome dad in army uniform with his arm round their mother's waist. She looked so happy. And one of Joyce with Frank and the children. Bobbie had only been a few weeks old when it was taken.

'I expect they're getting quite big now,' said Kay sadly. 'Perhaps we could go and live with Auntie Joyce. She lives in a big house.'

Shirley picked up the photograph of her gran, who was laughing. 'We're never going to see our gran again.' Slowly another tear ran down her face.

'And what if Grandad dies?'

'Don't!'

'I'm going home.'

'What about school?'

'I'm not worried about school. It might be very exciting dodging the bombs and doodlebugs. I wonder what they sound like?'

'They might show them on the newsreels,' sniffed Shirley, wiping her nose with the back of her hand. 'Stella said she was taking us to the pictures next week.'

Stella, Mrs Davies's daughter, was a happy young woman. She had moved in with her mother when her husband, like her father, had joined the navy. They had looked after the two London girls for four years now, and thought the world of them.

'Don't say anything to Mrs Davies. She's such a nice lady and I know she and Stella would be upset if she thought we was planning on running away.'

'Not "we". You,' said Shirley forcefully.

'All right then. Me.'

'You wouldn't, would you? Would you really go without me?' asked Shirley.

'I'll let you know.'

'Mrs Davies will be very worried about you if you go.

What if there was an air raid?'

'I'll go down a shelter.'

'Mum will be very cross.' Shirley opened the bedroom door. She stopped and turned. 'Kay, you wouldn't really go to London without me, would you?'

Kay looked at her sister and smiled.

Chapter 4

Ruth was waiting at the bus stop. It was early evening, and the sun was warm on her face. She didn't see a lot of sunshine as she tried to sleep through the day when she was on night duty. Two weeks had passed since her mother's funeral. Ruth clutched her handbag close to her, knowing that inside, as well as a note from Joyce, was a letter she had received from Alan that morning. Her husband's letter had been readdressed, and the date told her he hadn't got her letter telling him about her mother and father.

She had just spent two hours sitting with her father. It had been very hard work. He knew about his leg, and the nurse had told him about her mother.

'Should have gone with Betty. What bloody good am I with only one leg?'

'Don't talk like that, Dad.'

'I don't want to end up like those poor buggers after the last lot. Standing on the street corner with a tray of matches round me neck.'

Ruth laughed.

'It ain't funny.'

'Sorry, but can you honestly see me and Joyce letting that happen?'

He looked at her sheepishly. 'No.'

'Well then. Cheer up. Think of the pilot, Douglas Bader, he lost both his legs.'

'He's a lot younger than me.'

Twice during her visit she had helped the nurses to make sure the patients got under the bed when the doodlebugs came over.

Everybody was now tired of the sirens going and nothing happening, so most places had organized their own method of warning when their area was targeted. During the day, the hospital, like many other densely populated buildings, had watchers on the roof with binoculars. On a clear night, the flame that came from the tail of the V1 could be seen for miles. If the hospital watchers thought one was heading their way, they would phone down to the switchboard who gave every ward a long ring on the phone.

People were getting a little blasé about them now, only taking cover when the engine cut out. Everybody just wanted to carry on trying to live normal lives.

After saying goodbye to her father Ruth had left the building. Outside she looked about her. The windows of the hospital had been sandbagged up at the very beginning of the war and the building was looking a little like the people all around, battle scarred. Some of the sandbags had split open and their contents had trickled out, while others had wild flowers and weeds sprouting from them, as if they were window boxes. Most of them were a greenish colour; the sandbag had almost rotted away and the contents had set hard, like concrete.

When Ruth finally boarded the bus she couldn't help but admire the clippie, a young girl with long blonde hair and a lovely smile. Her lips were bright red. Everyone was trying to look like a film star these days. The cheery manner of these girls helped to lift some of the gloom. It was a job that suited Lucy.

Ruth sat down and stared at the green mesh stuck to the windows. It made it very difficult to see out properly. Even though the army was pushing Hitler back in France it didn't seem as if this war was ever going to end.

She let her thoughts go over the conversation she'd just had with her father. She had deliberately turned their talk away from her mother. 'I had letters from Joyce and Alan today. I'd told Joyce you were a lot better.'

'Frank brought me in one from her and he managed to get me a couple of eggs and some oranges.'

'What? How did he manage that?' Ruth was grateful that Frank, when he was around, popped in to see her father.

'I didn't ask. There's some apples as well. They come from the farm. Take a couple.'

'Thanks. I will.'

'Young Alice sent me a drawing. It's in there.'

Ruth reached into his locker. She laughed when she looked at the paper with squiggly lines over it. 'Is this supposed to be you?'

'Don't think so. It's got two legs.'

Ruth swallowed hard. 'I've been asking them about sending you out of London.'

'I know. That young slip of a girl who baths me told me. I don't like these young girls being so familiar.'

'I bet a lot of old men would like it.'

'Well, I ain't like that.'

'That's what you tell me.'

'I tell you, Ruth. I only had eyes for your mother.' He took a breath and once again tears filled his sad eyes. 'I loved her, you know.'

Ruth gently patted the back of his liver-spotted hand. 'I know. I was only kidding.'

Jack Harris rubbed at his eyes. 'I've had enough of this war. What about you, girl? You must have had more than enough be now with some of the things you've seen. Why don't you go and stay with your girls?'

'I'm not leaving you. Besides, I've got me job.'

'Is it that important?'

'I think so. Anyway I can't just up and leave. There's a war on, you know.' She smiled.

'I don't know how you can still be so bloody cheerful. Did you say you'd got a letter from Alan?'

'Yes.'

'Where is he?'

'He can't say, but I've got a feeling it's in Italy. He talks about the lovely beaches and blue sea.'

'You could be right.'

Ruth looked at her watch. 'I've got to go, Dad. I'm on duty.'

'OK.'

She kissed his cheek and left. She turned at the door to wave goodbye, but her father had settled down under the covers once more.

Ruth got off the bus and made her way to the Civil Defence building where she worked. As she passed the many bombed houses all round her, her heart sank. The feeling was all too familiar – she was getting very war weary. She knew she should get away for a short while. But more than that she wanted to see her daughters. A feeble smile lifted her mouth when she remembered how the girls now had a slight Welsh lilt to their voices. What would Alan say about that? Her dear Alan, she missed him so much. There was going to be so much building work to be done when this was all over. As a carpenter, he shouldn't have any difficulty in getting a job when he got back. Carpenters would be in great demand, so would houses. Where would they finish up? Would the government help? They didn't do much after the last lot. On the newsreels she had seen the new prefabs they were going to give people. At the time she'd said to Lucy, 'I'd like one of those. Especially now Dad's only got one leg. It would make everything so much easier.'

'All right then, Ruth?' asked Stan Page as he came out of the tobacconist and fell into step beside her.

'Hello, Stan. Not too bad. Just been to see Dad.'

Stan worked with Ruth and her father. She reckoned he was round about forty-four, ten years older than Alan. He had a mop of sandy-coloured hair and a sallow complexion. In all of the four years she had known him, his pale grey eyes had always looked sad. At times she wanted to hold him, to mother him, to make the expression go away.

'How is he?' asked Stan.

'A bit tearful.'

'That's to be expected. It was a bloody shame. I like Jack. I'll pop in and see him, that's if it's OK with you?'

Ruth smiled and nodded. 'He'd like that. I'll let you know when he can have visitors other than family.'

'Good. Fag?' he asked, offering her the packet.

'No thanks.'

'I know what it's like to lose your wife,' he said sadly. 'And it can't be nice losing your leg.'

Ruth remembered when Stan's wife, who was only in her late thirties, died in the blackout. She had been hit by a fire engine that had been returning to its depot.

That was always one of Ruth's biggest fears when they drove around at night with only tiny little slits cut into black metal shields that covered the headlights. She would be devastated if she hit someone. She saw enough death without contributing to it.

Stan, who had been invalided out of the army after Dunkirk, with a shrapnel wound, had been beside himself with grief over the loss of his wife. They didn't have any children and his parents, who lived in Rotherhithe, wanted him to go away, but he wouldn't leave them. It wasn't till after a very bad raid that he managed to persuade *them* to go to their daughter who lived at Brighton. As he was now involved with the Civil Defence he had stayed in Rotherhithe and promised them he would keep the house on.

'I was hoping I could get Dad away to some sort of convalescent home,' she said as they made their way along the road. 'They told me they didn't have any spare places. Too many service personnel, they said, and he ain't really ready to go from a hospital yet, it seems his leg ain't that good.'

'I'm really sorry to hear that.'

Ruth liked Stan. She was at ease and happy working with him. He was a warm, caring man with a sense of humour. When they sat in the van after being out all night, she could relax and talk to him. He had opened up to her about his troubles and she had told him all about Alan and her girls. He was the one who had driven her to the hospital and waited with her for news about her mother and father.

They turned into the office block that was now the warden's post, past the tall mounds of sandbags that fronted the building, and, going into the incident room, signed in.

The air was thick with tobacco smoke and Bill Clarke, who was sitting at his desk, flicked his cigarette ash into the overflowing ashtray.

'I expect the bastard will be sending over some more tonight,' said Bill, taking back the book they had just signed. Bill was in charge of the post. 'Everybody's getting really fed up with these bloody buzz bombs. It ain't as if we can shoot 'em down and kill the pilot, at least that gives you some sort of satisfaction. But these bloody things ain't got a pilot.'

Ruth shuddered at his callousness. Life was all about killing now.

'Any idea where today's lot finished up?' asked Stan.

'Croydon, Dagenham, Chelsea, Lambeth. Most of the usual places,' said Bill.

'What about round here?' asked Ruth.

'Been lucky today.'

'Ruth, how d'you fancy a game of crib?' said Stan, sitting at one of the tables. 'Or d'you want to get your head down while it's quiet?'

'Wouldn't mind. These night shifts take it out of me.'

'And it don't do your love life a lot of good either,' said Bill.

Gloria, another member of their watch, was filing her nails. She started to giggle.

Ruth gave Bill a withering look. 'That's all right if you've got someone,' she said sharply. She knew Bill wasn't the most tactful person around, but he was good at his job, and sometimes she wondered if his comments were just a form of bravado.

'Sorry,' he said, looking sheepishly at both Ruth and Stan. 'You know me and me big mouth.'

'Not to worry,' said Stan. 'I'll make a cuppa while it's quiet.'

Ruth lay on the camp bed and reflected on these people that she had almost lived with these past four years. They came from all walks of life, but shared the same hopes and fears. When this was all over she would miss the camaraderie they had built up, the tears when someone lost a friend or relation, and the dirty jokes that travelled from post to post with such speed.

When the telephone rang, it made Ruth jump. It had invaded her dreams. She sat up. Her back hurt from lying on the uncomfortable camp bed. It was the same every time she tried to get a little sleep. She wondered why she bothered.

Bill was talking down the phone. He replaced the receiver and looked up. 'Right, we're off. There's a couple of V1s heading this way.'

Ruth grabbed her gas mask and tin hat and followed Stan out to the van that had been made into a temporary ambulance.

'Who's driving?' she asked, adjusting the strap on her tin hat.

'Stan,' said Bill.

Ruth climbed in beside Stan. She glanced over her shoulder to make sure everything was in place, even though she knew that the van was always replenished as soon as they got back to the depot.

'Where to?' asked Stan. He stopped as the familiar putt putt sound filled the air above them.

As soon as the engine cut out, both Stan and Ruth fell from the van and lay on the ground.

The rushing noise filled her ears, followed by crashing masonry and the tinkling of glass. A blast of hot air filled her lungs. Dust and dirt clogged her nose and throat. The ground slowly lifted, shuddered and sank back down again. She felt that everything around her was moving past in slow motion. Leaves and branches fell from the trees. Paper and bits of debris floated by. She couldn't breathe. Was she going to die? Then something hit the side of her head and everything went black.

'Ruth. Ruth. Are you all right?' Stan was tapping the back of her hand.

She opened her eyes. 'What happened?'

'A piece of timber caught you a glancing blow. It don't look too bad.'

She put her hand to her head. It felt sticky. 'I'm bleeding,' she said in a surprised voice.

'I've had a look at it; it's not too deep. Your tin hat saved you. Do you want me to drive you home?'

She shook her head. 'No. I'm OK. Just give me a minute or two. Where did it fall?'

Stan nodded across the road. 'Those houses copped most of it. These trees saved us.'

Ruth looked at the trees. All the leaves had gone, blown away; bits of fabric that had been somebody's curtains and bed linen hung from the bare branches like Christmas decorations. 'Anybody been round there to see if there's any casualties?' she asked.

'Bill and the others are over there now.'

Ruth struggled to her feet. 'Sod it,' she said out loud.

'What is it?' asked Stan in a caring voice.

'Just torn me trousers. I'll have to try and get a new pair. The trouble is the WVS ain't got any in my size. And me new uniform and clothing coupons ain't come through yet. And these boiler suits don't do anything for you.'

'You look fine; after all, this ain't a fashion parade. I'll tell you what, I'll let you have some of mine,' said Stan as they picked their way across the road.

'What, trousers?'

He laughed. 'No, clothing coupons, you silly cow.'

It amazed Ruth that they could always find something to joke about, no matter how bad the situation was.

'Good job young Gloria went out earlier. She would have been livid if her make-up had got messed up.'

'Stan, that's not a nice thing to say. She's a very hard grafter.'

'Maybe. But she does plaster the old make-up on.'

'The boys like it.'

'And she likes the boys.'

'You're only jealous 'cos she don't pussyfoot round you.'

'No I'm not.'

'Don't give me that. I bet if she offered you a night of passion, you wouldn't say no.'

Stan grinned. 'She ain't got round to me yet.'

Everybody knew that Gloria would hop into any bed. Everybody noted how, since the Yanks had arrived over here, she only ever smoked American cigarettes. She laughed and said they were for services rendered. Gloria always insisted she only lived for the day, and since she wasn't married where was the harm? And nobody blamed her.

It was a long, busy night. Ruth and Stan were back and forth to the hospital, driving over hosepipes and negotiating all the diversions. She got angry on the occasions when they were too late and could only deliver a body. But when they helped dig someone out who was still alive, it was the most rewarding thing in the world.

Now the night was almost over and they were sitting in the van. The dawn was just beginning to lighten the edge of the sky. Even the black outlines, the skeletons of the bombed buildings, had a certain beauty at this time in the morning. It was very quiet and still.

'Looks like it's going to be another nice day,' said Ruth, bending down and looking through the windscreen.

'Not for some,' said Stan.

'That's true.'

'Any more tea left in that flask?' he asked.

Ruth shook her head. 'No, it's all gone.'

'It seems to have settled down. Let's get back and have a decent cuppa,' said Stan, starting the engine.

'I could certainly do with one. My mouth feels like a sewer.'

Stan laughed.

'What's so funny?'

'You wait till you see your face.'

'Why? What's wrong with it?'

'It's filthy dirty, and what with the blood, you look a bit of a mess.'

'Thanks.'

Stan turned off the engine. 'Ruth, I think you're smashing, what with all you've had to put up with.'

'No more than thousands of others.'

'But you've always got a ready smile and a kind word, and the way you talk to the victims and their families is fantastic.'

'It's me job.' She laughed nervously. 'Now stop all this old flannel and let's get back.'

'Ruth. I'm growing very fond of you.'

She turned and looked directly at him. 'Stan. I like you, and we work well together, so please, don't let's start to complicate things.'

'I'm sorry. You are so attractive and—'

'What, even with a dirty face?'

'I've got to say something.'

Ruth held up her hand. 'Don't. You know I love Alan, and I would never ever do anything to spoil what we have.'

'I know. I'm sorry.' He started the engine again. 'I promise I won't say any more.'

Ruth stared straight ahead. She was flattered, but frightened. With the thought that every day could be your last, it would be so easy to fall into someone's arms for love and

47

companionship. She mustn't think like this. She had to wait for Alan. But what if he didn't return? Little niggly thoughts were also creeping into her head. Ruth had had her leg pulled many times about Alan and the women who were grateful at being rescued from the Germans. Would he give in to temptation if it were offered?

Chapter 5

The following week Ruth collected her clothing coupons, and the allowance the government gave you for a few bits of furniture and furnishings. Very reluctantly, she had begun looking for somewhere to live, but everywhere seemed dirty and derelict.

'Don't know why you're bothering,' said Lucy when Ruth walked in one afternoon and told her about the flat she had just been to see. 'Ain't no point in you finding yourself a place till your dad comes out of hospital or Alan gets back. 'Sides, ain't it better to come home to a nice warm meal than to be stuck somewhere on your own?'

Ruth nodded. 'Course. And I suppose, knowing my luck, just as I got it looking a bit reasonable it would all be blown away again.'

'My, we are down today.'

'I'm sorry. But you know how it is and I don't want to impose.'

Lucy laughed. 'You, impose? Me and Mum really like having you here. And let's face it, when I'm on duty and you're around, I feel a lot better about Mum.'

Ruth smiled. 'Thanks.'

'No, honestly. But still I reckon you ought to try and get away from all this. Can't they give you some time off?'

'They have. I've managed to get a couple of days. I'm going to stay with Joyce, just for a night.'

'That's great. When you going?'

'Next week. I'll see if I can scrounge a few eggs from them while I'm down there.'

'Fresh eggs. That'll be something. I bet them in the country don't even know what dried egg tastes like.'

'It ain't that bad.'

'You can't put dried egg in an egg cup and dip your soldiers in it.'

'You are daft.'

'Have you told your dad you're going to see Joyce?'

'Yes. I'll only be gone for one night.'

'How you getting down there?'

'Frank was at the hospital and when I told him, he said he'd take me.'

'That's kind of him.'

Ruth sat at the table and played with the cloth. 'He's not a bad bloke really. Funny, Mum never did like him. Mind you, I think a lot of it was that he took her little girl away from her. And he didn't have a job she could boast about.'

'What did he do?'

'He was always very cagey about it. Mum always reckoned he was a rag-and-bone man.'

They laughed.

'Not like my Alan.'

'Did she like Alan?'

Ruth nodded. 'He couldn't do any wrong in her eyes. He'll be really upset when he gets that letter.'

'What does your dad have to say about Frank?'

'I think he always liked him, but wouldn't dare say so in front of Mum. When whisky started getting short and Frank managed to get Dad the odd drop now and again, well, that really gave him a boost.' A smile filled her face, but it soon faded.

'You look tired,' said Lucy.

'I am. I'm really looking forward to having a few days off.'

'Even though they've liberated Paris, there still ain't any let-up in these raids, is there?'

'No. And these buzz bombs are the limit. In some ways I'll feel guilty about going away. It's a bit like leaving the sinking ship.'

'The ship ain't sinking – well, not yet anyway. 'Sides, I reckon you deserve a break, especially after last week.'

Ruth stood up and looked in the mirror, which was now leaning against the wall. They hadn't put it back on the hook since the last raid, when it had finished up on the floor; Mrs Graham was worried that if it fell off again it would break and they would have seven years' bad luck. 'I don't think it'll scar,' she said, running her finger over the red weal under her hair.

'Have you heard from the girls?'

'Yes. They were really upset to hear about Mum and Dad. Shirley said Kay wanted to come home.'

'You won't let 'em, will you?'

'I should say not. 'Sides, we ain't got a home.'

'So, what you gonner do down in the darkest depths of Sussex?'

'I can't wait to take all me clothes off and then, after

sinking into a nice hot bath, get in a bed and sleep.'

'Shut up. You'll have me thinking about Charlie and making me come over all unnecessary.'

'No. This time I want to sleep. Mind you, I wouldn't say no to having a nice big box of chocolates and a good book beside me.'

'And that's all?'

Ruth grinned. 'Yes. For the time being.'

'I do miss me sweets. I can never make me ration last for long.'

'You'll have to find yourself a Yank. They always seem to have plenty to flash about.'

Lucy screwed up her nose. 'Chance'd be a fine thing – and it depends on what they're flashing.'

Ruth laughed. 'No, I can't see you falling for their charms, not you. You're too much of a Charlie's girl.'

'That's true. Ruth, do you ever wonder if Alan, you know, while he's away?'

'Sometimes.'

'I wonder about my Charlie. Not that he would, well, not intentionally. But what if they're in some port and these loose women come up to them and smother them with kisses and offer other things, d'you think they'd say no?'

'I don't know. I wouldn't like to say.'

They both sat quietly reflecting on what could happen.

'Life's going to be very humdrum when this is all over,' Lucy said suddenly.

'Well, you'll be able to settle down and raise a family. Believe me, you won't find life humdrum with a couple of little 'uns round you.' Ruth peered in the mirror again and put on her lipstick.

'Don't you feel angry at missing years of your girls growing up?'

Ruth straightened up. 'Yes I do. Bloody angry.'

'Would you like any more?'

'Don't know. Can't say I've even thought about that.'

'Well, you never know what's going to happen when all those blokes get back home.'

'It's going to be a lot different for them, and us. Christ, look at the time,' Ruth exclaimed. 'I'll be late. You know what the buses are like these days.'

Lucy went to throw a tea towel at her. 'Cheeky cow!'

'I ain't too early, am I?' said Frank when Ruth opened the front door to him.

'No. Come in.'

Frank followed Ruth down the passage.

'This is Mrs Graham, Lucy's mum,' said Ruth when they went into the kitchen.

'Hello, love,' said Frank. 'I hear you've been looking after our Ruth all right.'

'She ain't no trouble. In fact it's a pleasure to have her here. You got time for a cuppa?'

'No, thanks all the same,' said Frank. 'But I've got to come back. I'm on duty tonight.'

Ruth picked up her bag. 'Right then, we'll be—' Her sentence was cut short by a loud banging on the knocker.

'Who's that at this time of day?' Mrs Graham got to her feet. Her face turned grey. 'Please God, I hope it ain't one of those telegraph boys.'

Ruth went pale. That was everybody's fear. A telegram from the War Office.

53

'I'll go,' said Frank.

'No, it's all right.' Mrs Graham was out of the door.

They could hear voices and when the kitchen door opened, a policeman stood in the doorway.

Frank's face went ashen.

'You Mr Bentley?' The policeman asked Frank.

He shook his head.

'I'm Mrs Bentley. My husband is in the army. Why do you want him?'

'I don't want your husband. Do you have two daughters?'

Ruth slumped into a chair. She felt sick. 'Yes,' she whispered. 'What's happened to them?'

Frank put his arm round Ruth's shoulders.

'They're at the police station.'

'What? Here in London?'

'Yes. Can you come and get them?'

'What're they doing in London? They're in Wales.'

'It seems they wanted to come home. They were picked up this morning wandering round Paddington station. They were lost.'

Ruth began to cry. 'How did they get here?'

'I don't know that much, but I believe they came up on the night train.'

'Can you take me to them?'

'Sorry, but I've only got me bike.'

'Don't worry, Ruth, I'll take you.' Frank began to walk out of the kitchen.

Ruth was right behind him.

'That your car outside, sir?'

'Yes.'

'I presume you have got petrol?'

'Yes. I'm a warden and get an allowance.'

'I see. D'you mind if I look at your papers?'

Frank showed him his papers.

Ruth could see by the policeman's supercilious look that he thought, like so many people, that wardens of call-up age were scroungers and draft-dodgers who spent most of their time drinking tea and playing darts.

'Where were you going, if you don't mind me asking?'

'I do mind you asking. Can't you see this young woman wants to be with her daughters? And for your information I was going to work. And Ruth here is also a Civil Defence worker. Now, which police station are the girls at?'

'Ruth, you can bring them back here if you want,' said Mrs Graham following them down the passage.

Ruth was wiping her tears. She didn't know why she was crying. Was it because she was going to see her daughters, or was it because she was angry with them for coming home? Or was it relief that it wasn't a telegram? 'Thanks. I'll see what this is all about. I may take them to Joyce's.'

'I'll tell Lucy when she gets home. Bye.' Mrs Graham stood in the doorway and watched Ruth climb dazedly into Frank's car.

Frank finished talking to the policeman and got in the car beside her. 'Right, I know where they are,' he said to Ruth. 'Now come on. Dry your eyes.'

'What are they doing up here? What if a doodlebug had killed them last night? I would never have known. I'll kill them when I see them!'

Frank laughed. 'I don't think you will.'

She gave him a watery smile. 'No. Perhaps not.'

55

As soon as the car stopped, Ruth jumped out and went up the steps two at a time and into the police station.

'Mummy. Mummy!' Kay rushed to her and held her tight. She looked tired, dirty and dishevelled.

'Hello, Mum,' said Shirley, cautiously coming towards her.

Ruth put out her arms and Shirley too rushed into them and held her mother tight. All three were crying and laughing at the same time.

After a moment Ruth held them both at arm's length and tried to look stern. 'Just what the hell were you thinking of, coming up here? You could have been killed. You are very naughty girls. How did you get here? Does Mrs Davies know you've run away?'

Shirley nodded. 'We left her a note.'

'Why? Why? What are you doing here? Has she been ill-treating you?'

'No,' shouted Kay. 'And don't blame Shirl, it wasn't her fault. It was me,' she sniffed. 'I was ever so upset when you wrote to us about Gran and Grandad. I thought if you got killed, we wouldn't know and we'd never see you again.' Kay ran the back of her hand under her runny nose.

'But you shouldn't have come here. It's very dangerous. We have buzz bombs dropping on us all the time.' Ruth was angry, but she had difficulty keeping the joy out of her voice.

'We know. We heard them last night,' said Shirley.

'I was ever so frightened,' said Kay. 'Some man took us down the underground. We had to sit on the floor as it was ever so packed. Do those people sleep down there all the time?'

'Yes. My God. Anything could have happened to you. What if you'd been killed, how would we have known?' said Ruth.

'I'm really sorry,' sobbed Kay. 'But we always carry our identification cards and gas masks.'

'I should hope so. Just as long as you're safe, I suppose that's all that matters. Now come on.' Ruth turned to the policeman in charge. 'Thank you for contacting me.'

'That's all right missus. I know what it's like to have a couple of wayward kids. I couldn't keep my two away for long. The missus went mad when they wanted to come home. Anyway, look after them.'

'I will.' She put her arms round both of their shoulders and led them out of the station.

'What's going to happen to us?' asked Shirley.

'You're going straight back to Wales.'

'See. I told you Mum would be cross.'

Kay looked up at her mother and Ruth's heart melted. 'You won't send us back just yet, will you?'

Frank was waiting by the car. 'Hello, you two.'

'Hello, Uncle Frank,' they said together.

'Come here and let me give you a hug. You didn't half give your mum a fright.' He held them close and, looking over their heads, said to Ruth, 'I didn't come in, just in case they started to ask awkward questions.'

'I gathered that,' said Ruth. 'So, what are we going to do with these two?'

'Dunno. They look so grown up. It's a few years since I last saw 'em. Shirley's as tall as you now.'

Shirley gave Frank a beaming smile.

'We'd like to see Alice and Bobbie,' said Kay.

'Well, I was going to take your mum down there for a couple of days.'

Kay grabbed Ruth's hand. 'Can we come? Please?'

'No. I told you. I'm going to take you straight back to Wales.'

Shirley glared at Kay. 'I said it would be a waste of money coming all this way.'

'Where did you get the money from?' asked Ruth.

'We told Mrs Davies we wanted to give you a present.'

'You told that woman lies? You took money from her? That's dreadful. I'm very cross with you both.'

'We didn't tell her lies, we're the present. Don't you like it?' Kay twirled round.

Frank laughed. 'You've got to hand it to them, Ruth. They've got a lot of charm.'

'I'll give 'em charm. I *am* very angry. It's back to Wales for you two.'

'Can we have a drink first?' asked Shirley.

'And something to eat?' added Kay. 'We ain't had anything since yesterday.'

'Come on,' said Frank. 'We'll try and find a Lyons or somewhere that's still serving.'

The girls were full of smiles as they got into Frank's car and made their way to the nearest Lyons Corner House that was still standing, and open.

'Ever so many bombs must have dropped here,' said Shirley, looking out of the car window.

'Yes, and doodlebugs. It's not safe round here,' said Ruth.

They sat drinking their tea. Ruth's heart was bursting. She was so happy at seeing them again, but tried hard not to let them see it. She didn't want to send them away, but it was for their safety.

'How are you both doing at school?' asked Frank.

'Not bad. Sometimes the teachers try to get us to talk in Welsh, but we tell 'em we're Londoners and proud of it,' said Kay, grinning.

'Not "we",' said Shirley. 'You.'

'Ain't you proud of it then, girl?' asked Frank.

She gave him a grin and nodded. 'Course.'

'I love the way they talk now,' said Frank.

Ruth smiled. 'It is very attractive. But I don't know what your father's going to say when I write and tell him about this.'

'If we stay here we'll soon talk like you,' said Kay.

Ruth gave Kay a withering look.

'Sorry, Mum.'

'We didn't mean to upset you, Mum,' said Shirley. 'But you know what she's like – when she gets a bee in her bonnet there's no stopping her, and I thought it best if I come with her.'

'Yes, you did the right thing,' said Ruth. 'Right, now finish your tea and let's get you back to the station and find out what time the next train goes to Wales.'

Kay began to cry. 'Please, Mum, just let us stay for a few days. Please.'

Frank lit a cigarette and sat back.

'I said no. And I mean no. What's that poor Mrs Davies going to think?'

Shirley too began to cry silently.

Frank put his arm round Shirley's shoulders. 'Your mum's only doing what she thinks is right. It's very dangerous up here.'

'We saw a lot of kids playing,' sniffed Kay. 'Their mums let them stay here.'

'I don't care what or who you saw. You are not staying.' Ruth was beginning to get very agitated.

'Can't we go with you to see Auntie Joyce? I'm sure she'll be pleased to see us.'

'Kay. Stop it.' Ruth picked up her handbag. 'Come on. I'm not listening to any more of this.'

Shirley watched Frank shrug his shoulders at Ruth. Then he turned to her and gave her a wink.

Chapter 6

Kay was getting more and more excited as they sped along the country roads. 'They've not had so many bombs round here,' she said with her nose pressed hard against the car's window.

'No, we've been pretty lucky. It's just the odd one or two. It's mostly pilots who want to look good in the eyes of the Führer, and ditch their load before scuttling back home.' Frank turned the car into the tree-lined drive. 'Joyce is going to be that surprised.'

'I still can't believe that I let you talk me into this,' said Ruth.

'Thank you, Uncle Frank,' said Shirley.

Ruth looked over her shoulder at her daughters and smiled. 'But remember, it's only until tomorrow, then it's back to Wales for you two.'

Joyce was waiting in the drive for her sister, and running to the car, quickly opened Frank's door.

'You're late. Where have you been? I was that worried about—' She suddenly caught sight of Kay and Shirley sitting on the back seat. 'Oh my God. What are they doing . . .?'

Frank was out of his seat and at her side. 'Sorry, love. But we've had a bit of a morning.'

'I can see that. Where have they come from?'

'Don't ask,' said Ruth. 'Put the kettle on. I've brought some rations with me.'

'Hello, Auntie Joyce,' said Shirley as she got out.

Kay ran up to her auntie and held her close. 'It's really smashing to see you. Where's Alice and Bobbie? We've never seen him. Is he big now?'

'He's getting big. They're round the back.' Joyce's face was full of disbelief.

'I expect you want to talk, so can we go and see them?' asked Shirley.

'Course. But give me a big hug first.' She laughed. 'I don't believe this. You have certainly grown up, and into two lovely young ladies, I might add.'

Breaking away, Shirley smiled and, grabbing hold of Kay's hand, asked, 'How do we . . .'

'Just go round the side, but make sure you close the gate, I don't want Alice running out.'

'Thanks,' they said together and disappeared.

'Well. What's this all about?' asked Joyce, looking from her husband to her sister. 'How did they get here?'

As they went inside the house Ruth told her what had happened.

'So, what are you going to do with them?' asked Joyce, filling the kettle.

Ruth sat at the well-scrubbed, oblong deal table that stood in the centre of the bright airy kitchen. She could understand why her sister loved it so. Every time she came here, Ruth felt relaxed. And even though she did have to share a bed with Joyce, she always slept like a log. Whether she'd enjoy living here all the time though was a different matter.

'They're going back tomorrow. I'm going to see Bill and see if I can wangle another couple of days off. I think I can call it compassionate grounds. What do you think, Frank?'

'I reckon he could swing it.'

'What if you get tempted to stay with them?' asked Joyce.

'What, me stuck in the back of beyond? No thanks.' Ruth walked to the window and looked out at her daughters laughing and playing with Alice. Bobbie was in his pram grinning and, in his own way, excitedly shouting at them. 'They have certainly grown.'

'I should say so,' said Joyce, joining her. 'Young Kay's legs seem to go on for ever.'

'I wish this bloody war was over, then we could all be together again. Be a real family.' Ruth wiped her eyes.

Joyce put her arm round her sister's shoulder. 'Look, why don't we look for somewhere round here? It's reasonably safe, and I'm sure I can find someone to have them.'

'Could you? I reckon they'd like that. And I could come down here and see them.'

'I'll ask Mrs Cotton, she knows most of 'em round here. I know she would take them, but she's got land girls to look after.'

'Thanks, Joyce. That would be really wonderful.'

'Right, first things first. Tea, then we've got to sort out where you're sleeping tonight.'

'I can't stay. I've got to go back shortly,' said Frank, looking at his watch.

'I'll do you a couple of sandwiches and fill your flask.'

'Thanks, love. I don't know what we'd do without our cuppa.'

'It's part of being British,' said Ruth. 'Don't say anything to the girls just yet. Let's get it sorted out first. And besides, I want them to suffer a bit longer.'

'That seems very cruel,' said Joyce.

'Maybe, but I have to make them understand how silly they've been.'

Ruth found all the laughter and chatter while they were having tea wonderful. She wanted to tell her daughters the plan and was finding it difficult to keep a straight face. But she had to be sure her girls were going to finish up in a nice home, and with a decent family. She had heard so many stories about evacuated children being abused and treated as slaves.

Later when Joyce and Ruth came into the garden Kay asked, 'Where have you been?'

'We had to go to the shop in the village. I needed to get a few things,' said Joyce.

'Now, you two, go inside and sit down.' Ruth pushed them through the kitchen door.

Kay and Shirley looked very downhearted as they sat at the table in front of their mother and Joyce.

'As you both know I'm very cross at what you've done.'

'We've said we're sorry,' whined Kay.

'I promise we'll never do anything like this again,' said Shirley.

'I hope not.' Ruth was trying so very hard to keep a smile from breaking out.

'Are they going away?' asked Alice.

'We've got to,' said Kay angrily.

'I don't want them to,' said Alice, scrambling up on to Kay's lap.

'We don't want to either.' Shirley wiped her tears on the bottom of her dress.

Ruth began to laugh.

'I don't think it's very funny,' sniffed Kay.

'Come on, Ruth. Don't be so unkind,' said Joyce.

Shirley looked up.

'Your Auntie Joyce has found you a place in the village. You're going to stay with a Mr and Mrs Sharp. Mrs Sharp is the local guide mistress, so you'll have to join the girl guides.' Ruth was smiling at her daughters who sat with their mouths open.

'We're going to stay here?' asked Shirley in a low voice. 'In this village?'

Ruth nodded. 'Is that all right?'

'For ever?' added Kay.

'Well, till the end of the war.'

Shirley jumped up and, rushing round the table, threw her arms round her mother. 'Thank you. Thank you. Thank you.'

'Why is Shirley crying?' asked Alice.

''Cos we're going to stay here. We're not going back to Wales. We'll be able to see you every day.' Kay bounced Alice on her knee.

'You gonner stay with us? In this house?'

'No, love,' said Joyce. 'They are going to stay with Mrs Sharp. You know, that nice lady that used to have Roy and Rosy. Their mother and father were killed, so the gran decided to move right away from London and she took the children with her. They went to a daughter, up north somewhere. I know Mrs Sharp was very sorry to see them go.'

'What about all our clothes?' asked Shirley, ever practical.

'I'm going to write to Mrs Davies and explain all what's happened. I'll ask her to send on all your things. And I don't think it would hurt you both to sit down and write her a letter telling her how sorry you are.'

'I'm not sorry,' said Kay defiantly.

'Don't be so rotten, Kay. Mrs Davies was good to us.'

Kay pulled a face. 'I know. But if I hadn't said I was leaving, we wouldn't be here now, would we?'

'Well, you'll have to mind your Ps and Qs when you're living with Mrs Sharp,' said Joyce.

'Why?' asked Kay.

'Mrs Sharp is a pillar of respectability. Guide leader and a member of the church.'

'Oh dear,' said Ruth, grinning.

'I'll quite like joining the girl guides. Thank you, Mum. Thank you for letting us stay,' said Shirley.

'Don't thank me, thank Auntie Joyce. She's the one that's got it sorted out.'

'I think we're going to be very happy here.'

'Will you come and live down here?' Kay asked her mother.

'No, I can't. I've got my job to do.'

Kay turned down her mouth. 'Is your job more important than us then?'

'No, you know it isn't. But it's a bit like your father. He can't say, I'm sorry, sir, but I want to be with my daughters. None of us wants to be parted from one another. But till this war is over I'm afraid that's how it's got to be.'

'Can we go and see Grandad?' asked Shirley.

'I'll see if the hospital will let you. I'm hoping he'll be moved to a convalescent home soon, and who knows, with a bit of luck it may be near here.'

'I would like to see him,' said Shirley.

'I'll tell him when I go to the hospital tomorrow.'

'You look pleased with yourself,' said Stan when Ruth walked into the incident room. 'Did you enjoy your couple of days off?'

'I should say so. You're never going to guess what happened.'

'From the look on your face, it's got to be something good.'

'It was and it wasn't.' Ruth was pleased to see Stan was his usual self. She had been worried about working with him again, and him keeping his promise and not mentioning his feelings towards her. But somehow, deep down, she knew that he wouldn't jeopardize their friendship. 'My girls decided to come home. I can't tell you how worried I was when the policeman came and told me.'

'What? They came to London, from Wales, all on their own?'

Ruth nodded.

'Why?'

They sat at the table and she told him what had happened in just two short days.

Stan stood up and patted her shoulder. 'That's really great for you, Ruth, and them. Just as long as they're fine.'

Although the gesture had been no more than friendly, Ruth moved away. She felt herself blush and said quickly,

'Now. What's been happening while I've been away?'

'Nothing different I'm afraid. They're still sending those bloody doodlebugs over.'

'I gathered that. I wonder how long it'll be before our boys get to the sites and stop 'em.'

'Dunno. It seems to be going well over there, but I can't see it being over before Christmas.'

'Not another Christmas of sitting in an air-raid shelter and going short of life's luxuries. What you painting your nails with, Gloria? Is it that so-called stocking repairer?'

Gloria, who was sitting close by, looked up. 'Yer, it's good, ain't it? The way they get round all these shortages on so-called luxuries. I was talking to Bob, he's my American friend, he says that now they're over there it ain't gonner take long.'

Teddy, another warden, put the newspaper he was reading down. 'Shall we start singing "The Yanks are coming", and I mean in more ways than one?'

'You've got a filthy mouth,' said Gloria, flapping her hands about to dry her nails.

Stan tutted. 'Take no notice of him. But honestly, girl, Hitler ain't gonner give in till he really has to.'

'S'pose not,' said Gloria.

'It would be nice to get a few extra rations though, wouldn't it? But I can't see it, can you?' said Ruth.

'You should find yourself a Yank, Ruth. You wouldn't go short of anything then. D'you know, this bloody war's playing havoc with my nails.'

'It ain't giving you any trouble with yer love life though, is it, girl?'

Gloria was about to throw a hairbrush at Teddy who had

made that remark, when the conversation was interrupted by Bill Clarke yelling that a buzz bomb was heading their way.

'Right, girl, let's be having you.' Stan rammed on his tin helmet and made for the door with Ruth following close behind.

It was another long night and dawn was lighting the sky when Stan and Ruth made their way back to the post.

They bumped over pot holes and dodged hosepipes. Ruth was deep in thought at what Stan had said about Christmas. It was only August. A lot could happen in the next few months. Hopefully this year she would be with her daughters and her sister. But not her mum. Perhaps her dad would be able to come with them to Joyce's. If only she could be sure this was going to be the last Christmas without Alan. She needed love.

'You're quiet. A penny for 'em.'

Ruth turned to Stan. 'They ain't really worth a penny. I was just thinking about Christmas.'

'You've got a while to think about that. You spending it with your sister?'

She nodded. 'That's if I'm not on duty.'

'I reckon Bill will be a bit lenient. If I remember right, you did Christmas last year.'

'I couldn't get enough time off to go all the way to Wales. And Mum and Dad went down to Joyce's.'

'Why didn't you go with them?'

'Frank couldn't get enough petrol to make two journeys. I think he'd been given a warning about doing too many runs that weren't part of the job. Besides, it would have been a bit cramped with all of us there.'

'It's not like Frank to worry about things like petrol.'

'I know. Anyway, he was on duty as well.'

'Was he now? I would have thought he could have swung it as he's in charge.'

'What about you? Will you volunteer?'

'Might as well.'

Ruth sat back. 'What about going to see your mum and dad?'

'I'm quite happy being up here.'

'Have you thought about what you're going to do when this is all over?'

'Can't say I have.'

'Will your parents come back to live here?'

'I dunno.' Stan was peering through the windscreen. 'Does Frank behave himself?'

Ruth laughed. 'What d'you mean?'

'Well, you know what they say about when the cat's away and all that.'

'I shouldn't think Frank's like that for one minute. He loves my sister. Don't start reading things into it just 'cos he wasn't with her at Christmas.'

He touched her knee. 'Sorry. But you know men will be men. And who knows what can happen to the young 'uns with females like Gloria ready to pounce.'

Ruth gave him a quick glance. What if Alan was doing things? Would he ever tell her? Would he be able to control his manly urges? 'Stan, when you was abroad did you ever, you know?'

He laughed. 'Bloody hell no. We was too busy trying to get back alive. Didn't have time to stop and fraternize.'

'But would you, if . . .'

'Dunno. It's hard to say. I really loved my Jean.' He stopped. 'P'raps I might have done if the circumstances had been right. After all, men will be men,' he said lightheartedly.

'You haven't taken on Gloria.'

'I'm too old for the likes of her. 'Sides, it's the Yanks she's got her eyes on now.'

Ruth laughed. 'I'm sure you could find a nice person.'

'Can't say I'm looking. It'll take me a while to get . . . Well, not yet anyway. I miss her, you know.'

'I expect you do.'

'Here, you're not worried about your old man, are you?'

'No, course not,' she said sharply. But the way the Americans were carrying on over here, the seed of doubt had been sown.

Chapter 7

It was late September. Ruth, who was sitting in the depot reading the newspaper, looked up when Stan walked in. 'Stan, what do you make of these explosions? Do you believe the talk that he's sending over a new weapon?'

'Wouldn't like to say. Is there anything in the paper about it?'

'No. But then they can't say too much, can they?'

'Not really.'

'Surely they've got to tell us if they go on for much longer.'

'Bill was told it was a gas main that exploded in Chiswick, but we've had two or three now and that seems too much of a coincidence – that's, of course, unless it's sabotage.'

'You don't think that, do you? Not at this stage of the war?'

Stan shrugged. 'As I said: I wouldn't like to say.'

'Well, if the rumours are true, it's a bloody awful thing. The buzz bombs are bad enough. At least we know when they're coming. What do you think they are? Bill was saying something about rockets.'

'Could be. A lot of things have been invented during this war.'

Ruth sat back. 'I suppose there has, but this sounds a bit like something out of a Flash Gordon comic. Mind you, I would have thought with all our intelligence they could have found out where they're coming from.'

'Don't forget, he's very clever, and he ain't gonner go down quietly.'

Gradually the rumours were confirmed. The mysterious explosions were caused by V2s, unmanned rockets, dropping in and around London.

Everybody was terrified of these things that just fell out of the sky, without any sound or warning, and were causing a great many deaths and a huge amount of destruction. The only comfort people had, if any, was that if it was a direct hit, death was quick and painless.

As the months moved on, despite all that was happening around her, Ruth began to feel happy. When they were both home on the odd afternoon, she and Lucy would go to the pictures. They waited for the newsreels with just as much anticipation as the main feature. They sat on the edge of their seats when they saw pictures of the sailors on the convoys. They always lived in hope that one day they would see Charlie – or Alan when the army pushing up through Italy was mentioned. The smiling and waving Tommies often brought a cheer from the audience.

Now when Ruth had a day or two off she could go and see her daughters. Mrs Davies had been very upset at the girls leaving like they did but she had parcelled up all their things and had sent them on promptly. Ruth was surprised to see how many of their clothes they had grown out of and she spent the nights, when it was quiet while she was on duty, taking apart, sewing and altering as many of theirs and Joyce's bits as her sister could part with.

At the end of November Ruth's father learnt that the following week he was going to be sent to a convalescent home in Devon. Neither he nor Ruth were very happy about it.

'If only I had a house I could look after him,' Ruth moaned to Joyce at the weekend, when she had managed to get down to Sussex.

'How could you? You wouldn't leave him alone at night when you're on duty, now would you?'

'Suppose not.'

'He'll be all right once he settles in. Besides, you said something about him being fitted for an artificial leg.'

'They were talking about it, but I don't think he's that happy. He hasn't said that much about it. You know Dad. Sometimes it's like talking to a brick wall.'

'It's sure to be a bit strange for him at first. But I think he'll be in the best place.' Joyce picked Bobbie up from the floor and put him in his high chair.

'I know you're right. But to go all that way before Christmas. Last year it was Alan and the girls away, now this year it'll be Dad, and we ain't got Mum now.'

'Don't upset yourself. I'm sure he'll have a great time. He'll be with other men and that'll help cheer him up.'

'I hope so.'

'Will you manage to get to see him before Wednesday?'

'Yes.'

'I wish I could get up, but with the kids it's . . .'

'I know. Shirley wanted to see him, but it ain't worth the risk and Dad understands. 'Sides, as I said, he ain't that talkative.'

'Could you take him a few eggs and some bits I've got for him?'

Ruth nodded. 'I was going to try to get him a pair of slippers, but how can I? They don't let you have just one.'

'I've knitted a couple of socks. I've put different patterns on them and not put them in pairs.'

Ruth sniffed. 'I'm gonner miss popping in to see him.'

Joyce put a comforting arm round her sister. 'Of course you will. Buck up though, with a bit of luck this war will be over soon and you can start a new life with Alan, the girls and Dad near.'

'I'd like him to live with us.'

'I expect he will. But give him time to make up his own mind. Now come on, don't let the girls see you upset. Are you arranging to get Christmas off?'

'I'm keeping my fingers crossed. I've asked Bill and he said he'll let me know. What about Frank?'

Joyce shrugged.

'Joyce, do you ever wonder if Frank . . .'

'I know what you're going to say. But what about you? Do you ever get tempted?'

'No,' said Ruth quickly. 'But I ain't a man.'

'Has Frank ever said anything to you?'

'No. Course not.'

Joyce sat down at the table. 'I wonder how we'll feel after this lot? Will we all be able to settle down?'

'I don't know.'

Bobbie interrupted them with his shouting and banging on his tray with a wooden spoon.

'I'd better start the tea,' said Joyce. 'I think I know a little boy who's hungry.'

'You sure you don't mind giving the girls a bit of tea?'

'Course not. With everything they're doing they don't get to spend a lot of time with you.'

'What time did they say they'll finish their rehearsals?' Ruth had been tickled pink to find that her daughters were going to be in the village pantomime. The girls were almost too busy to see her – so much for her worrying about them!

'Any minute now,' Joyce replied. 'They're really thrilled at being asked and more so when Kay got the lead.'

'Well, she's blonde and beautiful and will make a lovely Cinderella. I can't tell you how happy I am at Kay and Shirley being here. Mrs Sharp has a way with her.'

The back door into the kitchen burst open and Kay and Shirley came bounding in.

'Guess what?' shouted Kay, her face flushed with excitement. 'They're going to have two real ponies to pull my coach – well, it's a cart really, but they're going to do it up to look like a coach.'

'That sounds lovely,' said Joyce. 'Alice will certainly like that.' She turned to Ruth. 'She can't wait to see Kay as Cinderella.'

'What about you, Shirley?' asked Ruth. 'You looking forward to playing Buttons?'

Shirley nodded and a broad grin filled her lovely face. 'Good job the local kids don't mind us taking the leads.'

'Let's face it, Shirl, they're not as good as us, even the other evacuees said that.'

'Well, don't get too big-headed, the pair of you,' said Ruth as she helped Joyce to set the table ready for tea.

'It's so lovely to see you, Mum. When will you be able to get down again?' asked Shirley.

'I don't know. Now we've got these rockets coming over it's not as cut and dried as planes and doodlebugs.'

Joyce looked worried. 'Frank was saying they do a terrible amount of damage.'

'Yes, they do.'

'Can't you come and live here with us?' asked Shirley.

'Believe me, I would if I could. Now come on and have your tea and don't you go worrying about me.'

On Wednesday Ruth was at the hospital to say goodbye to her father. She couldn't hide her tears as he clung to her. 'Now make sure you write as soon as you can.'

'Course love.'

'And remember, you mustn't open your presents till Christmas morning.'

'I won't. Thank your girls for me. I would have liked to see them and Joyce.'

'You will soon. You can drop them a line once you get settled.' Ruth hugged him for the last time as he was put into the ambulance.

She stood and watched the ambulance till it was out of sight. She knew it was the best thing that could happen to him, but that didn't stop the flood of utter despair that was washing over her. The strange happiness she had felt this autumn was gone.

The following Saturday morning, when Ruth came off duty,

she went to bed. In many ways she was pleased to be on night work as she could be with Mrs Graham during the day – albeit in bed. That way, Ruth felt she was helping Lucy.

She was in a deep sleep when someone banging on the front door startled her. Disorientated, she automatically grabbed her jumper and trousers and put them on over her pyjamas. She could hear voices when Mrs Graham answered the front door. Pulling her hair out from her jumper, she went into the passage and was surprised to see Stan standing there.

'What're you doing here?' she asked.

'Ruth, there's been a terrible explosion at New Cross.'

'I heard that. Made the whole place rattle,' said Mrs Graham as they made their way to the kitchen. 'I'm surprised it didn't wake you,' she said to Ruth. 'D'you fancy a cuppa?'

'I'd love one. What about you, Stan? Stan works with me. I must have been dead to the world, I didn't hear it.'

'It shook all the bloody windows. Thought we was gonner lose 'em again,' said Mrs Graham, putting the cups and saucers on the table.

'Is it bad?' asked Ruth.

Stan nodded.

'Was it one of these rocket things?' asked Mrs Graham.

'They think so. They said it's hit Woolies.'

Mrs Graham plonked herself down on a kitchen chair. 'No.'

'It seems it was packed with shoppers, mostly women and children.'

Ruth too sat at the table. 'That's awful.' She was suddenly filled with fear.

Her face must have registered her thoughts because Mrs Graham asked, 'Lucy. D'you happen to know what route my Lucy's on today?'

'I don't know,' whispered Ruth.

'Oh please God. You don't think she could be anywhere near . . .'

'I shouldn't think so. Don't worry, she'll come breezing in as usual.'

Tears were beginning to fill Mrs Graham's eyes. 'Can I come with you?'

'They want as many volunteers as they can gather to help dig the injured out. But I think you'd better wait here for your daughter,' said Stan, looking anxiously at Ruth.

'She should be off duty in a few hours, and she'll be worried stiff if you're not home.' Ruth was trying hard to say the right thing.

'P'raps you're right,' said Mrs Graham reluctantly.

'You ready, Ruth?' said Stan.

'I'll get me coat.'

'God only knows what we're gonner find when we get there,' said Stan.

'Ruth, what about your tea?' called Mrs Graham.

'Don't worry about it. I'll get a cuppa at the WVS stall. They're sure to be there.'

'That's a bloody wicked thing to do. Women and children.' Stan and Ruth left her wiping her eyes with the bottom of her pinny, sadly shaking her head.

Stan got the van as near as the police allowed.

'It ain't all that safe to go any further,' said the policeman.

'Is it bad?' asked Stan.

He nodded. 'Ain't seen nothing like this before. And by the way, no smoking. The gas main's been fractured.'

'I can smell it,' said Stan.

For years they had smelt and almost tasted the stench from the sewers, gas mains, vomit, dead bodies and burning flesh. These smells always hung heavy on the air after a raid.

When they finally picked their way through the rubble, Ruth couldn't keep the gasp escaping from her lips when she saw the devastation. It was vast. So many people crawling like ants over the twisted mound of concrete and metal. There seemed to be hundreds all pulling at masonry and iron girders and passing it to someone behind. Once or twice a piece of coloured paper was attached – was that part of the Christmas decorations?

Stan brought her back to reality. 'Come on, Ruth, don't stand there with your mouth open, give 'em a hand.'

Limbs and parts of bodies were being brought out. They were quickly put into bags. Ruth didn't have time to feel anything, she just kept toiling away. Lifting heavy timbers to release those trapped. Helping the badly injured to the fleet of ambulances.

Someone tossed a crushed bassinet aside. It was half its normal size; there wasn't any sign of a baby inside. Had it just been used for carting coal? A headless doll lay in the gutter.

Those being pulled out of the mess were mostly women and children. Some had lost their clothes and blankets were quickly used to cover them and preserve their dignity.

Ruth was told to attend to a woman who had been laid out in the road. She was still breathing although her eyes were closed and her face white with the dust and dirt. Blood was seeping through her clothes that were hanging in rags; she had obviously lost a great deal. Ruth gently brushed the muck from her eyes; they flickered.

Taking Ruth by surprise, the woman suddenly whispered, 'Help me. Help me.' She tried to move.

Ruth put her head closer.

'My little girl. Find my little girl.' She clung to Ruth's arm with her bloody hand. Her other arm was shattered, but the woman wasn't aware of it.

Ruth cradled the woman close to her. 'They're looking. Now they've got you she should be found soon.' Ruth tried to stanch the blood that was pumping from a gaping wound in her leg. 'I've got to get you to the hospital. I'll get someone to give me a hand.'

'Don't leave me. Please. I'll not go till they find my Mary.'

'How old is Mary?' Ruth wanted to keep her talking as she looked around for help. She felt the woman shudder and go limp. Ruth looked down at that tortured face and let her own tears fall.

'Come on, girl,' someone shouted at her. 'You ain't got time to sit and nurse a dead body, there's work to do.'

Ruth gently laid the woman back down in the road. She had seen so many terrible things during this war, but this was the worst. This had really got to her. These women were probably out Christmas shopping, looking forward to the festivities with their children. Searching for something to put into their stockings. Now it was all over for them.

She ran her sleeve under her nose and threw herself into helping. Would she find Mary? Was she just another tiny crumpled body now? Just another number to add to the growing list of statistics?

The bulldozers were brought in. All day Ruth worked. Her hands and legs were cut, but she felt no pain, just the urge to search and search until she found someone, hopefully alive. So many of the public were helping; some were frantically looking for their loved ones. There were tears of joy and tears of sorrow as more people were uncovered. The wailing when a body was identified was very sad. Often a shout would go up for everyone to be quiet, silence would fall, and ears strain to listen for any sound that would bring hope of finding someone living.

As usual the WVS ladies were there with cups of tea to quench dry and parched throats and quiet words to help troubled minds. The light was fading fast. Would they dare get some lights on the scene? When it began to get dark floodlights were brought in, regardless of the risk. Ruth realized she had been at the site for hours. Strangely, she didn't feel tired.

'Ruth. We've got to go. We've got to be on duty.' Stan was at her side.

'We can't go. You go and tell Bill. I'll stay and . . .'

'There's more than enough here. And fresh people are coming all the time. What if we're wanted somewhere else tonight?'

'But I can't go. I promised I'd look for Mary.'

'Who's Mary?'

'The daughter of the lady who died in my arms.'

'Now come on, Ruth. Even if you found her you wouldn't know it was her. How old is she?'

'I don't know.'

Stan looked at her anxiously. 'Let's go.'

'I can't. I promised.'

'Ruth. Be sensible.' He gently took her arm and pulled her away. 'I think it's about time we left and went back to the post. You might even have a chance to get your head down for an hour or two.'

'Stan . . .' She hesitated. She had said this many times before and knew there wasn't an answer, but . . . 'When will this end?'

'I wish I knew.'

'Thank God my girls aren't here. I couldn't bear it if they ever got injured.'

'They're fine where they are.' He put his arm round her shoulders and gently moved her towards the van.

They stumbled over the rough road. Exhaustion suddenly swept over her, and she felt so sad. As she went to open the door she began softly to cry.

'Ruth, what is it?' Stan put his arms round her and held her close.

She buried her head in his dusty clothes and let her tears fall.

'Come on, old girl. This isn't like you?' He gave her a smile as he removed her tin hat and looked at her. 'You look a bit of a mess.'

The smell of dirt filled her nostrils. She lifted her tear-stained face to him. She wasn't sure why, but she wanted him to kiss her. 'Stan,' she whispered. All she wanted was to be loved.

He was reading the message in her eyes, and bent down and kissed her waiting lips. It was a gentle, warm kiss at first; then they both began to feel the passion that had been simmering between them for a long while, waiting to explode.

Chapter 8

After Ruth and Stan left Mrs Graham, she had kept herself busy, but throughout the morning she had continually glanced at the clock. After lunch she had gone to sit in her front room, anxiously looking out of the window. It had gone three. Lucy should have been home at two. Should she go round to her friend Mrs Plater? She needed someone to talk to. But what if Lucy came home, she'd be worried if her mother wasn't around.

'I suppose I could leave a note,' said Mrs Graham out loud. 'I swear, if anything happens to my Luce, I'll end up going mad. I dunno what I'd do without her.'

Her thoughts went to Ruth. That young woman had been through so much. What had they found at New Cross? 'These girls will never be the same. What will happen to them when their men come home? Can they go back to being ordinary housewives and mothers again after all they've seen, and all this freedom?' Mrs Graham said out loud. She stopped when she heard the distant thud of another explosion. 'This lot's beginning to get to me. Hark at me. I'm starting to talk to me bloody self now.'

Mrs Graham's heart leapt when she caught sight of a

familiar figure in her navy blue uniform, with her hat perched on the back of her head, walking down the road swinging her gas mask. She rushed to the front door and threw herself into her daughter's arms.

'Mum. Mum. What is it?' Lucy took a step back in surprise and put her hand to her mouth. 'Oh no. It's not Charlie, is it?' Her voice was shaking with fear.

Her mother shook her head. 'No. No, love. I've been that worried about you. And you're late,' she reprimanded, wiping her eyes on the bottom of her apron.

'Sorry. But we had a lot of diversions and . . . Why are you crying?'

'That Stan came for Ruth. They went to that explosion at New Cross.'

Lucy put her arm round her mother's shoulders and gently led her back into the house. 'I heard about that. It's pretty bad, by all accounts.'

'When you was late I was so worried. I didn't know what route you was on.'

Lucy gave a silly nervous laugh. 'You ain't the only one. Half the time me and the driver don't even know if we were still in London, we've had that many diversions. Now, how about a nice cuppa?'

Stan was holding Ruth against the van and covering her face and neck with kisses. 'Ruth, I want you.'

She knew it was wrong but she didn't want him to stop. 'Can I . . .?'

With her arms round his neck, she let him kiss her eager mouth again. She knew his hand was cupping her breast, but she could hardly feel it through her thick boiler suit.

She wanted him to caress her body. She wanted him to make love to her.

'Come back to my place.'

She didn't argue when he took her hand and helped her into the van.

He leant over and kissed her once more before he started the engine and they moved off.

Slowly they made their way through the blackout towards Rotherhithe.

It was very quiet. Ruth watched the people with their heads down, pulling at their scarves as they hurried home. You didn't see happy laughing people carrying Christmas trees like the Christmas cards depicted. Next year Ruth vowed she would have a big tree with masses of fairy lights and baubles decorating it. Paper chains would be hanging from the ceiling. They would have a huge chicken and a Christmas pudding with a sprig of holly on top; she would pour brandy over it and bring it in, all alight. There would be plenty of laughter. Alan would be home and they would all be together. Ruth was confused. What was she doing? She quickly glanced at Stan. She liked him, but did she really want him to make love to her? Could she be unfaithful to Alan? No, she couldn't.

'Stan. I'm sorry.' Tears glistened in her eyes. 'I can't. I can't go home with you.'

Stan looked at her. He stopped the van. 'Why not?'

'Alan.'

'But, Ruth, he's probably having it away with some bird right now.'

'That's up to his conscience. But I can't. I'm sorry. I didn't mean to lead you on.'

Stan took hold of her hand. 'I'm very fond of you Ruth and I was, well . . .' He laughed but his voice cracked. 'And there's me thinking me luck had just changed,' he joked.

Ruth could see in the dim light that he was upset. 'Don't let this spoil our friendship.'

He shook his head. 'No. No course not.' He put the van in gear and they moved off again. 'Ruth . . .' he began. He wasn't looking at her. 'Remember I'll always be around if you ever want me.'

She nodded. 'I know, and thanks.'

'What for?'

'Being so understanding.'

'That's me. Dependable Stan.' And didn't say another word until they reached the depot.

'You two look a right mess,' said Bill when they walked in. 'I've had the posts round New Cross on the blower all day. I told them they'd already got some of me best crews. It's pretty bad then?'

Stan was signing in. 'Bloody bad.'

Ruth stood back and put her hands on the small of her back. 'I feel so tired.'

'Look, why don't you go on home? If we need you I'll get Stan to pick you up.' Bill flicked the ash from his cigarette on to the floor. He looked on edge and Ruth knew he was almost chainsmoking these days, but he never let on that their work might be getting to him. Despite his bravado, he was a very private man. Ruth guessed he was in his sixties. He never talked about his family, did he have a wife and children? Were they still in London?

'Would that be all right?'

'Go on home, girl, before I change me mind.'

'Thanks, Bill.' Ruth picked up her gas mask and left. She looked up at the night sky. 'Please don't let him send anything over tonight. Let's have a bit of a rest.'

Ruth knew Lucy was safe as soon as she opened the front door. She could hear her and her mother singing along with the wireless.

'Christ, you look a mess,' said Lucy when Ruth walked into the kitchen.

'Thanks, that's the second time I've been told that in the last hour.'

'Sorry. Shouldn't you be on duty?'

'Bill said I could come home, it's been a bit of a bad day.' Ruth brushed her hair from her face.

'I bet it has. Look at your hands.'

Ruth did as Lucy said. Her hands had been bleeding. 'I've lost all me fingernails again. Is there any chance I could have a bath?'

'Don't see why not,' said Mrs Graham who was standing at the table ironing. She put the flat iron back on the fire. 'I'll put a bucket on the gas.'

Ruth sat in the tin bath with her knees tucked under her chin. She closed her eyes and hugged her knees when Lucy offered to wash her back.

'Don't you go to sleep on me,' said Lucy, gently trickling the water over Ruth's back.

'I won't.'

'D'you want to talk about it?'

Ruth quickly opened her eyes. 'Talk about what?'

'The rescue.'

89

'Oh, that.'

'What did you think I meant?'

'Nothing.'

Lucy peered round at her; she was grinning. 'Here, you ain't been up to, you know, hanky panky, have you?'

Ruth laughed. She had to brazen this out. 'Who with? Besides, chance'd be a fine thing.'

'Well, you've got plenty of men at your post.'

'Oh yes. Those who are too old and infirm to do anything else. No, I fancy a man with a bit of go in him.'

'I know what you mean.'

'What about the men at the garage?'

Lucy laughed. 'As the song says, they're either too young or too old. Right. I've finished.' Lucy stood up. 'I'll leave you to get out. Look at the colour of that water.'

'It is pretty grimy. Thanks, Luce. I feel much better now.'

Ruth stood up and wrapped the towel that had been warming over the fire-guard around her. She buried her head in its warmth, then slipped into her pyjamas. She just wanted to sleep. Like most people these days, she wasn't going to the shelter tonight. If a doodlebug came over someone would wake her and if it was a rocket, well, at least it would be quick.

It was Saturday, 16 December and Ruth had the night off. She was so looking forward to seeing the first night performance of the pantomime the girls were performing in.

Travelling down on the train she had time to reflect on the past couple of weeks.

Since that night when Ruth had almost given herself to Stan, they had continued to work together. Nothing was ever said, but sometimes she caught him looking at her, and she felt guilty. There were times when she did wonder what it would have been like to have him make love to her, but the moment had passed.

Her thoughts went back to the first time she went to the wardens' post. It was after a very heavy raid; Ruth and her parents had been in the brick shelter in the back yard. When they finally emerged the following morning the front of their house had almost gone. The men at the post had been very helpful and had told her where to go to be rehoused and where to collect anything they required. She went back to thank them when they had settled in another house. It was then that she met Bill and he told her how short they were of help. Both herself and her father, who was out of work at the time through the docks being bombed, decided then and there that they would volunteer. She gave up her job in the shop and joined on a full-time basis. Stan had been with her since the very first day. He had taught her to drive and they had been a team ever since. She gave a little smile. He could have been her lover.

It was raining outside and, inside the dimly lit carriage, Ruth moved the green blind and cleaned the steamed-up window with her gloved hand. She smiled again, waiting for someone to start yelling, 'Put that light out.' It was a familiar saying, one she had used herself many times over the last four years. But now the end was in sight, the blackout, at long last, was being lifted.

When the train stopped she knew she was at Horsham, even though all the station names had been removed for security. She pulled at her coat and hastily made her way to the bus stop.

★ ★ ★

It wasn't long before, cold and wet, she was hurrying into the church hall, hoping she wasn't going to be late. She should have allowed more time to travel. She should have got Mrs Graham to wake her earlier.

Inside the hall it was warm and festive. She was told to sit in the front row as she was the star's mother. Joyce, along with Alice, Mrs Cotton and Bobbie, was already there; Ruth nodded and grinned at them all. Quickly she sat down next to Joyce just as the curtain was about to go up. Ruth was very excited and nervous.

She was so proud of her girls up there on the stage. They looked lovely and not once did they fluff their lines. Even the ponies behaved. It was Kay who stole the limelight and, at the party afterwards, much to her daughter's delight, everyone said how good she was.

Mrs Sharp came over to Ruth. 'I'm really pleased you could get time off to see the girls. They were first rate, looked almost professional.'

'Yes, they were,' said Ruth smiling.

'Young Kay has certainly got a lot of talent. Will you manage to get here for Christmas?' asked Mrs Sharp.

'I hope so, but you never know. These V2s are causing a lot of distress.'

'I know. I'm so glad we're not in the pathway.'

'So am I. Are my girls behaving themselves, Mrs Sharp?'

Mrs Sharp gave Ruth a warm smile. 'I should say so. It's a real pleasure to have them around.'

'That's good.'

'I'm so pleased you could make it, Ruth,' said Joyce.

'So am I. Did you get a letter from Dad telling you he's being moved?'

'Yes. Do you think he'll be all right?'

'I had a letter from the Sister. She said he was going to a sort of halfway house, just till I've got a place he can come back to. It sounds all right.'

'I hope so.'

Bobbie began to grizzle.

'Ruth, I'm sorry to be a killjoy,' said Joyce. 'But my two are done in, so do you mind if me and Mrs Cotton go on home?'

'No, course not. Do you want me to come as well?'

'No. You stay with the girls a bit longer and let them wallow in their glory.'

'Thanks. I won't be that long.'

Kay and Shirley kissed Bobbie and Alice goodnight. Alice was fascinated with the make-up they had on and her little fingers ran over their brightly painted lips.

'I'm going on the stage when I get a big girl.'

'Of course you are, darling,' said Joyce. 'But it's home to bed for you now.'

They said their goodbyes and Ruth stood and watched them walk away. She smiled to herself. At least her youngest daughter and niece had dreams and ambitions for the future.

Ruth was so happy, she *was* going to be with her girls over Christmas. With the end now in sight, the government had announced they would shortly be disbanding the Civil Defence, so Bill said she could have the time off.

Joyce had managed to get a mattress for Ruth and her

daughters and on Christmas Eve they were all sleeping on the sitting-room floor – or they were till Alice came bounding in at seven o'clock, followed by Joyce carrying Bobbie, and Frank carrying a tray of tea.

Frank switched on the tree's fairy lights. Mrs Cotton had given them the top of a small fir tree that was growing in the garden. Kay and Shirley had been busy for days making baubles and decorations from anything they could find – bits of silver paper, painted fir cones and berries. It even had a small fairy doll perched on top and it looked very festive. Frank had somehow managed to find the lights, and they worked. There was plenty of laughter and the meagre presents Ruth had managed to get were eagerly accepted and opened.

'I've always wanted a music case,' said Shirley. 'How did you manage . . .'

Ruth smiled and put her finger to her lips. 'I had a word with Father Christmas.'

'Of course,' said Kay, very pointedly looking at Alice. 'He was ever so clever to get me this skipping rope and a new set of crayons, and look at my skirt.' She held up a skirt that Ruth had made out of blackout material.

'I've got a new skirt as well,' said Shirley.

'I've got a doll with lots of clothes,' said Alice, her bright eyes shining.

'He is very clever,' said Joyce, remembering the nights she had sat knitting the tiny garments.

Frank was bursting with pride as he looked round the room. 'And what about you two?' he asked Ruth and Joyce.

'Chocolates and nylons,' said Ruth. 'I'm saving the nylons to wear when Alan comes home.'

'Let's hope Daddy's with us next year,' said Shirley.

Ruth swallowed hard. 'Yes, darling. We all hope for that.'

There was a brief silence as they all thought about Alan – what on earth was he doing this Christmas?

'What did you wish for when you stirred the Christmas pudding?' Kay asked her sister.

'I'm not telling.'

'You mustn't,' said Joyce. 'It might not come true.'

'I can't believe you managed to make a pudding,' said Ruth to Joyce.

'I hope it's all right,' said Joyce.

'Has it got any thruppenny bits in?' asked Frank.

'I'm not telling.'

'Well, I hope I don't break me teeth on one.'

'I hope it'll taste nice. I've never put potato and carrots in a pudding before, but it's a Ministry of Food recipe and that Marguerite Patten reckons it's all right.'

'Mrs Graham listens to her broadcasts, she uses some of her recipes.'

'Right,' said Frank. 'All this talk about food's making me hungry. What say we have some breakfast?'

'Yes, please,' came the chorus.

'Well, girl,' said Frank with his arm round Ruth's shoulder as they went into the kitchen. 'It looks like the end's in sight.'

'It's great we can lift the blackout. It seems funny knowing people can see in.'

'Taking those shields off the headlights is good. At least we can see where we're going,' Frank added.

'Have you heard anything about the running down of the Civil Defence?'

'We're waiting for our orders.'

'Does that mean you, Frank?' asked Joyce.

'Should think so.'

'What will you do?'

'I'll find something. There's going to be a lot of jobs going.'

'What about you, Ruth?' asked Joyce. 'Will you go back to work?'

'I don't know. I'll have to find a house and get it ready for when Alan comes home. Then there's Dad.'

'I hope he's having a good Christmas,' said Joyce. 'Pity he couldn't manage the journey.'

'There wasn't a lot of point really, not till I get a house.'

'Don't worry, Ruth. I expect he's having a great time. The locals in those out-of-the-way places are very keen to help those more unfortunate than themselves,' said Frank.

'According to his letters, he seems happy enough now he's settled in this new place. But he hasn't said a lot about his new leg,' said Ruth.

'He'll manage all right. He's a tough old boy.'

'All these changes he's had to face,' said Joyce.

'It seems we've all got to make changes. When are you going home, Joyce?'

She sat at the table. 'I expect it'll have to be soon. Can't say I'm looking forward to it after all this space. I might wait till these V2s ease up. Frank says they've had a few doodlebugs round Sutton and Cheam way. But what *do* you think you'll do, Ruth?'

'I'd like to stay at home. I'd like to go back to being a housewife again.'

'That'll be a bit tame after all the excitement you've had.'

'A lot of it I could have well done without. But we'll have to wait and see. If we get a house we've got to furnish it and that'll take a few bob.'

'It'll be wonderful for you to be a family again though. Will you stay in Rotherhithe?'

'I don't know. It'll be up to Alan.'

'At least he won't have to worry about getting a job with all the building work that's got to be done,' said Frank. 'They'll need plenty of carpenters.'

'That's true, but will he want to go back to that?'

'You'll have to give him time to settle,' said Joyce.

Ruth nodded. 'I know. We'll all need time for that.' What kind of war had Alan had? How would things be when they all came together again? The girls were growing up, would they resent a man telling them what to do?

Everybody's life was going to change next year.

Chapter 9

With the new year came the realization that, as Frank had said, the conflict in Europe would be over very soon.

Ruth had decided it was time she began looking in earnest for a home.

'I can't believe how lucky I am,' said Ruth excitedly as she told Lucy and her mother about the three-bedroom house she'd managed to get.

'We're really gonner miss you,' said Lucy.

'Where is it, love?' asked Mrs Graham.

'Lind Road. Do you know it?'

'That's a good few streets away,' said Mrs Graham.

'Will you still be able to pop in then?' asked Lucy.

'I hope so.'

'It's a bit posh round that way,' said Mrs Graham.

'It's not far from where me and Alan lived after we got married. God, that seems a lifetime ago.'

'What state's it in?' asked Lucy.

'Not bad, not bad at all. Needs a good clean, but it's got a roof and all its windows. The decoration's a bit, well, not my taste.'

'Alan will be able to sort that out, won't he?'

Ruth smiled at Lucy. 'I hope so. Guess what? It's got a bathroom. No more dragging the old tin bath in and filling with buckets. It's got an Ascot to heat the water.'

'That's lovely. Who told you about this one?' asked Mrs Graham. She knew how many places Ruth had looked at, and had turned down, including some that had been damaged and didn't look safe.

'Stan at work.'

'That was nice of him,' said Mrs Graham.

'Wasn't it? Stan lives near the pub and his landlord owns all the property round that way, so he knew who owned it. I get me rent book next week. Stan don't reckon he's a bad bloke and he does all his own repairs. I can't believe that after all this time I'll have me own place again.'

'When you bringing the girls back?' Mrs Graham asked as she smoothed out the tablecloth.

'When I've got it straight and some furniture. Can't have 'em sleeping on the floor. The last tenant left the lino and some curtains – they're a bit tatty, but they'll do. They left a sideboard too, so I've got a cupboard, but not a lot to put in it. It's OK for now. Mind you, the curtains might fall apart when I wash 'em.' Ruth laughed excitedly. 'It's like starting out again.'

'I can let you have a few bits.'

'Thanks, but I can't take anything . . .'

Mrs Graham held up her hand. 'Look, we've been lucky through this lot, and I've got more than enough sheets so I can spare you a pair, and I've a pair of curtains that might do as well.'

'But what about if Lucy wants—' Ruth stopped when she

99

caught sight of Lucy pulling a face behind her mother's back.

'I expect Luce will still live here even when her Charlie comes home. Ain't no point in her moving to another house and leaving me on me own, is there?'

'No. I shall be having my dad come and live with us.'

'That'll be nice for him,' said Mrs Graham. 'How is he?'

'Not too bad, or at least that's what he says in his letters. It's gonner be hard for him without Mum.'

'Will he be able to manage the stairs?' asked Mrs Graham.

'I don't know. We'll have to see when he gets here.'

'Will you go back to your old job?' asked Lucy.

'I'll have to. Mind you, selling clothes will seem a bit tame after what I've been doing these past years. Collins's is still standing, just about. I'll go and see if they want staff.'

'What about stock?' asked Lucy. 'Where do they get it from?'

'I don't know. They must still get some sort of allowance.'

Lucy grinned. 'Here, does that mean we might be able to get a frock without clothing coupons?'

Ruth laughed. 'Knowing Mrs Collins, I shouldn't think so for one minute.'

'I'd like to know where some of the market blokes get their gear. I know it costs a few bob more, but I'm more than happy to pay extra.' Lucy grinned. 'It's better than parting with your precious coupons.'

'I'll have to start scouring the second-hand stalls and shops for me new home. I'm going to ask Frank if he can get me some bits of furniture.'

'That should be interesting,' said Lucy.

★ ★ ★

It was April 1945. The sad news that President Roosevelt had died upset many people. He was well liked on both sides of the Atlantic. The news that Hitler and Mussolini were dead, however, was greeted with cheers. The terrible news of the concentration camps filled the newspapers.

So much was happening at once. Excitement filled the air as people started to think about their future. By now Ruth was no longer in the Civil Defence; Mrs Collins had taken her back but, like thousands of others, Ruth was finding a nine-to-five job wasn't very stimulating. She was missing the action and the camaraderie of working with people who, even in the darkest days, could laugh and make jokes. Everything had begun to seem very mundane. The only thing that pleased her was the enjoyment and challenge of finding furniture for the house. She was longing for the time when they could all be together again. When she had partly furnished the bedrooms she decided it was time to bring Kay and Shirley home.

It had been two weeks since Joyce had left the farm; she was now back in her home at Sutton and Ruth had gone to see her the first opportunity she had. This was the first time she had been to the house since Joyce left.

'Everything looks just the same,' Ruth had said as she walked in.

'It ain't as clean as I would like it. It's gonner take weeks to get it up to scratch.'

'You should see my place. It's gonner take me months.'

'I would have thought Frank's mum would have made a better job of keeping it clean. Don't look like the curtains have been washed in all this time.'

'That ain't fair. She's getting on a bit. 'Sides, Frank's not been living here that much, so it can't be that bad.'

'Suppose not.'

'By the way, where is he?'

'Out. Seeing a bloke about a lock-up to store some of his stuff.'

'What, on a Sunday?'

'You know Frank. I think this is going to be the story of my life from now on.' Joyce gazed out of the dining-room window. 'I shall miss living in the country. I used to love taking the kids for long walks in the woods. I'll miss a lot of things I used to do, like blackberrying and—'

'What a shame. My heart bleeds for you. At least you've still got your home and all your belongings.'

'I'm sorry. I know I shouldn't grumble.'

'No, you shouldn't. And you've got Frank. Sometimes I get fed up with your moaning.'

'Well, it's hard for me.'

'And it's bloody hard for me as well. I'm in a house that wants a good do through. I've got to scrimp and scrounge stuff that nobody else wants for me home, and still got to try to make it look something. My kids have got to cope with another new school, and my husband is Christ knows where. And you think you've got problems.'

'Ruth, I'm sorry. It's just that I feel so . . . I don't know. Trapped, I suppose. I'd like someone to come along and whisk me away.' A tear ran down Joyce's face.

'How do you think I feel? At least you've had a man around. I feel as if I've been in a convent for years.'

'Yes, but what about if Frank don't get a proper job and

says he's got to work late and don't come home till Christ knows what time?'

'Then you'll have to start looking for a knight on a white horse.'

Joyce sniffed. 'You don't know what it's like to be lonely.'

Ruth put her arms round her sister. 'We shouldn't be arguing. We've still got our health. We should think about Dad.'

'I know.' Joyce wiped her eyes. 'I do wonder how he's getting on.'

'In his last letter he said his tin leg was painful to walk on.'

'They'll get that sorted out, won't they?'

'I hope so. Come on, make a cup of tea, Joyce.'

Ruth followed her sister into the kitchen.

'It's a bit smaller than me last one.' Joyce grinned.

'At least your sink's a lot cleaner than mine. I'm buying bleach and Izal by the bucket load.'

'Ruth, would you like me to have Dad?'

'How could you? You've got two little 'uns running around. What if one of them bumped into him and knocked him over? No, it wouldn't be very practical.'

'It's just that I always feel I've let you do everything.'

'Well, you have.'

'Honestly. I would have him here.'

'I was only kidding. No, he'll be all right with me. Once some of his old clubs open up again and he meets his old cronies, he'll be as right as ninepence.'

Joyce filled the teapot. 'Do you see any of those you used to work with?'

'Sometimes.'

'Were there a lot of goings on?'

'I should say so.'

'Was you ever tempted?'

Ruth could feel her colour rising. 'Once. But I think too much of Alan. I'm very grateful to Frank for volunteering to bring the girls back,' she said, quickly changing the subject. 'They seemed to have collected so much stuff, we would never have managed on the train.'

'He don't mind. So who was this bloke then?'

'Someone I worked with. But it didn't go anywhere.'

'You dark horse. So how's work?'

Ruth screwed up her nose. 'It'll do for now. Good job Mrs Collins is Jewish and shuts on Saturdays. I don't know for how long though. She was saying when things look up a bit she's going to open on Saturdays and I'll be in charge.'

'That'll be good, won't it?'

'Depends on what she pays me. So, Frank's working then?'

'Yes. Well, he goes out and comes back with money, so he must be doing something.'

'I was really pleased with those beds he managed to get hold of.'

'I hope they didn't have any bugs hiding in the springs. What did he charge you?'

Ruth laughed. 'Only half a crown each for the girls' beds and five bob for the double. He threw in the mattresses, and I didn't see any bugs in 'em.' She looked through the kitchen window. 'She seems to be happy enough.' Ruth nodded towards Alice who was playing in the garden.

'Yes. I wish I was as adaptable as them.'

'Where's Bobbie?'

'Asleep. Ruth, if there's anything I can help you with . . .'

'You've given me quite a few bits already, but I never say no. D'you know, that Mrs Plater, who's a friend of Lucy's mum, she gave me a couple of pillows and an old bolster. I tell you, Joyce, people have been so kind.'

'So I'll have to try and keep up with 'em then!'

A few days later Ruth was surprised when she opened the door one evening to find Stan standing there. He was holding a bunch of flowers.

'These are from me garden. To welcome you to your new home. And to celebrate the fall of Berlin.' He thrust the flowers into her hand.

'Thanks, Stan, they're lovely. Isn't it fantastic news? Come in. D'you fancy a cup of tea?'

'Wouldn't say no.' He followed her down the passage. 'If there's anything I can do to help out, I'd be more than willing.'

'Thanks, but Frank has done a few bits for me. I could do with a flower vase.'

'I'll have a look and see what me mum's got.'

'No. I can't take your mother's. These will have to go in a milk bottle for now. How's work?'

'Not bad. A newspaper office is a bit boring after all this time. It seems funny working in the day after years of night shifts.'

'I know. It's a good job they took you back.'

Stan sat at the table. 'I was lucky, at least my firm's still standing.'

Ruth put a cup of tea in front of him.

'Thanks. I'm thinking of trying to get something down south somewhere.'

'What, move away?'

'Might as well. Mum and Dad ain't too keen to come back, so I ain't got a lot going for me round here now.'

'No, I suppose not.'

'My sister says she can put me up, but I'll try and get me own little flat. After being on me own all this time I don't fancy being in with a crowd.'

'How many kids has your sister got then?'

'Only two boys, but it seems like a crowd to me.'

'I expect it does. Would there be any work there?'

'I've got me union card and I can turn me hand to most things. It might be a good thing to start again.'

'Yes, I suppose it would.' Ruth felt very sad for Stan. She knew he missed his wife, but now he must miss the companionship they'd had in the Civil Defence. 'Thanks for helping me to get this place.'

'That's all right. When's your dad coming back?'

'I don't know. I've had a couple of letters from the doctor down there and they seem to think he should be able to make the move soon.'

'That'll be nice for him, back with his family.'

'I don't know. The girls might be a bit much for him.'

'When they coming home?'

'Saturday, I hope.'

'That'll be really nice.'

'Yes, it will.'

They went silent. It was strange, after all that had almost happened and all the years they had been together, now the atmosphere felt odd. It was like talking to a stranger. She felt ill at ease.

Stan must have felt it too. He stood up. 'I best be going.

Don't forget, I'm not that far away.' He stopped. 'Ruth, this might sound daft.' He shifted nervously from one foot to the other. 'But that night. You know? Well I'm glad nothing happened. I could never face your father or, come to that, Alan, when I finally get to meet him. Just as long as we can always be friends?'

'Thanks, Stan.' Ruth wanted to kiss his cheek, he looked so alone and vulnerable, but thought better of it.

She closed the door behind him and stood for a moment or two reflecting on what might have been. 'Thank goodness I came to my senses in time,' she said out loud.

Ruth was pleased to find Mrs Sharp out when she called for her daughters. They ran to her and first she hugged Kay then Shirley. 'Me and Uncle Frank have come to take you home,' she said enthusiastically.

'What home?' asked Kay pulling away.

'I told you. I told you we've got a house. We can be together again.'

'What, now?' asked Shirley. 'But the war's not over yet.'

'It will be any day now.'

'When have we got to go?' asked Kay.

'When Uncle Frank parks the car. Of course I'll wait for Mrs Sharp to come back. I won't just whisk you away.'

'What sort of house is it?' asked Kay.

'I've told you. It's very nice, it's got three bedrooms, a kitchen and a small scullery, and it's near to where we lived before.' Ruth was a little disappointed at their response.

'Has it got a lav indoors?' asked Kay. 'I don't like going in the yard at night with all those spiders.'

'You won't have to, and it's got a bathroom.'

107

'Will we each have a bedroom to ourselves?' asked Shirley.

'No, you'll have to share. We'll have Grandad living with us. Don't you want to come home?'

Shirley smiled. 'Of course we do. It's just that it will be different to living here.'

'Very different. Now, shall we start collecting your things?'

'Has it got furniture and stuff?' asked Kay.

'Of course. Not a lot at the moment, but we will get more in time.'

'Have we got beds?' asked Shirley.

'Don't be silly. Now, would I take you home if you didn't?'

Upstairs Ruth could see the girls were very reluctant to collect their belongings. 'This is such a lovely airy room,' she said looking out of the window.

'We know,' said Shirley.

'What sort of view will we have?' asked Kay.

Ruth was trying hard for the right words. How could she tell them the house looked over a bomb site? 'Well it's not the same as this. It wasn't that long ago you wanted to come home.'

Kay looked down sheepishly. 'That was before we came here.'

'Now that Joyce has gone I thought you'd be eager to come back.'

'It is a bit different now,' said Shirley. 'A lot of our mates have gone home.'

'Well then.'

Mrs Sharp came bustling up the stairs. 'I've just seen a car outside, is it Frank's?'

'Hello, Mrs Sharp. Yes, it is.'

'We've got to go back to London,' said Kay.

'Oh. When?'

'I thought we'd go today, while Frank's got the car and the time off.' Ruth could see she was upset at losing the girls.

'So soon? I didn't think it would be just yet.'

'I want to get them settled in school.'

'Of course.'

There were tears quietly running down the girls' cheeks, and Ruth noticed Mrs Sharp was swallowing hard.

'We'll come back to see you,' said Kay, holding her tight.

'Can we come in the holidays?' asked Shirley.

'Of course you can. You can stay as long as you like. But you'll soon forget me when you get back with your family.'

'No we won't,' said Kay. 'I promise we won't.'

Ruth was getting upset. All these years she'd wanted to be with her daughters, now they were reluctant to come with her.

'I wish we'd been here all through the war,' said Kay.

'And I wish I'd had you,' said Mrs Sharp, gently patting Kay's head.

'We could have, if Mum had asked Auntie Joyce.' Kay glared at her mother.

'Joyce didn't come here till after you'd been sent to Wales.' Ruth was now getting angry. She thought she had done the best thing for her daughters, and her good intentions were being questioned.

Frank poked his head round the door. 'Any more stuff?' he asked.

'No, that's it,' said Ruth.

There were more tears and hugs and Kay and Shirley waved out of the back window of the car till the house and Mrs Sharp had disappeared.

Ruth sat in the front in silence, wrapped up in her thoughts. *The girls are at a funny age, will it take them long to settle down? And what about when Alan returns, how will they deal with that?*

Ruth couldn't see any emotion on her daughters' faces as they got out of the car and looked around.

'Is this it?' asked Kay, looking up at the row of houses. 'It don't look very nice.'

'It will do,' said Frank. 'Your mum has done a lot inside. You wait and see.'

'All these houses are so close together,' said Shirley.

'I know,' said Ruth, pushing open the front door and making her way down the passage.

'What's in here?' asked Kay pushing open a door.

'That's the front room. I've not got any furniture in there just yet.'

Kay shut the door.

'It'll be nice and cosy in this kitchen in the winter,' said Ruth taking off her hat and putting it on the table. Under the green chenille cloth that Mrs Graham had given her was a battered old oak table with thick bulbous legs. It had definitely seen better days, but at only three shillings Ruth had found it too good a bargain to miss. She hadn't been able to get four matching chairs and had to make do with two pairs, but at least they had somewhere to sit.

In the scullery was a gas cooker and sink with a small

Ascot above it. 'So we'll have plenty of hot water,' said Ruth cheerfully.

'Can we see our room?'

Ruth could see Shirley wasn't over-impressed with her surroundings.

'I'll get their bits from the car and take 'em on up,' said Frank. 'Ruth, put the kettle on, there's a love. I'm parched.'

Ruth quickly filled the kettle and followed Frank and the girls upstairs.

'Which is our room?' asked Kay.

'This one,' said Ruth, hoping they would approve. She had tried to make it as attractive as she could. Two beds stood side by side with a small table in between. Ruth had scoured the second-hand shops for a dressing table with a mirror on top. The cover draped in front was made from an old lace curtain she'd got at a jumble sale. In the recess at the side of the fireplace, Frank had fixed a broom handle on top of the picture rail to hold their clothes. In front, Ruth had hung a piece of curtaining on a spring to hide the clothes. She was pleased with her efforts and thought the room looked rather nice. 'Do you like it?' she asked eagerly.

'Yes, it's all right,' said Shirley softly.

'It's a bit small,' said Kay.

The sound of the kettle's whistle sent Ruth scurrying down the stairs. She wanted to cry. This wasn't how she thought their homecoming would be. She wanted them to be happy. Would they really resent being here? She dabbed at her eyes.

'You all right, girl?' asked Frank, coming up behind her.

'I thought they'd be pleased to be back with me,' she sniffed.

'They will. Give 'em time. After all, it's a bit of a culture shock. I don't think Joyce has got over it yet, she still mopes around wishing she was back in the country.'

'What will it be like when Alan gets home?'

'I dunno, love. A lot of lives have been turned upside down, now we've just got to get on and try again.'

Ruth sat at the table and began to cry. 'I tried so hard to make it look nice. It wasn't easy.' She didn't notice her daughters standing behind her in the doorway, looking very guilty.

Three days later everybody was listening to the wireless as Churchill told the world that the war with Germany was now over.

Ruth couldn't stem her tears; they fell freely as she laughed and danced round the room holding Kay and Shirley close.

'When will Daddy be home?' asked Kay.

'I don't know. Let's hope it's soon.'

'Are we going to have a street party?' she asked.

'I think so. That Mrs Russell down the road has been collecting coupons and money for a few weeks now. Let's go and see Lucy.'

'All right,' said Shirley smiling. 'I like her.'

'She's been a very good friend to me.'

Since they had seen how upset their mother had been the day they came home, the girls had, to Ruth's relief, gone out of their way to accept that they were going to live in London from now on. Today they were definitely going to enjoy it.

All three quickly hurried to where Lucy and her mother lived.

Ruth didn't bother to knock. She hurried down the passage calling for Lucy.

The kitchen door flew open and they fell into each other's arms. Then Ruth hugged Mrs Graham.

'Mum, Mum. Everybody's out in the street, come and look.' Shirley's voice was high with excitement.

Flags people had kept tucked away were suddenly springing out of windows and church bells were ringing. People were singing. Kay was dancing with an old lady. The atmosphere was electric. They were all caught up in the euphoria.

'Shall we go up West?' said Lucy.

'Why not.' As Ruth danced about she was laughing and crying at the same time. She knew now that this was going to be the start of a wonderful life.

Chapter 10

Ruth, with her daughters and Lucy, spent the evening and half the night singing and dancing in the streets. It was magical. Bunting had appeared from nowhere, and anything red, white and blue was worn. They were all hugged and kissed by any member of the services that came past.

Arm in arm, along with thousands of others, they made their way along the Mall and joined the crush yelling for the King and Queen to come out on to the balcony of Buckingham Palace.

Ruth didn't want the night to end. She wanted to savour every moment. This was going to be a night she would never forget. She would tell Alan, and in years to come, their grandchildren.

Hours later all four of them sat on the kerb, happy but exhausted. Ruth, who was between her daughters, put her arms round their shoulders. 'What a night.' Her eyes were sparkling.

Lucy took off her shoes and began rubbing her feet. 'These feel like lumps of lead. One of those sailors that jumped in the fountain jumped on me foot first. My Gawd. Look at the colour of 'em, it'll take weeks to get them

clean, I should have gone in the fountain with him.' She
threw her head back and laughed.

'I think if I took my shoes off I'd never get them back on
again.' Ruth smiled at her daughters. 'I bet you're glad to be
in London on such a night.'

'It was fun. Thanks, Mum,' said Shirley.

'I enjoyed all the kissing,' said Kay.

'You would, you hussy,' said Ruth.

'Can't say I did,' said Shirley. 'One bloke, I think he was
Polish, wanted to take me home.'

'What?' Lucy, who was still holding her foot and laughing, yelled out. 'All the way back to Poland?'

Shirley was grinning as she nodded.

'Over my dead body,' said Ruth.

She giggled. 'I told him my mum would kill him.'

'What did he say to that?' asked Lucy.

'He reckoned he'd rather face the Germans than an angry
mum.'

They all laughed together.

'Come on,' said Lucy. 'Let's try and find a bus.'

'What about your shoes?' asked Kay as she watched Lucy
stuff them into her handbag.

'I'll put 'em on later. Want to feel the cold pavement, it
might help to cool 'em down.'

They made their way to a bus stop doing the conga. The
bus queue was long, but nobody seem to care. Nobody was
in a hurry to get home. Churchill had told the nation that
VE Day was going to be a holiday.

A few weeks later, once the street parties and the euphoria
had died down, people began to realize that, apart from no

bombs or blackout, nothing was going to change for a long while. Food was still short and the queues still long. There wasn't going to be a quick end to rationing, and the war with Japan continued. The one bright thing that everybody enjoyed was to see banners stretched across roads, and hanging from windows, announcing that someone's son, brother or husband was being welcomed home from the war.

Ruth knew she had to go to work every day, even though she found it boring and mundane. She told herself that when Alan came home things would be different, and with her dad to look after, she could stay at home and her days would be full. At the shop she seemed to spend hours dusting and standing around. Mrs Collins had very little stock to display and make look attractive. Then there was the hassle of clothing coupons. So many women pleaded with Ruth to take extra money if they didn't have enough coupons. She noticed Mrs Collins served some of her regulars and she was sure they didn't give up the correct amount, but it wasn't her business and she wasn't going to get involved.

Every morning Ruth eagerly waited for the postman to bring her the news she had been waiting for all these years.

'He's coming home,' Ruth shouted after quickly reading the letter that had just plopped through the letter box.

'Can we have the day off school?' asked Kay.

'He hasn't got a date yet. He said he'll let me know more in his next letter.'

'Can we make a flag?' asked Kay.

'And paint his name on it?' asked Shirley hugging her mother.

'Course,' said Ruth wiping her tears. 'We can use that old bolster case.'

'D'you think he'll remember us?' asked Kay.

'Don't be daft. In every letter I get he says he can't wait to see you again.'

'But we've grown up a bit. He might not like us.'

Ruth held Kay close. 'You are a silly girl. He loves you both as much as I do. It might take him a little while to adjust, just as it did when you first came back, but we pulled together, didn't we?'

Kay nodded.

'And you're happy enough now?'

'Course,' said Shirley smiling.

But deep down, Ruth too had her fears of what might happen when they were all together again.

Alan was coming home on Saturday and Ruth began making plans for a small welcome-home tea just for the four of them.

Shirley and Kay had helped her make a flag and it hung listlessly from the bedroom window.

'I like the flag,' said Lucy when Ruth opened the front door.

'Luce. This is a nice surprise.'

'Thought I'd pop in to see how things are going.'

'Alan's coming home.'

'So I gathered. Seeing that.' Lucy pointed to the limp bolster case.

'We tried to get it across the two windows, but I nearly fell out,' said Ruth. 'I needed someone to hold me legs.'

'Come on, I'll give you a hand.'

Upstairs there was plenty of laughter and giggles as between them, Ruth, her daughters and Lucy got the flag across the front of the house.

They were standing outside looking up at it when Lucy said, 'I can't wait to meet this handsome hunk. When's he coming home?'

'He reckoned about three, but a lot depends on the trains.'

'What, today?' said Lucy, her voice full of surprise.

Ruth nodded.

'I didn't think it was so soon. I'll go, you don't want me around.'

'No, please stay.'

'Are you sure?'

'I might need moral support.'

'Give over. I know you. You'll want me to take the girls out for a while.'

'Maybe. Let's go in and have a cuppa.' Ruth's smile lit up her face.

'I bet you're excited?' Lucy sat at the table. 'It'll be a few weeks 'fore Charlie gets here. He's still out on a convoy.'

Ruth sat next to her. 'I can't believe that after all these years, it's all over and we're going to have them home again.'

'Ruth. Are you worried about . . . What if they've changed?'

'I expect they have. I expect we've changed.'

'I know it won't be the same, but do you think we'll still . . . Will they still love us?'

'I don't know. I hope so.'

Lucy picked at the tablecloth. 'D'you know, I'm really

frightened. What if Charlie don't want me any more.'
Slowly tears ran down her cheeks.

Ruth patted her hand. 'Course he will.'

'You was married a long while before your Alan went
away. You really knew each other, but me and Charlie . . .'

'Yes, but a lot of water has gone under the bridge since
then. How will he feel about having two young women
around and not the two little girls he left behind? We've all
got a lot of adjusting to do. And we'll have me dad here as
well. I tell you, Luce, I'm really worried about it all.'

Lucy ran her hands over her wet cheeks. 'How is your
dad?'

'Not bad, be all accounts. He's in this halfway house now,
but he don't say a lot in his letters. They're going to
discharge him in a couple of weeks' time. They've been
waiting for me to get settled first.'

'Why didn't Joyce have him?'

'I couldn't let him go there, not with her little 'uns
running about. I'll make some more tea.'

As they sat drinking tea, both slipped back into their
own thoughts. The future, which they had so looked forward to, still seemed uncertain.

It was five o'clock and Lucy decided to leave Ruth and the
girls. She didn't want to intrude.

'We can have a get-together in a day or two.'

'But I wanted you to meet Alan,' said Ruth. 'Are you sure
you won't stay?'

'No, I'll leave you and the girls to greet him. Bye,' she
called as she went down the road.

Ruth stood in the gateway, waving goodbye to Lucy. She

looked at the two pieces of metal sticking out of the brick pillars; she assumed there had been a wrought-iron gate there before the war and had been taken away for scrap. Would the landlord fit another?

She looked at her watch; she was getting worried and impatient. Why was Alan so late? Had he run away? He wouldn't be the first serviceman to be scared at coming home. She had heard many stories of men who hid away, unable to face their family. After all this waiting, this was the longest and by far the worst bit. She wanted Alan home.

Suddenly she caught sight of him walking down the road. She took a quick intake of breath. He appeared a lot taller than she remembered. Her feet seemed stuck to the ground. She wanted to run up to him. 'Alan,' she said out loud. 'Alan!' she screamed out.

'Is it Dad?' yelled Kay who had been inside but was now pushing past her. 'Dad. *Dad!*'

Shirley, who had been on Kay's heels, hung back. Ruth could see she was shy and overwhelmed.

He dropped his kit-bag and first grabbed Kay, then Shirley.

Ruth could see him smothering their faces with kisses. Her feet became mobile and she was wrapped in his arms. Kisses rained down on her forehead, eyes, cheeks and mouth. Short quick kisses at first, then he devoured her with a long lingering kiss that brought back all the memories of years past. Tears ran down her face as they stood in an embrace, oblivious of all the stares and shouts around them.

'That looks good,' said Alan, with his arm round Ruth's waist, looking up at the flag.

'We did it,' said Kay.

'Mum nearly fell out of the window trying to put it up,' said Shirley.

Horror filled his face. 'You didn't, did you?'

Ruth grinned. 'No. Not really.' She tucked her arm through his. 'Come on. I expect you're dying for a good old English cuppa.'

'I should say so. Can you manage that, girls?'

Shirley and Kay were struggling along with his kit-bag.

'How did you carry this on your own?' asked Shirley.

'We had to learn. They didn't give us a wheelbarrow.'

Ruth laughed, her eyes glistening with tears. She looked at Alan. His hair had been cut short. She wanted to run her fingers down the lines on his face, lines that hadn't been there before. He looked different. What had he been through? What horrors had he seen? But it was over now and they had to learn to live again. This was the best day of Ruth's life.

In the kitchen, Kay and Shirley sat either side of their father as he drank his tea. Ruth watched them, smiling so hard she thought her face would crack.

'What country was you in when you was abroad?' asked Kay.

'Italy, for the last few years. This tastes good,' he said with his hands clasped round his cup.

'What was Italy like, Dad?' asked Shirley, looking up at him with adoring eyes.

'Rome has got some very beautiful buildings.'

'Did they get damaged?' asked Ruth.

'No, it seems they had an agreement not to bomb them.'

Shirley looked surprised. 'So buildings were more important than people.'

'Looks like it.' There was a short silence. The girls looked at him expectantly. 'In the summer it was very hot,' was all he added.

'Did you kill anyone?' asked Kay, who was sitting the other side of him.

'I expect so. I was a gunner.'

Ruth could see Alan was not prepared to go into a lot of detail of what he'd been through.

He looked at Ruth. 'From the damage I saw on the train it must have been pretty bad for you here.'

'We had our moments.' She was in no hurry to talk about their ordeal either. They had the rest of their lives to talk about the past.

After they finished their welcome-home tea, which included dried scrambled egg on toast and a fat-less sponge Ruth had made, they sat and talked. Ruth wanted to hold Alan. She wanted him to make love to her. Did he feel the same?

The girls wanted to know more about Italy and the old buildings they had learnt about at school, and Alan at last began to give them some details.

He was shown pictures of Frank and Joyce's children.

'I'm looking forward to seeing them all again.'

'They're coming round tomorrow,' said Ruth.

Alan, after inquiring about her father, said, 'I was really sorry to hear about your mum, she was a good old stick.'

'Do you mind Dad coming to live here with us?'

'No. He might have a bit of a job getting up those stairs though.'

'I don't know how mobile he is.'

'Well, we'll find out soon enough.'

Ruth sensed a little tension in his voice. 'You sure you don't mind?'

'I said so, didn't I?'

Ruth wasn't going to query it, not tonight, when everybody seemed to be feeling their way.

'I can't get over how you two have grown,' said Alan, quickly moving on to another subject. 'And I wasn't all that pleased to hear about you coming home from Wales on your own.'

They both looked sheepish.

'We was worried about Mum,' said Kay.

'From what I've gathered, your mother could look after herself.' He turned to Ruth. 'It must have been very different, doing a man's job. And you've learnt to drive as well. You'll be wanting a car next.'

'There were a lot of women doing men's work.' Ruth wasn't going to go on to that subject. 'I'm glad it's Sunday tomorrow. At least I don't have to go to work.'

'You've gone back to Collins's then.'

'For the time being.'

Ruth was pleased to see how much the girls were enjoying having their father home. They wouldn't leave his side.

As the evening wore on Ruth could see Alan was beginning to get tired.

'Come on, girls, I think it's about time you went up to bed. You've got all day tomorrow to talk to your father.'

'We've got more than that. I've got my leave and then I've got to go back to barracks and get my demob suit.'

Kay started laughing.

'What's so funny about that, young lady?'

'We've seen 'em at the pictures, some of the blokes look really funny in civvies.'

'Proper film fans these two are,' said Ruth.

'And you are as well,' said Kay to her mother. 'I want to be a film star when I grow up.'

Alan laughed.

'I'm sure you'll look just as handsome in a suit as you do in your uniform,' said Shirley.

'Of course I will. Now go on, up to bed with you.'

They kissed their mother and father and Shirley held Alan tight. 'It's lovely to have you home.'

'It's lovely to be home,' he said, nestling his head in her hair.

'I'll bring you a cup of tea in bed in the morning,' she said.

'Now that's what I call a luxury.'

'I'll help her,' said Kay, not wanting to be done out of anything.

'Remember to brush your teeth,' called Ruth as they finally made their way upstairs.

'I thought they'd never go,' said Ruth, cuddling Alan.

'Well, I must be a bit of a novelty.'

'Not to me.' She held up her face and ran her fingers through his short dark hair as he kissed her face, neck and throat.

'Shall we go up?' asked Alan.

'No. They won't even be in bed yet. I'll just close the kitchen door. Do you mind?'

'Mind? It took me all my self-control not to have you out there in the street.'

'That would have got the neighbours talking.'

Alan kissed her waiting lips again. He slowly removed her blouse and pulled her bra straps down.

'My God,' he said as his eyes and hands explored her. 'I feel I've waited for ever for this moment.' He kissed her breasts, gently at first, then with a passion that she had forgotten.

Together they slid to the floor in a frenzy of removing clothes and kisses. Then, all too soon, their passion was spent.

'I'm sorry.' Alan was towering over her. He lightly kissed her lips, cheeks and neck.

Ruth returned his butterfly kisses and gently ran her fingers over his bare chest. 'You mustn't be. I expect it's over just as quick for most blokes after all these years.'

He took hold of her fingers and put his lips to them.

Ruth started to laugh.

'What's so funny?'

'This is. You don't know how many years I thought about how today would be. I had visions of me floating round the bedroom in a posh nightie, and then getting into bed, and you gently making love to me. And what happens? We finish up grovelling on the kitchen floor.'

'And it's all over in a flash. I'll tell you what, Ruth. This floor's bloody hard on my knees.' He rolled on his back and stretched out next to her.

A tear slowly ran down her cheek.

'What's wrong?' he asked, sitting up.

'I'm so happy.'

'So am I.' He kissed her again and he found he could manage a repeat performance, but more tenderly and loving this time.

Chapter 11

Later that night, in the comfort of their bed, Ruth lay looking towards the window. She was so happy, she knew sleep wouldn't come easily. The gentle breeze moved the curtains, causing the lights outside to send patterns round the room. It was lovely to see streetlights on again. She smiled to herself. Some young children had never seen them before. Many times she'd put her hand out to touch Alan. She had to convince herself that he really was here, and it was his arm holding her. His warm smell and steady breathing were so very reassuring.

She must have finally drifted off, for, when she opened her eyes, it was daylight. Alan was propped up on his elbow, looking at her.

Ruth felt embarrassed. She sat up. 'I must look a right mess,' she said, trying to plump up her hair.

'You look wonderful to me.' He gently kissed her.

She nuzzled against him.

'This is like it used to be.'

'I know, and it's lovely.'

'D'you know, I was worried about coming home.'

'Worried? Why?'

'A new place to live. Nothing of what I remembered seems to exist.'

'I'm still the same.'

'Are you?'

'I hope so. I'm four years older though,' Ruth grimaced.

'And a lot wiser, I expect.'

'And so are the girls.'

'They have grown up.'

'What's the time?' asked Ruth.

'Why? You going somewhere?' His hands began gently to caress her body.

'No. It's just that Shirley might be in soon with our tea.'

'So what you're saying is that I'd better behave, just in case I get caught.'

'Something like that.'

Alan lay back. 'Ruth, I missed you so much. There were times when I was lying in the mud with shells exploding all round me . . . Well, I thought I'd never see you or the girls again. I was terrified.'

'I felt like that as well. Especially when the raids were really bad. And when Mum got killed. It was a dreadful time.'

'It must have been.'

'Thank God it's all over.'

'It used to break blokes' hearts when they heard that their loved ones had gone.'

'Well, you don't have to worry about that any more.'

'It upset 'em even more when they heard their wives or girlfriends had gone off with someone else.'

Ruth quickly glanced at him. 'That must have been awful.'

'It was. Poor buggers. D'you know, some of 'em even tried to top themselves?'

'No.'

'What was it like when all those Yanks were about?'

'Didn't have much to do with them. I was on night shifts most of the time.'

'Ruth, did you ever feel tempted to go astray? After all, you didn't have anyone to answer to, and you were living in a dangerous time.'

She swallowed hard. 'No, I didn't. I waited for you to come back.'

'What if I hadn't?'

'That's something I tried hard not to think about. Now I'll never have to worry about it. Will I? What about you? Was you ever tempted?'

He sat up, reached over to the small table at the side of the bed for his cigarettes, and after lighting it, blew the smoke high in the air.

Ruth waited anxiously for his answer.

'I behaved meself.' He grinned. 'Too bloody tired and worn out to do anything else. Now, where's Shirley with our tea?' He swung his legs out of the bed.

Ruth watched him put on his trousers. He hadn't really given her a very satisfactory reply. Had he been with another woman? What if she was an old pro and had some dreadful disease?

He came up to her and kissed her cheek. 'Don't look so worried, I've only ever wanted you. I'll go and see to the tea.'

When he left the room her mind went over and over his answer. She was being silly. She was trying to see something that wasn't there. At least she could answer him with a clear conscience – thank God.

Alan quickly returned. 'She'd put the kettle on, and got everything ready.' He put the tray on the bed.

'Sorry about that, Mum, but Dad beat me to it,' said Shirley, right behind him.

'That's all right, love. Come and sit here.' Ruth patted the bed.

'I thought I heard voices,' said a sleepy Kay, who came in rubbing her eyes. 'You are rotten, why didn't you wake me? I wanted to help. It's always the same, if I want . . .'

'Shut up,' said Shirley. 'Don't make such a fuss. Dad made the tea.'

'My God. It don't take three people to make a pot of tea,' said Ruth.

Alan looked at his wife, surprised.

'You sound grumpy,' said Kay.

'No, I'm not.' Ruth was upset – with Alan, but more with herself. This wasn't how she wanted things to be.

'So, what shall we do today?' asked Alan.

'I told you. I've invited Joyce and Frank over.'

'When are they coming?'

'This morning.'

'So soon?'

'They're coming to dinner.'

'Have you got enough rations?' asked Shirley.

Ruth smiled. Even the girls knew how difficult it was to feed people.

'Don't worry. I've given your mother my ration card,' said Alan as if answering Shirley's scepticism.

'And I shall use it tomorrow. It's just that after all this

129

time Joyce wanted to see you.'

'Her Bobbie and Alice are ever so nice,' said Kay.

'Oh yes. I forgot she's got two kids now.'

'You haven't seen either of them,' said Ruth.

'How's Frank? Still up to no good? I never did understand why he never got called up.'

'It was his ears.'

'We've all heard that one before.'

'He was in the thick of it round here.'

'I suppose someone had to stay behind and help,' Alan said grudgingly.

'He's been very good to us.' Ruth was getting upset at Alan's attitude.

'I bet he has.'

'He got me a lot of this furniture.'

'Did he charge you?'

'Yes.'

'Thought as much.'

'He has got a wife and two kids to look after.'

'Thought he could at least have given you this load of tat for free.'

Ruth was very upset that Alan should think like that. 'I've already lost two homes, and this is all I could afford.'

'Mum made our room look ever so nice,' said Shirley, quickly sensing the atmosphere.

'Come and see,' said Kay.

'When I get my gratuity through we can look for something better.'

'It's a job to find any decent stuff.' Ruth had tried so hard to make it homely, yet Alan obviously wasn't impressed. After all her hard work, it made her want to cry again. But perhaps he only needed time to settle. 'Come on, girls, move out. We've got to get up.'

The real reason for ushering the girls out, however, was that she didn't want them to see how upset she was.

Frank shook Alan's hand with gusto. 'It's great to have you back again, mate.'

Joyce passed Bobbie to Ruth and threw her arms round Alan's neck and kissed him. 'It's just lovely to see you again. I'm sure you've got a lot to tell us, and you seem to be taller. What they done to your hair?' Joyce ran her hands over his head.

'Had to have it shaved off. Might have got lice otherwise.'

'Yak,' said Joyce, screwing up her face.

'So, how was it?' asked Frank.

'Not good. Lost a lot of me mates.'

'That's rough. I expect you've noticed that it was pretty bad round here. And this one was a diamond.' Frank put his arm round Ruth's waist. 'Toast of her post, she was.'

Bobbie gave a little whimper and Ruth passed him back to his mother, then laughed nervously and pushed Frank away. 'Go on with you. I was only doing my job.'

'I tell yer, mate. This one has seen some really bloody awful things.'

Ruth noted Alan had clenched his teeth, causing his cheek to move in an agitated way.

'I was only working like thousands of other women,' she said.

'Are these your little 'uns?' Alan looked pointedly at the children.

Alice was hiding behind her mother's skirt.

Joyce smiled. 'That's right. Keep your eye on your brother, Alice.'

'Don't worry. We'll look after him,' said Kay. 'Come on, Alice.'

She ran to Kay her eyes shining.

'She thinks the world of her,' said Joyce. 'I've brought some bits, Ruth. Put that bag outside, Frank. I hope it ain't too much trouble, us staying for a bit of dinner.'

'No, I told you. I've made a vegetable and corned beef pie.'

'We got time for a drink, Ruth?' asked Frank.

'Should think so.'

'D'you girls want to come? Shirley can look after our two.'

'No thanks. Me and Joyce have got some nattering to catch up on.'

'D'you fancy a good old British pint then, Al?'

'I've had a few in the NAAFI before we came back, but it'll be good to be in a pub again.'

'The one round the corner's still standing. See you later, girls.'

'Well,' said Joyce as soon as the front door slammed. 'How's things? Has he changed much?'

'Christ, give us a chance, he only came home yesterday.'

'I know.' Joyce followed her sister into the scullery. 'I hope he's behaving like a long-lost lover boy should.'

'I ain't telling you.'

'He ain't . . . you know . . .?'

Ruth, who was at the sink, turned quickly. 'Know what?'

'Well, disappointed.'

'What about?'

'This place. Coming home. A lot of blokes are, you know.'

'We ain't had a lot of time to talk it over.'

'He didn't seem that keen to hear about what you've been doing.'

'Give him time. It's a big move. Fighting in a foreign country, then coming back to a new place.'

'S'pose so. Does he mind Dad coming to live here?'

'He hasn't really said. Anyway, it'll be me that'll be running around after him. When Alan gets a job I'm hoping I'll be able to give up work.'

'Won't you get fed up all day on your own?'

'I can't see me having time to get fed up.'

Joyce looked out of the kitchen window. 'I tell you, Ruth, life's bloody boring when you're stuck indoors on your own.'

'I won't be on my own, I'll have Dad here. You should have more than enough to do with your little 'uns to keep you company.'

'Big deal. Bobbie can't talk at all and Alice can't really hold an intelligent conversation.'

'Don't start again, Joyce. You've got a good husband and two lovely kids, what more do you want?'

'I'd like it if my husband took me out now and again.'

'I'm sure if you asked his mother, she'd look after your two sometimes. Could Frank afford it?'

'Course he can. He's always out drinking with his cronies. He calls it business meetings.'

'Perhaps they are.'

'He spends more time in the pub than at home.'

'I'm not surprised if you keep whingeing on at him all the time.'

'That's right, go on. Blame me. Take his side.'

'I'm not taking his side. Christ, you of all people should know Frank, he's always done a lot of deals in pubs.'

'I know.'

'You knew all this before you married him.'

'In many ways Mum was right. He is devious.'

'He looks after you and the kids all right though, don't he? You've never gone short of anything.'

'If you mean moneywise, well then, yes. But that ain't the be all and end all of it, is it?' Joyce looked very sad.

'Now it's my turn to ask. Does he keep you happy in bed?'

'Can't grumble on that score.'

'Well then, come on, cheer up, this is supposed to be a happy day. My husband has come home alive and well.'

Joyce smiled. 'I'm sorry.'

'I'll tell you what, give it a while then I'll ask Alan if me and you could go up West to see a film one Saturday, how would that suit you?'

'I'd love it.'

'I'll ask Lucy as well.'

Joyce smiled. 'I'd really like that. D'you see her much?'

'Not a lot. She popped in yesterday for a little while. I miss the talks we used to have.'

'When's her chap coming home?'

'He's with a convoy at the moment, but it shouldn't be long.' Ruth smiled. 'She can't wait. They hadn't been married long before he went away.'

'So, she's gonner find things strange then?'

'Just like the rest of us.'

134

Ruth looked at the wooden clock on the mantelpiece. The glass front was cracked – she'd bought it cheap in the second-hand shop – but it kept good time. She was beginning to get cross. 'I didn't expect them to stay till chucking-out time.'

'I told you what Frank's like these days.'

Roars of loud laughter came down the passage. The kitchen door burst open and Frank and Alan almost fell in.

'Mind the kids,' yelled Joyce, pulling Bobbie away.

'Sorry, girl. Didn't see him behind the door,' said Frank.

'My God, you've had a skinful,' said Ruth as she watched Alan swaying back and forth.

He grinned at her. 'Yes. You could say that.'

'He ain't used to it, that's the trouble,' said Frank.

'And, of course, you are?' Joyce was still holding Bobbie, who had started to cry.

'At least I can hold my drink, which is more than he can. He's just chucked up out front.'

'That's lovely. Thanks, Frank,' said Ruth, tutting.

'Now you know I wouldn't do a thing like that.' He grinned and put his arm round Ruth's waist. 'You know me. I won't part with anything.'

Alan, who was looking decidedly pale, went unsteadily up the stairs.

'What's wrong with Dad?' asked Shirley, coming into the kitchen. 'He's being ever so sick.'

'I hope it's in the bathroom, and down the pan,' said Ruth, glaring at Frank.

'Yes, he is,' said Shirley.

'How could you let him get in that state?' asked Joyce.

'It wasn't me. It was the blokes in the pub. They kept buying him drinks.'

'I suppose that's to be expected,' said Ruth. 'I'll get a bucket of water and throw it outside.'

'Shall I see to the dinner?' asked Joyce.

'I shouldn't bother with dishing any up for Alan.'

Ruth was now even unhappier than she had been this morning. This wasn't how she intended to spend their first proper meal together. Nothing about Alan's homecoming had been as she had hoped.

Chapter 12

Ruth anxiously tried to look beyond the sea of people waiting on the platform. She was straining to catch the first glimpse of the train that was bringing her father back to London.

Alan, who had been among the first to be demobbed, looked very smart at her side in his new faint grey-striped demob suit and dark grey trilby hat. He was beginning to look a little more relaxed these past few days. Since he had come out of the army, he had been having awful nightmares. They worried her hugely. At first he had tried to dismiss them, but when they got worse, he would wake up sweating and screaming for Josh. She had asked him so many times what was worrying him, but the only thing he'd told her was that Josh was his mate and he'd seen him die. But under what circumstances?

Alan said he was looking forward to going back to work next week, but was worried about it. Would he fit in? Would he remember his past skills? He had told her his concern was that the young lads who hadn't been away for four years would be out of their apprenticeship and probably in charge. Could he take orders from younger men? Ruth understood how he felt: it was to be expected after all this time.

With her father coming home, they could be a real family again. But would her father enjoy living with them? Everybody's life was having to change once again.

Frank was waiting with the car. Joyce, who had come to Rotherhithe with Frank, had stayed behind in Ruth's house with her children, while Kay and Shirley were at school.

Ruth had wanted a quiet homecoming for him, but as Frank had offered to collect him, she couldn't refuse Joyce the chance of seeing her father. Ruth had been hoping her sister could have left the children with Frank's mother, as she was worried that all this would be too much for Dad.

For so long Ruth had been wanting a house of her own so she could bring her father home, but knew she had to wait till all the conflict was over. It had been before Christmas when he went away. More than six months since Ruth had seen him. What did he look like now? She knew he wasn't happy with his artificial leg; he had only told her it was painful and he didn't wear it that often. Had he accepted the loss of his leg? His letters were always very short, just a page or two. Since he'd been moved out of the convalescent home and into a house with some ex-servicemen, he'd seemed fine, but that's all he had to write about, them and the staff.

How did he manage crutches? Would he ever be without them? The memory of that dreadful night came back to her. It was a year ago that her mother had been killed. Would he be angry with her for not having him home before this? She shuddered. In many ways it was a good thing she was taking him back to a different house, with different furniture and in a different road. There weren't any memories or ghosts in Lind Road.

Slowly the train snaked its way into the station. She'd been told he was going to be in the front carriage so at least she had some idea where to start looking. Then she caught sight of his face at the window as the train, which was slowing down, passed her. In that split second, to Ruth, he looked old and sad.

'Dad. Dad,' she called out, breaking into a run.

'Hang on, love,' said Alan who was beside her. 'Don't get too close to the edge, and mind those doors.'

When the train finally stopped, doors were flung open and its passengers, mostly servicemen and -women, were disgorged and quickly locked in their loved ones' arms. Tears of joy and laughter mingled with the porter's shouts; and the noise of slamming doors and steam from the train filled the station.

Ruth was trying to get on to the train, but it was proving to be an almost impossible task, like a salmon swimming upstream.

'Wait till they all get off,' shouted Alan.

'Do you think he saw us?' asked Ruth.

'I should think so.'

Finally she was able to make her way along the corridor and peer into every compartment.

'I'm in here, love.'

'Dad.' She fell on to the seat next to him and held him close. Tears ran down her face as he buried his head in her hair and, despite the hat pins holding it in place, he knocked her hat skew-whiff.

'All right then, Jack?' said Alan, shaking his father-in-law's hand when Jack let go of his daughter.

'Not too bad, son.' Jack pulled his crutches to him and went to stand up.

Ruth straightened her hat and put out her hand to help him.

'I can manage.'

Alan, who was behind the old man, shook his head at his wife and said, 'I'll take your bag.'

'Thanks.' Jack gradually got to his feet, but it looked very awkward.

Alan opened the carriage door; Ruth was right behind.

'Frank's got his car outside,' she said as Alan helped him down the high step.

'That's good. This is bloody uncomfortable.' He banged the side of his leg with his crutch.

'The car's not too far.' Ruth knew she was hovering round her father. She was amazed at how well he was managing.

As soon as Frank caught sight of them he hurried over and took the bag from Alan. 'Hello, Jack. How are you?'

'All right. Do you live far?' he asked Alan.

'No, not really. Mind you, it's a pig of a journey on the bus.'

Inside the car Ruth could see her father had aged. He used to be a broad, upright, well-built man, but now his shoulders slumped. His face was pale and drawn and his thick dark hair was more speckled with white than she remembered. He took his handkerchief from his coat pocket and wiped his wet brow.

'Joyce is waiting at home,' said Ruth.

'She said in her letter she was going to try and get to your place.'

'You should see her two, they're smashing.'

Her father didn't answer, he was busy looking out of the window.

'They had a lot of damage round here,' said Alan.

'They had a lot 'fore . . .' Jack stopped.

How difficult was this proving to be for him? As the journey continued they all became very quiet. Ruth wanted to talk, but was finding it hard going. Everything she said seemed trite and insignificant.

'Not long now, Dad,' she said when they finally turned into Lind Road.

'It looks very nice.'

As the car stopped the front door was flung open and Joyce, with Bobbie in her arms and Alice in tow, hurried to the car. 'Hello, Dad.' Her smile was beaming and there were tears glistening in her eyes.

Alan got out and helped his father-in-law.

'I've got the kettle on,' said Joyce as they went into the house.

As her father went clomping down the passage, Ruth was mentally going over things she must do to make it safer for him. That small mat would have to go in case he got caught up in it. This chair would have to be pulled out so that he could get round it easily. 'Sit here, Dad,' she said, helping him into an armchair.

'I ain't an invalid.'

'Sorry, Dad. It's just that I want you to be as comfortable as I can make you.'

'Just stop fussing, will you?'

Alice clung to her father. She couldn't take her eyes off Jack's leg, which was sticking straight out.

'This is your grandad,' Frank said to her.

'Why has he got those sticks to walk with?'

Both Ruth and Joyce were shocked when their father replied abruptly, 'This is a tin one.' He banged it again. 'They cut me real one off at the hospital.'

Alice's big blue eyes opened wide. 'Why? What did he do?'

'Come on, Alice,' said Joyce quickly. 'Help me make the tea. Grandad's tired. He's had a long day, so no more questions, there's a good girl.'

Joyce put Bobbie on Frank's lap and went out to the scullery.

'I'll take the tray in,' said Ruth who had followed her out.

'He don't seem very happy, does he?'

'I think you're right. He has had a long day and don't forget this is all new to him.'

Alice pulled at her mother's skirt. 'Why did they cut that man's leg off?'

'I told you, he's your grandad, you know, like Grandad Weston.'

'He's got two legs.'

'Well, Grandad Harris's leg went bad.'

Alice looked thoughtful and, pulling up her sleeve, pointed at the scab on her elbow. 'Will they cut my arm off if it don't get better?'

Ruth bent down and kissed it. 'Course they won't. How did you do that?'

'Racing up the garden on that old trike,' said Joyce.

'Well, now I've just kissed it to make it better,' said Ruth.

Alice smiled. 'Thanks.'

'Look, Alice, why don't you get your colouring pencils out, then you can show Kay how clever you are.'

'All right.' She scurried from the room.

'I don't think it was very nice of Dad telling her like that, do you?'

'No – but didn't you tell her?'

'I thought he'd be wearing his false leg, so she wouldn't notice. She'd only have started worrying and asking a lot of questions if I'd told her.'

'Give him time. He's probably forgotten how to handle kids.'

'Well, I hope he doesn't upset your two. Do you think you'll be able to cope?'

'Ain't got any choice, have I? He'll be all right once he's settled. I've told the girls to go a bit easy. It's the bathroom that's already started to cause problems with Alan home. At least Dad will still be in bed when they get ready for school, so it shouldn't be too bad.'

'God, I hope so, for your and the girls', and Alan's sake.'

Ruth put the cups and saucers on the tray. 'I'm worried about Alan.'

'Alan? Why? Is it because he's going back to work?'

'A bit. But he's been having terrible nightmares. We'll never know what he went through. Has he ever said anything to Frank?'

'Frank's never said.'

'I don't know what to do.'

'Give it time. We all need time to adjust; some more than others. I just hope Dad's not going to be too much for you.'

'So do I.' Ruth was beginning to worry that all her good

143

intentions may well put her and her family under a lot of strain. 'Come on, let's take this tea in.'

Ruth opened the door and led the way. 'Shirley and Kay have been looking forward to you coming home, Dad. They're young ladies now.' She began to fill the cups. 'Still take milk and sugar?'

'Course, they only chopped me leg off, they didn't take me taste buds out as well.'

Ruth heard Joyce take a breath, but she just smiled and said nothing.

'I'll take your bag up,' said Alan, obviously wanting to get away from the ghastly atmosphere.

'Can't I have a bed down here?'

'I don't know,' said Ruth. 'I thought it would be better for you as the bathroom's upstairs.'

'Well, we'll have to wait and see. But if I find those stairs a job, then I'll come down here.'

'OK.' Ruth wasn't going to argue at this point.

Jack stood up. 'Look, I'm gonner take this off.'

'I'll show you which room is yours,' said Ruth.

'I'll show you, Jack,' said Alan, picking up his bag.

When Alan returned Ruth and Joyce both said at once, 'Is he all right?'

Alan nodded. 'He'll be down in a tick.'

When their father returned he looked a lot easier and he had pinned up the bottom of his trouser leg. 'That's a bloody weight off me mind, or should I say stump.'

They gave a polite little laugh.

'At least you'll be home in time to vote then, Jack,' said Frank.

'I should hope so. We've got to have a change. We don't

want this lot looking after us.'

'Winnie did us proud though,' said Joyce.

'Well, it's over now and we don't need a warmonger in charge.' Nodding firmly, Jack Harris took his tobacco box from his pocket.

'Here,' said Frank. 'Have one of these.' He handed his father-in-law a packet of cigarettes.

'Thanks, mate.' After taking one he went to hand the packet back, but Frank shook his head. Smiling, Jack Harris put them in his pocket. 'Can only afford roll-ups now.'

They had just finished their tea when the kitchen door burst open and Shirley and Kay came bounding in.

'Hello, Mum,' said Shirley. She stood still for a moment, then went to her grandad and kissed his cheek. 'Hello, Grandad.'

To Ruth's relief he put his arm round her shoulder and smiled. 'How are you love?'

'I'm all right.'

Kay was still standing back.

'Say hello to your grandad then,' Ruth told her.

Kay then moved forward and also kissed his cheek.

'You've both grown up since I last saw you. Your gran would be that proud of you.'

Kay and Shirley looked awkward; they didn't know what to say to that.

'Where is his gran?' asked Alice loudly.

Joyce bent down and whispered, 'I told you. She's in heaven.'

Alice smiled. 'Oh, I forgot.'

Gradually everybody relaxed, however, and the mood improved. The small bottle of whisky Frank had brought with him helped. Kay and Shirley began to tell him all the things they did at school, and about when they were evacuated. At last Jack began to smile and look at ease.

When it was time for Joyce and Frank to take the children home, Joyce found Ruth in the scullery. 'He seems a bit brighter,' she said as she gathered together her children's bits and pieces.

'Thank goodness. I couldn't have stood too much of that.'

'I think your two will soon have him out and about.'

'I hope so, for their sakes.'

'Well, they're good girls. Right. I think that's everything.' They walked through into the kitchen.

'We're off, Dad. Frank will come up and see you, and I'll get up when I can.'

'Don't put yourself out.'

Joyce glanced at Ruth before kissing him. Then she went out to the car, followed by Ruth. 'Look. If he gets too much, I'll get Frank to collect him and give you a break.'

'I'll be all right.'

'We'll see. Even if I have him down for tea, or a bit of dinner sometime, at least you'll be able to go out and relax.'

'Thanks, but I'll manage. He ain't a baby,' said Ruth.

'What are you two plotting?' asked Frank.

'Nothing,' said Joyce as she slipped into the back seat. She took Bobbie from Frank and sat him on her lap; Alice was standing next to her.

Alan put his arm round Ruth's waist as they waved goodbye. 'Cheer up.'

146

'I'm all right.'

'So, what was you and Joyce planning?'

'Nothing.' She went to walk away.

Alan stopped her. 'Ruth, will you be able to cope?'

'Ain't got a lot of choice, have I?'

'Things'll get better.'

'Will they?'

'Give the old boy time. He perked up when the girls started talking to him.'

'I know. But what about when he's here all day on his own?'

'Don't look so down. I'm sure it'll work out.'

Ruth tried to smile, but she knew this was going to be an uphill journey.

Chapter 13

In the car, Alice turned to her mother and, with a puzzled look on her face, asked, 'Why did my new grandad have his leg cut off?'

Joyce put her arm round her daughter and pulled her on to the seat. 'When you get a bit older you'll understand.'

'Why can't you tell me now? I can understand.'

Joyce smiled. 'Yes, I think you can. It was in the war. He was bombed in his house, and his leg got very, very badly injured. And that's when your Granny Harris was killed.'

'I didn't know my Granny Harris. Was she nice?'

'Yes, she was.'

'She looks nice in the picture you showed me.' Alice was studying the backs of her hands; she was trying to make sense of it all. 'Is that why Kay's daddy has been away for years and years, 'cos of the war?'

'Yes, love.'

'I'm glad my daddy didn't go away. Well, only a few times, not for years and years. Kay said it's funny having a daddy in the house. I don't know if she'll like having a grandad living at their house. He moaned at her when she went in the bathroom. I heard him tell her to hurry up.'

Joyce smiled. She could remember how her father used to carry on at her and Ruth when they made up in the mirror in the kitchen. How they would both argue and push each other out of the way. They didn't have the luxury of a bathroom in their younger days.

At the traffic lights Frank turned. 'It must be hard for these little 'uns to fathom all this out.'

'Yes. Frank, do you think Dad has changed?'

'Course he has.'

'I'm really worried about Ruth.'

'She'll be all right. You know your sister, she can handle it.'

'I hope so,' said Joyce. But she looked far from convinced.

Things were changing on a national level as well as domestic. The Labour Party came to power with a huge majority, which pleased Jack.

The war with Japan came to a quick end when an atom bomb was dropped on Hiroshima, then another on Nagasaki. People were glad that it was the end of that war, but the newsreels at the cinema left everybody gasping at such a deadly weapon. The devastation would be talked about for weeks, and possibly years.

There were street parties again, but they didn't have the same impact as the end of the war in Europe. Japan was a long way away. Neither Ruth and her daughters nor Lucy went to the West End to celebrate this time. But they were all relieved that the war was really finally over.

The changes continued at home too. Ruth didn't see so much of Lucy now that Charlie had come home. Ruth had only met him once and he seemed a jolly sort of bloke, madly in love with Lucy. Ruth knew Lucy was still working; there wasn't any need for her to stay home all the while they lived with her mother. But Ruth didn't think it would be long before they started a family. That's what Lucy said she wanted more than anything.

Ruth guessed Stan had moved away as she hadn't seen him, and he hadn't been round to see her father as he'd promised.

Alan had gone back to work, but his nightmares continued, which meant they both suffered dreadfully from lack of sleep. So many times Ruth had tried to talk to him about the problem, but every time he dismissed it, telling her not to worry. But he said *he* was worried that he might not be able to settle at work so asked Ruth not to give up her job just yet.

Over the weeks Ruth tried to put on a brave face, but was finding it more and more difficult. There were arguments between her father and the girls. The front room had been made into a bedroom for him, which pleased the girls as they no longer had to share, but he still grumbled about how long they spent in the bathroom. The hair, clothes and wet towels they left all over the place were always a bone of contention and caused many arguments. Ruth was tired of constantly nagging at them and trying to be the peacemaker. Her father complained that they should remember it wasn't easy for him to get up and down the stairs and they should come out of the bathroom when he was waiting.

He spent all his time sitting in the chair reading the paper. He never attempted to wear his false leg and when Ruth commented about it he got angry and went to his room. Ruth tried to be understanding. After all, he had been master in his own house, now he was little more than a lodger. But it was getting to her – and the rest of the family. It made Kay sulk when he kept on at them. He was horrified when, one Saturday, she came down the stairs wearing bright red lipstick. Even Alan was cross with her and sent her upstairs to wash it off. Then he threw the lipstick away, which provoked many tears. Ruth was also very angry: it was her lipstick and they were hard to come by. Where would all this end?

Now Mrs Collins was talking about opening the shop on a Saturday. For Ruth, that would be the last straw. Monday to Friday was boring enough, and Saturday was the day she did her cleaning and washing. All week she spent most of her lunchtime queuing to get their rations and any perks that appeared in the shops. In the evening she had to rush home and try to make interesting meals out of the meagre amount of food that was available, but it was an endless grind which left no time for herself. She was getting to the end of her tether.

Ruth sighed as she pushed open the kitchen door and took her coat off. The tap, tap, tapping of her father's crutches as he came out of his room and followed her got on her nerves. She wanted to scream. If only he would try to wear his false leg. He only moaned that it was too painful and that she didn't understand. But he wouldn't go back to the hospital for them to sort it out.

'All right, Dad?' she asked out of habit. 'Had a bit of a lie down?'

She could mouth his answer with him.

'Not much else to do, is there?'

She kicked off her shoes and waited till he got settled in his chair, then gave him the evening paper.

She had just made a pot of tea when Alan walked in. Ruth stared at him. 'Look at the state of you,' she said. She slumped into the chair in disbelief.

Alan was covered with dust and his boots were white. 'Had a lot of plaster boards to shift.'

'How am I gonner get those things clean?'

'Sorry, love.' Alan began banging his trousers.

'Stop it. Stop it. Not in here. Look at all the dust flying about.' Tears welled up, and she couldn't control them.

'What's wrong?' asked Alan.

'Been bloody miserable ever since she came in,' said her father, looking up from the newspaper. 'Hardly spoke a word. I told her, she should try sitting in this bloody hard chair all day, then she'd have something to moan about.'

Ruth was out of the chair like a tiger. 'That's all the thanks I get.' She began wagging her finger at him. 'As soon as I get in I have to put up with your grumbling, it's the same day in and day out.'

'She must have had a bad day at work,' said her father, ignoring her and talking to Alan. 'D'you reckon we can go round the corner later, son, for a pint, and a bit of peace?'

'If you like,' said Alan, but he was staring at Ruth, who had, shockingly, begun to scream.

Ruth knew she was out of control. She knew she wasn't making sense, but she couldn't stop. Was she having a breakdown? The kitchen door flew open and Shirley and Kay were standing in the doorway, open-mouthed.

'*Mum!*' Shirley looked frightened.

Ruth didn't answer, she just stared at her daughter and carried on screaming.

'Mum, what's wrong?' asked Shirley, looking towards her father.

'Things are getting her down a bit,' said Alan. 'She's had a bit of a bad day.'

Ruth went quiet. 'That's it.' She put on her coat.

'Where're you going?' asked Alan.

She didn't reply, just slammed the front door as she went out.

Ruth stood at the bus stop and got on the first bus that came along.

She hurried up the stairs, relieved to find it almost empty.

The only other passenger stood up, rang the bell, then went downstairs.

'Fares, please,' said a familiar voice.

Ruth looked up and burst into tears.

'Ruth? What's wrong?'

Ruth stood up and threw her arms round a very surprised Lucy's neck.

Lucy patted her friend's back. 'What is it?'

The bus stopped.

Ruth sat down and, taking a handkerchief from her coat pocket, wiped her eyes and blew her nose. 'I've just walked out.'

Lucy looked down the stairs to make sure everybody had got off and on safely, then rang the bell. 'What? Why?'

'I don't know. I'm so fed up.' She sniffed. 'All I do is work and cook and clean. I wish the war was still on.'

Lucy looked at her friend in amazement. 'You can't mean that?'

'I was so happy when I was living at your house, doing a job I loved. Why did it all have to end?'

Lucy sat next to Ruth. 'Now you don't mean that for one minute. I reckon you've got those Monday blues.'

Ruth sighed. 'You could be right.'

'You've got your girls and Alan home, and your dad. I thought that's what you always wanted.'

'I thought I did. But now I'm not so sure.'

Lucy grinned and bent her head nearer. 'Are you getting enough . . . you know?'

Ruth looked down. 'Yes. Of course. Except we have to remember that Dad is sleeping underneath us.'

'That can be a bit off-putting.'

'At times. Then there's Alan's nightmares.'

'He still having them?'

Ruth nodded.

'Look, we're on the way back to the depot, then I've finished for the night. You can come back home with me and we'll have a nice long talk.'

'Will Charlie be there?'

'I should think so. Why?'

'I'd rather I didn't . . .'

'Charlie don't mind.'

'Could we go somewhere on our own?'

'If you like.'

'I can't pay my fare, I didn't pick up me bag.'

Lucy smiled. 'That's all right. Have this one on me.'

Shirley stood and looked at the closed door. 'What's wrong

with Mum? Why has she run off like that?'

'I don't know,' said Alan.

'Women can be bloody funny at times,' said Jack.

'But that's not like Mum. She's normally ever so brave and—'

'I think that's a large part of the trouble,' said Alan, putting his arm round Shirley's shoulders. 'She's led such a busy and different life these past years that she's finding it hard to settle down.'

'She's not the only one,' said his father-in-law. 'She should remember what I've been through.'

'She does, Grandad.'

'We've all been through a lot one way and another,' said Alan, raising his voice. 'And we should all pull together, to help each other.'

Kay, who had been quiet throughout this conversation said, 'I don't think any of us knows what Mum did.'

'No,' said Alan. 'And I don't suppose we ever will.'

Jack stood up. 'Look, I know I'm in the way, so I'll find out if I can rent a place of me own.'

'Mum's not going to like that,' said Kay.

'Oh, I don't know. I reckon you and her will be glad to see the back of me.' Jack made his way to the front room.

'I'm sorry we upset you, Grandad,' called Shirley.

He didn't reply. They only heard the tap, tap, tapping of his crutches up the passage, and the click of his door closing.

'Mum will be ever so cross if Grandad goes,' said Kay. 'And it's not all our fault.'

'What are we going to do, Dad?' asked Shirley. Her face was full of fear.

'Wait till your mother comes back.'

'What if she don't?' asked Kay.

'Don't say things like that,' said Shirley.

'She'll be back,' said Alan. 'Besides, where can she go?'

'Her friend Lucy's. She was happy there,' said Shirley.

'Or she could go to Auntie Joyce,' said Kay.

'Don't worry about it now. She'll be home soon. See if you can find something to eat. I'm starving.' Alan felt the teapot. 'This is stone cold. Put the kettle on, Kay, there's a good girl.'

Ruth was hugging the cup like a comfort blanket; she had long since finished the tea.

'Well, are you going to tell me the real reason for all these dramatics?' said Lucy.

'Nothing to tell really. It's just that I've had enough.'

'You ain't given it a lot of time, have you?'

'No, suppose not.'

'How long is it? A couple of months?'

'It seems like a lifetime.'

'I can remember, and it ain't that long ago, when all you did was dream about you and Alan and the girls all being together. Now it's here, you calmly sit there and tell me you've had enough.'

'I know. I don't know what I was expecting. Do I sound daft?'

'Is it your dad getting you down?'

Ruth nodded and let her tears run down her face. 'And my job, and the rationing, and the cooking and the washing Alan creates.'

'I don't suppose you're the only one,' said Lucy.

'I don't care about anybody else. It's me I feel sorry for.'

'Oh dear. We'd better try and sort this out.'

'How?'

'First things first. I reckon you should give up that job.'

'But we need—'

Lucy put up her hand. 'Hear me out. Give it a try. Alan must be earning a decent wage.'

'Yes, it's not bad, but what with what the girls want and—'

'I know about you wanting nice things and all that, but I think your sanity comes first.'

Ruth sat back. 'Thanks. So you think I'm going round the bend?'

'You might do if you carry on like this.'

'Like what?'

'Walking out on your family when things don't go your way.'

Ruth was stunned. Nobody had ever spoken to her like this before. 'What can I do?' She was almost pleading.

'As I said. I think you should give up your job.'

'I don't know if I could stand being with me dad day in and day out.'

'Take him along to one of these clubs that are starting up again. There must be one near you. He must like a game of cards, or dominoes or something.'

'Suppose so.'

'Then I suggest you try and find a little part-time job. Something that will give you a bit of time at home.'

'I could try.'

'Make sure it's interesting, though.'

'Such as?'

'I dunno. Your job must be pretty boring most of the time.'

'It is.'

'Well then. But at the end of the day, it's you what's got to make the decision.'

Ruth smiled.

'What's so funny?'

'You. You're talking to me like some old woman. But you're making a lot of sense.' She leant across the table and kissed Lucy's cheek.

Lucy blushed and rubbed at her face. 'Give over. You'll have this lot thinking we're a couple of . . .' She looked round the café. 'You know?'

'Can I have another cup of tea?' asked Ruth.

'Yes. Then I've got to get home.'

'I'm sorry. I shouldn't have . . .'

'Yes, you should. That's what friends are for. And I always think of you as a very good friend. We've faced some good and bad times, and we've got through them together.'

Ruth swallowed hard. 'Don't go getting all poetic on me otherwise you'll have me blubbing again. And, as a friend, do you think you could lend me my bus fare?'

Lucy laughed. 'Come off it. Don't push your luck, Bentley.'

Chapter 14

Ruth sat on the bus and let her thoughts turn over and over. Lucy was right, she had to get a part-time job if she wanted to keep her family together and her sanity.

She looked through the window. The green mesh that had been covering bus windows all these years had been stripped away. You could now see the flowers that sprouted from the bomb sites. The leaves on the trees that had survived were beginning to turn a rich golden colour now autumn was fast approaching. When the bus stopped and the lights in the houses were being switched on, Ruth could see into people's front rooms. In a way it was a bit like looking into their lives. Everybody could see the real person now they had been stripped of their uniform. People who had been heroes and heroines throughout the war were now plain husbands and wives, fathers and mothers. How were they all managing? Were they having the same problems adjusting?

She felt guilty when she saw families sitting together. She knew she had to get home. What would her family be thinking? Were they worried about her? Were they all out looking for her?

Although Alan was at work, and there was plenty for builders and carpenters, he still had this fear that he might not be able to hold down a job. He talked about the demanding youngsters who were in charge. He had begged her not to stay at home just yet, at least till he was settled.

But what about her? She wasn't settled. She had waited for years for them to be together, to be a happy, laughing family again, but it was all going wrong. There was always this tension when she got home from work or shopping. As soon as she walked in her father would complain about the girls and the bathroom and Kay dancing about all the time. Then he'd sit and mope in the chair. Even Alan would yell at the girls for trivial things. It seemed to be up to her to make a better home life for all of them, and the first thing she knew she had to do was get a part-time job.

Joyce was angry. She looked at the clock. It had gone nine. Where was Frank? He had been out since early this morning. His dinner was still on the side. The gravy had congealed round the rim of the plate, and the corned beef had dried up and was curling at the edges. He said he would be home early tonight. Why did he do this to her?

Bobbie cried out, and Joyce hurried up the stairs to him. He had filled his nappy and the smell was nauseating. She felt his forehead; he was hot and his cheeks were burning. He was cutting the last of his back teeth and his constant grizzling was getting to her. She changed her son's nappy, and with soothing noises lulled him back to sleep. She then looked in at Alice, who was sleeping soundly. She didn't remember Alice being such a fretful baby. Joyce smiled at her daughter who looked so peaceful. Her steady breathing was the only sound in the room. Her blonde hair had spread over her pillow. Joyce didn't want to cut it but wondered if it was going to be worth the trouble with the problems she had trying to get a comb through it in the mornings. Joyce didn't know if she could stand those scenes every day when Alice started school.

She gently closed the door and went downstairs. She loved her children, and Frank, but she was sad and lonely. It was all right for Ruth, she had a houseful. Joyce wanted to go out, she wanted to be with people, but where could she go? All she wanted was to talk to grown-ups.

Ruth turned into Lind Road. What would she say when she got home? Part of her didn't actually *want* to go home. She loved Alan, and her daughters, and her father, yet she couldn't help feeling there had to be more to life than looking after all of them all the time. But what?

She was surprised to see the front of the house was in darkness. There wasn't a light on in the passage. Ruth's heart was thumping. Where were they? Were they out looking for her? She opened the front door.

'Mum. Is that you?' Shirley's voice came through the darkness.

Ruth turned on the light.

Shirley, who was sitting at the top of the stairs, blinked rapidly at the light. She had her nightgown pulled tight over her knees. Her long dark hair was falling round her shoulders. She looked so young and so vulnerable, yet she would be fourteen in November and leaving school at Christmas. Then she'd be going to work, out into the big wide world.

'You should be in bed.'

Shirley ran down the stairs and threw herself into her mother's arms. 'I thought you'd run away for ever,' she sobbed.

Ruth held her close. 'Don't be silly. I just needed to get out for a bit.'

'Where have you been?'

'With Lucy.' Ruth gently eased her daughter along the passage and into the dark kitchen. She switched on the light.

'Where's your father?'

'Out. Why was you screaming at Grandad?'

'Where's he gone?'

'Him and Grandad have gone to the pub. Mum, why was you . . .?'

'They've gone to the pub?' Ruth slumped into the chair. So much for her worrying about them.

'D'you want a cup of tea?' asked Shirley, running the back of her hand under her nose.

'That'll be nice.'

Shirley went into the scullery. 'Mum.' Her gentle voice drifted into the kitchen, interrupting Ruth's thoughts. 'Grandad said he was going to move.'

'What?' Ruth was out of the chair and in the scullery in a flash. 'When did he say that?'

'Tonight, after you went. He said it was his fault, but . . .'

'That's just like him. Got to show off. Make everybody feel sorry for him.'

'Me and Kay are ever so sorry if we upset you and Grandad.'

Ruth pulled her daughter closer and held her. 'It wasn't just you two, love. It's . . . I don't know – everything.'

The whistling kettle made Ruth put her hand out and turn off the gas. She kissed Shirley's head and let her go.

'I'm going to give up my job so that I'll be able to spend more time at home.'

'That'll be nice. We could go out then when we're on holiday.'

'Yes, but not for much longer. You'll be at work next year.'

'I know.'

'Is there anything you want to do?'

Shirley shook her head. 'I don't want to go into a factory.'

'And I don't want you to. What about an office?'

Shirley screwed up her nose. 'I don't know if I'm clever enough for that.'

'Well, you've got a few months yet to make up your mind. Now I think it's time you went to bed.'

Shirley put her arms round her mother. 'Goodnight. I love you ever such a lot.'

Ruth kissed her daughter's cheek. 'And I love you. Now off you go,' she said, gently patting Shirley's bottom.

Ruth sat in the chair and thought about their future. Her daughter was going out to work next year. It only seemed a short while ago she was a baby. She had missed four years of her growing up. Would this separation have any effect on her in future years? Shirley was a sensible girl, but how would Kay handle the big wide world?

Ruth began to think about herself. What kind of job could she find that would please everybody? Like Shirley, she didn't want to go into a factory, and she wasn't clever enough to go into an office. There must be something for her. What about driving? Stan had said she was a good little driver, and she'd had plenty of practice during the war. That was worth pursuing.

Ruth was reading the newspaper when she heard the key being pulled through the letter box. The voices told her her father and Alan were home.

When the kitchen door opened she put on a big smile. 'Hello, you two.'

'So, you've come home then,' said her father.

'I only had to get out for a bit.'

'Where've you been?' said Alan.

'I went to see Lucy. Why?'

'I was worried. You went off in such a huff.'

'Well, yes. I'm sorry about that.'

'Look, Ruth . . .' Alan began clearly agitated.

Ruth could see he was trying to say the right thing. He glanced at her father who was sitting silently in the chair carefully rolling a cigarette.

'I think we all said things we shouldn't have, so now the air's cleared I think we should just get on with our lives,' continued Alan.

'I've been giving it a lot of thought,' Ruth replied, 'and I'm going to get a part-time job. That way the shopping and everything won't be too much for me.'

'Part-time?' Alan looked down but quickly recovered. 'That's a good idea.'

'It'll give me more time at home.'

'Course. I wish I could say give up. But you know how I worry about keeping this job.'

'I'm still going to look for somewhere to live,' said her

father, leaning forward and sticking a piece of rolled-up paper in the fire to light his cigarette.

'Why? You don't have to, Jack,' said Alan.

'I know I'm in the way.'

'Look, Dad. Give us a bit of time. This is a whole new lifestyle for all of us, and it's caused, well, a bit of a strain. I'm sure we can work it out. Please, don't go.'

Jack looked closely at Ruth. 'Well, all right, I'll give it another go.'

Ruth sighed.

'What d'you reckon you'll do?' asked Alan.

'I don't know. I was thinking of perhaps getting a driving job.'

'That's man's work,' said her father.

'It was once,' said Ruth.

'Well, I don't reckon it's right, taking men's jobs.'

Ruth was about to retort when she caught sight of Alan shaking his head behind her father. Alan was right. It wouldn't do to start another row.

'I'm off,' said Jack, carefully getting up out of the chair.

As soon as the door closed Alan said, 'I know things have been difficult, but, Ruth, you have got to try.'

'*Me!* Why does it always come back to me? It's very hard trying to run a house and a job.'

'I find it difficult as well, you know, after being in the army all these years. Always being told what to do – and being in the thick of the fighting, never knowing if you're going to see another day. Cradling your mate's head and watch his brains spilling out.'

Ruth took in a sharp breath. 'I didn't know. You never said.'

Alan put his head in his hands. 'I tried to keep it to meself.'

'It was a bit like that for me as well,' said Ruth softly.

He looked up sharply. 'I had a pretty rough time. I've seen things . . . It was bloody hard watching me mates get killed. Hiding from shells and bombs. Being stuck in a dugout with shells flying over your head day and night. Going days without sleep. The noise driving us all mad. So don't give me all that stuff about what you, and him, went through.' He pointed his thumb at the door.

Ruth sat open-mouthed. Alan had never spoken to her like this before. He had never told her about his war. 'I'm so sorry,' she whispered.

He ran his fingers through his thick dark hair. 'We've all been through a lot. We mustn't keep it all bottled up.'

Ruth went over to Alan and put her arms round his neck. 'I do love you.' She put her lips to his and let her tears run.

'I'm sorry, too, Ruth. But I was so worried when you left.'

She wanted to say: But you didn't come looking for me, but thought it wise not to pursue that any longer.

Alan held her close and kissed her passionately. She kissed him back. This is what they had both, in their own way, been fighting for.

Joyce was asleep in the chair when she heard Frank come in.

'I thought you'd be in bed.'

'No, I ain't.'

'My, my, we do look angry.'

'Angry? I'm bloody livid. Why can't you come home at a decent time?'

''Cos I've been busy.'

'Busy my arse. Have you got a bit on the side?'

He laughed. 'Now would I do that?'

Joyce wiped her tears. 'I don't know. I don't know you any more.'

Frank pulled her to him. The smell of drink on his breath almost took her breath away.

'I worry about you in that car when you've had a few.'

He kissed her gently. 'You don't want to worry about me. Now, how about a nice cup of coffee?'

'I don't believe you at times,' said Joyce, pulling away from him. 'Is that all you want? A cup of coffee? What about your dinner?'

'I had something out. But I'll tell you what – when we get to bed, I'll want me afters.'

Although Joyce was angry, she knew it wouldn't last long. She went into her kitchen and put the kettle on.

Frank followed her and put his arms round her waist. 'You know I'll always come back to you and the kids.' He kissed the back of her neck. 'I love you so much. I couldn't live without you. Turn the kettle out. I can't wait for coffee.'

Chapter 15

The next day during her lunch break, Ruth went along to the labour exchange.

'I'm sorry,' said the young girl behind the desk. 'We don't have any driving jobs.'

'Nothing? Nothing at all?' asked Ruth.

'Not at the moment. Not till petrol rationing comes to an end and things really begin to improve. You see, most of the boys who come back can drive now, and they snap them up. And I'm afraid that most employers prefer men in that job.'

'I see.' Ruth went to turn away.

'I'll put your name down and if you'd like to call in next week, we may have something then.'

'Thanks.' Ruth gave her name and address, but she didn't hold out much hope.

Back at the shop she did her usual dusting and straightening the garments on the rails – not that that was very hard with the meagre amount of stock they had – feeling more frustrated and bored than ever. She needed something more exciting – but what?

Mrs Collins let her go a little early and as Ruth walked home she noticed a queue outside the butcher's.

'What they got?' Ruth asked the woman she automatically stood behind.

'Sausages, so the old dear at the front said. Mind you, he
might have sold out or be shut be the time we get to the
front.'

'I'll wait, just in case.'

'Story of our lives, ducks, ain't it? Always standing
around waiting and hoping. You just finished work?'

Ruth nodded as they moved two steps nearer the shop
door.

'I must say, you look very nice. Can see you don't work in
no factory.'

'No, I work in Collins's, the dress shop.'

'Oh, her. I know all about her.'

'You do?' said Ruth, not really taking a lot of notice of
what the woman was saying. The things women talked
about while they were queuing were usually so mundane.

'Is she still as tight as she was?' The woman gave Ruth a
nudge. 'Does she let you have a few things off coupons?'

'No. It would make the job a sight more interesting if she
did.'

'Didn't think she would. Mind you, old Ma Collins can
be a funny cow if you upset her. I used to be her cleaner,
but she chucked me.'

Ruth suddenly looked closer at this dumpy round woman
who had a bright red headscarf knotted under her chin.
'You were? When?'

The queue shuffled forward again and two more women,
deep in conversation, joined it behind Ruth.

'It was years ago, when she first opened. Before your
time.'

'Yes. I started there after my youngest was born. Me mum used to look after my girls.'

'That's nice. Was you there all through the war?'

'No. I was in the Civil Defence.'

'Round this way?'

'Yes.'

'You must 'ave seen some pretty rotten things then.'

Ruth nodded. 'It was part of the job.'

'I expect you find shop work a bit tame now.'

'Yes, I do. In fact I'm looking for something else.'

'I would have thought there was plenty of work around.'
They moved a few more steps towards the butcher's door.

'There is if you're qualified. But I only want part time now my husband's home.' Ruth looked along the line of women. 'D'you think we'll be lucky?'

'Wouldn't like to say.'

The butcher's boy came out of the shop and slowly began to walk along the queue, counting. 'Sorry, ladies,' he said, stopping about four people in front of Ruth's new-found friend. 'Only got enough for this lot.'

'I've been bloody well standing here all this time,' called the woman who was the first one behind his outstretched arm. 'Surely you can find me just a couple for me old man's tea.'

'Sorry. Mr Newman's only letting 'em have a pound each. There's no point in you staying.'

There was a lot of mumbling and the queue was very slow to disperse.

'Ah well,' said Ruth's companion, clutching her handbag to her chest. 'Better luck next time.'

'Might see you in the next queue,' said Ruth.

'Dunno about that. Here, what sort of job you looking for?'

'Anything that's part time. Why, do you know of something?'

'I do part time. It ain't as interesting as working in a shop, and it ain't as exciting as the Civil Defence, but it ain't bad, and you get a lot of time off when the kids are on holiday.'

'Sounds good. What is it?' asked Ruth eagerly.

'School cleaner.'

Ruth felt her interest fall away. 'I don't think I'd want anything like that.'

'Didn't think you would be. Must be off. Tat ta.'

Ruth watched the woman walk away. A school cleaner. Slowly she began to think about it. They could only work when the children weren't there, so that must mean after school. That would give her all day to do what she wanted. She turned and began to move in the same direction as the woman.

'Excuse me,' she called.

The old lady stopped.

'That job you was talking about, where is it?'

'The school near the park. Rayfield Place. D'you know it?'

'My daughters go there. Do they really want staff?'

'Dunno about staff, but they want cleaners. Not many stick at it.'

Ruth was a little apprehensive. 'Who do I have to see?'

'It's what, Wednesday tomorrow, is that half-day closing at Collins's?'

Ruth shook her head. 'Not yet. She still closes on Saturday.'

'I'll have a word with Mr Walsh, he's the one that hires and fires. I'll ask him to hang on till you finish. I'll wait and take you to see him.'

'Thank you. I'll be there. Who . . .'

She smiled. 'The name's Daisy. And yours?'

'Ruth. Ruth Bentley. I'm pleased to meet you, Daisy.'

'Likewise, I'm sure. I reckon we could get on a treat.'

'I think so.'

Ruth was smiling as she walked home. There was a spring in her step. She would have been even happier if she'd got some of those sausages for tea as well.

'Hello, Dad, everything all right?' Ruth handed her father the newspaper. She was pleased they had patched up their differences, even if the peace was fragile and most of the time she felt she was walking on eggs.

'You sound cheerful.'

'I'm going to try for a new job.'

'Oh yes. And where's that then?'

Ruth could see he wasn't very interested as he opened the pages of the paper. 'Well, I haven't got it yet, but I'm going to see about it tomorrow. I'm hoping to be a cleaner at the school.'

He looked over the top of the paper. 'A cleaner. Alan's not gonner like that.'

'Part-time jobs are hard to come by. And that way I can be home a bit more and not have to—'

Her father struggled to his feet. 'Is this 'cos of me?'

'No.'

'It is. I know I'm in the way and causing a lot of work.'

'No, you're not. It's the rationing. The shopping, the

172

bloody queuing for everything. And the cleaning.' Ruth was trying hard to keep her temper under control. 'If I go part time it'll be for me, myself. That's all.'

'Well, Alan won't like it.'

'I don't care. I've got to do something to bring in a bit . . .' She stopped. She didn't want her father to know that Alan was worried that he might not be able to hold down a job. 'Anyway. I shouldn't have said anything. I ain't got it yet.'

'I know I'm a burden to you.'

'Don't talk daft.'

'I know you get fed up with me round your feet. Well, let me tell you, it ain't a bed of roses for me living here.' Her father stood in the doorway. 'What with those girls in the bathroom all the time, and that Kay dancing about all over the place.'

'They're only young, Dad. You should be used to it, after all me and Joyce—'

'Your mother had more discipline over you two. And you didn't answer back.'

Ruth didn't want to argue. She could have added: You were at work most of the time, so you didn't see what went on. She decided against that, as it would lead to more trouble.

He went out of the kitchen leaving the door wide open.

The tap, tap, tapping of his crutches on the lino as he moved along the passage was beginning to sound like a taut drum in her head. Ruth wanted to stamp and shout again, but knew that wouldn't do any good. Despite everything, she loved her father and hated to see him so unhappy.

She busied herself setting the table. She'd take him a cup

of tea as soon as the kettle boiled.

With the tea in her hand Ruth stood outside his door. She was about to knock when she heard sniffing. Putting her ear to the door, she could hear her father crying. Guilt enveloped her like a great cloud. She pushed open the door. Her father quickly turned away.

'Dad. Dad. What is it?' She put the tea on the table and went to put an arm round his shoulder, but he pulled away.

'Go away. Leave me be.'

'Dad. I'm so sorry. I don't want you to be unhappy here.'

He sniffed and blew his nose. 'D'you know what the date is?'

Ruth put her hand to her mouth. 'September twenty-fifth,' she whispered. 'Your wedding anniversary. Dad, I'm so sorry. I didn't think.'

He wiped his eyes. 'That's a lot of your trouble. You don't think. But then I shouldn't expect you to.'

She sat on the bed. She didn't know what to say. Why hadn't she been a bit more patient with him?

'As soon as I can find something I'll be gone.'

'I keep telling you, you don't have to, and if I manage to get this part-time job it'll work out, you'll see.'

She watched a tear slowly run down his sad face. There were even more lines there now.

'I should have gone with Betty. I'm no bloody good without her.'

'Don't say that.'

The key was being pulled through the letter box.

'That's the girls.' In some ways she was glad of an excuse to leave him as she knew he didn't want to talk. 'I'll leave you for a bit. Don't let your tea get cold.'

He didn't answer.

All evening Ruth watched her father. She had decided not to tell the family about her job till she was sure she was getting it. Her father didn't mention it, so she guessed he had dismissed it.

The next afternoon, as soon as Ruth left work, she hurried eagerly to the school. It was very quiet: the children had long gone home. At the gate she looked around for Daisy.

'You've come then,' said a voice behind her. 'Didn't think you would.'

Ruth smiled at Daisy. 'Where have I got to go?'

'Mr Walsh. Come on, I'll take you.'

Mr Walsh was a pleasant man. He told her she could be on three months' trial. 'That's for both of us,' he added.

Ruth thanked him and Daisy, and, walking home, thought about what she'd done. She would give her notice in on Friday. She smiled. She would be home all day. She could take her father to see Joyce. Many plans began to go round her head. She had to start early in the morning, before the children started school, and she had to go back again when they finished. The pay wasn't very grand, but thirty shillings a week would help, and she would be paid a retainer through the holidays. That's if she stayed that long.

On her way home she called into the tobacconist's for some tobacco for her father. Perhaps that would help to heal the breach that was sadly getting wider.

'Hello there,' said a familiar voice.

Ruth turned. A broad grin spread across her face. 'Stan. Stan! What are you doing here? I thought you'd moved away.'

'I did give it a try, but I didn't like the job and as I'd still kept the house, decided to come back. What about you? You still living in Lind Road?'

She nodded. 'Look, I'm just going home. Why don't you come round and see Dad?'

'He's home then? How is he?'

'He gets very down.'

They began to walk along together slowly.

'How's life treating you then, Ruth?'

'A clothes shop's a bit mundane after what we did for all those years.'

'Yer. I know what you mean.'

'I'm changing me job.'

'That's good.'

'I hope so. It's only a cleaning job, but it's part time, so I'll be home most of the day. What about you? You still in the print lark?'

He laughed and nodded. 'And I'm still on nights. How's your old man? Alan, wasn't it? How's he settling down?'

'It's a bit hard for him.'

'It's hard for most of us. Still, at least you can go to bed and sleep all night. I think that was the worst part, when we did get the chance of going to bed. Even in the day when they came over, we'd finish up down the shelter.'

'That's all over now, thank God,' said Ruth.

They turned into Lind Road.

Ruth knew her girls wouldn't be home. As it was a cold but fine afternoon, they would be hanging round the park swings. That was another worry: Kay. She was growing to be very attractive and Ruth knew she liked the boys . . .

'Dad. Dad,' called Ruth as she walked up the passage.

'I've got a visitor for you.' She pushed open the kitchen door. 'He must be up in the bathroom,' said Ruth looking at his empty chair. 'Have a seat while I put the kettle on.'

'Thanks,' said Stan, nervously turning his cap over and over. 'What time does your Alan get home?'

'Depends a lot on the weather,' Ruth called from the scullery.

She took the crocks from the dresser and put them on the table. She suddenly felt ill at ease. Where was her father? He must have heard them come in.

'Do you see anything of Gloria these days?' asked Stan.

'No. I expect she's finished up in America.'

He nodded. 'I would think so.'

Ruth sat at the table. 'Stan, are you finding it hard to settle?'

'Yes. It's coming home to an empty house. I didn't really miss Jean at first. Well I did but . . . You know what I mean, not with all what we was doing. But now . . .'

'Would you ever get married again?'

'Might. If I found the right person. What about you, Ruth? Are you happy?'

The kettle whistling its heart out made her jump to her feet.

When she returned with the teapot, the giggling in the passage told her she didn't have to answer him.

'Hello, Mum.' Shirley stopped in the doorway.

'Move over,' said Kay, barging past her sister.

'This is Stan. I used to work with him. He's a friend of your grandad's.'

Both girls looked at Stan, then at their mother.

'Where's Grandad?' asked Kay.

'He must be upstairs,' said Ruth.

'I'll go and find out,' said Shirley, quickly leaving the room.

'No, don't. Leave him,' called Ruth, but she was too late: Shirley was halfway up the stairs. 'He gets so cross with the girls and that bathroom,' she said to Stan.

He smiled at Kay. 'I expect you spend a lot of time in there?'

'No. Not really.'

Shirley came clattering down the stairs. 'Grandad ain't up there.'

'He's probably in his room then. Mind you, with all the racket you two make I'm surprised he ain't come out.'

'Don't you start nagging us,' said Kay. 'We get enough from Grandad.'

'Kay,' said Ruth, embarrassed at her daughter complaining about her grandfather in front of Stan. 'I'll go and give him a knock.'

Ruth gently tapped on his door. 'Dad,' she called.

There was no reply.

She tapped again. 'Dad. Dad. Stan's come to see you.'

Still no noise or movement. Ruth slowly opened the door, apprehensive about what she was going to find.

Please don't take him from me, she said silently. Once inside she looked round the empty room. It was very tidy. His coat had gone from behind the door. Something made Ruth open the cupboard he used as a wardrobe. His suit and trilby had gone. The bag he had used to bring his bits and pieces here was missing. Only his false leg, with its shoe and sock on, stood there, all alone.

Chapter 16

Ruth ran from the room with tears in her eyes. She burst into the kitchen. 'He's gone,' she cried out. 'He's gone.'

'Ruth, you don't mean he's . . .'

She looked at Stan; his face was full of sorrow and grief. 'No, he's left us. Gone away.'

'What?' said Shirley. 'Where?'

'He never goes out,' said Kay.

Stan stood up. 'Can I help? Is there anything I can do?'

Ruth shook her head. 'I don't know. I've got to try and find him.'

'Perhaps he's just gone out for a walk,' said Stan.

'What, in this weather?'

'He only ever goes to the pub with Dad,' said Kay.

'I can't think where he would go.' Ruth ran her fingers through her hair and sat down.

Stan was still standing. He moved awkwardly from one foot to the other. 'Look. I don't want to be in the way, so I'll be off. I can call in another time.'

'No, Stan. You don't have to go. You see, me and Dad, well, we've been at loggerheads for weeks, and he's always threatening to leave, and now it looks as if he has.'

'Has he taken all his things?' asked Stan, getting practical.

'I don't know. I didn't look. But his bag's not there.'

'I'll go and look,' said Shirley.

She was back in the kitchen very quickly. 'There's only a few bits left in the drawers, and only his false leg is in the wardrobe.'

'Well, there you are,' said Stan. 'He wouldn't go out without his leg, now would he?'

'He never wears it,' said Ruth. 'Where could he have gone?'

'Are you going to call the police?' asked Kay.

Ruth looked at her, then at Stan. 'Should we?'

He shrugged. 'I wouldn't like to say. What time does Alan get home?'

'About five these nights.'

'I'd wait till then. The old man might even be home by then.'

Ruth gave him a weak smile. 'You could be right. He might even have done it just to worry me.' But deep down, somehow she knew her father had left them.

Stan appeared very uncomfortable. 'Look, I've got to be off – you know, work tonight. I'll call in tomorrow to see if there's any news.'

'OK. Thanks for coming round. Take care, Stan.'

'I'll see meself out.'

Shirley went with Stan to the front door. When she returned she said, 'He seems a nice man.'

'He is,' said Ruth. 'He is.'

It was well past six o'clock. Ruth was upstairs anxiously looking out of her bedroom window. Where was Alan? He should be home. Ruth couldn't even concentrate on getting the evening meal ready. The only thing that filled her head was her father. Where was he? Was he safe? Why did he do this to her?

When Alan turned the corner, she suddenly noticed how hunched his shoulders were. He looked tired. She had been so busy these past weeks worrying about herself that she hadn't noticed that those she loved were also beginning to feel the strain of trying to fit into family life.

She rushed down the stairs and, flinging open the front door, threw herself into Alan's arms. He looked bewildered as she held on to him and cried bitterly.

'Ruth? Ruth, love, what is it? What's wrong?'

Shirley and Kay came to the door.

'Grandad's gone,' said Shirley.

'Gone?' asked Alan, easing Ruth from him. 'Gone?'

'He's left us,' said Kay.

'Ruth, let's go inside.' Alan gently guided her along the passage. In the kitchen he took off his jacket and hung it on the hook behind the door. Sitting at the table he asked, 'Now, what's this all about? You two been having a go at each other again?'

Ruth shook her head. 'No,' she sniffed. 'He wasn't here when I got home from work.' She took her handkerchief from the pocket of her skirt and wiped her eyes.

'Mum's friend Stan was here, and he said we should wait till you got home before we called the police.' Kay began looking around. 'Mum, what's for tea?'

'I don't know. I can't think of anything like that at the moment.'

'Who's this Stan?' asked Alan.

'It's someone me and Dad used to work with when we were in the Civil Defence. He came to see Dad.'

'I see. Well, I think we ought to give the old man a bit of time before we start sending the police out after him.'

'But what if he's been taken ill, or been run over?' pleaded Ruth.

'You'd hear soon enough. Now, as Kay just asked, what's for tea?'

'I'll put the kettle on,' said Shirley.

Ruth couldn't believe how they were dismissing the fact that her father had left home.

'Look, Ruth,' said Alan as if reading her mind. 'He won't thank you for dragging him from where he's staying. After all, he is a grown-up. We'll look in his room and see if he's left any clues. Then, later on, I'll go down the pub and see if anyone there knows where he might be.'

'I don't know how you can just brush it aside like that.'

'When you went storming off the other night, we knew you'd be back, and I expect the old man will as well. He's just done it to give you a fright.'

'He's done that all right. I hope he ain't been knocked over and finished up in hospital.'

'As I said, you'd hear soon enough. Now, what's to eat? I'm starving.'

Ruth cooked some dried egg and the few streaky rashers of bacon she had. She hacked off some slices of bread and put a pot of watery strawberry jam on the table, hoping that would satisfy them. She couldn't face anything to eat herself till she knew her father was safe.

She was in the scullery washing up when there was a loud knocking on the front door. Her face turned ashen as she walked into the kitchen wiping her hands on the bottom of her pinny.

'I'll go,' said Alan, jumping to his feet.

Shirley and Kay sat at the table, white-faced and perfectly still.

Ruth stared at the closed kitchen door; she couldn't move. Voices drifted down the passage. When the door opened she could hardly contain her fear.

'It's Frank,' said Alan.

'*Frank*? What's wrong?'

He grinned. 'We've got a lodger. The old man decided to pay us a visit. He wants to stay for a few days. Joyce told him that was all right.'

'He went all that way on his own?' said Ruth.

'Seems like it,' said Frank.

'But how did he manage the bus and train?' asked Alan.

Frank shrugged. 'Christ knows. Remember, he's a determined old bugger.'

Ruth sat down in the chair and cried.

'Dad, I'm so pleased you managed to get over here. I think you was very brave tackling that journey all on your own. You must have been frozen waiting for buses.' Joyce was fussing round him, plumping up the cushion behind him. 'Just let me know if there's anything you want.'

'No, everything's fine, girl.'

Alice, who had been sitting at the table playing with Joyce's button box, was studying her grandfather. 'Are you going to live with us for ever and ever?'

'I don't know. Do you want me to?'

Alice didn't answer. She continued putting the buttons into different piles.

'You should have told Ruth you was coming over here, she'll be worried sick about you.'

'Dunno about that. Me and her have been at each other's throats for weeks now. What with her and those girls always in the bathroom . . .'

Joyce laughed. 'I expect you would have been moaning at us if we'd had a bathroom. You used to go on enough about us and the mirror in the kitchen.'

'That's 'cos it wasn't nice, always combing your hair when there was food on the table. Your mother was too soft with you.'

'All mums are soft with their own kids, but she could be strict when she wanted to. I don't think Ruth means to upset you, after all she has enough to do what with going to work full time and all.'

'She reckons she's got a part-time job.'

'That'll be nice for her, did she say where?'

'No. Just that she was going cleaning. I don't reckon Alan will be that pleased about that.'

'*Cleaning?*' said Joyce. 'That's a bit of a come-down from a dress shop.'

Bobbie began banging his tray with his spoon.

'It's his teatime. I'll just give him a bit of jelly.'

'You sure I won't be in the way?' called her father.

'No. I told you. We can move Alice in with Bobbie. There's a bed in there, but he's still using his cot. You can have her bed.'

'I don't want to sleep in his room,' said Alice. 'He cries and smells.'

Joyce laughed. 'So did you when you was his age.'

'Where's your leg?' asked Alice.

'Can't wear it. It hurts.'

Joyce could see by Alice's puckered brow that she was ready to ask a lot of questions. 'Right, you can both play for a little while, then it's bed.'

Later, as Joyce was tucking Alice into bed, the little girl asked, 'Will it be all right if I use the bathroom while Grandad's here?'

Joyce smiled. 'Of course, love.'

'Kay said he tells her off every time she goes in there.'

'Well, I expect she spends a long while in the bath. Now close your eyes and try to sleep.' She kissed the top of her head and pulled the bedroom door to.

At last they were alone and Joyce sat down near her father. Deep down she felt sorry for her sister. She must be going mad with worry. 'I hope Frank's not going to be too late tonight.'

'Why? Is he?'

'Sometimes. When he gets in I'll get him to go and tell Ruth you're here.'

'Please yourself.'

Although Joyce was upset at the way he'd left Ruth, she was happy he'd come. At last she was holding a conversation with a grown-up and perhaps she would learn more about him. They had never been really close: here was an opportunity to remedy that.

The girls had gone upstairs, and they ought to have been in bed, but Ruth knew they were probably sitting at the top of the stairs listening to the conversation, as they'd left the kitchen door ajar.

'Did he say how long he was going to stay at your place?' Ruth asked Frank.

'Dunno. He's brought a bag with him, so I reckon he must be thinking of a few days.'

'I'd like to know how he managed to get over there on his own,' said Alan. 'What with his crutches and a bag.'

'He's a stubborn old fool,' said Ruth. 'If he'd said, I could have gone with him, or Frank here would have taken him, but no, he has to do it on his own. Anything to make out I'm the wicked one. Did he mention that me and him have been having a bit of a disagreement lately?'

Frank shook his head. 'Not really. He just said he wanted a change of scenery.'

'Well, I only hope Joyce can cope. He can be so bloody obstinate at times.'

'She'll be all right. In fact I think she'll quite like having someone to talk to. She's always going on about only having the kids round her.'

'Thanks, Frank, for letting us know,' said Alan. 'I was even thinking of going round to the police station.'

Frank laughed. 'Don't worry. Why don't you come down to us on Sunday? I'm sure Joyce will be able to rustle up something for tea. And after I'll run you home, and if the old man wants to come back, I can bring him as well.'

'That would be nice, wouldn't it, Alan?'

'Yer. Why not.'

'Right, that's settled. I'd better be off. See you on Sunday.'

'Thanks,' said Ruth. 'I'll see you out.'

Alan had turned the radio on and soft music was drifting round the kitchen when Ruth walked back in. She carefully closed the door behind her.

'Well, at least I'll be able to sleep tonight, knowing he's safe.' Ruth sat in the chair opposite Alan. 'I still can't believe he went over there on his own.'

'At least it'll give you a break.'

'I hope he don't get too much for Joyce.'

'Don't worry. I bet he'll be on his best behaviour.'

'I hope so.'

'Ruth, this Stan. Is he married?'

'No, not now. His wife was killed in the war.'

'Did he really come here to see your dad?'

'Yes, course. Why?'

'You looked a bit embarrassed when Kay mentioned him.'

'Alan, me and Stan worked together for many years. He worked with Dad as well. You didn't think . . .'

'No. Course not. Now, how about a cuppa?'

But Ruth wasn't convinced Alan had fully accepted her explanation.

On Friday Ruth handed in a week's notice to her employer.

'I can't believe you're going cleaning,' Mrs Collins said disdainfully. 'What does your husband have to say about it?'

'He doesn't mind, and after all it is part time.'

'So you said.'

Ruth didn't want to say she had forgotten to tell Alan. With all that had been going on, it had slipped her mind. She knew she had to tell them tonight.

They had finished their meal and the girls were sitting at the table making clothes for Alice's doll.

'What d'you think, Mum?' Shirley held up a small dress.

'Will it go over her head?' asked Ruth.

'I think so.'

'By the way, I forgot to tell you, what with all the problems we had the other night, but I've got a new job. I'm going part time.'

Alan looked up from the newspaper. 'That's nice. Where is it?'

'The school.'

Shirley and Kay both looked up.

'What school?' asked Kay.

'Yours.'

'You're gonner be a teacher at our school?' asked Shirley.

'We'll play you up if you're in any of our classes,' said Kay grinning.

'I'm not going to be a teacher. I'm a cleaner.'

Ruth couldn't believe the look on all of their faces.

'What did you say?' Alan began folding the newspaper. 'You're gonner be a cleaner at the school? Surely you could have found something better than that.'

'What's wrong with it?'

'I don't want my wife to be a cleaner. Some sort of *skivvy*.'

'How could you, Mum?' asked Kay. 'What am I going to tell me mates if we see you?'

'I go after you've finished.'

'I know. But sometimes we bump into them. This will be so embarrassing.'

'What have you got to say about it, Shirley?'

'It won't affect her for long, will it? She'll be leaving soon,' said Kay.

'I don't mind,' said Shirley. 'If that's what you want.'

'It's not what I want, but part-time jobs are hard to come by.'

'I suppose this is all my fault,' said Alan, stuffing the paper under the chair.

'No,' said Ruth.

'Look, you know I'm worried about my job. Especially now the winter's here. All I asked was for you to bear with me for a while. Just till I was sure of meself.'

'And that's what I'm doing.' Ruth knew her voice was rising.

Alan stood up. 'I'm going out for a drink.'

'That's it,' yelled Ruth. 'Go off. You men are all the bloody same. If one thing don't go to your liking, you're off. You're as bad as me father.'

He stood in the doorway. 'Yes, and I had a lot of sympathy for him stuck in a houseful of females.' He slammed the door behind him.

Ruth turned on her daughters. 'And I'm sorry for you, Kay, if I don't fit into any of your plans. Anyone would think I'll enjoy going out to work cleaning.'

'Perhaps you won't have to when I start work,' said Shirley.

'And what sort of money do you think you'll be earning?'

'I don't know, but it will help out, won't it?'

'You don't even know what you want to do.'

'I have been thinking about it.'

'Now's not the time to worry about it. Just clear all this away and go on up to bed.'

Silently Kay and Shirley put the scraps of material in the shoe box and left the room.

Ruth sat at the table looking at her fingers. Slowly a tear

ran down her face. Why did everything she tried to do go wrong?

'Mum?' Shirley, who was in her nightgown, came into the kitchen.

'Yes, what is it?'

'Can I talk to you?'

'Yes, if you want to. But you won't get me to change my mind.'

'That's not what I want to say. It's about the job I want to do.'

'Oh yes, and what is it?' Ruth wasn't really concentrating on what her daughter was saying.

'I think I'd like to be a hairdresser.'

'What? Why?'

'I like doing Kay's hair and she reckons I'm good at it.'

'So? That's not enough reason to make a career out of it.'

'Don't you think I should then?'

'I don't know. We'll talk about it some other time.'

'All right then. Goodnight.' Shirley kissed her mother and left the room.

Ruth sat staring into space. She hadn't taken a lot of notice of what Shirley had been saying. Suddenly it began to sink into her mind. This was her daughter's future and she had calmly dismissed her. Once more she was full of guilt. How could she have been so insensitive? She went up the stairs. Shirley was sitting up in bed crying.

'Shirley, I'm so sorry.' Ruth held her daughter close. 'I wasn't listening.'

'That's all right. I picked a bad time.'

'I told her that, but she wouldn't listen.' Kay was standing in the doorway.

'Come here. Come and sit on the bed.'

Kay did as she was told.

'Now, we mustn't fall out. I know you don't want me at your school, Kay, but I promise I will never talk to you if I see you.'

'But what if my friends see . . .'

'You never bring them home.'

'Well, you've always been at work.'

'That's true.' She turned to Shirley. 'Look, if this is what you really want to do, we'll go to the labour exchange and find out all about it and see if there are any jobs going. You know you'll have to be an apprentice, and it'll be hard work.'

Shirley smiled and wiped her nose. 'Thanks, Mum. I really do want to do it.'

Ruth held her close and patted her back. She couldn't believe her daughter was growing up and talking about going out to work. 'Right, now,' she said, straightening up, 'time to go to sleep.' She kissed Shirley, and taking Kay's hand led her into her room. 'Come on, poppet, let's get you settled down too.'

Chapter 17

'He's not saying much, is he,' said Ruth, inclining her head towards the doorway. It was Sunday, and she was helping Joyce with the washing-up.

'I think he might be feeling a bit ashamed of the way he left your place.'

'Is he behaving himself?' asked Ruth.

Joyce nodded. 'At the moment.'

'Do you mind him being here?'

Joyce turned from the sink. 'Ruth, I don't want to sound, you know . . . but I don't think I could have him here permanently.'

'I don't expect you to.'

'You see, it's when Alice starts school. I'll be back and forth and I'll have Bobbie to see to. He's getting to be a right pickle, he's in to everything. I don't know how long Dad will put up with him clambering over everything.'

'So how long do you reckon you'll put up with him?'

'I don't know. I'm dead worried the kids will trip him up, what with the way they rush about all over the place.'

'It would help if he used his leg instead of those bloody crutches.'

'I know. And they do get in the way. I've nearly fallen over 'em a few times meself.'

'So, what do you reckon then, next week?'

'Oh no. Give it a bit longer than that. Give it till after Christmas. Alice goes to school then.'

'Christmas? Blimey, Joyce, d'you know what you're saying?'

'Yes. I know it's a few months away, but you know how quick time creeps up on you.'

'I know. Look, Joyce, if he does get too much for you before then, get Frank to bring him back.'

Joyce wiped her hands on the towel. 'I feel awful, we're talking about our father as if he was some sort of parcel, a delinquent.'

'Believe me, he can behave like one at times.'

'He's still our dad.'

'I know.'

They were silent for a moment or two.

When Joyce began putting the crocks away, she asked, 'So what about this new job then. When do you start?'

'Monday week. Can't say I'm that thrilled about it.'

'What about Alan?'

'You should have heard him, and Kay, going on about it. He don't like the idea of his wife being a cleaner and as for Kay, she's worried to death I might bump into her at school. She reckons she'll die of embarrassment.'

'What about you? Do you have to go to work?'

'It's Alan. For some reason he's worried he won't be able to stick at work.'

'I wonder what makes him think that?'

'I wish I knew. He's still so very insecure, and, let's face it, the building trade can be a dicey one at this time of the year.'

'Does he still have those nightmares?'

'They're not so bad now.'

'Look, we'd better go in the front room, otherwise they'll be out looking for us.'

'The old man ain't got you to bring the bed down here then?'

Joyce laughed. 'He did talk about it.'

Alice was sitting on the sofa between Kay and Shirley when they walked into the front room.

'Auntie Ruth, Kay was telling me she's going to be a dancer when she leaves school.'

'So she tells us, Alice. Did Shirley tell you she wants to be a hairdresser?'

'No.' Alice spun round to Shirley. 'Will you do my hair? My mummy pulls it when she combs it, and it hurts.'

'I'll have to see.'

'So where are you hoping to go then, Shirley?' asked Joyce.

'I don't know. Me and Mum's gonner go to the labour exchange to find out, but it won't be till after Christmas.'

'So you'll be fourteen next birthday. Will you have a celebration?'

'Don't think so. It's not for ages, anyway.'

'I thought we could go and see a show,' said Ruth.

'That would be great,' said Kay. 'What one shall we see?'

'It will have to be Shirley's choice, that's if she wants to go.'

'We'll study the paper,' said Kay. 'I'll tell you which one I think will be best.'

'Kay,' said Ruth sternly. 'I said, it's Shirley's choice.'

'I know. Sorry.'

'I don't mind where we go,' said Shirley.

'That'll be dead handy, having a hairdresser in the family,' said Joyce, trying to ease the situation.

'I might even get free haircuts,' laughed Alan.

Shirley grinned. 'I reckon you will, and you, Grandad. After all, I'll have to have someone to practise on.'

'You can't do much with this lot,' Jack replied, smiling and running his fingers through his hair.

For once, Ruth felt happy. It was lovely to see all her family together, and all getting on. Even Bobbie, who had managed to get on to his grandfather's knee, was giggling as her father tickled him. But would all this last?

The morning Ruth had to start her new job she was up very early. It was cold, damp and very dark as she hurried to the school. Despite her gloves her fingers were almost dead. She was pleased to see Daisy waiting at the gate for her.

'Good to see you're not late. Mr Walsh don't like that. Come on, I'll show you where we keep our brooms and things, and then he'll tell you which classrooms will be yours. And Gawd help you if any of the teachers complain. Tell you what, it's bloody cold this morning.'

They made their way across the playground. After Ruth was told what to do and where to go, Daisy said, 'Don't worry. I'll keep me eye on you.'

'Thanks.'

Ruth had to take down all the chairs from off the desks and dust them. She was surprised how long it took and looked up when she caught sight of Daisy in the doorway of the last classroom Ruth had been allocated. This was the first time Ruth had seen Daisy without her headscarf. Her short salt-and-pepper grey hair was parted on one side and held off her well scrubbed face with a kirby grip.

'Nearly finished then?' Daisy asked, walking in and putting a chair on the floor.

Ruth nodded. 'This is the last room. It seems to take for ever.'

'Don't worry, you'll get quicker.'

'I hope so.'

'You have to come back again after the kids have gone home this afternoon and put all these chairs back up again. And sweep. Some of the teachers get 'em to put the chairs up, and that's a big help, but not all of 'em. I tell you, some of these kids can be dirty little buggers. Think that all we've got to do is run around after them.'

Ruth's back was aching, but she wasn't going to let on. She realized she must be getting soft when she remembered all the lifting and pulling she'd done during the war.

'We'll see you here at three-thirty,' said Mr Walsh when she went to tell him she'd finished.

'Yes.'

'Think you made a bit of an impression,' said Daisy as they walked out of the gate together. It was still dark and her breath was forming little clouds. 'Do you live near here?'

'Down there, past the park.'

'I go the other way. Tat ta for now, see you later.'

'Thanks,' said Ruth as she hurried home to get the girls out of bed and ready for school.

'Well,' said Alan when Ruth walked in. 'How was it?'

'Not bad.'

'Did you have to do any scrubbing?'

'No. It's mostly sweeping and dusting. I'll get the girls.'

Kay and Shirley sat at the table eating their porridge.

'What classrooms did you clean?' asked Kay.

'I think they were the little ones'. The chairs and toilets were very small.' Ruth noticed a look of relief came over her face.

'I'm glad it's not ours. I don't want you going into my desk and reading my work books.'

'I wouldn't have time for that. That's of course if I knew which was your desk. Now come on, get a move on, all of you.'

'What you gonner do with yourself all day?' asked Alan as Ruth helped him with his jacket.

'Have you seen that pile of washing and ironing sitting upstairs? Besides, this will give me time to catch up on a lot of jobs before I go and try and find something for us to eat.' She kissed his cheek.

The girls came clattering down the stairs.

'See you tonight,' Kay yelled as they went out the door.

Suddenly it was quiet. It felt odd. This was one of the few times she had been in this house completely on her own. She poured herself out another cup of tea, turned the radio on, and began to sing along with it. Life was great, and she had all day to do her chores.

Although the work was hard, Ruth was happy. By the end of the week she had managed to do so many things at home that she knew had been neglected. She'd even cleaned all the windows and washed the curtains.

It was when she was hurrying home on Friday evening that she bumped into Stan again.

'Sorry I ain't been round before but I've had a rotten cold,' said Stan as he fell into step beside her.

'That's all right.'

'Wanted to come and find out what happened to your dad.'

'He went to Sutton, to stay with my sister Joyce.'

'How did he get there?'

Ruth laughed. 'Bloody determination.'

'Is he back home?'

'Not yet. He will be when Joyce gets fed up with him.'

They reached the top of Lind Road. Neither made a move to walk on in their different directions.

'Let me know when he gets back. I'll take him for a drink.'

'I'll let you have his address if you like.'

'That'll be great. I might even see if I can get over there to see him.'

'Thanks, Stan. He'd like that. He's got to come back after Christmas as Joyce's little 'un will be starting school.'

'Have you started your new job yet?'

'Yes. Just finished a stint.'

'Is it all right?'

'Well, not a lot can be said about cleaning a school.'

'No, suppose not.'

Ruth stamped her cold feet. 'I'm frozen. And you shouldn't be standing about if you've just got over a cold.'

He smiled.

'What's so funny?'

'I was thinking. It must be nice to have someone worrying about you.'

Ruth felt herself blushing. 'I really must go.'

'OK. I'll be seeing you. I'll pop in sometime for your sister's address.' He touched the brim of his trilby and walked away.

Ruth stood for a moment. She felt really sorry for Stan. It must be awful not to have anyone who cared about you.

On Saturday 24 November, Ruth and Alan took the girls to the London Palladium for Shirley's birthday treat. The show, 'Happy and Glorious', starring Tommy Trinder, was slick and fast.

Ruth couldn't take her eyes off Kay who sat gazing in wonderment.

'Did you enjoy it?' Ruth asked her daughters as they waited for a bus home.

'It was lovely. Thank you both.' Shirley kissed her parents.

'I think we could find somewhere to have a cuppa 'fore we go home, don't you?' said Alan.

'Why not.' Ruth tucked her arm through his and they made their way to the nearest café.

Ruth could see Kay was hardly able to contain her excitement.

'That's really made up my mind,' she said eagerly as they sat at a table. 'I'm going on the stage.'

'Oh yes?' said Alan.

'Yes,' she said, full of confidence. 'Did you see the way those girls all kept in line and those costumes? That's what I want to do. I'm going to find out about dancing classes.'

'And who's going to pay for them, young lady?'

Kay looked down. 'I don't know. Perhaps I could do some jobs for you, Mum.'

'I'm sure we could find you a few extra pennies.' Ruth smiled. 'So I'm going to have a hairdresser and a showgirl in the family.'

'Over my dead body,' said Alan.

Ruth looked at him in surprise. She leant closer. 'Alan, just humour her. She's got a couple of years yet, and you know how often she changes her mind.'

'I won't. I really mean it, Mum.'

'Of course you do,' said Ruth.

'You didn't see me on the stage when we was evacuated Dad, I was very good. Everybody said so. Didn't they, Mum?'

'Yes, they did. Now eat your bun.'

Kay slowly took bites out of the bun she was holding. Her eyes were shining. She was lost in her own dream world.

Chapter 18

Joyce was standing in the hallway. 'I've really got to go, Dad.' She leant over the pram and tucked a blanket round Bobbie's legs. Alice, who was holding on to the pram's handle, looked up at her mother.

'Can we go and see Nanny Weston after?'

'I should think so. You'll be all right then, Dad? I must take Bobbie to the welfare for his check-up. They only have the doctor in on a Friday and a Monday and I don't want to wait till Monday.'

'I told you, go on then. Stan should be here about four.'

'Are you sure you'll be all right on your own till then?'

'Course. Now go on. Stop fussing. I was on me own all day when I was with your sister. 'Sides, it'll be a change to have a bit of peace and quiet.'

Joyce knew that the children sometimes got on his nerves, even though she was aware that he went to great lengths not to let her know. Was he worried she might throw him out? Joyce was pleased Stan had written to tell him he was coming to see him. It would be good for him to have another man to talk to. He was sometimes in bed when Frank got home, and even then Frank couldn't always hold a decent conversation as he was usually three sheets to the wind.

'Right. I've left the tea things out, and there's a bit of cake for you both. I'll see you later.'

'Bye, Grandad,' said Alice.

'Bye, love.'

Joyce left the house.

Jack Harris sat back in the armchair and let his thoughts drift on. What could he do with his life? He had had enough of Joyce's kids, but he didn't have the guts to tell her when she had been good enough to take him in. It wasn't that they were bad, but he couldn't cope with the noise and all the running about. He knew he could go back to Ruth, but would she want him? He knew the answer to that, but she couldn't say no. What else was there? He didn't want to be in a place of his own – he wouldn't be able to cope. He realized he was turning into a moaning old bugger, but he couldn't help it. He felt fate had dealt him a rotten blow, leaving him on his own with only one leg.

If only he weren't so stubborn. Tears misted his eyes as he thought about Betty. Dear Betty, she was always going on about what a stubborn old fool he was. He missed her so much. All the years they had planned for their old age together – now she wasn't here to share it with him. He felt like a spare part. He didn't seem to fit in anywhere.

He began to roll a cigarette, thinking that he should have persevered with that leg. If he were walking he could do so much more. Now he was feeling angry with himself, the war and the world. Being on crutches was such a sodding nuisance. Getting on and off buses, even going to the shops and getting money out of your pockets was a bore, you almost had to be a trapeze artist to balance on one leg.

He struggled out of the chair. He had to do something with his life, but what? He couldn't spend the rest of his days sitting in a chair waiting to die.

He slowly eased himself up the stairs and into the bathroom. 'Even having a bloody piddle is a bloody work of art,' he said out loud. 'And I know Joyce gets annoyed when I dribble on the floor.' He came out of the bathroom and, balancing at the top of the stairs, looked down. One thought was filling his head: *I could break me neck if I fell down this lot*. He closed his eyes. *That's got to be the answer*. 'Help me, Betty love,' he whispered. 'Please help me.'

It was late; Ruth and Alan were in bed. She sat up. She was disorientated. What time was it? She looked at the clock. It was half past twelve. And what was that noise?

Alan mumbled and turned over. 'What's that racket?'

Ruth was out of bed and running her hand underneath feeling for her slippers. 'It's someone at the front door.' She pulled on her dressing gown.

Alan sat up. 'Where you going?'

'To find out who's making all that bloody noise.' She wrapped her dressing gown round her, shivering as she went downstairs. It was so cold. She opened the front door and was taken aback to see Frank standing there. 'Frank? What're you doing here at this time of the night?'

'It's your dad.'

Ruth held on to the front door. She felt everything slipping away. She mustn't pass out. 'Dad?' she asked, getting everything back into focus as the cold night air hit her. 'What's wrong with him?'

'Can I come in?'

'Sorry.' She stepped to one side to let him enter.

'Frank?' said Alan, who was at the top of the stairs. He started to make his way down. 'What on earth are you doing here?'

'It's Jack. He's had an accident.'

Ruth let out a little noise. 'Oh no.'

'Come into the kitchen,' said Alan, easing Ruth along the passage. 'It's bloody cold out here.'

'Sorry it's so late, but I've been at the hospital all evening, then I had to take Joyce home and she reckoned I should let you know. I don't think she realized it was so late.'

'What happened?' asked Alan, raking at the dying embers, trying to will some life into them.

'He fell down the stairs.'

'How bad is he?' asked Ruth.

'Pretty bad. He's cracked a couple of ribs and he's badly bruised, and he's suffering from concussion.'

Ruth began to cry. 'What made him fall?'

'We don't know. He was on his own and Joyce didn't get home till gone six, so we don't know how long he'd been lying there. He was still unconscious when she found him hunched up at the bottom of the stairs.'

'Where's Joyce now?' asked Ruth.

'Home. There isn't anything we can do till tomorrow.'

'Who looked after the kids?' she asked.

'My mum.'

'D'you fancy a cuppa?' asked Alan.

'No. Thanks all the same, but I'd better get back to Joyce. She blames herself. She reckons she shouldn't have left him.'

'He's not a baby,' said Ruth, wiping her nose.

'That Stan was supposed to be coming to see him this afternoon, but he didn't turn up.'

Ruth looked up quickly. 'Stan? He must have. He wouldn't let Dad down.'

'He might not have been able to make Jack hear, unless he was trying to get down the stairs quickly to answer the door,' said Alan.

'But wouldn't Stan have heard Dad fall?' asked Ruth.

'He can't have done. Anyway, I'm sorry to bring you bad news.'

'I'll go to the hospital tomorrow,' Ruth declared.

'He's in St Helier. It's a fair way for you to traipse.'

'Don't matter.' Ruth dabbed at her eyes again and Alan put his arm round her.

Frank stood up. 'I'll see meself out.'

'No, I'll come to the door with you.'

Alan and Frank left Ruth and she put her head in her hands and cried.

When Alan walked back into the kitchen he looked at Ruth, who had her head down. She hadn't heard him come in. He was filled with guilt. She had had so much to deal with in her life. Everybody took her for granted. She was always there. All through the war she had been in the thick of it. Twice she had lost her home and all her possessions, but she hadn't complained. He knew from Lucy how she had lived. Then he had brought his problems home with him, his nightmares, and wanting to run away from his job. And her father had just sat in a chair complaining. She coped with going to work, rationing and queuing. She was one in a million, and she was his.

'Ruth,' he said softly. 'Why don't you go on up to bed?'

She looked up. 'I don't think I'd be able to sleep. Good job it's Saturday tomorrow and I don't have to go to work. I wouldn't mind a cup of tea.'

He smiled. 'I think I can manage to do that.' He kissed the top of her head. 'I love you so much.'

'Alan, will we ever be free of worry?'

'I shouldn't think so for one moment.'

Shirley and Kay sat open-mouthed while Ruth told them what had happened last night.

'I thought I heard a noise,' said Kay.

'Why didn't you wake me?' said Shirley.

'I wasn't really sure. I thought I was dreaming.'

'As soon as you've finished your breakfast you can wash up,' said Alan. 'Me and your mother are going over to see Joyce this afternoon when I finish work, and then on to the hospital. I don't know how long we'll be out.'

'Couldn't we come with you?' asked Shirley. 'We could look after Bobbie and Alice for Auntie Joyce.'

'That's kind of you,' said Ruth. 'But we'll find out more today, then we can make plans after that. I'll leave you something to eat.'

The morning dragged for Ruth, and she was glad when at last she and Alan were on the bus. She stared silently out of the window.

Alan touched her hand. 'I'm sure he'll be all right. He's a tough old bugger.'

Ruth gave him a weak smile. 'He's more trouble than both our girls put together.'

'I know. Ruth, you mustn't blame yourself for him going off, you know.'

'That's easier said than done.'

The journey to Joyce's was long and involved changing trains and buses.

'I still don't know how Dad managed to do all that on his own,' said Ruth, when at long last they were walking up Joyce's path.

Joyce flung the front door open and threw herself into her sister's arms.

'I'm so sorry,' she sobbed. 'I wouldn't have let this happen for the world.'

'I know,' said Ruth, gently easing her sister's arms from her neck. 'It wasn't your fault.'

'I shouldn't have left him.'

'Joyce,' said Ruth sternly. 'He's not a child.'

'Hello, Ruth, Alan,' said Frank, coming to meet them. 'I've put the kettle on, I expect you'll fancy a cuppa, or would you rather have something stronger?'

'No, tea will be fine, thanks,' said Ruth, sitting at the table. 'Now tell me what happened and, more important, how is he? I couldn't really take it all in last night.'

Joyce sat opposite Ruth and Alan. 'Well, he was waiting for that Stan. I don't know if that's what made him fall when Stan knocked, or whether he was already at the bottom of the stairs. I didn't get home till late. I went and had a cup of tea with me ma-in-law. I didn't want the kids to interrupt Dad and Stan. When I came round the corner I could see his car wasn't there, so I thought he'd gone.'

'Stan hasn't got a car,' said Ruth.

'Oh,' said Joyce. 'Anyway, it was about six when I finally

came home.' She stopped to dab at her eyes. 'And there he was – just lying at the bottom of the stairs. I thought he was dead when I couldn't wake him. I didn't know what to do.' Tears ran down her face.

Frank put the cups and saucers on the table and put his arm round his wife's shoulders. 'She went running back to me mum's. Mum took the kids in and me dad came back with Joyce. He went up the road and phoned for an ambulance. I didn't get home till gone ten. Me mum was here. She'd put the kids to bed and I went up the hospital.'

'I waited till they strapped him up. They said they are only hairline fractures. It seems he's got good bones. But it was a long, cold, lonely wait.'

As Ruth listened to her sister, it was as if history was repeating itself. She remembered when she had sat all night in a cold hospital, waiting for news of her father and mother. Although there had been plenty of people about she still felt very alone. 'What about his concussion?' she asked.

'They reckon he'll be all right. They took quite a few X-rays, but there's nothing cracked or broken. They said his ribs would be a long job and of course he won't be able to use his crutches – it'll be too much strain under his arms.' Joyce looked tired and drawn.

'What we gonner do?' asked Ruth.

'Well, at least we've got the car.'

'Where are the kids?' asked Alan, looking round.

'Me Mum's got 'em,' said Frank. 'I can take you to the hospital whenever you're ready.'

'Thanks, Frank. I've been thinking. I reckon it's about time I got a car.'

Ruth looked at Alan. 'Can we afford one?'

'What sort of money we talking, Frank?'

'I'll ask around. You won't want anything big, will you?' Alan shook his head.

'Have you got a licence, Alan?'

'Got it in the army. That's about the only good thing that came out of all those years.'

'But . . .' said Ruth. 'You only get three pounds a week.'

'I know. We can use my gratuity as a deposit, and hopefully, when the better weather comes, I should be able to pick up quite a bit of overtime.'

'But . . .' said Ruth again.

'Look, Ruth. If you've got to keep coming backwards and forwards over here, then I reckon the answer has got to be a little runabout.'

'You still got your licence Ruth?' Frank asked.

Ruth nodded.

'Well then. I'll find out what I can, and I'll get you the best deal.'

'Thanks, mate,' said Alan.

Ruth stood at the door of the ward her father was in. She was reluctant to go in, even though the doctor had told both Ruth and Joyce that he was now conscious and cheerful.

'Cheerful?' questioned Ruth.

The doctor smiled. 'There shouldn't be any complications. But we need to keep him under observation. He'll be pleased to see you both.'

Joyce took hold of her sister's hand. 'Come on.'

'Will he really want to see us?'

'Course.'

Ruth pushed the door open. As they walked down the ward it was Joyce who caught sight of him first.

'Dad,' she called out and ran to his bed. She kissed his cheek. 'What sort of game you been playing at?'

'Hello, Dad,' said Ruth, also kissing him. She looked at him propped up in bed. He had a nasty bruise on the left side of his face. 'You look as if you've just gone ten rounds with Joe Louis.'

'I feel like it.'

'Are you in a lot of pain?' asked Joyce.

'Not too bad.'

'So, what happened?' asked Ruth, sitting on a chair next to his bed.

'I fell down the stairs.'

'So I gathered. Did Stan come to see you?'

'Don't know. I only remember having a jimmy riddle, and then the next thing I knew, I was in here with me chest all strapped up.'

Ruth couldn't believe how cheerful he was. 'Frank and Alan are outside.'

'Good lads, the pair of 'em.'

Joyce and Ruth looked at each other.

That bang on the head must have done something to him, thought Ruth.

'The doctor said I'll be in here for a few weeks.'

'Looks like it,' said Joyce.

'Can you bring me shaving and washing things in?'

'I've got them here,' said Joyce, putting a brown paper bag on his locker. 'And I've brought you your own pyjamas.'

'Good girl.'

When Frank and Alan came in the sisters had to wait outside.

'I can't understand it,' said Joyce, looking through the glass door at the men by the bed talking. 'Why isn't he angry?'

'Beats me,' said Ruth. 'But whatever it is, it's certainly made him different.'

'Let's hope it lasts,' said Joyce.

'I'll drink to that,' said Ruth with a very puzzled expression on her face.

Chapter 19

The journey to and from the hospital was going to be easy now Ruth had the car. She was in her element sitting behind the wheel of their lovely little blue Morris Eight that Frank had managed to get them. Some of the money came from Alan's gratuity, and the rest Frank had arranged for them with a finance company. Ruth's only worry, as the windscreen wipers swished backwards and forwards, was: would they be able to keep up the payments?

At the weekend Alan drove, and Ruth could see the girls were very proud that they were the owners of a car.

Ruth tried to get over to see her father when she could. She had managed to persuade the sister to let her visit at lunchtime. She soon found herself helping out in the ward, cutting up dinners for those with their arms in splints, and thoroughly enjoying herself. The laughing and jokes reminded her of when she was in the Civil Defence. Her part-time job couldn't have come at a better time. As Ruth sat and talked to her father, she found she was learning more about him and her mother than she had ever known before. He told her how he met her mother. They were on a day trip up the Thames.

'I didn't know that,' said Ruth.

'I knew she was the one for me the minute I saw her. She was having trouble keeping her hat on and her lovely long dark hair was blowing in the wind. She was so lovely. Always laughing.'

Ruth noticed her father had a faraway look in his sad eyes. She too remembered her mother's laugh. 'She was a good mum,' she said softly.

'She wouldn't stand for no nonsense, mind, but yes. She was a good woman. When you arrived I didn't see that much of you as I was always working. Things were hard in those days. Then when little Joyce came along, I had another mouth to feed.' He stopped. 'She shouldn't have gone before me.'

'I'm sure she's looking down on you.'

'I know she is,' he said confidently.

Some mornings Ruth would collect Joyce and they would visit together. Amazingly, he was taking this in his stride, but it was his cheerfulness that worried his daughters more than anything.

Nearly two weeks passed before Ruth had a chance to let Stan know what had happened.

She had been to his house once before. It was just after her father had been injured and her mother killed. They had finished their shift and had gone back for a cup of tea. But that was a long while ago. She was very apprehensive when she knocked.

'Ruth, what brings you here? Come in.'

'Just for a minute. I can't stay, I'm on my way home from work. I was hoping I'd catch you before you went off. It's about me dad.'

'D'you fancy a cuppa?'

'No thanks.'

He sat and listened to what Ruth said about her father.

'I thought it was odd when I didn't get an answer. I even wondered if he'd got my letter. Mind you, I wasn't all that pleased at traipsing all the way over there, as I thought, for nothing.'

'He was looking forward to seeing you.'

'If only I'd looked through the letter box. I might have seen him lying at the bottom of the stairs.'

'You wasn't to know.'

'I should have thought. He wouldn't have gone out, not Jack.'

'I've got a car now.'

'Have you? That's great. Really coming up in the world then.'

'Alan thought it best, now I have to go over to visit Dad. I can always take you if you wanted to go and see him.'

'I might take you up on that. Will he be in long?'

'We don't know. The hospital are concerned he may not be able to get about.'

'I'd like to see him again, but it would have to be the weekend.'

'That's OK. Can you come on Saturday?'

'I'd like that, that's if I'm not stopping anybody else.'

'No. It'll just be me and Alan. Frank and Joyce are going in on Sunday.'

'Thanks. I'll look forward to that.'

In many ways Ruth was happy now she knew her father was on the mend. Also, despite the early mornings and it being hard work, Ruth was pleased with her new job. Kay had got over her initial fear of seeing her mother when she was on her way to work, as Ruth always managed to keep well away from her. Daisy was proving to be a good friend, helping her out whenever she got behind. So, the next thing she had to get settled was a job for Shirley.

With less than two weeks to Christmas, Shirley took the day off from school and Ruth and she went along to the labour exchange.

'So, you want to be a hairdresser,' said the woman behind the desk.

Shirley nodded.

'You know you don't get a lot of money?'

Again Shirley only nodded.

The woman turned to Ruth. 'They do get a wage now, before the war you had to pay to become an apprentice. It could cost anything up to a hundred pounds.'

Ruth took a breath. 'Thank goodness times have changed.'

The woman studied the papers in front of her. 'We have two requests for young ladies. The first is from Madam Dorina's in the High Street. Do you know it?'

'Yes,' said Shirley, her lovely brown eyes glistening with excitement.

'And the other,' continued the woman, looking up, 'is from Brown's, the department store. They have a very good hairdressing department. If you want my opinion, for what it's worth, I would try Brown's first. It has been a family-run store for many years.'

'Yes, I know,' said Ruth.

'Could we go now?' asked Shirley.

'I'll give them a ring.'

Soon it was settled and they made their way to Brown's.

They wandered through the many departments, stopping now and then to admire the expensive items that were on display.

'I wish I had some coupons,' said Shirley, holding a dress at arm's length.

'Look at the price. And I thought Collins's was pricey.'

'But they are exclusive.'

'Come on,' said her mother, walking on.

Ruth hadn't been in a hairdresser's for years, and then it had only been the little one at the bottom of the road. This was very different. The first thing that struck her when they walked into that department was the smell: a mixture of perm lotion and heady perfume.

A pretty young lady, who had far too much make-up on, was behind the desk. 'Can I help you?' she asked.

'This is Shirley Bentley. She has an appointment to see Miss Gillman.'

The girl ran her finger down the appointment book. 'I don't see your name here.'

Ruth laughed genteelly. 'No, she hasn't got a hair appointment, she's here about a job – sorry, the vacancy.' For a reason known only to herself, Ruth found she was trying to speak a lot better than she usually did.

'Oh, I see. If you'd like to take a seat, I'll get her for you.' With that the girl walked into one of the many cubicles that led off the reception area. The cubicles all had light wood doors with a small window, so offering a very discreet domain for their customers. After seeing the price list, Ruth guessed they had to be well off and didn't want to be seen having perms and sets and sitting under the dryer.

'Nervous?' asked Ruth.

'A bit,' whispered Shirley.

'Miss Bentley,' said a woman in her late thirties. She came and shook Shirley's hand. 'Come into my room.'

Ruth was holding back.

'Are you Mrs Bentley?' the woman asked.

'Yes.'

'Then, please, do come along.'

Ruth was beginning to feel very intimidated. She hoped Shirley would make the right decision.

Miss Gillman told them the hours they worked and what she expected from Shirley. 'And you'll be pleased to hear the wages have just gone up to eighteen shillings a week.'

Ruth noted that Shirley looked a bit down at that.

Miss Gillman stood up. 'Now, can you let me know your decision as soon as possible, as we do need an apprentice rather urgently. Since the end of the war our business has been expanding rapidly.'

'Yes, I will,' said Shirley. 'But I don't leave school till Christmas.'

'Yes. I'm aware of that. Do you have far to come?'

Shirley shook her head.

'That's good.' Miss Gillman held out her hand. 'You look a pleasant and intelligent young lady. I hope we have the pleasure of seeing you after Christmas.' She shook Shirley's hand and turned to Ruth. 'We come back on Thursday the twenty-seventh. We may not be very busy so that will give Miss Bentley time to settle in and find her way around.'

When they got outside Ruth burst out laughing. 'Well, Miss Bentley. Shall we go along to Madam Dorina's?'

'No,' said Shirley firmly.

'But you're not thinking of . . . Do you think you'll like it there? Do you think you'll fit in? It's a bit posh.'

Shirley nodded and tucked her arm through her mother's. 'I reckon it'll be smashing, much better than Madam Dorina's.'

'But they all talk so much better than us.'

'So what? I'm just as good as them. And I like their overalls.'

Ruth patted her daughter's hand. 'Of course you're as good as them. In fact, in my eyes, you're better.'

That evening Shirley was full of what she was going to do after Christmas. She told her father and sister everything that had happened that afternoon.

'Don't reckon we'll be able to retire on your wages though,' said Alan.

Kay sat and watched her sister getting all the attention. 'Is it very posh?' she asked.

'Looks like it,' said Ruth.

'So what are you going to do when you leave school?' asked Alan.

'I told you. I'm going on the stage,' said Kay.

Alan laughed. 'Oh yes. I forgot.'

Ruth had picked up Joyce, and they were on their way to the hospital.

'That was nice of Stan, going last Saturday to see Dad,' said Joyce.

'We could see them talking away. It was good for him to see other people.'

'Alice was saying she wanted to come with us, but I told

her children aren't allowed. She's got ever such a soft spot for Dad.'

'I can see that. Strange, ain't it? He can be such a miserable old sod at times.'

'I must admit he was on his best behaviour when he was with me.'

Ruth laughed. 'Then it must be me what brings the worst out in him.' Ruth parked the car. 'Guess what? I had a Christmas card from Lucy. I haven't seen her for ages. I never seem to catch her at home with her being on shift-work. She's going to have a baby.'

'That's great. When?'

'June.'

'She'll make a lovely mum.'

'I'll have to go round and see her. I feel so guilty. They looked after me so well when I was really down.'

'They know how busy you've been with dad and working. They'll understand.'

'I hope so.'

'So, what're we going to do about Christmas this year?'

'I thought you'd like to come to me, that's if we can get Dad home.' With Christmas only ten days away, Ruth had been thinking about the things she wanted to do.

'I can't believe that Dad might be in hospital again this Christmas,' said Joyce.

'Perhaps not.'

'What can we do about it?'

'I'm going to ask the doctor if we can have him home for the holiday.'

'D'you think they will?' asked Joyce.

'I would think so. He may even be discharged by then.'

'You know it's going to be hard for him to walk.'

'I know. Perhaps we can hire a wheelchair.'

'That's a good idea.' Joyce touched Ruth's arm. 'Look, do you think you'll be able to cope with him?'

'Course.' But deep down Ruth did have her doubts, and what about her father? Would he be as cheerful when he got home?

It was Christmas afternoon. The washing-up had been done and everybody sat quietly listening to the King make his broadcast. Ruth had been a bit concerned that the men would stay in the pub till closing time. But Alan, Frank, Stan and her father had insisted they wouldn't be late, and to her surprise they had kept their promise and they all sat down to a one o'clock dinner. After the King's speech, the excitement rose again as everybody began opening the rest of their presents.

Ruth was smiling so hard she thought her face would crack in two. She looked round the room. She thought back to a year ago. This was just how she hoped and imagined it would be. The years of being apart were behind them. Everybody was laughing. It was such a happy sound. Even her father sitting in the armchair was wearing a bright red paper hat.

When Joyce and Ruth discussed Christmas, it had been decided they would all spend the day at Ruth's. The week before Frank had brought round a large chicken and plenty of drink. Ruth didn't ask where it came from. On Sunday, Alan and Ruth had collected her father, complete with wheelchair. Alan had put his bed up in the front room, but today it had been taken down and hidden away upstairs.

Ruth sat looking at her Christmas tree. It didn't reach the ceiling but it was decorated with baubles and twinkling fairy lights. Her pudding had been sprinkled with brandy and, to everybody's delight, was alight when she brought it to the table.

Everything was perfect. Just as she had prayed it would be.

Bobbie was sitting on the floor playing with a truck that somehow Frank had managed to get hold of, when Kay's voice startled everybody.

'Wow,' she shouted. 'Thank you, Auntie Joyce. How did you manage to get them without clothing coupons?'

Ruth looked over at her daughter who was positively glowing with happiness. She was clutching a pair of red tap shoes to her chest.

'Look! Look at the taps!' Kay was stuffing the shoes under her mother's nose.

How? Ruth was about to ask her sister, but Joyce quickly shook her head.

'I know it's something she's always wanted,' said Joyce.

Alice rushed over to Kay who was sitting on the floor. 'Can I try them on?'

'They'll be too big for you,' said Kay, taking off her slippers. She tied the red ribbons into large bows, and began tapping round the room.

'Thanks, Joyce,' said Alan. 'Can we send her over to you at least once a week?'

Joyce laughed. 'Don't be such a spoilsport.'

Kay hugged Joyce and kissed her.

Ruth noticed that Alice's mouth had turned down; she ran and sat next to her grandfather. He smiled at her and patted her head. 'Don't worry, I expect you'll have a pair like that before long,' he said.

Alice looked at him and, holding his hand, smiled.

Ruth felt her tears welling up. Her father was certainly showing a side she hadn't seen for years. She also knew that Joyce had given Kay the best present ever.

That night, as they were getting ready for bed, Alan suddenly kissed Ruth's cheek.

She laughed and rubbed it. 'What's that for?'

'For giving me the best Christmas I've had in years.'

'It's the best Christmas any of us has had.' She snuggled down beside Alan.

He put his arm round her and held her close. 'Ruth, I know this is a silly question, but you are sure you don't have a soft spot for Stan?'

Ruth was taken back. 'What makes you ask that?'

'The way he looks at you.'

She laughed. 'Don't be daft.'

'So why did you ask him here to spend Christmas with us? Why didn't he go to Brighton, to stay with his family?'

'I don't know. He just said he was going to be on his own, and I thought it would be nice for Dad. That's all.'

'You're a sucker for any hard luck stories.'

'I couldn't let him be on his own, not over Christmas, now could I?'

'No, I suppose not.'

As Ruth lay looking towards the window the clouds flitted across the moon. Had she given Alan any reason to be jealous of Stan? She did have a soft spot for him. As far as she could see, after all the years and the traumas they had been through together, it was only natural. He was a friend, a very good friend. Why couldn't men accept that they could be just friends, without any strings attached. She had proved to herself and to Stan a long while ago that she could never love him. It was Alan, and only Alan she could ever love.

Chapter 20

Ruth felt sorry for her father. She knew his ribs still hurt. At times he looked thoroughly exhausted from the sheer physical exertion of heaving himself up on his crutches, and she worried he would go back to his old miserable ways. Sometimes she saw sadness in his eyes. She wanted to hold him and make things better for him. But now, with her part-time job and a lot of effort, she found things were a lot easier than before. Jack was pleased when Stan offered to take him to his house some afternoons for a game of cards, and he always sat in his wheelchair eagerly waiting for him. And now that some the working men's clubs were reopening, he'd have some more outings.

Ruth at last managed to visit Lucy and Mrs Graham, and she was welcomed with open arms.

They sat and talked for hours about the past and the future.

Lucy and Mrs Graham were really sorry to hear about Ruth's father.

'He's a poor old bugger. Cracked ribs can be bloody painful. He must think Him up there' – Mrs Graham raised her eyes to the ceiling – 'has got it in for him.'

Ruth smiled. 'Something like that.'

'Is everything all right now you've got this part-time job?' asked Lucy.

'Yes. And I'll be eternally grateful to you for pointing me in the right direction that night.'

Lucy laughed. 'Don't forget, you never did give me the money you borrowed for your fare.'

Ruth laughed too. 'I'd forgotten all about that.'

'I bet you did.'

'Tell you what. I'll give you the tuppence and you can start the new baby's money box with it.'

'Saucy cow,' said Lucy. 'No, honestly, it's really good to see that everything is going all right.'

'I'll tell yer, girl. We was both really worried about you that night when she came home and told me all about it,' said Mrs Graham.

'I was gonner pop round, but I didn't want your lot to know you'd been that upset and had talked to me about family matters,' said Lucy.

'Well, it's all water under the bridge now. Are you still working?'

'No. I gave it up. Running up and down those stairs all day was making me legs swell, and besides, I think they wanted to get rid of the clippies so they could give the blokes back their jobs.'

'Well, I think it's only right. After all, most of 'em have got their wives and kids to feed,' said Mrs Graham.

'That's true,' said Ruth. She turned to Lucy. 'And look at you. You're positively blooming.'

Lucy grinned. 'I know. I was ever so sick at the beginning, but I feel great now. And I'm so lucky to have Charlie and Mum. I get really spoiled. Waited on hand and foot.'

'She deserves it,' said Mrs Graham.

'You're very lucky,' said Ruth. 'But you wait till it's born and you have all those sleepless nights.'

'I can't wait to find out what I've got.' Lucy gently patted her round stomach.

'You'll have to. Mother Nature's like that.'

'I hope it don't get too hot in the summer. Don't fancy waddling around with this lot.'

'It shouldn't be, when's it due?'

'June.'

'It'll be lovely having a baby in the summer. Both mine were winter babies, and I didn't have much of a chance to show them off. You'll let me know when it's born?'

'Course. I'll send Charlie round. But we'll have to go out before that.'

'I'd like that,' said Ruth. Ruth felt a little reluctant when it was time for her to leave. Although reminiscing always made her feel a little down, she knew the future, for all of them, was more important now. As she walked home she was thinking of Lucy and how well she looked. She remembered how she had felt when she was having her babies. She suddenly thought that she would like to start again. It would bring the family together, but would Alan accept another baby in the house? And what about the girls? Ruth had a smile on her face and a spring in her step. This was something they would definitely have to talk about.

Shirley had now started work and was loving every moment. Every night she would come home with tales of the customers, and the women she worked with. Some of the customers were very well off and they gave her very good tips. She would tell them how she was allowed, first thing before the store opened, to wander through the departments gazing at all the things they had on display, even though most were on coupons.

She also tried to practise what she was learning on her sister and mother, although sometimes she had trouble with the tongs and made them too hot. Ruth did worry that they could finish up bald, and Kay screamed if her sister got them too close to her scalp.

The young girl who had been sitting at the desk when Shirley went for her interview was Miss Rita Jones; she had taken a liking to Shirley. Although only seventeen, she looked a lot older and was very worldly. It made Shirley's eyes open wide to hear Rita's tales of her outings with her Canadian airmen friends.

One day at the end of February, Shirley was home and sitting at the table reading the *Picturegoer*, her favourite magazine. As it was Wednesday, it was her half-day.

Ruth was getting ready to go to the school and Stan had taken Jack out in his wheelchair.

'I hope Stan don't keep your grandad out too long. It's so cold.'

'He said he was only taking him back to his house for a game of crib.'

'I'm so glad he don't mind being pushed about, it's a lot easier than him walking.'

'I think he quite likes it.'

'Well, it does get him out more now.' Ruth looked in the mirror over the fireplace and pushed her hair into place. 'Just as long as Stan wraps that blanket round him.'

'Mum, I'm sure Grandad would tell him if he was cold.'

Ruth smiled. 'Course, but you know how I worry about him.'

'You worry about everybody.' Shirley hesitated. 'Mum, Rita wants me to go to the pictures with her on Saturday night when we finish work.'

'That's nice of her. Where're you thinking of going?'

'Up West.'

'That's a bit of a trek. What if the weather turns really bad? You may have a job to get home. Can't you go to one of the local ones?'

Shirley began fiddling with her fingers. 'Rita wants me to make up a foursome.'

'What?'

'She wants me—'

'I heard, and I don't think so. Is she that fast one who goes out with Canadians?'

Shirley nodded.

'You're only fourteen.'

'So?'

'Well, I don't approve.'

'Why not?'

'As I said: you're only fourteen. I don't think you should be going out with men, especially Canadian soldiers.'

'They're in the air force. And I'll be fifteen this year.'

'Not till November.'

'Oh, for goodness' sake. We're only going to the pictures.'

'Mind what you're saying, young lady.'

'Well . . .' Shirley looked sulky.

'I'm not going to stand here and argue with you. You'd

228

better ask your father. Mind you, I don't think he'll be very happy about it.'

'We're only going to see a film.'

'Yes, so you said, but where's he taking you after that?'

'We might go for something to eat, as we're going straight from work.'

'I don't like the idea of it.'

Shirley pulled a long face. 'You won't let me do anything. Look how you carried on about me using make-up.'

'Oh come on, Shirley, you looked like a clown. I'm glad you saw enough sense to stop wearing it.'

'I only want to look like all the others at work. I don't want to go round looking like a silly schoolgirl.' Shirley didn't let on that she still wore make-up at work, but made sure she'd wiped it off before she got home.

'Give yourself time. Mind you, I still don't think I should have let you go to work there. Can't have you getting ideas above your station.'

'I love it.'

'As I said, I'm not going to argue with you, I've got to go to work. Let your father decide.' But Ruth was talking to the air. Shirley had left the room, slamming the door behind her.

As Ruth walked to work, her mind was going over and over their conversation. This was the first big row she'd had with Shirley. What would it be like when Kay started work? Where would she finish up? Ruth knew her daughters were growing up, and they would have to let go one day. Being evacuated had given them a certain amount of freedom and they had made big decisions before, like when they left Wales. To come home all that way on their own had been a big step. They would surely resent not being in control now they were getting older.

Ruth had known what Alan's answer would be, and Shirley hardly spoke to them for a week after that refusal.

Despite the war being over things still weren't getting any easier for housewives. Food shortages was the thing most talked about, and queuing up day after day in the cold for so little was beginning to get everybody down.

The cold weather had created a coal shortage, and Ruth's regular coalman was very cagey about how many bags he left her, and sometimes it was barely enough to get through the week. Vegetables were getting hard to come by too.

'You should see the taters I got this morning. Bloody great lumps of dirt stuck to 'em,' said Daisy as they walked out of the school together. 'I told the bloke I wanted to eat 'em, not grow 'em.'

Ruth laughed. 'I bet that didn't go down too well.'

'No, that's the trouble. They think they can do as they like with us.'

'I bought some sprouts yesterday. There was ice in them and half of them were rotten.'

'It's the weather,' said Daisy.

'Someone in the queue said we were going to get bananas again.'

'I heard that,' said Daisy, pulling her scarf tighter round her neck. 'Just think, some poor kids don't know what a 'nana looks like.'

'I think my two may have forgotten what they taste like.'

'Just as long as they remember to peel 'em. See yer tomorrow.' Daisy waved as she went on her way home.

Kay was waiting for Ruth when she got in from work.
'Mum, Mum,' she said excitedly. 'Can I have dancing
lessons?'

'Give me a chance to take me scarf off.' Ruth undid the
knot that was tied under her chin and removed her headscarf. She shook her dark hair and ran her fingers through
it. 'Now, what's all this about?'

'Well, I was talking to Sally, she's a mate at school, you
don't know her. She has tap-dancing lessons. It's a proper
place with big mirrors on the wall and all that. Well, Miss
Fox, she's the teacher, wants to start a really proper dancing
troupe. She may even get us on the stage.'

Ruth was busy raking the fire she had built up with
potato peelings before she had left for work, trying to get
some warmth in the room. 'That'll be nice,' she said, not
bothering to look up.

'So can I join?'

'I don't know. How much will it cost?' asked Ruth,
straightening up.

'I don't know. But I've got my shoes and until we do a
show I've only got to have a short skirt. You can make me
one.'

'Hold on. You'd better ask your father.'

Kay sat down at the table. 'I knew you'd say that. I bet he
won't let me. He's always going on about me dancing
about.'

Ruth looked at her sad face. 'It's the dancing round the
room that gets on his nerves. Find out how much this Miss
What's-her-Name charges for lessons and then we'll go
from there.'

Kay jumped up and hugged her mother tight. 'Thank

you. This is something I've always wanted to do.'

'I know. Now I've got to lay the table. Your father will be in soon and Stan's bringing Grandad back about six, so I've got to get on with the meal.'

'What we got?'

'Dried egg, chips and spam.'

Kay screwed up her nose. 'I don't fancy that.'

'Well, my girl, it's that or bread and jam.'

In some ways Joyce had been happy when her father was in hospital. It had given her a chance to go out and talk to others who were visiting patients. Now Alice had started school and despite the backwards and forwards every day in the bad weather, she was enjoying meeting other mums, and was in her element when she found a soulmate in Laura.

Laura was the same age as Joyce. She had two children: a boy, Richard, who had just started school and a girl, Susan, just a year old. Laura was married to the owner of the ironmonger's. Her husband, like Frank, was always working. Joyce had seen her a few times in the shop when she had gone in there for paraffin for the heater. As they got to know each other Joyce learned that Laura had a car and could drive. When the weather began to improve, Laura had suggested that perhaps they could all go off for the day at the start of the Easter school holidays, and began making arrangements.

Frank put down the newspaper he was reading. 'What did you say?' It was one of the rare evenings he was home early.

'I said, I'm going to Brighton for the day next Wednesday.'

'Who with?'

'Laura and her two children.'

'Who's she?'

'I told you, her husband's got the ironmonger's. We're going in her car.'

'Who's driving?'

'Laura.'

'Well, I don't like the idea of that.'

'Why?'

'I don't like women drivers, bloody menace they are.'

Joyce laughed. 'You don't say that about Ruth.'

'She's sensible. Besides, she ain't got four kids in the back all buggering about.'

'Laura is a very good driver. And I'm going with her whatever you say.'

'What if I want me tea when I get home?'

Joyce was angry. 'Tough. You swan in and out of here just when it pleases you and expect me to be here waiting on you hand and foot. I've had enough.'

'Have you now?'

'Yes. I'm going on Wednesday and that's that.'

Frank carefully folded his paper and put it on the floor. 'I work bloody hard for you and the kids.'

Joyce laughed. 'D'you call sitting in a pub half the day hard work?'

'You don't know what I do.'

'No, that's true.'

'Me mum always stayed at home and looked after me dad and us kids, and I expect my wife to do the same.'

'There's been a war, in case you didn't know. Things have changed.'

'Not for me they ain't.'

'That's a laugh. There's you wants me to stay at home, and Alan wants Ruth to go out to work. You blokes should make up your minds what you want us women to do.'

'What they do is their problem. Mind you, I can't understand Alan.'

'Pity you didn't marry Ruth then. All she wants out of life is to be the happy homemaker.'

'And you don't?'

'I like a bit of life, and with you out all the time I feel it's passing me by.' Joyce was angry. For the first time since she had Alice she was doing something she wanted to do, and now Frank was being difficult. No matter what he said, she was going out with Laura next Wednesday.

Chapter 21

It was the Wednesday before Easter; Joyce had got up early. The first thing she did was to check on the weather. Round about this time of the year it could be very changeable, but thank goodness today the sun was shining.

She was singing softly as she prepared the children's breakfast and did all the sandwiches. She was having difficulty in keeping chattering Alice quiet.

'Shh, there's a good girl. Daddy's still in bed and—'

'No I ain't,' said a bleary-eyed Frank as he walked into the kitchen rubbing his stubbly chin. He was only wearing the bottom half of his pyjamas. 'What's all this bloody noise down here?'

'We're going to the seaside, daddy,' said Alice excitedly. 'Mummy's doing sandwiches and we've got a bottle of lemonade and . . .' Alice stopped when she saw the anger on her father's face.

Bobbie was holding on to Frank's leg.

'What? I thought I told you I didn't want you to go. Let go, son.' He gently pushed Bobbie to one side and tightened his pyjama cord.

Joyce ignored her husband and continued to put the children's bits into a bag.

'Will you listen to me?' He slammed his fist hard down on the table making them all jump and Bobbie, who had been trying to climb on the chair, fell down crying.

Joyce quickly put her hand out to stop the milk bottle from falling over. 'I don't believe you've just done that,' she said softly. She picked Bobbie up from the floor and held him close, whispering soothing noises in his ear.

Alice looked terrified and backed away when Frank moved towards her.

'I'm sorry, Alice love, I didn't mean to upset you.' He held out his hand but she didn't move.

'What's wrong with you?' asked Joyce. 'All we're doing is going out for the day.'

'I've had a bit of a bad time. I'm worried, that's all.'

'What about?'

'Nothing for you to worry about.'

'See? *See!*' she screamed. 'I try to understand and what happens? You push me aside as if I'm not able to handle any problems. I never know what time you're coming in or anything about what you do.'

'I'm sorry, love.'

'Get your coat, Alice, and wait by the front door with Bobbie.'

'Joyce, don't go.'

'I told you. I've promised Laura.' She went up the passage and strapped Bobbie in his pushchair. She came back, and gathering up the sandwiches and drinks began putting them into the bag.

Frank held on to her hand. 'Let *me* take you out for the day?'

Joyce pulled her hand away. 'Frank, you're always saying you'll take us out, but nothing ever comes of it.'

'It's the weather. When it gets better we'll go away for a weekend or something. I promise.'

Joyce stopped what she was doing. 'Why don't you want me to go out with Laura?'

'I thought it would be nice if we could all be together for the day.'

'That is just a silly excuse to get me to stay. Come lunchtime and you'd be off again. You forget, I've heard all this before. Besides, we've got all Easter, you can take us out on Sunday.' She picked up her bag. 'I don't know what time I'll be home, so get yourself something to eat.'

'My daddy didn't want us to come out with you today,' said Alice as she scrambled into the back of Laura's car.

Laura, tall and slim, brushed a blonde strand of hair back from her face. She was standing holding the front seat up so that the children could clamber in. She turned to Joyce. 'Is that true?'

Joyce smiled and nodded. 'He was just having a funny five minutes.'

'Well, you're here now, so hop in, Joyce.'

Joyce sat in the front seat with Bobbie on her lap.

'Are you all right with him?' asked Laura.

Joyce smiled. 'He'll be OK.'

'He's getting to be a big boy.'

'He's still my baby.' Joyce tried to kiss Bobbie who was struggling to get free.

Alice and Richard were standing behind and Susan was strapped in her carrycot on the floor.

'Richard, sit down,' said Laura, looking through the rear-view mirror. 'I don't want you falling on Susan if I have to brake quickly.'

'Alice. That goes for you as well,' said Joyce as Bobbie settled down. 'It's lovely to have a day out, and it's really nice of you to ask us along.'

'He gets under Bill's feet if I let him go in the shop, and I get fed up in that flat upstairs all day on me own, with no one to talk to. Sometimes these two almost drive me mad. I thought it would be nice to have a day out, and to have some intelligent conversation for a change.'

Joyce was still smiling. 'I should say so. And I know exactly how you feel being cooped up all day on your own.'

The sun was shining as they headed towards the sea.

'Mum, will we be able to go paddling in the sea?' asked Alice.

'Shouldn't think so. It'll be too cold.'

'Richard said he was going in.'

'I don't think so,' said Laura.

'See, I told you,' said Alice with a smug look on her face.

'So why did you bring a towel?' asked Richard.

'To wipe your dirty face.'

'I ain't got a dirty face.'

'You will have.'

Joyce was so happy as they sped along, passing fields with sheep and cows lazily grazing. The banks at the side of the road were dotted with yellow primroses. The plants and trees were beginning to get ready for spring. It brought back all those memories of when she was evacuated to the country. She was so happy then, being part of a small community. Her thoughts went back to Frank. Why was he so angry at her going out for the day? He was normally so easy-going. If only she knew what he did. Could he be in some kind of trouble?

Ruth was in their small back yard. She had hung the mats over the clothes line and started banging them with a stick. Spring was definitely in the air and she was making the most of the fine weather.

She was singing away when her father came hobbling into the yard.

'You sound happy, girl.'

'It's the weather.' Ruth put the stick on the ground. 'Is Stan coming round today?'

'No. But I might take meself up the pub at lunchtime. A couple of us are starting to play dominoes.'

'That's good. Can you manage on your own?'

'Now don't start.'

'Sorry, Dad.'

'It's nice out here now. Could you get me a chair so I can sit out here for a bit?'

'Course. I've finished beating the mats so the dust should soon settle.'

Ruth lifted the mats off the line and took them indoors. She returned a few minutes later with two chairs. 'I've put the kettle on so I thought I'd join you.'

They both sat back with their eyes closed. The sun was warm on their faces.

'That little car's been a godsend for you,' he said out of the blue.

Ruth sat up. 'It was while you was in hospital.'

'Stan's talking about getting one. I told him to have a word with Frank.'

'That's a good idea. He'll be able to visit his mum and dad more often then.'

'I think that's the idea. He said he'd take me out sometimes. We get on well, me and him.'

'That's good. He's a nice bloke.'

The whistling kettle sent Ruth hurrying into the scullery.

She was carrying a tray when she came back into the yard.

'Dad, I hope Kay's not getting on your nerves with all this tap dancing?'

'No, she's all right.'

'Even Alan gets fed up with her practising.'

'You could send her out here.'

'We could do. Mind you, she's certainly taken to it.'

'You managed to get Alan to agree to the lessons, then?'

'Only 'cos I said I'd pay for them. Her teacher's supposed to be putting on this show after Easter.'

'You'll have to go and see that.'

'I hope we all go.'

He laughed. 'What, me go and sit through a lot of kids jumping up and down?'

'Don't let her hear you say that. She takes it all very seriously. I'm pleased you don't mind.' Ruth laughed. 'I don't know what that bang on the head did, but you've changed your tune.'

'It was your mother.'

Ruth stopped pouring the tea and looked at him. 'But . . . Mum . . .'

'I know this might sound daft – that's why I ain't said anything before – but, you see, I wanted to kill meself.'

'What?'

'When I stood at the top of Joyce's stairs, I'd had enough. I'd fallen out with you, after all you'd done for me. I know I was a miserable old bugger, but I couldn't help it. I had nothing to do. I couldn't work, and I miss your mother so much. I didn't want to be here without her. There didn't seem any point to me life.'

Ruth sat with her mouth open.

'I wanted to be with Betty,' he said softly. 'I felt so out of place. I would like to get something of me own, but I know I couldn't manage.' He took his tin of tobacco from his cardigan pocket and began rolling a cigarette. 'As I said.' He licked the end of the paper, then studied the finished article for a few moments before getting the matches out of his pocket to light the cigarette.

All the while Ruth sat silently watching him. She didn't want to interrupt. She wanted to know more.

He blew the smoke in the air. 'As I stood there and looked down those stairs I prayed she would help me. I was a bit of a hypocrite really, as you know I don't go to church. Well, while I was falling I heard her say, just as clear as I can hear you. She said . . . ' He stopped and took a deep breath. 'She said, "You've got to make your peace with the girls before I come for you. Look after our girls for me. Be kind to them 'cos they really love you." '

Ruth let her tears fall.

'So when I woke up in hospital I thought of her words, and knew I had to make a change if I still wanted to be part of the family.' He drew long and hard on his roll-up. 'Right.

Now I'm off.' He struggled to stand up. 'I should be back at closing time.'

Ruth jumped up. She held her father close. 'Thank you for telling me this,' she sniffed. 'At least we all know where we stand now.'

He laughed. 'Well, with me, girl, it's only on one leg.'

With misty eyes, Ruth watched him tap, tap, tapping away. She had no answer to that.

When everybody had gone to bed that evening, Ruth told Alan of her father's confession that morning. He was a little more cynical.

'I reckon it was the bang on the head that made him suddenly realize which side his bread was buttered.'

'Well, I don't think so.'

'Your mother talked to him? Come off it, Ruth. Anybody can tell you anything and you'd believe it.'

Ruth didn't answer that. 'By the way, I don't think you heard Kay telling us that the dance studio was doing this show next month.'

'That's all right. I should be able to find some excuse.'

'You'd better not.'

'You can't expect me to sit through all that?'

'I can, and you will.'

'That look tells me I have to.'

Ruth nodded.

'Perhaps that will get this nonsense out of her system.'

Ruth didn't answer that remark either, as she knew that nothing, at the moment, would get the stage out of Kay's system.

★ ★ ★

Frank put the newspaper down and looked at the large clock standing in the corner of the room. He pulled hard on his cigarette. Where was Joyce? It was six o'clock. She should be home by now. He moved out into the kitchen and began looking in the cupboard for something to eat. He took out a tin of beans and slammed the door. He was hungry, angry and anxious as he hacked at the bread he found in the bread bin. What did they know about this tart she'd gone out with? Her old man's shop would be shut by now otherwise he would have gone up there and seen him, but what good would that do?

Frank was suddenly filled with fear. What if something had happened to them? Did Joyce have any identification on her? Would they know who she was and where she lived? Why did they have to stop using identity cards? And what about the kids? *If anything's happened to my kids* . . . Frank wouldn't let such thoughts into his mind.

He quickly threw his cigarette into the sink and, picking up his coat, ran up the road to the ironmonger's shop.

Chapter 22

Although Webber's ironmonger's was only a few streets away, Frank had been running and was breathless when he reached the shop. The blinds were down and the sign said 'Closed', but he ignored that and banged on the glass door.

Nobody came to open it, so he banged again, much harder this time.

'You'll end up breaking that glass if you ain't careful, mate,' said a man walking past with his dog. The dog had stopped and, after sniffing round the lamppost, cocked his leg. 'He don't open till morning,' said the man, who was obviously out for an evening stroll.

Frank stood back and looked up at the window. 'Where's the way into the flat?'

'Down that alley and along.' He took the wet dog-end from his mouth and spat out the bits of tobacco that had stuck to his tongue. 'Blimey, you must be desperate. What is it, run short of candles? Mind you, I don't reckon old Webber'll be that pleased to be disturbed this time of night.' He moved on, calling to his dog as he went on his way. 'Come on, boy. Let's be 'aving you.'

Frank ran down the alley and went up the concrete stairs

two at a time. He tried to remember how many shops along was the ironmonger's.

'Does Webber live here?' he asked as the first door he'd knocked on was opened.

'No. Next door but one.'

'Thanks, mate.'

Frank was trembling as he lifted his hand to the knocker. Was the husband home? What would he tell him?

The door was pulled open immediately.

The laughter from inside told him Joyce and the kids were safe.

'Yes?' said the bloke holding the door.

He was a lot younger than Frank had imagined. 'I'm looking for Joyce Weston.'

'Daddy, Daddy,' yelled Alice, running to the door. Her face was flushed with excitement. 'We've been to the sea-side, and we've had ice cream, and we played on the stones, they didn't have sand.'

Frank bent down and, closing his eyes, held her against him. 'That's nice,' he whispered.

The bloke who'd opened the door went back inside.

'Frank? What are you doing here?' Joyce was standing over him.

'I was worried. You didn't say what time you'd be home.'

Joyce looked behind her and moved outside. 'Alice, go and keep an eye on Bobbie.' She pulled the door behind her. 'I didn't bother to hurry home as most of the time you ain't around. So why all this big concern about me all of a sudden?'

'As I said, I was worried.'

'Well, as you can see, I'm fine. I'll be home a bit later. Bye.'

Frank's mouth dropped open.

The door was pulled out of Joyce's hand and Laura was standing there. 'Alice said her daddy was here. Why don't you ask him in, Joyce? By the way, I'm Laura.' She held out her hand to Frank. 'Would you like to come in and have a drink?'

'Well, yes.' He looked at Joyce, whose face was like thunder. 'Yes, thank you,' he said, stepping into the small hallway. 'That would be very nice.'

Frank followed Laura and Joyce into the living room where the children were playing on the floor.

Laura introduced Frank to her husband. Bill, who was a lot older than her, remained seated, giving Frank a nod. Bill was short, balding, with a paunch and red-veined cheeks.

She told him the man who'd opened the door was her brother. He was tall, with fair hair that had darkened; he was good looking in a boyish sort of way.

'Pete's here for Easter. He works up north,' said Laura.

He was standing next to the fireplace. 'So you're Joyce's husband. Been hearing all about you from your daughter.'

'All good, I hope.'

'Yes, it was. I'm pleased to meet you.' He put out his hand to Frank.

Frank shook his hand.

'Whisky OK?' Laura asked Frank.

'Yes, thanks. That'll be fine.'

Frank sat and watched as the children argued and played together. Bobbie scrambled on to his father's knee; Joyce said nothing, but the look she gave him said it all.

When the squabbling was beginning to get out of hand Joyce said it was time to go.

'Thank you so much, Laura, for a really lovely day,' said Joyce.

'No, thank you. I've enjoyed it as well. We'll have to do it again.'

'I'd like that. Come on, Alice, you're tired.'

Alice took hold of Frank's hand while Joyce put Bobbie in his pushchair.

'I reckon he'll be asleep before we get home,' said Joyce.

'Well, it's been a long day for them.'

They said their goodbyes.

Laura stood at the door waving while Frank and Joyce carried the pushchair down the stairs.

When they were out of sight Joyce turned on Frank. 'What the bloody hell do you think you're doing? Coming out after me as if I was a child.'

'I was worried about you.'

'You came to make me look a fool. Well, I think you did that well enough.'

'Joyce, believe me. I didn't mean to . . .'

Joyce wasn't listening, she was too angry. She began striding out and Alice cried as she tried to keep up with her mother.

'Come here, love,' said Frank, hoisting Alice onto his shoulders. 'Slow down a bit, Joyce.'

He only got the cold, hard look.

On the Saturday after Easter, Ruth had managed, after quite a struggle, to persuade Shirley, Alan and her father to come to the show Kay was going to be in. As they settled down in their seats Ruth looked along the row to her father and Alan. She noted that Shirley was looking radiant. She was wearing just a hint of make-up and her eyes sparkled. Her hair had been styled in the latest pageboy bob. Ruth knew she was so happy in her job.

The music started and the curtains opened.

Ruth sat riveted. She couldn't believe that was her daughter up there on the stage. She was so full of energy and confidence as she danced and sang. She was absolutely wonderful. Ruth's hands hurt, she was clapping so much. She also noted Alan and her father were applauding with gusto.

At the end they sat and waited for Kay. To Ruth's surprise Kay was accompanied by a woman who must have been in her forties, but looked a lot younger. She stood in the background for a moment or two.

'Well?' said Kay. 'What did you think?'

'Really good,' said her father, standing up and holding her close.

'I loved it,' said Ruth, next to him.

Shirley hugged her sister. 'You were really great.'

'This is Miss Fox,' said Kay when she broke away from Shirley.

Miss Fox gave a little nod to all of them. 'You must be very proud of Kay, Mr and Mrs Bentley. She's our star pupil.'

Ruth looked at Kay, who was beaming. 'She was very good. And so was the show.'

Alan stepped forward. 'It looked nearly as good as a professional.'

'It was, very professional,' said Miss Fox. 'My Moonbeams are going to go far.'

Ruth could see Alan was having a job to suppress his smile breaking into laughter.

'Shall we sit down. I have something to ask you.'

Jack was already sitting, but Ruth and Alan quickly sat back on the seat behind them.

'I have been approached by one of the top producers.' Miss Fox smiled. 'He wants some of my girls to be part of the chorus in his pantomime this year.'

'What, already?' said Alan. 'It's only April.'

'All these things take a while to set up.'

Ruth gave Alan a look that told him to shut up and listen. 'That will be very nice,' said Ruth. 'Kay was in a school panto when she was evacuated. She was in the lead. She was Cinderella.'

'She did tell me,' said Miss Fox. 'We will have to have your permission for her to perform as she is under age.'

'I see,' said Ruth.

'I'll make all the arrangements, but if you say yes, then I can go ahead.'

'I can't see any reason not to,' said Ruth.

'Don't they do matinées?' asked Alan.

'Usually in the middle of the week they have one, and on Saturdays.'

'What about her schooling?' asked Alan.

'I'll be leaving next year at Easter,' said Kay.

'All right, but I'm not happy about it.' Alan stood up. 'Are you ready then, Kay? I expect Miss Fox has other parents to see.'

There were lots of giggles from the girls as Alan drove home.

'I'm so happy,' said Kay. 'This is what I want to do more than anything else.'

249

'We'll all have to come and see you in this pantomime,' said Ruth.

'I hope so.'

They were still laughing when they arrived home, with Kay singing some of the songs from the show.

'I didn't realize you had such a nice voice,' said Ruth.

'Well, I don't get much chance at home, do I? I'm always being told to shut up that caterwauling.' She stood with her hands on her hips. 'But now I'm going to be a professional. I shall get paid.'

'Paid?' said Alan. 'Who says so?'

'It's going to be a top show.'

Alan laughed. 'You'll probably get about as much as your sister does.'

'I don't care. It's a start. I'll have one foot on the ladder of fame.'

Shirley burst out laughing. 'Hark at you.'

'I can't see how that Miss Fox can look down her nose and talk about being a professional when you're only going to be performing in the local town hall's pantomime. She tried to make it sound really something,' said Alan.

Kay looked astonished. 'It's not the local town hall. We're going to Margate. We're going to the theatre. We're going to be on stage with the top stars.'

'Oh yes. And I suppose you think me or your mother will be running you down there for your little one-off.'

Kay sat at the table. 'It's not a one-off. It's going to be for six weeks.'

'Six *weeks*?' said Ruth. 'Where will you stay?'

'Miss Fox will get the digs. I expect I'll have to share, but I don't mind. Me and Sally are really excited about it.'

'You're not going,' said Alan.

Kay looked at him with wide eyes. 'Why?'

'I'm not having a daughter of mine parading herself on the stage.'

'But . . . you said yes . . .'

'That was before I found out you're going away. And what about school?'

'But you told Miss Fox.' Kay was fighting to keep back the tears.

'That woman didn't say anything about you going away and sleeping in some grotty doss house.'

Ruth looked from one to the other.

'She would make sure it was all right,' said Kay.

'How do you know? Besides, who's paying for all this?'

'The company,' sniffed Kay.

'That's what I thought. So they ain't gonner put you up at the Ritz, are they?'

Kay began to cry.

Ruth put her arm round her daughter and turned to Alan. 'Don't you think we should find out more about all this before we say no?'

'I've heard about what goes on with those stage door Johnnies,' said Jack, who up to now had been silent. 'After all the young girls they are, promising them everything and when they've got what they want, they leave 'em.'

'How do you know?' Ruth quickly asked.

'I've heard, that's how.'

'Anyway,' said Alan. 'I've made up me mind. She ain't going on some run-down stage, half naked and sleeping in some flea-ridden doss house. Who knows where all this will lead to?'

'I'm hoping it'll lead to me being a star,' said Kay, breaking away from her mother and holding her tear-stained face defiantly high.

Alan laughed. 'You can dream, ducky.'

Kay, with tears running down her face, said, 'I'll run away.'

'And where to?' asked Alan.

'I'll go and stay with Mrs Sharp.'

'Who's she?'

'The lady we was evacuated with,' said Shirley softly.

'She'd let me go on the stage.'

'I bet she will.' Alan picked up his paper. 'And remember, I can always bring you back again. Till you're twenty-one you'll do as I say.'

Kay ran from the kitchen. Shirley glared at her father and followed Kay.

'I think you was being a bit hard on her, Alan,' said Ruth.

'I don't think so. She'll get over it. We all have disappointments in our lives. Besides, as Jack just said, what about all those blokes what hang about waiting to pounce on young innocent girls?'

'I'm sure Miss Fox wouldn't let anything like that happen.'

'Don't you believe it.' Her father rubbed his forefinger and thumb together. 'Not if there's money involved.'

'I don't want her to run away,' said Ruth.

'She won't. She's not daft. She knows what side her bread is buttered.'

But Ruth was worried. She knew Kay was determined. She had run away from Wales, so it would be wrong to underestimate her. In fact she was terrified, but she wouldn't let Alan see that. This could be Kay's big chance. Would she ever forgive him? Ruth knew it would be wiser not to mention it for a while. She had to find out more first.

At the end of May, Ruth was delighted to open the door to Charlie.

'It's a boy,' he said, beaming from ear to ear.

'Come in. Is Lucy all right?'

'She is now. Had a bit of a rough time though.'

'Dad, this is Lucy's husband Charlie. I told you about him. Lucy's just had a baby boy.'

'Congratulations, mate.'

'Thanks.'

'I've got a drop of port. Let's have a drink to wet the baby's head.'

'That's a good idea,' said her father.

'I can't stay long, but I promised Luce I'd tell you.'

'I should hope so. It's a pity they won't let friends in, but as soon as she's home I'll pop round.' Ruth handed him a glass of port. 'Cheers, and lots of love and best wishes to . . .'

'Simon.'

'Simon!' said Ruth and her father.

Ruth's thoughts went back to when she had told Alan she would like another baby. As with most things that might bring a change to their lives, he'd quickly pooh-poohed it, and told her to get that foolish idea right out of her mind. She'd been disappointed, but not surprised. She smiled, remembering the naughty thought that had suddenly come into her head that night: I bet I wouldn't have any difficulty in getting Stan to oblige.

★ ★ ★

It was a warm sunny Sunday in June, with hardly a breath of air. Alan had taken the girls, Ruth and her father to spend the afternoon with Frank, Joyce and their children.

Ruth had been telling Joyce about Lucy's new baby. 'He's lovely.'

'All babies are lovely,' said Joyce.

'I know. I love the smell of new babies.'

'Not when they fill their nappies.'

'Don't be such a defeatist.'

'The real trouble is that they grown up too quick.'

'I know, and that's when the trouble starts. When Lucy got pregnant I suddenly realized I would have liked another.'

'What? What did Alan say about that?'

'Said I was too old.'

'He could be right.'

'Oh, I suppose. Maybe it was a mad idea, but it would have been rather nice.'

'I wouldn't like to tie meself down again when those two grow up.'

Ruth and Joyce were in the kitchen. Joyce was gazing out of the window watching Kay trying to teach Alice some dance steps.

'I wish I'd seen Kay's show. Shirley was telling me how good it was.'

'It was. Did Shirley mention the set-to we had over Kay wanting to go away?'

Joyce nodded. 'I can't understand men at times. Look at that performance I had with Frank when I went out with Laura.'

'What is it with blokes?'

'I think it's called having your cake and eating it.'

'They do like things to go all their way. You haven't been tempted to do it again then?'

'We're going out when Alice and Richard break up for the summer holidays.'

'What's he got to say to that?' Ruth nodded towards the garden where Frank, Alan and their father were all lying back on deckchairs.

'He don't know.'

'Is that wise?'

'What he don't know won't hurt him. I'm not having him carrying on just yet. He'll know soon enough, he can moan then. I can't understand what he's got against Laura.'

Joyce had told her sister what happened when they got together over Easter.

'That was so unlike Frank,' said Ruth. 'He's normally so easy-going.'

'I know. I must admit I did get a bit worried. For one thing he was home quite a bit around that time. Which, as you well know, ain't like Frank, but whatever it was it's all blown over now. I think he'd been involved with something dodgy.'

Ruth laughed. 'He's always been involved with something dodgy.'

'I know. But this must have been a bit more. Thank goodness it's finished now.'

'D'you want me to ask Alan to find out.'

'You could do.'

'I suppose we'd better take these drinks out for them,' said Ruth, picking up the tray.

'Laura said her brother was coming down in August, and he wants to take us all out.'

'Oh yes, and what's he like?'

'Very nice.'

'Will Frank go?'

'Dunno. But I will.'

Ruth looked at her sister as she went into the garden. She certainly seemed a lot happier. Ruth looked at her family all around her. They were laughing and enjoying life, but she wondered how long all this tranquillity would last. She knew that the trouble between Kay and Alan was certainly going to flare up again, and it could be very soon.

Chapter 23

Miss Fox was perched, with her long legs crossed elegantly in front of her, on the edge of a pale green velvet armchair. Her face was discreetly made up and her dark hair pulled back into a bun. She was tall and slim. Her pale green floral summer frock clung to her and, when she walked, she still had the grace of a dancer. 'I was very disappointed to hear that your husband is against Kay going to Margate. She is very upset.'

'I know. That's why I'm here. He's worried about where she'll be staying, and I hope that if I can put his mind at rest, well, who knows?' Ruth, in her beige blouse and navy skirt, felt fat, frumpish and uneasy sitting near this woman. She began fiddling with her handbag.

'I can understand her father's reluctance, but you know it's her big chance? It could lead to all sorts of openings. She is very talented and I would be willing to help her every step of the way. Is there any chance of him changing his mind?'

'I'm hoping there is.' Ruth and Miss Fox were sitting in the teacher's beautifully furnished lounge. Ruth had been admiring the photographs of this woman. They were dotted all around the room; many were taken with famous people when she was a dancer. Ruth wanted to ask her if her parents had objected when she started out, but decided it was too personal. 'We don't want to stop Kay doing what she wants, but we are worried about what sort of people she'll be mixing with.'

'I can assure you I will be supervising the girls at all times. I can't ruin my reputation, now can I?'

Ruth shook her head. 'What sort of accommodation would they have?'

'It's very good. I shall be taking six girls, and they will probably be sleeping three to a room. They all come from decent homes, so you have no worries there. But when your girls were evacuated, didn't you worry about that? We've heard some dreadful tales of what happened to some of the youngsters.'

'Yes, I did worry, but it was for their safety. The raids were very bad.'

'That's true. I was away with a show most of the time.' She smiled. 'If you and your husband would like to go to Margate sometime, I can give you the address of where the girls will be staying. That might help to dispel any fears you may have.'

'That sounds a very good idea. Thank you for seeing me, but I really must go. I have to go to work.'

Miss Fox glanced up at the marble clock on the wooden mantelpiece. 'So late?'

Ruth nodded. Immediately she knew she shouldn't have said that. Kay would be horrified if she thought Miss Fox knew her mother was just a cleaner at the school.

Ruth decided not to tell Kay she had been to see her dance teacher, she didn't want to raise her hopes unnecessarily.

That night, when the girls and her father were in bed, she told Alan where she had been, and the conversation she'd had.

'What did you do that for? You know I'm dead against it.'

'I thought if we went to see the woman she'll be staying with, it might make a difference. We could just go and look.'

'I ain't going down there.'

'I think we ought to find out what she could be letting herself into.'

'I thought you'd given up that idea.'

'I don't think we should stop Kay from doing what she really wants to do. She might get fed up with living in digs and working till late at night.'

'And what if she don't?'

'Then I think we'll have to resign ourselves.'

Alan stood up. 'Well, I don't like it. And I ain't gonna sign no form.'

'Alan, please try and see it from her point of view.'

'The trouble with you is that you're too bloody soft with those girls.'

'I want them to be happy.'

'What if she comes home up the spout because some pimply bloke took a fancy to her?'

'She could just as easy get pregnant here, at home.'

'On no she wouldn't, because when she starts going out with boys I shall want to know all about it.'

Ruth sighed. 'Well, can't we at least go to this address and see for ourselves?'

'No.'

'We can't keep them under wraps for ever. They'll both leave home one day.'

'Ruth, I don't want to hear any more about this nonsense. D'you hear?'

Ruth nodded, but although she knew she was defeated with this argument, it wasn't going to stop her from finding out more for herself.

The following week Ruth decided to go and see Joyce.

'This is a pleasant surprise, is Dad with you?'

'No.'

'Thought you might be fed up with him again.'

'No, he's certainly a lot better now he plays dominoes at the pub. They've got a team up apparently, and they go to other pubs. Some afternoons Stan takes him back to his place for a game of cards. When Stan gets his car I don't reckon I'll be seeing much of him at all. In fact, he's getting quite a social life.' At Easter Ruth had told Joyce about their father's change of heart, and Joyce said she didn't care who he had talked to as long as it made him happy to think it had been their mother.

It was lunchtime and Joyce was seeing to Bobbie and Alice, who were eating their dinner.

Ruth sat next to Alice. 'It's about this to-do we're having with Alan about Kay. I've come to ask you if you'd come to Margate with me?'

Joyce was beginning to dish up some apple and custard. 'Want some?' she asked Ruth.

Ruth shook her head. 'No, thanks. I want to go down to see this Mrs Mills.'

'That the woman who's gonner put the girls up?'

'Yes. I don't want Kay or Alan to know I'm going there, not till I've sussed it out. It'll have to be in the week.'

'I'll come with you, but it'll have to be in the holidays.'

'I know, that goes for me as well, don't forget.'

'Come on, Bobbie, stop playing about with that dinner, we've got to take Alice back to school.'

'Leave him here with me while you run Alice back.'

'Thanks, that'll be a big help.'

'Have you fixed a date for that Laura to take you out again?'

'Her brother Pete might be coming with us.'

'Where does he live?'

'Up north somewhere. He's something to do with this new Coal Board.'

'What, he works down the mine?'

Joyce smiled. 'No, he's an official, he works in the office.'

'So what's he doing down here?'

'He comes to stay with Laura when he's on holiday.'

'Is he married?'

'No. And I tell you something . . .' Joyce broke off, busying herself washing Alice's face.

'Mummy, don't be so rough. You hurt,' said Alice, trying to back away.

'Right, we're off.' Joyce threw the flannel in the sink. 'I'll only be a few ticks.'

'What was you saying? He's what?' asked Ruth eagerly.

'He's very nice.'

'Is he now,' said Ruth as her sister went out of the door.

261

It was hot the day Ruth and Joyce decided to go to Margate.

'I feel really guilty not telling Kay or any of them where we're going,' said Ruth as they made their way down to the coast.

'So what did you tell them?'

'I said we were going to see someone you knew when you was evacuated.'

'Thanks. So what do I say when they ask who it was?'

'I don't know. You'll think of something.'

'Didn't Kay want to come?'

'No, she's got dancing lessons.'

'And what about Dad?'

'He's got a domino match.'

Joyce, who was sitting in the back seat between Bobbie and Alice, relaxed. 'You know, you can be a crafty cow at times.'

'I know,' said Ruth smiling.

It was late morning when they finally found the address Miss Fox had written down. Ruth parked the car but, they didn't move, they just sat looking up at the three-storey house.

'It looks very posh and clean enough from the outside,' said Joyce, craning her neck to get a better view. 'Got nice curtains.'

'I suppose I'd better go and see this Mrs Mills.'

Joyce started laughing. 'Here, I wonder if she's the one what plays the piano.'

'Shouldn't think so. Have you got any of her records?'

'No. A lot of my records got broken when I came back from the farm.'

'Mine all went the first time we was bombed, and I didn't bother to start again. Kay keeps on at us to get a record player.'

'Will you get one?'

'I don't know. It's having somewhere to put it. Look, I'd better go and find out about this woman. You coming?'

'No. I'll wait here with the kids.'

Ruth walked up the steps to the front door. She turned to look at Joyce after she'd rung the bell. She suddenly had a thought. What if the woman wasn't home?

The door opened and a short round woman stood in the doorway. 'Yes?' she asked.

Ruth smiled. 'Are you Mrs Mills?'

'Yes, I am.'

Ruth felt awkward and embarrassed. How could she tell this woman she'd come to see if her house was good enough for her daughter? 'I'm Mrs Bentley. My daughter might be coming to stay with you at Christmas. She's hoping to be in the pantomime . . .'

Mrs Mills's face broke into the widest grin Ruth had ever seen. 'Come in. Come in.' She looked along the road. 'Is that yours?' She pointed to the car.

Ruth nodded.

'Is your daughter inside?'

'No. It's my sister and her . . .'

Despite her size, Mrs Mills bounded down the steps and opened the car door. 'Come on in.'

Joyce, who looked a little bewildered, got out. Ruth took hold of Alice's hand, and Joyce grabbed hold of Bobbie.

'This way,' Mrs Mills shouted over her shoulder as she entered the house and led them into a large, bright, airy room. 'Would you ladies like a cup of tea?' she asked. 'And would the children like a cold drink?'

'Yes, please,' said Alice.

Mrs Mills patted her on the head. 'Nice manners. I like to see children with nice manners. I've had some right ones here, I can tell you. Sit yourselves down.' She left the room.

Ruth and Joyce looked at each other.

'Well,' said Joyce, trying to restrain Bobbie who was fighting to get down. 'Sit still. I'm not having you touching anything.' She glanced round the room. 'This looks good enough. Wouldn't mind staying here meself.'

'It is nicely furnished. It's much better than my place.'

'Is Kay going to live here?' asked Alice.

'We don't know,' said Joyce. 'I like that sideboard. And look at all those photos on the piano.' She jumped up, still holding on to Bobbie. 'Look, that's Tommy Trinder, and Max Miller.'

'I see you're admiring my pictures,' said Mrs Mills as she re-entered the room carrying a tray. 'I've had some of the greats here at times. What's your name?' she asked Alice as she gave her a glass of lemonade.

'Alice. Thank you.' Alice took hold of the glass.

'Be very careful,' said Joyce. 'Don't spill it.'

'Here, you can put it on this little table,' said Mrs Mills, pushing a small table in front of Alice. She began pouring out the tea. 'Is your daughter one of Jane's Moonbeams?' she asked Ruth as she sat down in the armchair opposite Ruth and Joyce.

'Yes. Kay Bentley. You see, the reason I'm here is my husband is very worried about Kay being away from home. She's not yet fourteen.'

'I understand that. But I can assure you and your husband that Jane will keep a very strict eye on her girls. She's been in this business for a long while, and she knows all the pitfalls.'

'Does she dance now?' asked Joyce.

'No, it's her knees. They're a dancer's problem. But she just couldn't stay away from the business. That's why she started the dance school.'

'Have you known her long?' asked Ruth.

Mrs Mills grinned. 'All her life, she's my daughter.'

Ruth gasped.

'I know what you're thinking. I've been married twice, and I wasn't always this size. But I never had the talent. I was upset when Jane wanted to leave home; that's when I decided to start this boarding house. That way I could have some of her friends around me. Been doing it for years.' Mrs Mills leant forward. 'You must let your daughter go on the stage. If Jane can see talent, then she'll do her best to get her noticed.'

Ruth was smiling. 'I'm so glad I came to see you. I feel so much happier now. Thank you.'

'It's my pleasure. I'll tell Jane you came. She's a good girl. Never caused me any trouble.'

On the way home Ruth was full of what they'd seen.

'Do you think you'll be able to get Alan to change his mind?' asked Joyce.

'I'm gonner have a bloody good try. He can't stop Kay, it ain't fair.'

'Would you have liked to go on the stage?'

Ruth laughed. 'Good God, no! I couldn't get up there and prance about.'

'I would have,' said Joyce wistfully.

'D'you know, I could just see you.'

'We didn't get the chance.'

'Today's kids will get a lot of chances. That's what the war was all about. Freedom.'

'I'd like to go and live with that lady,' said Alice.

'Oh would you,' said Joyce, looking over her shoulder.

'Would Daddy let me go on the stage?'

'We'll have to wait and see.'

'Alice,' said Ruth, looking through the rear-view mirror when they stopped at the traffic lights, 'don't tell Kay – well, not just yet. There's a good girl.'

She laughed. 'Is it our secret?'

'Yes,' said Joyce.

'I like secrets. I know a lot now.'

'Do you? That's good! I was just thinking,' Joyce went on, 'we got over one war and in some ways we still have to do battle with those around us.'

'I know. Even those we love.'

'I'm sure it will all work out fine.'

'I hope so,' said Ruth. 'I really do hope so.'

Chapter 24

'Where have you been?' asked Alan when Ruth got home.

'Out with Joyce. I told Dad.'

'He's not in.'

'I didn't think you'd be home just yet. I thought you was working overtime.'

'I was. Then I was taken off the job. I had to go to a meeting.'

Ruth stopped taking her coat off and looked at Alan. 'You haven't got the sack, have you?'

'No. I could be one of a crew that's being put on a new job they're starting. I've got to go with the boss tomorrow and look the site over.'

'That's great. Where?'

'I don't know yet, but I think it's over the water some-where.'

'Will we have to move?'

'No, course not. I'm going along at the beginning and if I don't fancy it, well, I can always find work here. There's plenty going on round this way.'

Ruth looked at Alan. This was the first time she had heard him sound so positive.

'So, did you have a good day with Joyce?'

She nodded.

'Where did you go?'

Not thinking, she said, 'Margate.' As soon as the word had left her mouth, Ruth knew she had said the wrong thing.

'Margate? What was you doing down there?'

She went to go out of the room. 'I'll tell you later.'

Alan stood in the doorway blocking her. 'You can tell me now. You've been to see that woman?'

'Alan, you've got to sign that form. We mustn't stand in Kay's way. It ain't fair. We let Shirley do what she wanted.'

'She only works a bus ride away. She ain't going to be gallivanting on the stage with all those blokes ogling her.' His voice was rising. 'Ruth, she's only thirteen, for Christ's sake.'

'She'll be fourteen in January. I've been to see Miss Fox's mother. She's the one they'll be staying with. She's a very nice lady and she's got a lovely home. In fact it's much better than this.' Ruth pushed past Alan and walked out of the kitchen.

Alan followed her up to the bedroom. 'I'm surprised at you going behind my back. I thought all this nonsense had been sorted.'

'Listen, Alan. I didn't want to, but I had to see for myself.'

'And who's gonner pay for all this then? It's bad enough paying for her so-called dancing lessons. What about for her digs?'

'She told you. The company's paying for them; besides, I don't think Mrs Mills will be charging them that much.'

'She'll still want pocket money.'

'Oh, for God's sake, Alan, stop making it so difficult.'

'I'm just being practical.'

'I'm working, remember.'

'All right. You don't have to keep rubbing it in. You won't have to soon if this new job works out.'

'But if it don't?'

'I told you. I'll find something else.'

'So why are you being so bloody-minded?'

Alan stood looking out of the window. 'It's just that I don't like the idea of her going away.'

'Do you think I do. But I don't want to stop her. She's been given a chance and I think we should give her all the encouragement we can. These girls have been through enough. Do you really think I want her to go away after I missed years of them growing up? But I can't tie them to my apron strings for ever. They'll grow up, get married and leave home one day. And I want them to know they can always come back here. I don't want them ever to go away with bad feelings. I've been through all that once before with Dad, remember.'

Alan sank on to the bed. 'That was quite a speech.'

'I didn't mean to go behind your back, but if it had been a horrible place, and the woman an old bag, then I wouldn't have let her go, and I wouldn't have said any more about it, but it's not like that. Can't we let her give it a try? Please? After all, it is only for six weeks.' Ruth sat down next to him.

'I don't know.'

'We live in a different world now. These girls have had to grow up very quickly.'

'I can't help worrying about it, Ruth.'

'I know. But she's a sensible girl. Please, Alan.'

Alan gave her a faint smile. 'I don't like it, but it looks like I've got to give in.' He wagged his finger at her. 'All right then. But at the first hint of any trouble, and if she's unhappy, then she's back here.'

'Thanks.' Ruth threw her arms round his neck and kissed him long and hard.

When they broke apart, she whispered, 'I don't want you to go away again.'

He pushed her back on the bed and laughed. 'I'll only be the other side of the Thames. What time will everybody be back?'

'You've got about half an hour.'

He grinned and, taking off his shoes, said, 'That's more than enough time for me.'

They had just finished their meal. Shirley got up to help clear the table.

'Sit down, Shirley,' said Ruth. 'Your father has got something to say.'

Shirley quickly sat back down; her face had turned scarlet.

Kay looked at her and grinned. 'What have you been up to then, Sis?' she asked.

'Nothing.'

'This is not to do with Shirley,' said Ruth. 'It's to do with you.'

'Me? What have I done?'

Alan laughed. 'Don't look so worried. Your mother has been to Margate today, and—'

'Margate? What was you doing down there?' interrupted Kay.

'Let your father finish,' said Ruth.

'Well, it seems she went to see a Mrs Mills.'

'That's Miss Fox's mother,' said Kay softly.

'Yes, I know. And your mother liked what she saw and we've decided to let you go . . .'

Kay was out of her chair like a bullet. She threw her arms round Ruth and then Alan. Tears ran down her face. 'I can go? I can go with the Moonbeams?'

'Yes,' said Alan, recovering from almost being crushed. 'But if you're at all unhappy, you've got to come home.'

Kay wiped her eyes. 'I won't be unhappy.'

'So, you changed your mind then,' said Jack, struggling up from the table.

'I was put under a lot of pressure,' said Alan, glancing at Ruth.

Shirley looked at Kay. 'I'm really happy for you, but you do realize this is the first time in our lives that we'll be parted.'

Kay went and held her sister. 'Don't worry. I'll write and tell you all what's happening.'

'Would I be able to phone you?' asked Shirley.

'If Mrs Mills has got a phone I don't see why not. Miss Fox will be ever so pleased. Thank you, Mum and Dad. I promise I won't let you down.'

'It's not us you'll be letting down.' Ruth began clearing the table, then put the plates back down and straightened up. 'We just want you to be happy, and if you want to come back, just let us know.'

'Well, I will be back for Christmas and when the show

finishes. But you will come to see me, won't you?'

'Of course.' Ruth picked up the plates again. She knew that if her daughter had found her true vocation, they wouldn't be seeing much of her in the future.

It was a hot August day in the school holidays and Joyce was waiting for Laura. She had told Frank she was going to Littlehampton for the day and knew that this time he was resigned to it. He was back to his old self now, and Joyce had been delighted to find out why. Frank had confided in Alan, and Ruth had passed it all on to her sister. He had been involved with some young villains, but they'd been put away.

'What about when they come out?' Joyce had asked. 'Will they come after him?'

'He said there wasn't any worry about that as they were well-to-do blokes and their parents were going to make sure they stayed out of trouble.'

Ruth was happy Frank and Alan got on so well.

Alice was playing in the front garden while Joyce was getting Bobbie ready. Joyce heard her daughter squealing with delight when she caught sight of Laura's car.

Joyce smiled to herself. 'I think your sister has got a soft spot for Richard,' she said to Bobbie, who just shouted out, 'Lis, Lis.' He was having difficulty saying Alice.

'Come on then, young man.' Joyce took hold of her son's hand and led him outside.

'Hello,' said Pete, jumping out of the car. 'It's great to see you again. Here, let me take that.' He took the bag Joyce was holding and went round and put it in the boot.

'Will you be all right in the back with all the kids?' asked Laura.

'Yes.'

'Give me a shout if they start clambering all over you,' said Pete, getting in the car. 'Then I'll get in amongst them. I'll sort them out.'

Joyce laughed. She knew today was going to be a great day out.

Eventually they reached Littlehampton and everything for their picnic was laid out on the beach.

'Watch where you put your feet,' said Laura to her son. 'We don't want sand in our sandwiches.'

The sea was cold, but that didn't stop them all from dipping their toes.

They had their sandwiches, followed by ice cream, and everything was accompanied with giggles and yells of delight.

Joyce was so happy. With her skirt held up well past her knees she paddled with the children, then they made sandcastles. She had laughed at Pete, with his knotted handkerchief on his head and his trouser legs rolled up. He helped her collect shells and stones to decorate the castle.

The sun warmed them when they lay back, then all too soon it was over.

'It's been a great day,' said Pete as they began to collect everything up. 'I don't know when I've enjoyed myself so much.'

Joyce stood waiting to put the buckets and spades in the boot of the car. 'Don't you go out with Laura when you come down?'

'Sometimes. But Richie's always been a bit too young to play with, and besides, I think he got bored with just me and his mum around.'

'I must admit, kids make all the difference to a day out.'

'Not only the kids,' said Pete. 'It's the adult company as well.' Joyce let his hand linger on hers for a moment or two as he took the buckets and spades from her.

'Alice, brush all that sand from your feet,' said Joyce as they began to scramble into the back of the car. 'Look at your face. You've certainly caught the sun.'

'I think we all have,' said Pete, picking up the travelling rug.

Joyce could feel her face burning, but she wasn't sure if it was from the sun. 'Thank you, Laura. I've had a really wonderful day. Keep still,' she said to Bobbie squirming on her lap. She was having great difficulty in brushing the sand from his feet.

'As Pete just said. I think we all have.' Laura gave her brother a knowing look.

'I don't go back till the end of next week, could we do this again?' asked Pete.

'I don't know,' said Joyce.

'Frank might not approve,' said Laura.

Joyce felt herself blush again. She didn't want Pete to know Frank had been difficult. 'Oh, he don't mind. It was just that the last time he was having problems at work.'

Laura smiled at Joyce. 'Well, you can let me know what day suits.'

'Any day,' said Joyce.

'I can pop round and tell you,' Pete said eagerly. 'If Laura can't make it, perhaps I can borrow her car.'

'We'll see. Right, everybody, let's head for home,' said Laura, starting the engine.

Pete turned and smiled, then sat back.

Joyce looked at the back of his head. All sorts of thoughts were filling hers – none of which she would ever be able to tell anyone. Not even her sister.

Chapter 25

On Monday of the following week, Joyce was surprised to open the front door and find Pete on her doorstep. He had called round with the news that they couldn't go out for the day on Wednesday as planned, as Laura's daughter Susan had a cold.

Joyce made him sit in the garden and entertain Alice while she put on a clean frock and some make-up.

'You didn't have to do that,' he said when she joined him and Alice.

'I wanted to. I don't like looking a mess.' Joyce knew she was being silly and schoolgirlish, but he had that effect on her.

'You certainly didn't look a mess.'

Although Joyce wasn't sure how easy it would be talking to him without Laura around, she was still very happy to see him. 'How bad is Susan?'

'Not too bad, but Laura thinks that if we're all on top of each other in the car we might all catch it.'

'That's very thoughtful of her.'

'Yes. I did ask her if I could borrow the car and take you out for the day, but she wasn't too happy about it.'

Joyce wondered why, but didn't pursue it. Instead she asked, 'Do you get down this way very often?' She knew this was a silly question, and she already knew the answer as she had asked him when they first met.

'I can't get away now till Christmas.'

'My niece is going on the stage at Christmas.'

'Is she?'

'Yes. She's going to be in a pantomime in Margate.'

Why on earth had she said that? Pete wasn't interested in Kay.

Joyce knew she was rambling, desperately trying to make small talk.

'That's nice.'

'You haven't met her. Alice loves Kay and . . .'

He took hold of her hand. 'Joyce, I must ask—'

She pulled her hand away and quickly stood up. She knew from the look in his eyes he was going to ask her something she couldn't answer.

'I want to see you again, alone.'

'Please, Pete. Don't ask me to do anything I might regret later on.'

'I must. Please, Joyce, just listen to what I've got to say.'

She sat down again.

'I could get very fond of you.'

Joyce looked away. 'Don't.' She was hoping Alice would come bounding up, but she was absorbed in playing. Perhaps Bobbie would wake up from his morning nap. Joyce's mind was in turmoil. She did – and didn't – want him to say things like this to her. Had she been giving him the wrong signals? 'How can you say that? You've only met me a few times.'

'I know. But I've never met anyone like you before. You're so full of life.'

She laughed. 'You've only seen me when we've been out enjoying ourselves. You haven't seen me on a bad day.'

'Joyce, can I write to you?'

She shook her head. 'I don't think that would be a very good idea.'

'If there is any chance . . .'

'Pete. I know I shouldn't say this, but perhaps under different circumstances I could get fond of you. But I'm married and Frank is a good husband. I love him. And you've only known me for a short time.'

'I know. Yet I know how I feel, even though I never believed in love at first sight. I know it sounds stupid, but if there's any hope . . .'

Joyce stood up again. 'No, Pete. Please go.'

He also stood up. He was very close to her. She could feel the warmth of his body. It was exciting and disturbing. 'Can I kiss you?'

'No.' She quickly turned away. But inside she wanted him to kiss her. She wanted him to hold her. 'Please go.'

Pete held her hand. 'I'll be back. I don't give up that easily.'

Joyce watched him walk away. She loved Frank, but to have another man interested in her this way was very flattering. It could be very dangerous though. She looked around her. Was she prepared to lose all this for a fling with a man who was years younger than her husband, and had never been married? She'd be mad to take the risk – but she was very tempted.

★ ★ ★

It was a Sunday evening and everybody was standing outside Ruth's house admiring the car Frank had just brought over for Stan.

'It's really smart,' said Stan, sitting in the driver's seat.

'There was a choice of two, but I thought this one was a better buy.'

Stan grinned. 'I'll be able to take you out for a spin now, Jack.'

'I'm looking forward to that,' Jack replied as he wedged himself against the garden wall.

Frank stood next to him and, after offering everyone a cigarette, lit his own. 'I'm in with this bloke now and we've started getting a few cars for people. It means a bit of running about.'

'Are they kosher?' asked Alan.

'Course.' He blew the smoke high in the still air. 'In fact I was hoping it might cheer Joyce up a bit now she knows I'm doing something she can talk about. She's been that bloody miserable just lately. I don't know what's wrong with her. Always moaning.'

Ruth looked at Frank. This wasn't like Joyce these days. She had been so happy since Alice had started school and she had been going out and about with Laura. 'I'll go over next week and have a word with her. I'll try to find out what's wrong.'

'Thanks, Ruth. Look, why don't you all come over next Sunday? I'm sure that'll be OK.'

'We could do. In fact that's a good idea. The kids all go back to school next week and neither of us will get much of a chance after that.'

'Now I've got the car I might take it for a run down to

Brighton next Sunday. D'you fancy a run out, Jack?'

'Thanks, Stan. I'd like that,' said Jack. 'That all right with you, girl?'

'That's fine,' said Ruth.

'We could go and see me mum and dad.'

'How's the new job, Alan?' asked Frank.

'Not bad. The money's better.'

'So, you thinking of upgrading the car?'

'No, I bloody well ain't.'

Frank laughed. 'It was just a thought. I've got to look after me interests these days. Anyway, I best be off. See you all next Sunday. And Stan, I'll get this over to you as soon as the paperwork's done.'

Ruth watched him drive away. What was getting her sister down this time?

'We're going to go to Auntie Joyce's next Sunday,' said Ruth when the girls got home.

'That's good,' said Kay. 'I can show Alice my dance routines – she loves that. We've started rehearsals for the Christmas show.'

'What, already?' said Shirley.

'Miss Fox said we have to be perfect. We've got to be able to do it in our sleep.'

Ruth laughed. 'Well, don't wake me up then.'

Shirley pulled a face. 'I'm glad I don't have to sleep in the same room now.'

'Yes, but when I go away you'll miss me.'

'You're only going for six weeks.'

'That depends.'

Ruth was pleased neither her father nor Alan were in the

room otherwise there might have been a few more words.

Shirley stood up and walked towards the door. 'Mum, I won't be coming on Sunday.'

'Oh, why is that?'

Shirley didn't look at her mother. 'I'm going out.'

'Who with?' Ruth had always been a bit suspicious of Shirley's friends since she first wanted to go out with those Canadians. Ruth had since learnt that that girl had left the salon.

'Mrs Little, she's one of the women at the salon, she's having a tea for her daughter's birthday, and she's invited me.'

Ruth smiled. 'That's nice of her. Where does she live?'

'Near Southwark Park.'

'There's some posh houses round that way. Perhaps we can drop you off.'

'No, that'll be all right. I can get the bus.'

'As long as you're sure. It wouldn't be any trouble.'

'No, that's all right.' She went out.

Kay also left the room and, upstairs in their bedroom, asked, 'Are you really going to tea with this Mrs What's-her-name?'

'Yes. Of course.'

'Then why have you gone all red?'

'I haven't.'

'Is it that boy at work you told me about?'

Shirley smiled. 'He'll be there. It's his mother's I'm going to, she works in our salon and he works in the soft furnishings department.'

'That's all very cosy. What's he like?'

Shirley sat on the bed. 'He's very nice.'

'What's his name?'

'Andrew.'

'Have you been out with him?'

Shirley shook her head. 'No. But we talk in the canteen.'

'Why don't you tell Mum?'

'Let them get over you going away before I say anything. Besides, it might not come to much.'

'Do you want it to?'

Shirley nodded.

'So why are you so miserable?' Ruth asked when she and Joyce were alone in the kitchen.

Joyce put the plate she was holding back on the table. 'Who told you that?'

'Frank. He said he was worried about you.'

'I'm not miserable.'

'Is he staying out half the night again?'

'No. In fact since he's gone in with this bloke, Alf something, he's being a model husband.'

'And you're worried it won't last?'

'No, it's not that.'

'So, what is it then?'

Joyce looked embarrassed. 'You remember when Alan was away and you told me that you could have had an affair with Stan if you'd been that way inclined, and not loved Alan so much?'

Ruth nodded. 'Don't remind me . . .'

'Well, Laura's brother came round here the other Monday and . . .'

Ruth looked shocked. 'Oh my God. Joyce, you didn't, did—'

'No! But I could have. Quite easily.'

'Well, we all get tempted.'

'Ruth, if he asked me again, I would willingly go away with him.'

Ruth stared at her sister with her mouth open. 'You can't mean that? You couldn't throw away all of this?' Ruth waved her arms around her. 'It would be devastating for Frank. And what about the kids?'

'Don't think I haven't thought about that. It would only be for a weekend. I was wondering if you would look after them . . .'

'No, I won't. I'm not encouraging you to have a dirty weekend.'

'It wouldn't be like that.'

'What else is it then?'

'It would be nice to be somewhere without the kids.'

'And what if you finished up the spout?'

'I don't know.'

'Joyce. Don't even think about it.'

'I can't stop thinking about him.'

'Is he writing to you?'

'I did tell him not to, but now I regret that.'

'When's he coming down here again?'

'Christmas.'

'Please, Joyce. Be sensible.'

Joyce looked out of the kitchen window. 'That's the trouble. I don't want to be sensible.'

'So you're the Shirley my mother's always talking about?' said Mary Little when Shirley walked into the garden and was introduced by Mrs Little, who had quickly moved on.

'Cake?' Mary handed Shirley a piece of her birthday cake. 'I've heard a lot about you.'

Shirley gave her a smile; she felt embarrassed and tongue-tied. She took the cake and thanked her. Mary, who was tall and dark, walked on to the next group. It was Mary's eighteenth birthday and there were many of her friends and relations sitting in the garden chatting. Her mother, Elizabeth, had told Shirley that Mary worked in her father's office.

The house stood on its own in a garden that was a blaze of autumn colour, so different to her back yard. Shirley was feeling very unsure of herself and awkward as she struggled with her plate and drink. She was looking around for somewhere to sit when Andrew came and stood next to her.

'I'm so glad you could make it. I'll get you a chair from the garage.'

'Thank you.'

He returned almost at once with two chairs and sat next to her. 'Mum said you're really good at this hairdressing lark.'

'Yes, but I've only been there nine months, as I said. I've got a three-year apprenticeship before I can do it for real.'

'So I shall be seeing a lot of you then?'

'Yes. I expect so. That's if you don't change your job.'

'Can't see me doing that.'

They both sat silent for a moment or two.

'Can I take you out one night, the pictures or something?' asked Andrew quickly.

'That would be nice. Thank you.'

'You're a funny thing.'

Shirley was taken back. 'What d'you mean?'

'Well, most of them in that department are so stuck up.'

'Your mum's not.'

'I'm talking about most of the others. And I think there's one or two who'll go out with anyone, but you're not like that.'

'How do you know?'

'I've been keeping my eye on you.' He laughed. 'Don't look so worried.'

Shirley wanted to tell him that she too had been keeping an eye on him, but she couldn't until she got to know him better.

All afternoon Shirley sat with Andrew. She found out he was nineteen and his father owned a furniture factory. Andrew was more interested in the selling than the making and was working at Brown's to increase his knowledge and experience.

When the party began to break up and it was time to leave she was very reluctant to go. Andrew had insisted on taking her to the bus stop.

'Can we go to the pictures next Thursday?' he asked as they walked along the road.

'I don't see why not. Shall we go straight from work?'

'That sounds a good idea to me.'

They stood at the bus stop and again were both lost for words.

'This is my bus. Thank you for a smashing afternoon.'

'I'll see you tomorrow.' Andrew went to kiss her, but she quickly jumped on the bus – and immediately regretted it.

He stood waving at her, then the bus moved off. She was so happy. She really did like Andrew, but what would her mother and father say? Their first words would be that she was too young to have a boyfriend. But Andrew was nice, and she did like him, and his father had a small furniture factory, which must be in his favour.

When Kay bounded in, she quickly got her sister on her own and asked her how it went.

Shirley grinned and told her.

Kay hugged her sister. 'All you've got to do now is tell Mum and Dad.'

'I'll do that when I'm sure of him, and besides, let them get over losing you first.'

'Wow. We ain't talking wedding bells here, are we?'

Shirley blushed. 'Don't talk daft. Mum would have a fit if she heard you. Besides, I don't know if . . .'

'If what?'

'His house is very grand and his mother used to have her own shop before it got bombed.'

'They're not stuck up, are they?'

'No. They're very nice.'

'So what's your problem? You're just as good as them.'

'Our house isn't.'

'Oh come on, Shirl, it ain't Mum and Dad's fault. Did you tell him how many times Mum had been bombed out?'

'Yes. And he thought that must have been awful to lose everything.'

'Well, that shows he's got a caring nature.'

Shirley laughed. 'You sound like an old woman some-times.'

'Someone's got to keep an eye on you. I don't want you marrying any old Tom, Dick or Harry. But Andrew sounds nice.'

'He is.'

November twenty-fourth fell on a Sunday this year. Joyce and her family had been invited to Shirley's fifteenth birthday tea. The person Shirley wanted to be there more than anyone else was Andrew. She still hadn't told her family about him and every time she went out she told them it was with someone from the department store. She hadn't the courage to tell them it was a young man from soft furnishings.

'You are daft,' said Kay. 'This would have been a golden opportunity. You could have invited a couple of them from work, including this Andrew. I tell you, I'm dying to meet him.'

Shirley smiled. 'You will soon.'

During tea the main topic of conversation was Kay going away. Everybody was happy for her. Shirley sat and watched. Kay would always be the centre of attention, whatever she did. Was this the reason that, deep down, she was frightened of bringing Andrew home? Would he be able to resist her sister's charms?

All afternoon Ruth had been trying to get Joyce on her own. She knew Joyce was deliberately avoiding her. Ruth had to find out if she had seen or heard anything from Laura's brother. It was almost time for them to go when Ruth finally cornered her.

'Well?' asked Ruth, closing the scullery door. 'Has he written?'

Joyce nodded. 'It was just a card.'

'Did he give you his address?'

'Yes, he did.' Joyce was very blasé about it.

'Did Frank see it?'

'No.'

'Did you write to him?'

'Give over, Ruth. This sounds like the bloody third degree.'

'It is. I don't want you to throw away everything you've got on a silly whim.'

'For your information, it ain't a silly whim, and when he comes down here at Christmas, I'm going to see him.'

'Joyce, please don't.'

Joyce looked at her watch. 'It's about time we went. It's Bobbie's bedtime.'

Ruth stood and watched her sister go and talk to Frank. He was laughing as he picked up Bobbie and ruffled Alice's hair. Her heart was pleading for her sister to see sense. But when Joyce turned to wave, Ruth could see by the cold look on her face that she was determined to do exactly what she wanted to.

Chapter 26

Ruth put her head down against the bitter wind and, pulling her scarf tighter at her throat, made her way to the school. She had been toying with the idea of giving up her job for weeks now that Alan seemed to be settled. He was one of the foremen on this new building site. The money was good and he didn't have a lot of travelling expenses. She didn't feel it was necessary for her to go out on these cold winter mornings any longer. It was Kay she had been working for recently. She wouldn't ask Alan for money for the bits and pieces she had had to get her. But Kay was set up now, and would soon be earning herself. The house would be very quiet next week with Kay going away. As she turned the corner and the school came in sight, Ruth pondered would she be bored at home all day? Her father was always out with Stan or at his club, which had started up again. He'd be able to get about much more if he'd only try to get used to his false leg, but every time Ruth mentioned it, it caused an upset, so she let the matter drop.

How things had changed over the past year. Shirley was happy at work, and Kay was going on the stage. It was her sister that was now causing her to worry. She knew Joyce had received a card from this Pete, but was she making arrangements to see him over Christmas when he was going to stay with his sister?

'Hello there, girl, all right?'

She was greeted cheerfully as usual from Daisy.

'Yes, thanks.'

'Be glad to have a bit of time off over Christmas. It must be me age, this cold and damp goes right through to me bones.'

'I would think it goes through anybody at this time of the morning.'

'I think you're right. I saw my milkie this morning.' Daisy laughed. 'Well, I think it was him under all his clothes. He said some places are having snow.'

Ruth shuddered. 'Oh don't. Let's hope we can still get some coal.'

'I don't think me old legs will be able to put up with standing in a queue for coal as well as everything else this year.'

As they made their way to the classrooms they cleaned, the thought of trudging through snow when she could still be snuggled up in a warm bed really convinced Ruth that it was time to be thinking about being a lady of leisure.

It was Sunday, ten days before Christmas. Ruth was fighting back tears as she and Alan stood on the platform to see Kay off.

'You will write?' asked Ruth.

'I've told you I will. Gosh, Mum, I'll be home next week. And besides, now I've given Shirley Mrs Mills's phone number, she'll phone me on Sunday morning to find out what train I'll be on on Tuesday. I told her not too early though.'

Ruth could see that although her daughter was almost beside herself with excitement she still looked sad. And this morning when she said goodbye to Shirley, they had both shed a few tears at the thought of being apart.

When a train came chugging into the station Miss Fox gathered her six Moonbeams together. 'Right, girls, this is our train.'

With high-pitched giggles, the girls, struggling with their cases, gave their parents hurried kisses and cuddles.

Ruth and Alan watched their youngest daughter clamber on the train to start a new life.

'See you next week,' yelled Ruth above the din of the station. Kay was coming home just for Christmas Eve and Christmas Day. The show was opening on Boxing Day and they needed this time to be on the stage for rehearsals.

'Don't worry. We'll arrange for me or your mother to be here to meet you,' shouted Alan.

The whistle was blown, the green flag waved and they watched their daughter slowly being taken away from them.

Ruth dabbed at her eyes. 'I feel I'm always saying hello or goodbye to someone.'

Alan put his arm round her shoulders. 'Remember it was you who twisted my arm to let her go.'

She smiled up at him. 'I know.'

On the Saturday before Christmas Ruth went to see Joyce. But before she did, she went along to the ironmonger's, to have a word with Laura.

'Excuse me,' she said to the balding, plump man behind

291

the counter. 'Is Laura home?'

'Yes. She's upstairs.'

'Could I have a word with her?'

He looked puzzled.

'I'm Ruth, Joyce's sister. I think your wife goes out with . . .'

'What's wrong? Is Joyce all right?'

Ruth smiled, surprised at his apparent look of concern. 'Yes. Yes, she is.'

'Go through the back of the shop and up the stairs.' He held up the flap of the counter and let Ruth through.

She gingerly pushed open the door at the top of the stairs. 'Hello,' she called. 'Laura, are you there?'

Laura came out of a room. 'Yes?'

'Laura, I'm Ruth, Joyce's sister.'

Laura's face broke into a smile then almost at once turned to alarm. 'Is something wrong?'

'No. I just wonder if I could have a little talk, if that's all right.'

'Course. Come in. Take a seat,' said Laura, quickly grabbing a pile of ironing from off a chair. 'Can never keep this lot down.'

'It's the drying of it in this weather that gets me,' said Ruth.

Laura smiled and sat in a chair opposite. 'I know what you mean.'

Silence fell. Ruth began fidgeting with her handbag. 'I've come about Joyce. I'm worried about her.'

'Why? What's wrong?'

'This might sound stupid, but I think she might be thinking of having an affair with your brother.'

Laura began fussing with some papers. 'What makes you think that?'

'She's been very funny since he went back after the holidays, and I know he's written to her . . .'

'The sod. Sorry about that. I told him not to.'

'You know?'

'I did have my suspicions.' She stood up. 'I'm very sorry about this.'

'It's not your fault.'

'I thought there was something. When he was here in the summer he wanted to borrow my car and take her out, but I wouldn't let him. He got very angry about it. I think he went to see her.'

'Is he coming here at Christmas?'

Laura nodded. 'Today until Thursday. It's only for a few days.'

'That's all it takes,' said Ruth.

'He's on his way so I can't tell him not to come. I'm the only family he's got. Our parents died a while back, and he never married. He only seemed to find gold-diggers. He's got a very good job. It takes him all over the country. He was worried he couldn't find a girl he could love for himself.'

'It seems he has now.'

'Does her husband know?'

Ruth shook her head. 'All he knows is that she's miserable. Poor Frank, he thinks he's to blame. He's ten years older than Joyce and I understand your brother is about the same age as her.'

'Yes, he'll be twenty-nine next month. I'll have a word with him. But I don't know if it'll make any difference, they are both grown-ups.'

'I know. I feel awful going behind Joyce's back. You didn't mind me coming to tell you this, did you?'

'No. I'm glad you did. I'm really sorry. You must be very fond of your sister to worry about her like this.'

'Yes, I am.'

'I can't see how they'll be able to get away on their own, not over Christmas.'

'I hope not.' Ruth stood up. 'Thank you for talking to me and being so understanding. I was worried you might tell me to bugger off and mind my own business.'

'I wouldn't do that. I'm being very selfish, you see I like being in your sister's company and if she goes off with my brother, I'll never see her again!'

Ruth gave her a slight smile. 'Don't even think about things like that.'

'Go out through this door, that way you don't have to go through the shop. It's been nice meeting you.'

'And you. Merry Christmas.'

'And to you.'

Ruth made her way down the stone steps. The thought that was filling her head was that it wouldn't be a very merry Christmas for Frank if he ever found out what his wife might be thinking of doing.

Joyce was looking harassed when she opened the door. 'Thought it was you, saw the car.'

Ruth walked in. 'Well, how are you? Did you have a good journey? I'm so glad you've come over.'

'Sorry. I'll put the kettle on. It's just that I'm having a bad day.'

'It looks like it.'

'Auntie Ruth!' said Alice, running up to her. She had red eyes and was sniffing. 'My mummy smacked me.'

Ruth bent down and gave her a cuddle. 'Did she now. Why did she do that?'

'I was a naughty girl.'

Ruth stood up.

'Go on. Go on. Tell Auntie Ruth what you did.'

Alice hung her head and began to wander away.

'Alice,' said Joyce firmly.

'I bit Bobbie,' she whispered.

'That wasn't very nice. What will Kay say about that?'

Alice looked up with wide eyes. 'Don't tell her. Please don't tell her. He broke my doll. I won't do it again. I promise.'

'That's all right then. Show me your doll, perhaps we can mend it.'

'He pulled its arm off. What brings you over here?' asked Joyce.

'I must say I like your way of greeting people and making them feel welcome.'

'Sorry. But with them round me feet all day and . . .' Joyce suddenly burst into tears.

Ruth ran to her sister and held her close. 'What is it?'

Joyce broke away and wiped her eyes on the bottom of her pinny.

Alice looked at her mother with horror. 'Mummy. Mummy. I'm ever so sorry. I won't do it again. I promise.' Tears ran down her bright red cheeks.

Joyce gave her a watery smile. 'It wasn't you, darling. Mummy don't feel well. Now you go and play in the front room with your doll's house. And don't touch that electric fire.'

Alice reluctantly moved away.

'What's wrong?' asked Ruth.

'I've had a Christmas card from Pete.'

'So what's to get upset over that?'

'There was a letter as well. He wants to see me over Christmas.'

Ruth sat at the kitchen table. 'You can't. You mustn't.'

Joyce also sat down. 'For the first time in my life I'll be doing something exciting.'

'It could also be the ending of your marriage if Frank found out.'

'I can always say I'm going away with Laura.'

'Laura won't like that.'

'I can talk her round.'

'I don't think you will. I've just been to see her and—'

'You've what?'

'I've been worried about you so I thought . . .'

'You've got a bloody cheek checking up on me!'

'I wasn't.'

'Thought you'd find out what I'm up to, I suppose?'

'No, Joyce, it's not like that.'

'So why did you go to see her?'

'I told you. Please, Joyce, be sensible. Don't throw all this away just on a silly whim.'

'It's not a silly whim, Ruth. I could easily fall in love with him.'

'Don't talk like a silly schoolgirl.'

'I'm serious.'

'So when are your thinking of having this illicit affair?'

'I'm seeing him the Saturday after Christmas. He's not going back up north, his office is moving to London.'

'He told Laura he was going home on Thursday.'

'He told her that to cover his tracks.'

'He said all this in one letter?'

Joyce shook her head. 'We've been writing to each other.'

'Joyce, you are being so bloody stupid!'

'You can't shout. You nearly had an affair, remember.'

'Nearly is the right word. Thank God I came to my senses in time.'

Joyce turned away.

Ruth stood up and walked to the door. 'Well, I don't approve, and I know Laura doesn't.'

'So what are you going to do about it? Are you going to tell Frank?'

'No. I'll leave that up to your conscience, but I won't help to make it easy for you.'

'I didn't expect you to.'

'Please, Joyce. Really give it a lot of thought.'

'I have, and I want to see him again.'

As Ruth drove home she was in turmoil. *What about Bobbie and Alice? What is Joyce thinking of? Why does she always want some excitement in her life?* Her father would kill her if he found out. Ruth knew she had to be very careful what she said. And she had to think of something to keep her sister busy all over Christmas, and the weekend after. *Oh, why is this Pete being moved to London?* Hopefully he would be moved away again soon and out of Joyce's life.

Chapter 27

It was Kay who, on Christmas Eve, came up with the answer to Ruth's immediate prayers.

From the moment she had met Kay from the train, Ruth knew the excitement and babble would last all over the short time she was home.

Ruth had bought a Christmas tree and the decorations were up ready for the big day. Frank, Joyce and their children, along with Stan, were all spending the day with them, just as last year. But Ruth was still worried about Joyce, although she had kept her fears to herself and had not mentioned it to Alan.

Since her sister had told her about Pete, whenever she looked at Stan she was so pleased that she hadn't given in to temptation all those years ago. But her moment of madness would have been due to the circumstances they had found themselves in at the time. It wasn't something they had planned, and she knew Stan felt the same.

Kay hadn't stopped talking since she'd stepped off the train. Ruth could see that even in just over a week she had grown in confidence. She waved her arms about describing the large stage, the sets and costumes. 'In one scene we wear these lovely pink dresses, and a little matching pill-box hat. They are gorgeous. I bet you say our skirts are too short, Dad, but we have to have them short, we have to show off our steps.' With that she launched into a display of tap dancing. Her eyes were bright as buttons and her enthusiasm overwhelming.

'What are your digs like?' asked Alan, getting practical as they sat down to their evening meal on Christmas Eve. 'Can she cook as good as your mother?'

'Mrs Mills is wonderful. She gives us breakfast and a packed lunch, then when we get back home she's got a hot meal for us. But I don't know what it'll be like when the show opens. We won't get home till about eleven.'

Ruth felt hurt when she called Mrs Mills's house home – perhaps it was just a slip of the tongue.

'Did you miss us?' asked Shirley.

'Yes. We all missed home. Sally cried some nights. But I didn't. I told her she should have been evacuated. That was worse.'

'Wasn't she sent away?' asked Ruth.

'No, only to her grandma. I think it was on the Isle of Wight or somewhere.'

'I thought you were happy when you were evacuated,' said Alan.

'We were. I was lucky. I was with Shirley all the time. But we did worry about Mum. And you.' She seemed to add that as an afterthought. 'I've got you all a present.'

'You'll have to wait till the morning,' said Ruth.

'It's not a Christmas present. It's from the theatre. It's tickets to come and see our performance.'

'That'll be nice,' said Shirley. 'When?'

'Next Saturday afternoon. Please say you'll all come.'

Shirley looked dismayed. 'I can't go. I'll be at work.'

'I know and I'm really sorry about that. It was the only ones they would let us have. Couldn't you have a Saturday off?'

'No. I couldn't do that.'

'Perhaps you can come some other time, but you'll have to pay.'

'I'm not going all that way on my own.'

'Look, perhaps we can sort something out later. That's very nice, Kay. How many tickets did they let you have?' asked Ruth.

'Four. You and Dad, Shirley and Grandad. Perhaps Auntie Joyce would like to come in Shirley's place?'

Ruth smiled. 'I'll ask her. I'm sure she'd love to come,' she said enthusiastically. Ruth knew Frank would mind the children, so Joyce couldn't get out of it.

Christmas Day started early. Everyone was happy exchanging presents. Things were still on ration, so presents had been hard to come by. For weeks Ruth had spent most of her evenings knitting gloves for everyone with the wool she'd got from all the old jumpers she'd unpicked. They all appeared very pleased with her handiwork.

As the chemist was the only shop where you didn't need coupons, it seemed both Kay and Shirley had been there for presents, and tins of cough sweets, wintergreen ointment and sticking plaster were nicely wrapped and given.

When Joyce and her family arrived Ruth couldn't wait to tell her that she was going to Margate with them on Saturday.

'That's great,' said Frank. 'It'll do you good to have a day away from the kids.'

Joyce was scowling at Ruth. 'I don't know if I can make it,' she said.

'Why not?' asked Ruth, trying to look innocent. 'What else have you got in mind?'

'I was going to go out with Laura.'

'Laura won't mind,' said Frank. 'Besides, you can always go with her another day.'

'But I promised her.'

'Laura's a reasonable woman. She'll understand. Besides, whatever it is surely can wait another week or two.'

'I don't know.'

'It's all free,' said Ruth feeling slightly guilty at making her sister suffer.

'Please come, Auntie Joyce,' said Kay. 'I know you'll like it.'

'Can I go with Mummy?' asked Alice. 'I like panto-mimes.'

Kay bent down and cuddled Alice. 'I'm sorry, poppet, not this time, I've only got the four tickets.' She looked up at Frank. 'Perhaps you can get your daddy to bring you down to see me another time.'

'Daddy, Daddy, could you do that?'

'That would be a great idea,' said Joyce, perking up. 'We could all go together the following Saturday. It'll be nice going out as a family. Kay, could you give our tickets to your mother when you see her next week. Frank will pay you for them.'

'What shall I do with this one?' asked Ruth pathetically.

'You'll be able to find someone to take,' said Joyce with a

self-satisfied look on her face.

When it was time for dinner, to Ruth's delight, the day took on a familiar pattern. After the chicken and Christmas pudding, they listened to the King's speech. Jack and Stan settled in the armchairs and nodded off. Their snores brought hoots of laughter from the children, especially when Kay found a feather and kept putting it under their noses.

The evening was full of laughter and games. Kay went through some of the things the company had been rehearsing.

'I reckon we'll see you in the lead before long,' said Frank.

'If only,' said Kay, wringing her hands in a very theatrical way.

At the end of the evening Joyce and Ruth found themselves alone in the kitchen.

'I'm disappointed you won't be coming with us on Saturday.'

'I bet you are. At least you got rid of the ticket.'

'I know. I only hope Stan enjoys it. Joyce, please don't do anything stupid.'

'I've got to see him again. So whatever you say won't stop me.'

'I didn't think it would. But at least think about Frank.'

'Who's taking my name in vain?' asked Frank, coming into the kitchen. 'You ready, Joyce? Bobbie's fast asleep, and Alice is having trouble keeping her eyes open.'

'I'm just coming.'

'It's been a long day for them,' said Ruth.

They all gathered on the doorstep to wave them goodbye.

'Have a nice time on Saturday,' said Joyce, smiling as she climbed into Frank's car. Ruth knew that remark was made especially for her.

'And, Kay, I really hope you can get us the tickets for the Saturday after.'

'Shouldn't think that will be any trouble,' said Kay, waving them off.

'Quick, indoors,' said Shirley. 'It's freezing out here.'

Stan and Jack were sitting quietly talking when they all burst into the front room.

'Well, that's another Christmas over,' said Alan.

'We've got the New Year next,' said Kay.

'I wonder what 1947 will bring?' asked Ruth.

'Hope,' said her father. 'I saw in the paper that they're nationalizing the coal mines. So that's a start. It's health they've got to think about next.'

'That'll come,' said Alan.

'What are you going to do at New Year?' asked Kay.

'Same as usual,' said Alan. 'Nothing.'

'Oh I think you *should* do something. Make a change,' said Kay.

'But it's a Tuesday, I have to work the next day,' said Shirley.

'And so do I,' said Alan.

'It'll come in without us lot sitting up half the night,' said Jack.

'Well, I'll be having a good time. The cast all have a big party after the show,' said Kay.

'Do they?' said Alan. 'Well, no drinking. Just you remember you're under age, young lady.'

'I know, and I'm sure Miss Fox will be keeping her beady eye on all of us.'

'I hope so,' said Alan. 'Otherwise she'll have me to answer to.'

Shirley giggled. 'You sound like a Victorian father.'

'Theirs wasn't such a bad idea, keeping their daughters locked away till they got them married off,' said Jack.

'Is that what you did with your daughters then, Grandad?'

'Fat chance of that,' he laughed. 'Your grandmother would have let them out.'

Kay grinned. 'Do you want to get us married off then, Dad?'

'No, I don't. Well, not yet anyway.'

'That's a pity,' said Kay, plonking herself down on the sofa next to Shirley. 'Looks like you'll have to wait a little bit longer then, Shirl.'

'What's she talking about?' asked Alan, nodding his head towards Kay.

Shirley's face was crimson. 'I don't know. I'm going up. You coming, Kay?'

The girls kissed everyone goodnight and left the room.

Ruth was looking very thoughtfully at Shirley.

'I reckon that young Kay will bring you grief one of these days.'

'Don't say that, Dad.'

'What's she gonner do when this 'ere stint down in Margate finishes?'

'I don't know. She'll be going back to school till Easter, then she'll have to go out to work. I'm glad you're coming with us on Saturday, Stan,' said Ruth.

'It'll make a nice change. I ain't been to a pantomime since I was a kid.'

'I expect it'll be very noisy.'

'It'll be a bit of a laugh though.'

'Kay Bentley, I could thump you sometimes,' said Shirley as she pulled her nightgown over her head.

'Why? What have I done?' asked Kay as she sat on her sister's bed.

'You know why. Why didn't you say outright: By the way, Mum and Dad, did you know Shirley was seeing this boy from work. They go out every week.'

'Well, it's the truth. And I think you're daft not telling them.'

'I will – in me own good time. I reckon Mum knows.'

'How?'

'The way she looked at me.'

'She can certainly pick up on things.' Kay laughed. 'Here, do you reckon it's 'cos she got up to all sorts of things in the war?'

'No. Not our mum.'

'Kay,' said Shirley. 'Even though you had other girls in the room, did you miss me?'

'Yes, I did. It seemed really funny not having you around. I couldn't talk to the others like we do.'

'I'm glad you missed me. I really missed you. I don't have anyone to talk to here at home now.'

'I'll be home in six weeks.'

'I know, but what if you get asked to do another show?'

'I'll go.' She eagerly sat up higher. 'I tell you, Shirl, it's wonderful. I know that this is something I want to do. I really do.'

'Are there any nice boys in the show?'

'Some.'

'And?'

'I'm not interested.'

'You used to be. You was always hanging round the park with them.'

'Shirl, I just want to be on the stage. All I want is to see my name in lights. Nothing is going to get in the way of that.'

Shirley jumped out of bed and cuddled her sister. 'I'm so proud of you. I'll phone every Sunday.'

Kay swallowed hard. 'I'll look forward to that. You must try and come to see me. We have a matinée on a Wednesday.'

'I couldn't get down there in time. Not if I have to work in the morning.'

'The evening performance will be too late for you.'

Shirley clambered back into bed and pulled the blankets up round her neck. She smiled. 'Andrew can drive. Sometimes he borrows his father's car. Perhaps we could come down on a Wednesday and see the evening performance and then come home.'

'It's a long way, and it would be ever so late. I don't think Dad would let you.'

'I'll ask Andrew first and if he says yes, then I'll tackle Mum.'

'I'm dying to meet him.'

'It might be sooner than you think.' Shirley lay gazing up at the ceiling with a smile on her face. She wasn't ambitious like her sister. All she wanted out of life was to be with Andrew.

Chapter 28

'Will you be all right? We may not be home till late.' It was Saturday morning. Ruth was on her knees raking out the grate and Shirley was getting ready for work.

'I'll be fine. Don't worry.'

'I'm dreading the bad weather with all these coal shortages. If the coalman cuts me down any more, I don't know how we'll manage.'

'Mum, I might be going to the pictures straight from work.'

'That's good.'

Shirley was waiting for her usual question: Who with? But it didn't come. Ruth was too busy sorting through the ash for any reasonable bits of coal she could use again. 'Give Kay a big hug from me.'

Ruth looked up and smiled. 'Course I will.'

'I wish I was coming. Don't forget to get me a programme.'

'No, I won't. I'll bank up the fire with potato peelings. It should still be in when you get home, but go careful with the coal. Perhaps you can do yourself something on toast, there's a tin of fish roe in the cupboard. I'll leave it out.'

'Don't worry. You go and enjoy yourself.'

'We will. Mind you, I don't like the look of the weather.'

'Oh, Mum, stop worrying.'

If only she could. Ruth's mind was flitting from one problem to another, but it was Joyce that was worrying her most. *Where is she going with this Pete?*

Joyce was in the bedroom anxiously getting herself ready.

'You're getting a bit dolled up just to go out with Laura,' said Frank, sitting up in bed watching her.

'I think we're going to get something to eat out and I'm not sure where we're going.'

Frank laughed. 'Here, you're not going to meet your fancy man, are you?'

Joyce felt the colour start at her neck and rush up to cover her face. She laughed too, a silly giggle. 'Chance would be a fine thing.'

'What time will you be home?'

'I don't know. But it shouldn't be too late.'

'I'll take the kids out.'

'Where to?' Joyce quickly asked. The last thing she wanted was to bump into them with Pete on her arm.

'Don't know. I expect Alice will think of something.'

'I don't think that's such a good idea. Bobbie has got a bit of the snuffles. He might be coming down with a cold.'

'Don't worry. I'll wrap him up well.'

Joyce knew she couldn't insist they stay in. She felt very nervous, she knew that what she was doing was going to be very dangerous. Would Frank ever forgive her if he found out? 'Right. I'm off.'

'Is Laura coming here?'

'No. I'm going round to her. It ain't that far. I'll say goodbye to the kids.' She picked up her handbag, kissed his cheek and left the room. She gave the children a big hug and made her way down the stairs.

'Joyce?'

She froze when Frank called her name. She turned to see him standing at the top of the stairs.

'Have you got enough money?' he asked.

She let out a sigh of relief and nodded. 'Yes, thanks.'

'Well, have a good time.'

Despite the cold Joyce was glowing as she hurried to the Odeon cinema where she had arranged to meet Pete. She wasn't sure what they would do, but she wasn't worried any more. She just wanted to see him, to be with him without his sister and the kids around.

Her thoughts went to Ruth. She knew her sister was angry with her, but she didn't care. This could well be just a one-off. He might not want to see her again. He might not even turn up today.

'You're very quiet, Ruth,' said Alan as they made their way through the Kent countryside.

'I was just thinking how drab everything looks at this time of the year.'

'Well, let's hope it don't snow. It might make the place look pretty,' said her father, who was sitting in the front, 'but I don't want to have to help push this.'

Alan laughed. 'Fat lot of good you'd be.'

'How're your parents?' Ruth asked Stan, who was sitting next to her.

'Not bad.'

309

'They've got a nice little place,' said Jack.

'So you said.'

'Have you any idea where this theatre is?' asked Alan, quickly glancing over his shoulder.

'No, but it must be near the front. I'm sure someone will tell us the way.'

Slowly they drove down the streets and then Ruth caught sight of it. 'It's in that road you've just passed.'

Alan parked the car and they made their way to the foyer.

'Look,' said Ruth pointing at a poster. 'The Moon-beams.'

Alan laughed. 'I still reckon that's a daft name for a lot of kids prancing about.'

'Don't you let Kay hear you say that – she'd go mad.' Ruth stood admiring the poster. She wasn't interested who was in the lead, or what panto they were doing. All she knew and could see in her mind's eye was that one day her daughter's name would be in large letters on a poster.

The panto was loud and noisy. Kids were shouting and screaming, but when Kay was on stage everything else paled into insignificance for Ruth. Her daughter was wonderful, not once did she falter or miss a step. She shone out. Ruth had tears in her eyes as she watched with a pride that only a mother could feel. She wasn't surprised when her father and Stan told her they didn't want to return after the interval. Alan wanted to stay with them in the bar but Ruth had given him one of her looks, so he changed his mind.

At the end, when they finally managed to get out, they hurried round to the stage door. Alan was upset to see so many young men hanging about.

'See, I told you about all these stage door Johnnies,' said Jack.

'Don't talk daft, Dad. I expect they've got family in the show.' Ruth retorted, although she had to admit to herself that it was a bit off-putting to see all these young men in smart suits and Brylcreemed hair waiting for someone.

Inside they were ushered into a room. It was dirty, cold and damp. It smelled of drains and, amongst other things, unwashed bodies. Kay rushed in, the sound of her tap shoes echoing on the concrete floor. She hugged them one by one. 'Did you like it?'

'Not really my cup of tea,' said her grandfather.

'It is a bit loud,' Kay giggled.

'You were very good,' said Ruth. 'I was that proud of you.'

'Miss Fox said I'm one of the best students she's ever had.'

'You've still got all that muck on your face,' said Alan.

'I know. I'll take it off later.'

'It's a bit, well, not what I thought backstage would be like,' said Ruth, looking round.

'It is a bit rough, but I don't care. I love it and when I get out on that stage, I'm transported into another world.'

Stan laughed. 'You must admit, she's even beginning to talk like one of those actresses now.'

'Come, on,' said Alan. 'Let's take you out for a bite to eat.'

'OK. Just give me a bit of time to get ready. I'll have to tell Miss Fox, she don't allow us to go anywhere on our own.'

'Thank goodness for that,' said Ruth.

★   ★   ★

'I'm sorry I'm late,' said Pete. 'I've had a bit of a barney with Laura.'

'That's all right. What is it with sisters that they think they can rule your life?'

'You had trouble with yours?'

She nodded. 'Where shall we go?'

'I don't mind.'

'There's not a lot to do in Sutton.'

'We could always get the bus to Kingston or Hampton Court.'

'It's a bit cold for walking about. What about London?'

'That sounds great. We could go to one of the museums. It should be warmer in there.'

Museums weren't exactly what Joyce had in mind.

Pete was being a perfect gentleman: holding her elbow as they crossed the road; taking her hand and helping her on to the bus and train. When they sat on the underground train, he smiled and, taking hold of her hand, gently patted it. Joyce felt her heart leap. She knew she was being silly but couldn't help it. Frank had been the only man she'd ever been out with. This was something new and exciting.

When they got to the museum he put his arm round her waist as he explained things to her. Not that she was really interested. Just being here with him was all she wanted.

After a while they sat down and talked.

'I don't know how long I'll be in London. Now everything is moving with the new national Coal Board, I might have to spend a lot of time back up north, or even go to Wales. Joyce, would you be willing to come with me?'

She went to speak, but the words wouldn't come.

'I realize that this is a bit sudden, but I can honestly say I've never wanted to be with anyone like I want to with you.'

'But you've only seen me a few times. You don't know nothing about me.'

'What I've seen, I like.'

'I'm very flattered. But I've got two children.'

'I know that, remember? I would be willing to take them on.'

'Pete, you don't know what you're saying.' Joyce was getting worried. This wasn't what she'd been expecting. She thought he only wanted to take her out, to have some fun. She had no idea he was going to get so serious. Her thoughts went to Frank. 'I'm sorry, but I couldn't leave Frank.'

He looked disappointed. 'I was worried you might say that. Couldn't we spend a weekend together, just so we can get to know each other better?'

'I'm sorry, Pete. I don't think that would be such a good idea.'

'Joyce. I love you. I want to be with you.'

'Don't.' She looked around, embarrassed. At that moment they were alone. She was getting nervous. She didn't know how to handle a situation like this. 'Please, Pete. Don't spoil it. I like you and I do want to be with you but—'

He quickly pulled her to him and kissed her full on the mouth. She was breathless when they broke away, pleased that nobody had seen them.

'You've got lipstick round your mouth,' she whispered.

'Joyce, I've got to see you again.'

She took her hankie from her handbag and gently wiped the lipstick away.

He took hold of her hand and kissed it. 'I mean it, Joyce. I'm not going to take no for an answer.'

She was beginning to get a little alarmed at his tone of voice. 'This is all so sudden. I can't think about anything like that at the moment.'

'I'm not going to give you up.'

'But, Pete. I'm married.'

'That doesn't matter these days.'

'It does to me.' She stood up.

'I thought you were interested in me. I thought you liked me.'

'I do.' Joyce looked at her watch. 'I think we should start to make our way back home.'

'I'm hoping to be back next week. Let's meet next Saturday.'

He was standing very close to her; she could feel his body was almost touching hers. Part of her wanted to be in his arms, but her conscience told her it was wrong. She knew she was playing with fire. Could she extract herself from this before it got out of hand? 'I can't,' she said, at last finding her voice.

'Why not?'

'We're all going to see my niece in the pantomime down at Margate. I told you about her, remember?'

'Can't you get out of it?' There was a hint of irritation in his tone.

'No.' At the back of her mind she was beginning to regret she hadn't gone with Ruth today.

'I'll find out when I'm down this way again. Perhaps you

could get your sister to mind the kids and we can go off for the day. I could find somewhere for us to stay.'

Joyce didn't answer. She wanted to laugh at the thought of asking Ruth to have the children while she was having it away with Pete.

They slowly began to move on. Outside the museum Pete stopped and pulled Joyce to him. He kissed her again. This time it was an aggressive and hungry kiss.

'Cor, look at them,' shouted a boy.

'Go on, mate, enjoy yourself,' shouted another.

Joyce broke away and quickly walked off. Immediately, he was at her side.

'I wish you hadn't done that,' she said angrily.

'Why? I know you enjoyed it.'

She couldn't answer, because part of her agreed with him.

Chapter 29

Ruth was hoping she would see Joyce before they all went to Margate. She wanted to know what had happened when she had met Pete. Was she going to see him again? But it was Frank who came, alone, to collect the tickets to the pantomime.

'The kids will love it,' said Ruth.

'Too bloody noisy for me,' said her father.

Frank laughed. 'Alice can't wait. She's so excited.'

'It'll be right up her street,' said Jack. 'I bet her face will be a picture when she sees young Kay up there dancing about.'

'Kay was very good,' said Ruth. 'Did Joyce enjoy her day out with Laura?'

'She didn't say a lot about it, just that they went up West. They looked in the shops, then went to the pictures.'

'That was nice,' said Ruth.

'She said she couldn't buy anything. Moaned about not having any coupons.'

'I know the feeling,' said Ruth.

'She needed a change. It did her good to do something without the kids in tow.'

'Is she any happier lately?'

'She seems to be.'

'That's good,' said Ruth slowly. Deep down she was now even more worried. What had happened to make her sister so happy?

At the end of January, all the signs of it being a hard winter were really beginning to bite. There were many shortages and they were causing a lot of unrest. A strike by road hauliers brought about a massive meat shortage and the government had called in the army to help get the meat into the shops. The bad weather had even prompted some greengrocers to ration potatoes to two pounds per person. Everybody was very fed up.

'I saw in the paper that they've cut the meat ration to a shilling a week. How you gonner manage, love?' asked Alan.

'I don't know. Like everyone else does, I suppose.'

Alan threw a lump of wood that he'd managed to bring home from the building site on to the fire.

'Watch those sparks,' said Ruth, covering her legs. 'That last lot caught my stockings and I ain't got enough coupons for a new pair.'

'The landlord at the Beak told me they're cutting back on beer production; they need the grain for bread. It makes you wonder who won that bloody war,' said Jack when they were sitting discussing the developments after listening to the news on the radio.

'So, we're going to get two penn'oth of corned beef to eke out the meat ration. I suppose I'll be able to get a dinner out of that. When will it all end?'

'I dunno,' said her father. 'It's this snow I'm worried about. Those crutches slip and slide all over the place, and the last thing I want is to fall arse over head on me way to the pub and break the only leg I've got.'

'You know I'll always take you for a drink,' said Alan.

'I know, son. It's not so much the drink, it's me dominoes, and Ruth here won't like you being out all evening.'

'I can take you and then come and get you. Blimey, it's only a couple of streets away.'

'I should move in with Stan, he only lives next door.'

Ruth quickly looked up from her knitting. 'You're not thinking of doing that, are you?'

Jack laughed. 'I don't think so. I might have to help him with the washing-up. Besides, I don't reckon he can cook as good as you.'

Ruth looked at him suspiciously. She wondered. Had they been talking? Had Stan made any suggestions?

When Shirley came home, the open door sent a cold draught through the room. Her nose was red with the cold.

'I thought I'd freeze to death waiting in that bus queue. I don't know how our Kay can jump about on the stage in those silly little frocks,' she said, warming her hands in front of the fire even before she'd taken her gloves off.

'I'm surprised you bother to go to the pictures. Would have thought you'd want to get home,' said her father.

Shirley rubbed her cheeks. She would have stood naked in the middle of the Arctic if it meant she could be with Andrew. 'I had to go and see *The Best Years of Our Lives*. It was such a good film, it was worth it. I cried all the way through.'

'I thought you went to the pictures to cheer yourself up,' said her grandfather.

'No. I like a good cry.'

'Bloody daft if you ask me.'

Shirley sat on the floor in front of the fire. 'I wish I'd been able to go and see Kay.'

'I'm a bit worried about her coming home. They say we're gonner have snow,' said Alan.

'It shouldn't affect the trains, surely,' said Jack.

'It will if the railway blokes go on strike.'

'What's happening to this country?' asked Ruth. 'We all stood together in the war, now it seems that everybody's out to cause as much hardship as they can.'

'I think it's 'cos everybody's fed up with all the shortages,' said Alan. 'We thought we'd be better off when it was all over . . .'

'Just like the last lot,' said Jack. 'Thought it would be a land fit for heroes. Bloody politicians. I'm gonner go to bed.'

'Hang on a minute, Dad, I'll put your hot-water bottle in first,' said Ruth.

'Thanks, girl.'

The snow had been falling for days. Unsettling news of drifts blocking the roads reached Alan and Ruth as they paced up and down the platform, waiting for Kay's train. The pantomime's run was over.

'It's having a job to get through,' said a man in army uniform.

'I don't know why you bothered to come with me,' Alan said to Ruth, banging his hands together.

'I wanted to. I've really missed her.'

At last the train slowly edged its way into the station.

Kay looked frozen when she jumped down on to the platform and ran into her parents' arms. 'I'm so glad you've come to meet me. It was so cold on that train. Have you got the car?'

'Yes, but it'll take a while to get home with all this snow.'

'I know. It's ever so thick in the country. It looks really pretty though.'

Alan picked up her case. 'You gonner say goodbye to your mates?'

'I'll be seeing them all tomorrow when we go to class.'

'Why?' asked Alan.

'We've got to go and see Miss Fox.'

'Why?' Ruth echoed her husband.

'She thinks she's got us in another show.'

Alan put Kay's case back on the ground. 'Now wait a minute, young lady. I didn't think we'd be going through all this again.'

'Alan,' said Ruth, looking round. 'Don't make a fuss, not here. Let's wait till we get home before you . . .' She was going to say 'start', but didn't think that would be very wise.

As they slowly drove home, Alan had difficulty seeing through the windscreen. The wipers were having a job to take the snow away.

'I don't like this. I shan't be sorry to get home,' said Ruth, peering through the windscreen.

'We couldn't have any matinées last week because of the power cuts,' said Kay.

'I know. It's affecting so many people. A lot of the

320

children are being sent home from school when it gets dark. They can't do their lessons by candlelight.'

'How do you manage?' asked Kay. 'You can't do the sweeping in the dark.'

'We have to do it all in the morning as soon as it gets light. Shirley came home early the other afternoon. They didn't have any hot water or electric. She said they've been turning out cupboards and cleaning, but when it got dark they had to come home.'

'Bet she didn't like that, cleaning cupboards. I'm really looking forward to seeing her again. It seems ages. I really missed her.'

'She missed you as well,' said Ruth.

'It's Shirley,' shouted Kay when she heard the key being pulled through the letter box. She ran to meet her.

Ruth smiled as they stood in the passage hugging each other.

'You look so good,' said Shirley, standing back to admire her sister.

'And so do you. I love your hair.'

Shirley touched her hair. 'I've had it permed. It's the latest style. I really have missed you. D'you know that it was the first time I didn't see you on your birthday?'

'I know. It seemed ever so funny.'

'Did you get my card?'

Kay nodded. 'Yes thanks. I've got such a lot to tell you. The company was ever so nice. They got me a cake and I had lots of presents, make-up mostly.'

'How did they manage to get that?' asked Shirley.

'It seems you can get make-up when you're on the stage.

You have to go to a special place. I can let you have a lipstick.'

'That'll be great.' Shirley stopped and looked at her mother. 'I only wear it now and again.'

Ruth noticed Kay nudge Shirley. She went into the scullery. She knew they wanted to chat and their giggles would be heard all evening. It was such a lovely sound.

All the while they were sitting having their corned beef and potato pie, Kay talked.

'I know you don't want me to, but I must go and see Miss Fox tomorrow.'

'You're not going away again, are you?' asked Shirley.

With her mouth full of food, Kay looked at her father and shrugged.

'You know how I feel about this,' said Alan.

'Dad, just let me find out where it is first.'

'With all these power cuts I can't see how you'll be able to perform on a stage,' said Ruth.

'That's gonner be one of the problems,' said Kay. 'But not to worry. It won't last for ever.'

Ruth smiled. Her daughter was like a breath of fresh air.

Joyce was waiting for the postman. She knew that because of the bad weather the post had almost ground to a halt. She had had one letter from Pete; he didn't come on the Saturday, but told her he would be in Sutton very soon. She didn't write back, she didn't want him to think she cared, but she knew deep in her heart she did. She felt her life was in a turmoil and the more her sister and Laura told her to stop, the more she wanted to flirt with danger.

On the journeys backwards and forwards to school

Laura had been very offhand. Joyce knew Pete had told his sister he wanted to see her again and as she didn't approve, things were getting very strained between them.

'I don't know why you're so cross with me. It's not like I'm thinking of running away with him or anything,' said Joyce one morning as they battled their way through the snow. She was getting fed up with Laura's attitude.

'That's not what he told me.'

'Well, I'm telling you I wouldn't.'

'So why did you bother to go out with him?'

'I thought it would be exciting. I didn't think he would get so serious.'

'Well, he has. And he's very upset you turned him down. He's not going to give up, you know. I told him what a silly sod he was, but he reckons he's in love with you.'

Joyce looked in the pram at Bobbie. Although he was nearly four years old he was still in his big pram as Joyce found it easier back and forth in this weather. He was well wrapped up and with all the clothes and warm cosy hat he was wearing, hopefully he would be having trouble hearing, and not repeating all that Laura was saying. Next year he'd be starting school, then she would be on her own for a few hours.

'Joyce, don't break his heart.'

'Sorry, I wasn't listening.'

'Pete. After all he is my brother and I don't want to see him hurt.'

'That's up to him, he's a grown-up. I've told him how I feel.'

'At least with this weather he'll have a job to get down here.'

'I thought he was coming down *because* of his job?'

'He was. But now I think he's talking of giving it up so that he can move down here permanently.'

'What?'

'Didn't he tell you?'

'No.'

'Well, that's what he said the last time I heard from him.'

'Please, Laura, don't let him do that.'

'As you just said, he's a grown man. I can't tell him what to do.'

Joyce felt the tears sting her eyes. Her mind was in turmoil. She had to tell him that she didn't want him. She would never leave Frank, and she couldn't let Pete give up his job and home for a dream that she might have been willing to share.

Chapter 30

The following evening when Kay burst in from her dancing lessons she was very excited. 'Miss Fox wants us to be in a revue in Croydon. It's going to have a lot of top stars in it. The company only wants four of us, and I'm going to be one of them.'

'Who said so?' asked Alan.

'Miss Fox.'

'You're not going away again.'

'Croydon's not too far away,' said Ruth.

'What about her schooling?'

'Dad, I'm fourteen now. I shall be leaving at Easter.'

'But that's not now, is it? I don't want you to go and that's that.'

'Why?'

'It's not a proper job. Prancing about on a stage.'

'Mum!' Kay looked at her mother with pleading eyes.

'You know I don't hold with this, Ruth.'

Ruth stood up. She wasn't going to argue with him. Kay was fourteen and she felt that, up to a point, he should let her do what she wanted.

'Mum,' pleaded Kay. 'Can I? *Please*.'

Ruth didn't answer, just walked out into the scullery.

Kay quickly followed, anger filling her face. 'I don't care. Whatever Dad says, I'm not going to work in a shop. Or a factory.'

'What will you do if I can't get your father to say yes?'

'I don't know. Sit at home all day. That'll upset him.'

'Come on now, Kay, don't be silly.'

'Please, Mum. Try to make him understand.'

'I'll do my best. Will you have to have any new things?'

'I shall need another pair of tap shoes, black ones.'

'What about coupons? I don't have any spare.'

'We get an allowance, but I'll have to stay in lodgings.'

'I see. Do you know how much?'

Kay nodded. 'Miss Fox said it would be about seven and six a week. That's for everything, all our food and washing. We do get paid.'

'How much?'

'One pound ten shillings a week.'

'That's a lot of money for a fourteen-year-old. Much more than Shirley gets.'

'But I do have to buy make-up and stuff like that. And I like to have some money when I go out with the girls. Also, I have to spend some of it on – personal things. You know.' She blushed.

Ruth smiled; she knew what Kay was talking about. Now both her daughters were young women. 'I'll try to persuade your father, but I don't make any promises.'

Kay threw her arms round her mother's neck and kissed her. 'Thank you. If I can go, will Dad give me the money for my shoes?'

'Don't worry about that.' Ruth knew then that she

wouldn't be able to give up work just yet; she had a daughter to keep.

To everyone's relief, spring brought a thaw. Kay was performing in Croydon and Ruth collected her on Sunday mornings so that she could spend the day with them. Twice they went to the Saturday evening performance, then they brought her back home with them afterwards. The show went very well; Ruth was delighted to see that Kay seemed to be dancing better and better.

She was even more pleased when Joyce told her she had written to Pete telling him he mustn't give up everything to be with her, as she wasn't going to leave Frank.

Ruth's world had fallen into a pleasant routine as spring gave way to summer. When Kay's show moved to Bournemouth and they got the list of theatres the troupe would be performing at, Ruth knew she wouldn't be seeing very much of her daughter, but she vowed she would never let her, or Alan, know how much that distressed her. Shirley was also very upset and phoned her sister every Sunday morning to keep in touch.

The thing that lifted Shirley's spirits was that she was now officially going out with Andrew. When she'd received the invitation to his sister's wedding, she knew the time had come to tell her parents about him.

'It looks as if it's going to be a very posh do,' Ruth had said, admiring the card.

'They've got a lovely house. But I can't go till the evening as I'm working.'

'You say she is nineteen?'

Shirley nodded.

'What has her mother got to say about that?'

'Mrs Little's ever so pleased.'

'Well, I wouldn't be very pleased if one of you wanted to get married when you were only nineteen.'

'Why not?'

'It's much too young.'

'They've got a place to live and it's better than being apart.'

'That's a silly excuse. This Mrs Little must think a lot of you to invite you.'

'She does. I get on well with her, and I've been out with her son, Andrew,' Shirley said casually.

'What?' said Ruth. 'When?'

'We've been to the pictures.'

'You told me you went with someone from work.'

'That's right. Andrew works in soft furnishings.'

'That was a bit sneaky. You didn't say it was a boy.'

'You didn't ask.'

'How long has this been going on?'

'If you mean how long have I known Andrew: a long while. I met him in the canteen just after I started at Brown's, but we've only been going out since I went to his sister's birthday party and that's only to the pictures once a week straight from work.'

'You might have told us.'

'I didn't think Dad would approve.'

Ruth smiled. 'Well, he'll have to know now, that is if you intend to go on seeing him.'

'I do.'

'Sounds like you're treated as one of the family.'

Shirley blushed. 'I'd like to be.'

'I take it you really like him.'

'Yes. Yes, I do.'

'Well, in that case, we'd better meet him.'

'What will Dad say?'

'I don't suppose he'll be very happy at his girl growing up.'

'Will you tell him?'

Ruth nodded.

'Wait till he's in a good mood.'

'Has Kay seen this what's-his-name?'

'Andrew. No, but she knows all about him.'

It was Ruth's turn to smile. It was nice to know that the second generation of sisters was clinging together.

It took a while to convince Alan that Shirley had a boyfriend and wanted to bring him home. They went through all the familiar conversations they had had when Kay wanted to go on the stage. Ruth worried that Alan wouldn't approve on principle, and it wasn't until late summer that Andrew finally came to tea. Both Alan and Ruth instantly liked him. He was a shy, good-looking lad with a mop of dark hair; he was polite and Ruth noted that he never took his dark expressive eyes off Shirley.

After he left Ruth looked sad.

'What's the trouble?' asked Alan. 'Don't you like him?'

'Yes I do.'

'I'm glad he's not a yob. Seems like quite a nice boy.'

'I only hope Shirley don't leave us too soon.'

He laughed. 'What makes you say that?'

'It's bad enough only seeing Kay now and again, I

couldn't bear it if Shirley left home.'

'Why should she?'

'If she gets married.'

'What? She's not up the . . .'

'No.'

'Christ, he's the only boyfriend she's ever had!'

'That don't make any difference. You was the only one I went out with, remember.'

'I know, but you was much older. She's much too young. Has she said anything to you?'

'No, but the way she looks at him . . .'

'You read too many books. And I've got to give my permission till she's twenty-one, remember.'

Was it Princess Elizabeth's forthcoming marriage that was running through Ruth's mind? Was everybody thinking about weddings?

Ruth wasn't very happy over Christmas as Kay was away and couldn't get home. When Ruth questioned Joyce about Pete she said she'd only had a Christmas card from him, but Ruth wasn't one hundred per cent sure she was telling her the truth. Would Laura know? Would it be wrong for Ruth to interfere?

When winter gave way to spring Ruth's father dropped a bombshell. She was very shocked.

'Why?'

'I dunno. We just seem to hit it off all right.'

'That's no reason.'

'I'm sure you'll be glad to see the back of me.'

'No I won't. I thought you was happy here. We get on all right now – don't we?'

'Yes. Me and Stan have been talking about this for months.'

'You might have told me.'

'It took a while for me to come to this decision.'

Ruth sat in the chair. 'So when're you moving in with him?'

'Thought I'd leave it till the weekend, when Stan's home.'

'I'm really gonner miss you, Dad.'

'Christ, girl, I'm only round the corner.'

'I know, but it won't be the same. What with Kay being away, now you. It only wants Shirley to go then me and Alan will be like Darby and Joan.'

'It'll be a nice change for you two to be on your own. Ever since Alan came out of the army you've had someone round you.'

'I know, but that's what families are all about.'

'Anyway, it'll be nice for me to have someone to look after for a change.'

'How will you manage the shopping and all that?'

'We will, don't worry.'

'I will worry. You'll have Joyce thinking I've kicked you out.'

'No, she won't. Besides, I think she's got enough on her plate, she never looks very happy lately.'

'That's true.' Ruth was still worried that over these past months Joyce had been in contact with Pete. But she never mentioned it and when Ruth asked her she quickly brushed it aside.

Jack had moved in with Stan and appeared to be very happy. Summer had arrived and for the past year the New

Look was making young girls, after years of utility, very fashion conscious. With Ruth's help, as clothes were still on coupons, Shirley had to cut up some of her frocks to lengthen others. She wanted to be in fashion.

Ruth had carried on working as she liked to send Kay money to help her out. Kay had been away when she had her fifteenth birthday and continued to be in shows all over the country. Sometimes she was near enough to home and they could go and see her, then she would be with them all day Sunday. If she was at Worthing, Mrs Sharp would go with them to see the show. Ruth was pleased that both girls still wrote to her occasionally, and they all sent Christmas cards. Even Alan had had to admit that his daughter's determination to be a star one day was impressive, and had told Ruth and Kay he wasn't going to stand in her way.

Shirley had now blossomed and at the end of the year she would be seventeen. With her three-year apprenticeship almost behind her, she was now well on the way to being a fully fledged hairdresser. She had grown up so much and had officially been going steady with Andrew for over a year now.

Over the years everybody's lives had forged ahead, while Ruth still remained a cleaner at the school. Like her sister, she too wanted something more interesting and exciting in her life. But what? She'd had that crazy idea of having another baby, but that hadn't been the answer. Maybe a better job? Something stimulating that she would look forward to going to every day? Not a lover, that was for sure. She couldn't stand all the intrigue.

Ruth hadn't seen Joyce for a few weeks, although Frank often popped in with any news. Ruth had a strange feeling something was wrong with her, and decided to pay her a visit.

It was then that Joyce dropped another bombshell.

'What do you mean, you're going to leave Frank?'

'I told you. Pete wants me to go and live with him.'

'I thought you told me you hadn't seen him.'

'That was at Christmas. I sent him a card and then we exchanged letters, then he came to see Laura. We went out for a drink and that's when we decided we wanted to be together.'

'Just like that?'

Joyce was smiling. 'It was seeing him again. I did a lot of soul-searching, but yes, just like that.'

'Does Frank know?'

'Not yet.'

'What about Bobbie and Alice?'

'I'll take them with me, of course.'

Ruth had tears running down her face. 'I don't believe you're telling me this. Where will you go?'

'Pete's gonner get a house in London. He said the Coal Board was settling down and his particular job's moving down this way shortly, then he'll start looking.'

'Don't do it, Joyce. Don't throw everything away on a silly whim.'

'It's not a silly whim.'

Ruth held her sister close. 'Please, Joyce, think again.'

'Why are you crying, Auntie Ruth?' asked Alice, coming into the kitchen.

Ruth quickly brushed her tears away with her hand. 'It's nothing, love.'

'My mummy's been crying.'

Ruth looked up. 'She has? Why?'

'I don't know.'

'Go away and play,' said Joyce. 'I'll get you a biscuit.'

'And don't forget to get one for Bobbie.'

'Course. As if he would let me forget him.'

'Why have you been crying?' asked Ruth.

'It has taken me a while to make up my mind. It wasn't easy.'

'That's not the way it sounds.'

'You won't say nothing to Frank, will you?'

'I should say not, that's your job. When are you going to tell him?'

'When we've got everything settled.'

'That's a bit cruel.'

'Is it? Do you want him to stew for – I don't know, it could be weeks. He might even chuck me out.'

'He wouldn't do that. He thinks too much of the kids. What about their school?'

'They'll manage. After all, yours did all right, even with all the moves they had.'

'That was because of the war, remember?'

'Well. Yes. Pete has got to find us a nice house first. I'm not living in a hovel.'

Despite feeling wretched at the situation, Ruth wanted to smile. Joyce wasn't going to put up with any old place. Would this Pete be willing to give Joyce everything she wanted?

'By the way, how's Dad settling in?'

'I'm glad you can think of other people now and again. He's all right. In fact he seems very happy. The pub's only next door and he's been made captain of the domino team.

Stan and him go out quite a bit. All in all he's coping very well.'

'That's good,' Joyce said vaguely.

Ruth wanted to hit her sister. She was only thinking of herself.

'What has Laura got to say about all this?'

'I don't think Pete has told her everything.'

'I see.'

'No, you don't. We want to make sure everything is right before we go round shouting about it.'

'Are you sure you won't change your mind?'

Joyce bit her lip and shook her head.

'Haven't you got any doubts at all?'

Joyce didn't answer.

'This is not a game, Joyce.'

'I know.'

'Do you?' Ruth picked up her handbag. She was certain her sister was going to burst into tears. 'You will let me know where you finish up, won't you?'

'Course.'

'Driving home, tears blurred Ruth's vision. *Why does Joyce always think the grass is greener on the other side of the fence? And poor Bobbie and Alice, how will they react to having a new daddy? And what about Frank? This could really destroy him.* Ruth knew that he wouldn't let those kids go without a fight. 'Joyce,' she shouted out loud. 'For Christ's sake, come to your senses.'

Chapter 31

For weeks, every time Ruth saw Frank she felt guilty. She knew he hadn't any idea what was going on, since he always appeared so cheerful. How could her sister be so cruel and thoughtless?

Ruth knew she had to go and see Joyce again, so as soon as her sister's children had gone back to school after the summer holidays, Ruth called in on her.

Joyce appeared cheerful when she opened the door. 'This is a surprise.'

'You're still here then?'

'You'll know soon enough when I do go.'

'So, what's lover boy up to?'

'He's still trying to find us a place, but he can only come down here when he has to attend a meeting.'

'I thought he was moving down here.'

'He will be eventually, but at the moment all this is very new, the Coal Board has got a lot of work.'

'I see. He's not trying to put you off, is he?'

'No, he's not. In fact he wants me to divorce Frank.'

'What? On what grounds?'

'He said he'll sort that out.'

'Joyce, I don't like this. Are you sure you're not getting in too deep?'

'I know what I'm doing.'

'Do you? You don't know him. Why does he want a ready-made family?'

'Let's drop the subject, shall we? Where's Kay these days?'

'Birmingham.'

'Is she still enjoying it?'

'Yes.'

'Don't look at me like that. I'm not some kind of ogre.'

'Sorry, but I can't help it. All the years . . .'

'Ruth, stop it.'

'But why?'

'I can't spend the rest of my life wondering if there is anything better. I think it was the war that made me feel so unsettled.'

'That's a bloody load of rubbish, and you know it. You had Frank round you most of the time, and your kids. Think about me and what I went through. If anyone should be unsettled it's me.'

'Well, you had your moments.'

'Yes, and thank God I came to my senses.'

Joyce didn't answer; she busied herself at the sink.

'I only hope you come to your senses before long,' said Ruth quietly.

'Don't keep on, you're getting to be a right old moaner.'

'You've got a lot to shout about.' But Ruth knew she was upsetting her sister and decided to change the subject. 'How's Bobbie settling down at school?'

'He likes it. It seems funny being on my own.'

'I would have thought that's what you wanted. Don't you go out with Laura now?'

'No. We had a bust-up over Pete.'

'I'm not surprised.' For the first time in their lives, Ruth was finding it difficult to talk to her sister. Pete, and what he stood for, was coming between them and hanging over the conversation like a dark cloud. 'I'd better be going. Why don't you come over on Sunday? I think Andrew's coming to tea.'

'He's a nice lad. I can see Shirley marrying him.'

'She's a bit young, and he's the only boyfriend she's ever had.'

'Bit like me then.'

Ruth couldn't answer that. 'I'll ask Dad and Stan round. Your two don't see that much of Dad now.'

'OK. That'll make a nice change.'

'Joyce. If . . . if he . . .'

'Don't worry. He won't be here this weekend.'

On Sunday when Ruth saw her father playing with his two youngest grandchildren her heart felt it would break. *Will he see them if . . .* She tried not to let those thoughts enter her mind.

Although it was autumn, it was a lovely morning and Ruth had been shopping for the weekly rations. She decided to take the long way back through the park. She sat on a bench next to an old man. He turned.

'Hello. It's Ruth, ain't it?'

'Bill. Bill Clarke,' she said smiling. 'How are you?'

'Not too bad. Mustn't grumble. Miss the old wardens' post though.'

Ruth could see he didn't look very happy. 'Is everything all right?'

Slowly he shook his head and reached into the inside pocket of his jacket. He handed her a piece of paper. It was a death certificate.

'The wife.'

Ruth could see a tear running down his cheek. This was the man who had held the post together through the thick of the war; now he looked old and broken. 'I'm so very sorry, Bill.'

'Funny, ain't it? Went all through the war, and now she's gone.' He stood up. 'She was all I had. Take care of yourself, girl, and look after that family of yours. They're very precious.'

Ruth watched him walk away. She didn't ask him to stay, she could see he wanted to be alone with his grief. She hadn't even known he was married. She sat for a while and let her mind go back to the war. They had been heady days. All that had kept them going had been the thought of being a family again. How quickly they had forgotten that. She was lucky: her girls, Alan and her father were settled. Although she would like a more exciting job, it gave her some spending money; she didn't have to ask Alan for every penny. It was Joyce who was now causing her the most concern. Would she give up the idea of going off with Pete?

A couple of months later Ruth was sitting quietly in front of the fire, sewing. She had to get ready for work, but she didn't really fancy going out in the fog that seemed to have been closing in around them all day. She looked up when she heard the key being pulled through the letter box. That must be Alan. She stood up to go into the scullery to put the kettle on but stopped when the kitchen door opened. It wasn't Alan; it was Frank.

As soon as he walked in, she knew what had happened. He was glassy-eyed and his face ashen.

'What is it, Frank?'

'She's . . . She's gone. She's left me. She's taken the kids and gone off. What have I done?'

'Here, sit down.' Ruth led him to the armchair.

He buried his head in his hands and wept.

Ruth put a comforting arm round his shoulder, but it seemed so inadequate. What could she say? 'I'm so sorry, Frank.'

She looked up at the clock on the mantelpiece and after a quarter of an hour of Frank silently weeping and crying out, 'Why? Why?' she said, 'Look Frank, I'm sorry, but I must go to work.'

He raised his head. 'I'm sorry, Ruth. I shouldn't burden you with my troubles.'

She gave him a slight smile. 'That's what families are for. Look, you stay here till I get back. Have a bit of tea with us.' She hurried up the passage and put on her coat. She was dreading him realizing that she hadn't seemed shocked. 'I'll be as quick as I can,' she called out.

As soon as she arrived at the school she found Daisy working away and singing loudly.

'Hello there, girl. All right?' she said as soon as she set eyes on Ruth.

'Not really. Daisy, do you think you could help me to finish up early today? I wouldn't ask but we've got a bit of a problem at home.'

Daisy straightened up and, leaning on her broom, said, 'Course, girl. Nothing bad, I hope?'

'The worst. My sister's just up and left her husband and taken the kids with her. He's round at my place, in a bit of a state.'

'No. That is bad. Look, don't worry about this, you get off home.'

'I can't leave you to do it all.'

'I remember, and it wasn't all that long ago, you helped me out.'

'That was different, you was ill.'

'That's as may be, but I don't forget a favour. Now be off with you.'

Ruth kissed her cheek. 'Thanks.'

Daisy smiled and rubbed her cheek. 'Silly cow.'

Ruth pulled her headscarf tighter and made for the door. 'I hope it all works out,' called Daisy.

'So do I.'

Outside it was very quiet as the dense yellow fog swirled round. Suddenly Ruth was frightened she might lose her sense of direction. Alan should be home, but it would take Shirley a long while to walk as the buses had stopped.

Her thoughts went to Joyce. *Where is she? Why has she gone on such a dreadful day? What about the children? I hope the place is well aired.* Her thoughts seemed to echo loud in her head. *What can I say to Frank? Should I have warned him?*

Approaching the house, guilt almost overwhelmed Ruth. When she opened the front door she heard voices coming from the kitchen, and gave a sigh of relief. Thank goodness, Alan was home.

'It's really bad out there,' said Ruth, walking into the kitchen and taking off her headscarf. 'I'm a bit worried about Shirley, do you think she'll find her way home all right?'

Frank, who was sitting in front of the fire, looked at her. His eyes seemed to bore right into her. 'You knew, didn't you?'

She nodded. 'I'm so sorry.'

'How long has it been going on?' he demanded.

'I don't really know.'

Frank stood up. 'Come off it. I wasn't born yesterday. It must have been going on for months. Do you know who he is?'

'I've never met him.'

'Where's he come from? Where did she meet him?'

'Frank, take it easy,' said Alan.

Frank ignored him. 'Come on, Ruth, tell me the truth. Where is she?'

'I honestly don't know.'

'I don't believe you.'

'Now, come off it, Frank. If Ruth says she doesn't know . . .'

'Why wasn't she upset when I walked in? Go on, answer me that.' Frank took another cigarette from a packet that was on the mantelpiece, and Ruth could see by the dog ends in the grate that he'd already had quite a few.

'Can we sit and talk about this?' asked Ruth nervously.

'Sit down, Frank,' said Alan. 'I'll go and pour you out another cup of tea.'

'Got anything stronger?' asked Frank, sitting at the table.

'There's a drop of whisky.' Alan went to the sideboard

and took out a bottle. 'Do you want one, Ruth?'

She shook her head.

Alan came to the table and poured a small drop of whisky into two glasses. 'Cheers,' he said absent-mindedly.

'I ain't got nothing to cheer about.' Frank quickly downed his drink.

Ruth sat at the table. Where should she begin? How much should she tell him?

When she told him who Pete was Frank jumped up.

'I've met that little shit. He was at that Laura's when I went round there. They'd been out for the day. I was worried about her. If I'd known I'd have broken his sodding neck. So where are they?'

'Honestly, Frank, I don't know.'

'But you knew she was leaving me?'

'I did try to talk her out of it.'

Frank poured himself another whisky. 'Well, you didn't do a very good job, did you?'

They sat in silence for a while.

'I'd better start to get the tea. You are going to stay, Frank?'

'Might as well. Ain't got no family to go home to.'

Ruth wanted to hold him. She wanted to cry for him, and she wanted to kill her sister for bringing everyone so much unhappiness.

Pete put his arm round Joyce's slender waist. 'I can't believe we're actually here.'

She looked up at him and let him kiss her eager lips.

'I can't wait till the kids are in bed,' he said, nuzzling his face in her neck.

343

'Well, you'll just have to.'

'When are we going home?' asked Alice, walking into the room.

Joyce quickly jumped back from Pete. 'This is home now, darling. We're going to live here.'

'It's ever so foggy out there. Will Daddy be very late?'

'Daddy won't be coming here.'

'Why not?' Alice's eyes were wide open.

'Because Pete's going to look after us.'

'But what about Daddy?'

'Daddy will be fine on his own.'

Her face crumpled and tears slowly trickled down her cheeks. 'But I want my daddy.'

'Now come on, Alice. Don't be silly. We didn't see that much of Daddy, he was always at work. And we were on our own in the war, you only saw him now and again.'

'Is there going to be another war?'

'No. Come and show me where you've put your things in the lovely bedroom Pete's furnished for you.' Joyce took hold of Alice's hand and led her upstairs.

She pushed open a door to a room that if the sun had been shining would have been bright and airy. The furniture was lovely. With its kidney-shaped dressing table, it was definitely a little girl's room. For weeks she had admired Pete's choice of furnishings, even if they did seem expensive to her. As soon as the children had gone to school she had been here helping him move in the furniture, hang curtains and do a million and one other things that had been necessary. She had even seen about a new school. She was so excited, she felt like a young bride again, and although Pete had been desperate to make love, somehow Joyce had managed to stall him. She wasn't sure why. Was it fear of becoming pregnant? Or was it because she was ridden with this guilt thing?

Alice scowled at her mother. 'I don't like this room, it's dark.'

'That's because it's foggy outside.' Joyce went over to the window and looked out. She drew the curtains. 'You wait till the sun shines, it'll be lovely then. And you'll be able to see there's a park just across the road.' Joyce was a little upset that Alice wasn't a bit impressed. Why did it have to be such a miserable day? This fog was making everything feel damp and dirty. 'After we've had tea I'll read you a story.'

Alice didn't answer. She made her way downstairs to her brother. Thank goodness Bobbie seemed to be taking all this in his stride. Joyce knew she wouldn't be able to cope if both of them had been stroppy.

As soon as the children were in bed Joyce and Pete sat down together on the beautiful antique pale-green brocade sofa. Joyce ran her fingers over the material. She loved the feel of it. When she first saw it, like everything else he'd bought, she had told him it was the wrong colour and far too expensive to have when there were children around. But he was adamant: that's what he wanted. She did admire his taste. This was the first real home he'd ever had. Being a bachelor for so long and living in lodgings had enabled him to save as he had a good job.

She sat up very straight.

'Drink?' he asked.

She nodded. She felt like a schoolgirl on her first date, and needed some Dutch courage.

After a few drinks they nestled down in front of the fire and Joyce cuddled closer to him.

She knew that when the children were asleep they would make love. This was going to be the first time. She was nervous; she'd never had another man. When she had been with Pete she had asked him to wait till they were settled. What was he expecting? Would she be able to please him? He was such a kind, considerate man. Everything she'd asked for he'd provided. To take on her and her children proved that he must love her very much.

Gradually, as they kissed, they began passionately exploring each other's bodies. Suddenly there was a crash from upstairs. They broke away and Joyce quickly pulled on her blouse and ran up the stairs two at a time.

'It came from Alice's room,' she said when she reached the top.

As soon as Joyce opened the door, Alice scrambled under the bedclothes.

'What was that crash?'

Pete picked up a blackboard and easel. 'I think it was this,' he said standing it upright.

'Come on now, you should be asleep. This light should be off.'

Joyce went to turn the bedside light off when Alice sat up and screamed out, 'No. Leave it on.' Her eyes were red and puffy.

'What's wrong?' asked Joyce.

'Don't leave me, Mummy. I'm frightened,' she sobbed.

Joyce sat on the bed and Alice threw her arms round her mother and held her close. She was squeezing Joyce so hard it almost took her breath away. 'Don't be such a silly girl. I'll only be in the next room.'

'Where's he going to sleep?' Alice looked accusingly at Pete, who was standing in the doorway.

'Don't worry your pretty head about Pete, he'll be all right. Now come on, settle down.' Joyce untangled her daughter's arms.

'Please don't leave me.'

'Alice,' said Joyce, her voice rising. 'Lie down and go to sleep. You'll wake Bobbie.'

'I'll make a cup of tea,' said Pete, moving away.

'I won't sleep. I want to go home.'

Joyce wanted to cry. She knew the moment she'd been waiting for had gone. 'All right. I'll stay with you.'

As she lay next to Alice and turned out the light, all that was going through her mind was: *I have to be here for my daughter. There will be other nights, but will Pete be prepared to wait?*

Chapter 32

Ruth was worried. Two weeks had passed and she hadn't heard from her sister. Where was she? Frank was also waiting for news of his wife and children. He was going out of his mind with worry and looked dreadful. He spent so much time with them that Ruth was thinking of asking him to stay permanently, but when she suggested it to Alan, he said: No, Frank had to learn to stand on his own two feet. Ruth thought he was being a bit hard, but she could see his point. She hadn't told her father what had happened; deep down she was hoping that it would all be over soon and Joyce would return with the children. Those poor kids, they must be missing their dad. How were they reacting to a new home? Ruth looked at the presents she had bought them and let out a deep painful sigh. Christmas was in two weeks. Would Joyce get in touch with her before then?

A few days later, the Christmas card Ruth received from her sister brought tears to her eyes. Why hadn't she given her an address? The postmark said London, so she must be near. She also said she would write in the New Year. Ruth looked at the card. Surely she hadn't sent one to Frank like this, she couldn't be so cruel as to wish him a Merry Christmas.

Ruth had been upset months ago when Kay had told them she wouldn't be able to get home for the festivities for the second year running, and when her father told her he was going to spend it with Stan's parents, Ruth could see her world beginning to collapse. Christmas meant everything to her.

Shirley came home from work and found her mother crying.

When Ruth told her the reason she sat and held her mother's hand. 'You can't always have things go the way you want them to. Everything has to change.'

Ruth wiped her eyes. 'I know. But I love Christmas. I've always loved Christmas. That's what I used to look forward to throughout the war.'

'Everybody must do what they want.'

'I know. Don't tell me you want to be somewhere else.'

'No, course not.' Shirley hadn't the heart to tell her mother that Andrew was going to ask them if they could get engaged at Christmas. They were thinking of getting married next year. But could she? Not till she found out where her Auntie Joyce was.

Everybody was in bed very early on Christmas night. It had been a very long gloomy day, and Ruth was glad to see the back of it. She had felt sorry for Shirley, who'd had to put up with all the moaning, and as she had pointed out to her mother, was just as unhappy as Ruth that her sister wasn't with them. Ruth lay on her back.

'You all right, love?' asked Alan.

'No.' Tears ran into her ears. 'It was a bit of a disaster, wasn't it? There's Frank downstairs stoned out of his mind. He looks terrible.'

'The dinner was nice.' Alan held her tight. It upset him to hear her cry. 'Don't worry, I'm sure Joyce will be back soon.'

'Will she?'

'At least Frank had a shave. I've never seen him look so scruffy.'

'I offered to do his washing, but he said he could manage.' Ruth wiped her eyes. 'Where's all this going to end?'

'I wish I knew, love. I really do.' Alan turned on his back. 'I wonder how those kids are?'

This brought more tears from Ruth.

'I'm sorry, love.'

'This has been the most miserable Christmas of my life.'

'Let's hope your dad enjoyed himself. When you gonner tell him?'

'I don't know. I was waiting till I heard from her.'

'He thinks the world of those kids.'

'I know,' sniffed Ruth. 'Good job he don't see that much of them now they're both at school.'

'I would think our Kay's had a good time.'

'Shirley said she was enjoying herself when she phoned her. Why do people have to grow up?'

'Now come on, Ruth, you've still got Shirley at home.'

'But how long for?'

'What d'you mean?'

'Andrew's coming to tea tomorrow and I've got a funny feeling he's going to ask us if they can get engaged.'

Alan sat up. 'What makes you think that?'

'Woman's intuition, and Shirley did drop a hint. When I asked her what Andrew had bought her for Christmas, she said I was to wait and see on Boxing Day.'

'Oh bloody hell. I suppose this means more tears.'

In the darkness Ruth couldn't help but give a little smile. 'Do you realize that when Shirley does go, we'll be on our own for the first time since she was born?'

Alan snuggled up close to Ruth. 'Perhaps that wouldn't be such a bad idea after all.' He gave her a long lingering kiss that held the promise of something more exciting.

Alice had been standing on a chair looking out of the window since early morning. 'When is Daddy coming?' she'd asked every five minutes since opening her eyes.

She was cuddling her old worn teddy. The beautiful doll's pram and doll Pete had bought her had been discarded very quickly.

'I keep telling you. He's not.' Joyce was beginning to get angry with her daughter. Every morning since they had moved here there had been a wet bed to contend with. And then there were the scenes she had to put up with on the way to the school. Why wasn't Alice like Bobbie? She smiled down at her son, who was playing on the carpet with his new cars. He had accepted this move so readily. Joyce looked at the huge tree Pete had bought. It stood in the corner of the lofty room, covered with twinkling lights and decorations. He was trying so hard to please her and the children, but she was worried his patience might wear thin. Should she let Alice go back to Frank as Pete had suggested? But it would be his mother that would have her when she wasn't at school. Joyce was at her wits' end with her. Suddenly she decided she would write to Ruth and invite her here; her sister might have a solution to her problem.

Pete came into the room and put his arm round Joyce's waist. 'You were miles away. A penny for them,' he whispered in her ear.

She nestled against him. 'They're not worth a penny.'

Alice spun round. 'You mustn't do that to my mummy.'

'Alice,' said Joyce sternly. 'Behave. Pete has bought you lots of lovely things and you haven't even thanked him.'

'That's 'cos he took you away from my daddy.' She jumped down from the window and ran from the room in tears.

Joyce went to go after her, but Pete put out his hand.

'Leave her. Give her time.'

Joyce could see his jaw was clenched with anger. She was worried. How long would it be before Alice would accept him? And would he be prepared to wait that long? She prayed that this would all soon blow over and Pete and Alice would be happy together.

On Boxing Day Alan sat back and patted his stomach. 'That cake was excellent. I don't know how you managed to get hold of the ingredients.'

'Been saving the coupons for months.'

Andrew gave a little cough and stood up. Ruth could guess what was coming and was pleased Frank had gone to the pub instead of staying for tea. He would probably have said something hurtful.

Andrew cleared his throat and said in a very soft voice,

'Please, Mr and Mrs Bentley, would you give us permission to get engaged?'

Ruth didn't know whether to laugh or cry. He could be such a serious young man, but she did like him. And Shirley was looking up at him with so much love in her eyes.

Ruth looked across at Alan. 'Well, you're the head of the household.'

Alan laughed. 'Now that's something I never knew before. You're very young, Shirley.'

Ruth noted her daughter's mouth turn down.

'But I don't suppose you'll be thinking of getting married just yet,' Alan added, looking very pompous.

'We've got a lot of saving to do before we think of anything like that,' said Shirley.

'So will we if you want a white wedding,' added Ruth. She knew that any ideas she'd had about giving up work were once again put on hold.

'Does that mean we can?' asked Shirley.

Alan looked at all of them. 'I don't see why not.'

Shirley jumped up and hugged her mother, then she rushed round the table and did the same to her father.

Andrew took a ring box from his jacket pocket. He opened it to reveal a two diamond ring, which he put on Shirley's finger.

'That's a surprise, it fits,' said Alan.

Shirley laughed. 'Andrew bought it last week.' Her eyes were shining.

'You'll have to tell Kay,' said Ruth.

Shirley blushed. 'She knows.'

'Good job I said yes then.' Alan stood up. 'I think this calls for a drink.'

Shirley looked at the ring on her finger. 'I won't wear it to work. I don't want to get perm lotion on it.'

'What about your parents, Andrew? Do they know?' asked Ruth.

'Yes. And they approve. They like Shirley very much.'

Ruth smiled. At least Shirley and Andrew were happy, but Ruth knew she would always remember this Christmas for the other, less happy, reasons.

When the letter arrived in the New Year, Ruth read it over and over again. She was looking for some hint of how Joyce was feeling, but the note just said she wanted to meet Ruth in the West End next Friday. She also asked her not to mention this letter to Frank.

'So, what are you going to do?' asked Alan when Ruth told him.

'I'll go, of course. Don't tell Frank though, not till I've seen her.'

'Why won't she tell you where she's living?'

'I don't know.'

'Unless it's some run-down place.'

'No. I can't see that. Not Joyce.'

Ruth decided not to take the car. While she was sitting on the bus, she was trying hard to keep her anger under control. She had found it very difficult in the past week to keep this meeting from Frank.

When she reached the café, Ruth walked up and down outside waiting for her sister. She was cold. She looked at her watch. Joyce was late. That's it, she would go inside and have a cup of tea then she'd be off home again. Ruth pushed open the door and suddenly stopped. She was taken back to see her sister sitting at a table in the far corner of the room.

She stormed up to Joyce. 'What's your bloody game?' she said through clenched teeth. 'I'm half frozen to death hanging about outside for you and you're in here in the warm.' She sat down, banging the chair.

'I'm sorry. It's just that I was trying to get up courage to talk to you.'

'Since when have you had to have courage to talk to me?' Ruth snapped. She gave her order and continued. 'What's all this about? You know you ruined my and everyone else's Christmas, don't you?' Ruth was seething so much that she failed to notice her sister looked distressed. 'You've always been bloody selfish.'

'Have you finished?'

'No, not really. So is lover boy as good as you thought he'd be?'

'How's Frank?'

'He looks dreadful. He's been staying with us.' Ruth let her voice soften. 'He really misses the kids, you know.'

'I'm having a bit of trouble with Alice.'

'In what way?'

'She won't accept Pete at any price.'

'Well, whose fault's that?'

'All right, I know.' Joyce took a handkerchief from her bag and dabbed at her eyes. 'Pete's being really nice about it, but I don't know what to do.'

'Have you thought about going back home?'

'No.'

'Can Frank see the kids?'

Joyce looked up. 'You didn't tell him you was meeting me, did you?'

Ruth shook her head. 'No. Grant me with a bit of common. He would have followed me all the way here, then he would have probably knocked your block off, then he would have gone and found Pete, and killed him.'

'He's that angry?'

'He is that angry,' repeated Ruth.

'It's Alice I'm worried about. She's having a bad time.'

Ruth leant across and put her hand on her sister's. 'Please, Joyce. You've had your little fling, now come on home.'

Joyce quickly pulled her hand away and buried her head in her handkerchief. 'I can't,' she sobbed.

Ruth looked round. Fortunately they were in the corner and none of the other customers had noticed them. 'Why can't you?'

'I'm fond of Pete, and he loves me. Why can't we be in love with two people, like we love two children?'

'Don't ask me.'

'Bobbie accepts Pete.'

'He's a lot younger.'

Joyce wiped her eyes. 'I don't want to keep the children away from Frank.'

'So why don't you get him to meet you somewhere?'

'Where do you suggest?'

'The zoo, or somewhere like that.'

'What if Frank starts shouting and carrying on?'

'I don't know, that's a chance you'd have to take.'

'I was hoping I could bring them to your place.'

'What? I don't want any trouble.'

'Please, Ruth. Frank thinks the world of you and he wouldn't do anything to upset you. Besides, I'd feel a lot safer.'

Ruth looked at her sister. She could see she was really upset. 'Well . . . all right then. Mind you, I don't know what Alan's going to say.'

'Thanks.'

'So where are you living now?'

'Not too far away. It's a lovely house. When I'm really sure of myself and Pete I'll invite you over. When can we bring the children over?'

' "We"? Did you say "we"? Joyce, I'm not having him in my house.'

'Pete can bring me to the top of your road then wait for me somewhere else.'

'You've got all this planned.'

'We have talked about it. And we both think that this is the best thing.'

'Who for?'

'All of us, I hope.'

'I'm not so sure about that.'

'Please, Ruth.'

'Well, OK.'

'When shall we come?'

'You'd better make it a Saturday. Shirley won't be home. By the way, just in case you're interested, her and Andrew got engaged at Christmas.'

'That's lovely. I'm really pleased for them.'

'Makes me wonder if you'll still be around when they get married.'

'Please, we mustn't lose touch.'

'That all depends on you, Joyce.'

Chapter 33

'Hello, girl,' said her father as he hobbled in. 'Did you have a nice Christmas?' He eased himself into the armchair.

'Hello, Stan,' said Ruth, not answering her father's question.

'His parents really made me welcome. They've got a lovely little place. Felt like one of the family. Did me proud they did.'

'That's good.'

'So what about you?'

'It was very quiet without Kay.'

'I expect it was. Did the kids enjoy their presents?'

Ruth looked uncomfortable. Did she want to say anything in front of Stan? It was Sunday and Ruth had invited them to have a bit of dinner, her usual corned beef and potato pie. She had been waiting for them and Frank and Alan.

'Where's Alan?' asked Jack.

'He's up the pub with Frank.'

Her father looked round. 'So, where's Joyce and the kids?'

'Dad. I've got something to tell you.'

Her father's face went from joy to sadness in a second. 'Oh my God. Don't tell me, they've been in an accident.'

'No. No, it's nothing like that.' She glanced at Stan.

He shuffled his feet and looked uncomfortable. He could sense something wasn't right. 'Do you want me to go?'

'No. It's all right.' She gave him a smile. 'You're almost one of the family now. It's Joyce, Dad. She's left Frank.'

It took a second or two to sink in, then her father's face went red with anger. 'What?' he yelled. 'She's left Frank? And where's the kids?'

'She's taken them with her.'

'Is it another bloke?'

Ruth nodded.

'What's Frank doing about it?'

'We don't know where she's living.' Ruth wasn't telling anyone that Joyce was coming here in two weeks' time. She hadn't even told Alan.

'She wants her bloody arse kicked. He's always been too soft with her.'

The kitchen door opened and Frank and Alan walked in.

'Hello, son,' said Jack. 'I'm really sorry to hear about our Joyce buggering off.'

'Not nearly as sorry as me.'

'D'you know who the bloke is?'

'I did meet him once.' Frank looked at Ruth. He guessed Joyce had told her about that incident. 'I went round to see his sister as soon as I found out who it was. But she ain't heard from him. I think she's nearly as upset about it as we are.'

'I'm really gonner miss those kids,' said Jack. 'You'll let me know when you hear something, won't you?'

Frank nodded.

'Right. Dinner's ready,' said Ruth.

'Where's young Shirley?' asked her father.

'Right now I expect she's phoning Kay.'

'Where's *she* these days?'

'Still doing the pantomime in Bristol.'

'She certainly gets around.'

'I missed her over Christmas.'

'I expect you did. Will Shirley be back soon?'

'No. She's out with her young man. Her and Andrew got engaged at Christmas. They've gone over to his parents for dinner today.'

'So, we gonner hear wedding bells then, Ruth?' asked Stan.

'Not just yet, I hope. Weddings cost a few bob these days.'

'He's a nice lad. Let's hope it lasts when they get round to tying the knot.' Jack sat at the table. His good humour had evaporated. His daughter had let him down.

'I don't know why you're so worried,' said Alan as he watched Ruth go backwards and forwards to the front room to look out of the window.

'I thought Frank would be here by now, he knows Joyce should be here at one. You don't think he's up the road waiting to pounce on that Pete, do you?'

'Shouldn't think so.'

'Alan, go and look for him.'

'I'm not doing that. I'm not his keeper.'

'But if he catches him, he'll kill him.'

'I don't think so. Not in front of the kids.'

The key was being pulled through the letter box.

'Is that him?'

'I can't see through doors, can I?' said Alan.

'Frank!' said Ruth when he walked into the kitchen. 'You look very smart.'

'Thanks. Do you think she'll like these?' He was holding a bunch of roses.

'They're lovely.' Ruth was feeling very upset. Frank was really going to try hard to get his wife back.

'She did say one o'clock, didn't she?'

'Yes.'

'Do you want us to go out?' asked Alan.

'No. No, course not, this is your house.'

'Look, we'll go in the front room,' said Ruth.

'We can look after the kids if you like,' said Alan.

'No. Thanks all the same, but I want them with me all the time.'

'I've made some tea, and got some biscuits.'

'Thanks, Ruth.'

They all looked up when somebody banged on the knocker.

'I'll go,' said Ruth.

She opened the door to her sister. 'Why didn't you use the key?'

'I didn't like to.'

Ruth looked up and down the road. She was hoping that Pete's car was well out of sight.

'Don't worry. He's gone back home.'

'Hello, Auntie Ruth,' said Alice, rushing into Ruth's open arms.

'Hello, darling.' She held her close and kissed her.

'Alice,' called Frank.

'Daddy. *Daddy!*' She ran down the passage as fast as her legs could carry her.

Frank swept her up in his arms and buried his face in her neck. 'I've missed you so much.' There was a catch in his voice.

'Daddy. Daddy,' Bobbie echoed his sister, coming up to his father.

Frank bent down and picked him up.

'Hello, Frank,' said Joyce.

He only nodded a reply.

'Look, go into the kitchen. Me and Alan will be in the front room,' said Ruth.

'It's good to see you, Joyce,' said Alan, kissing her cheek.

'And you, Alan.'

Ruth watched Frank, with both his children in his arms, go into the kitchen. She said a silent prayer for them. She desperately wanted them to be back together again.

Ruth was glad she had made them go into the kitchen, which was warm and cosy, not like the front room. 'Do you think she'll come back?'

'Wouldn't like to say. She don't look all that happy.'

Ruth shuddered. 'It's so cold in here.'

'I should have lit the fire,' said Alan.

'I can't really spare the coal for two fires. I wonder what they're talking about.'

'Stop pacing and come and sit here.' Alan put his arm round Ruth's shoulders.

'I'll just pop upstairs and get a thicker cardigan.' As she went into the passage she could hear Frank's raised voice. She stood at the bottom of the stairs. Should she go and get the kids? Should they be listening to all this?

The kitchen door was suddenly flung open.

'Ruth,' shouted Frank. 'Come and see if you can talk some common sense into this silly cow.'

Alan came out of the front room. 'Frank, let me have the kids.'

'Alice, Bobbie, come in here with your Uncle Alan,' said Ruth.

Joyce stood pale-faced as she watched Bobbie trot up the passage. He was all grins, but Alice was clinging to her father's leg.

'I don't want to,' she sobbed. 'I don't want to leave my daddy.' She looked up at him. 'Please, Daddy, don't make me go and live with that Pete.'

The rage that filled Frank's face was frightening. He turned on Joyce. 'What's he done to her?'

'Nothing.' Joyce looked bewildered. 'He ain't done nothing.'

Frank took hold of Joyce's arms and shook her. 'If he's so much as shouted at her, I swear I'll kill him.'

'Frank,' shouted Ruth. 'Stop it.'

'Frank. Don't. You're hurting me,' cried Joyce.

'Frank, let her go,' said Alan.

Alice was crying and Bobbie was looking confused. He was holding Alan's hand very tight as he looked from one to the other.

Joyce began to cry. She rubbed the tops of her arms. 'It's not that I don't love you, Frank.'

'You've got a bloody funny way of showing it.'

'Look,' said Ruth. 'Let's all go back into the kitchen.'

Joyce turned and went through the door, but Frank took

his jacket off the hook in the passage. 'I ain't staying here. There ain't no point in trying to talk to her.'

'Please, Frank, calm down,' said Alan.

'Sorry, mate.' He picked up Alice. Tears were streaming down his face. 'I'm taking her with me.'

Alice put her arms round her father's neck and clung to him.

'*No. No*,' screamed Joyce. 'You can't take her.'

Frank roughly pushed Joyce to one side and opened the front door.

'Frank,' shouted Alan. 'You can't do that.'

'Who says so?'

Ruth picked up Bobbie who was crying. 'Come on, little feller.'

Joyce was running after Frank as he went to the gate. When he put Alice down to get his car keys from his pocket, Joyce pounced and, taking hold of her arm, dragged Alice back inside and slammed the door behind her. Alice threw herself on to the floor screaming and Frank was banging his fists on the front door.

'Open this bloody door,' he yelled.

Ruth was trying to comfort Alice.

Joyce, looking wildly from her daughter to the door, suddenly moved away and went into the kitchen. She picked up the flowers Frank had bought her and came back to the doorway.

It seemed like for ever before the banging stopped. They all stood in the passage waiting for the car to start. Alice's sobs were breaking Ruth's heart and she held her very close.

When they heard the sound of the engine, Joyce walked up the passage with the flowers.

'What are you going to do with them?' asked Ruth.

'Chuck 'em at him.' She opened the front door.

In a flash Alice broke away from Ruth and raced outside past her mother. 'Daddy. Daddy,' she cried out.

Frank didn't see her as he pulled away from the kerb. She must have been in a blind spot. Alice ran into the road, and straight into his car.

The sickening thump as she was hit and the screech of brakes turned Ruth's stomach. For a split second she stood paralysed. Then reality hit her and she ran to Alice who was lying very still. Blood was slowly seeping from her head and her leg was wedged under the car.

Frank was out of the car and sitting in the road cradling his daughter's head. His wailing was blood-curdling.

Joyce stood holding the roses, silently watching. It was like she wasn't there. She was in shock. Bobbie was holding onto her skirt, wide-eyed, calling out, 'Lis, Lis!' It was still his nickname for his sister.

'Quick, get a jack,' yelled Alan.

From nowhere a jack appeared, and Alan began feverishly pumping it up to get Alice out from under the car.

'I've phoned for an ambulance,' someone in the crowd that had quickly gathered said.

Slowly they eased Alice out. Ruth had fetched towels for her head. Frank was covered in blood, but refused to let go of Alice. Joyce sat next to him on the kerb. No words had left her colourless, trembling lips. Tears streamed down her face as she rocked back and forth.

A neighbour had taken Bobbie away.

Ruth and Alan stood watching the ambulance take Alice,

Frank and Joyce away. 'She won't die, will she?' Ruth asked softly.

'I shouldn't think so,' said Alan.

It was then the shock hit Ruth, and she began to shake uncontrollably.

Ruth had collected Bobbie from the neighbour and was giving him his tea. She wanted to try to keep things as calm as she could. 'I'll have to go round and tell Dad.'

'Wait till Shirley gets home, she'll look after Bobbie and we can go round together.'

'Good idea, Alan. Thanks.' Ruth tried to smile, but her face was taut. 'Poor Frank. He's never ever going to forgive himself.'

'It was an accident.'

'I know. Do you think Joyce will come back after this?'

Alan shrugged. 'Wouldn't like to say.'

'Can we phone the hospital?'

'I don't see why not. We'll do that on the way round to your dad.'

'We could pop in. They might let us see her.'

'No. Let them get her sorted out first. I should think that Frank and Joyce will come back here.'

'Perhaps you're right. I'm glad she's not going to be too far away. At least we'll all be able to go and see her. Even Dad, as the Royal Hospital is only up the road from him.'

Shirley dissolved into tears when she was told. 'I'll have to tell Kay.'

'Yes, but leave it till we have some news.'

'All right,' sniffed Shirley. 'I'll write her a long letter.'

'Look, if Frank and Joyce get back here before we do, make them a cup of tea.'

'Course.'

Ruth put on her coat. 'I'm really dreading this.'

'Come on,' said Alan. 'We don't want him hearing it from someone else, do we?'

She shook her head, then kissed Bobbie. 'Shirley will read you a story.'

'Are you going to get Lis?'

'I think she'll be away for a little while.'

His face puckered. 'Will you bring my mummy and daddy home?'

'I'm sure they'll be here as soon as they can,' said Ruth.

Shirley took his hand. 'Come upstairs with me and we'll see if there's anything we can find for you to play with.'

'Shirley,' said Ruth, suddenly remembering. 'All their Christmas presents are still here. They're at the bottom of my wardrobe.'

'Well that's it,' said Shirley. 'We've got lots to play with.'

Bobbie's sad face was suddenly wreathed in smiles.

'Don't worry, Mum, he'll be all right.'

Ruth and Alan left the house. This was something that had to be done, but neither of them wanted to do it.

Chapter 34

Jack Harris cried into his handkerchief. 'I'm sorry,' he said, wiping his eyes.

'Don't worry about it, Dad. We understand.'

'That poor kid. She must have been that desperate to go with Frank. When will you know how she is?'

'We phoned the hospital before we got here. They said she's still sedated.'

'Frank must be beside himself,' sniffed her father. 'I could murder that silly cow of a daughter. None of this would have happened if she'd been home looking after her old man.'

'Dad, it's no good blaming anyone. It was an accident. It's happened and we've all got to help them as much as we can.'

'I know you're right, girl, but I can't help it. I think the world of those kids.'

Ruth patted the back of her father's liver-spotted hand. 'I know you do.'

'What's gonner happen to young Bobbie?'

'I'll look after him till they get themselves sorted out. In fact I should be putting him to bed right now. Look, why don't you come round tomorrow. We should have a bit more news then. Will that be all right with you, Stan?'

'Yes. Ruth, I've got some pork chops we was going to have. Would you like them? You'll have to feed Frank and Joyce.'

'I can't take those. What about you two?'

Stan gave her a grin. 'One of the blokes at work has gone and bought a quarter of a pig, and he couldn't use it all. He's worried it might go off.'

'Not in this weather it won't.'

'There's only him and his missus.'

'I'll never say no to a bit extra. How many have you got?'

'Six.'

'*Six*!' repeated Ruth. 'I can't take all of them.'

'Course you can. We could come round and you could cook them for all of us.'

'Are you sure?'

'I'll just go and get them.'

Ruth stood at the window and watched Stan go into the yard. He turned and smiled at her, then took the pork chops from the meat safe that hung on the wall.

'He's a good lad,' said her father. 'Always bringing in bits and pieces he picks up at work. They're a double-dyed lot, those newspaper blokes.'

'Sounds good to me,' said Alan.

Ruth was relieved. At least she'd be able to give everybody a decent meal tomorrow. She looked round the room. It was sparsely furnished, as Stan's parents had taken some furniture when they moved to Brighton, and it needed a woman's touch, an ornament here and there. But she knew her father was happy here, and that's all that mattered.

'Thanks, Stan,' she said when he reappeared.

'It'll make a nice change from spam or corned beef and potato pie,' said Alan.

It was very quiet. Bobbie was fast asleep in Kay's bed, and Shirley had gone up to her room. Ruth and Alan were in the kitchen watching the coals make pictures in the fire, each with their own thoughts. They didn't speak; words weren't necessary. The radio was softly playing, but they weren't really listening to it.

'Look, why don't you go on up?' said Alan after a while. 'I'll stay down here for a bit longer.'

'They will come back here, won't they?'

'One of them will, there's Bobbie to collect, and don't forget Frank's car's outside.'

'Alan, you don't think anything's . . .' Ruth gave a little sob.

'No. They're just waiting till she's fine and they can leave her.'

'I hope so.' Ruth kissed Alan goodnight and made her way up to bed. As she lay down she knew sleep wasn't going to come easily. Her mind was going over and over the day's events.

'Ruth. Ruth.'

She sat up. 'What's happened?'

Alan was standing over her. 'They've just come back.'

Ruth grabbed her dressing gown and rushed down the stairs and into the kitchen. She threw herself at her sister and held her close. 'How is she?'

Joyce sat at the table. Her normally elegant blonde hair was a tangled mess and her face drawn and grey-looking.

Her blue eyes were red and puffy. Ruth glanced at Frank. He too looked terrible; he needed a shave and his shirt was covered with his daughter's blood. Alan brought in the teapot and began to pour out the tea.

'How is she?' Ruth asked again.

'She's conscious now. We wouldn't leave her till she'd come round,' said Frank. 'They've taken loads of X-rays. Her head's all right, just concussion. It's her foot they're worried about. They're talking about amputating.'

Ruth took a sharp breath. Tears filled her eyes and she grabbed her sister's hand. 'No,' she whispered. 'They can't.'

'They're going to try and see if it's possible to pin it, but they don't hold out much hope.' Frank was having difficulty speaking, it seemed the words were sticking in his throat. He shook his head. 'I'll never forgive myself.'

'It wasn't your fault,' said Ruth softly.

Joyce looked at Frank, then at her sister. 'How's Bobbie?' she asked.

'He's fine. He's sparko,' said Alan. 'He's been as good as gold. Shirley's been playing with him, and he's had all his Christmas presents.'

'Thanks,' said Joyce, her voice barely above a whisper.

'Joyce, would you like to stay here for dinner?'

She shook her head. 'No. Thanks all the same, Ruth, but I'd better be . . .' She stopped. 'Where can I go?' Tears ran down her sad face.

Frank rushed to her side and knelt next to her. 'Stay here with Ruth for now. We can go and see Alice this afternoon, then we can sort something out later.'

'I can't. I look such a mess.'

'Don't worry about that. We can find you something to wear,' said Ruth.

'All right. I feel so tired.'

Ruth looked at the clock. It was six in the morning. 'Go on up to our bed. I'll call you later.'

When she didn't argue, Ruth realized how exhausted Joyce was. There wasn't any fight left in her sister.

Frank stood up. 'Look, I'll go on home and get cleaned up.'

'But come back here for dinner.'

'What about your rations? I can't take your food.'

'Don't worry. Stan gave me some pork chops. But if you've got any veg I'd appreciate that.'

'Sounds great. Thanks, Ruth, and you, Alan, for everything.' He finished his tea and left.

Joyce was asleep as soon as her head touched the pillow.

Once again Ruth and Alan were alone in the kitchen with their thoughts and their fears.

It was nine o'clock when Shirley came down to find them in the kitchen. She was holding Bobbie by the hand. 'Has Auntie Joyce come back yet?'

Ruth nodded. 'Don't wake her, she's been up all night.'

'Where's Uncle Frank?'

'He's gone home, but he'll be back later.'

'How's Alice?'

'She's come round, but—' Ruth stopped. 'They may have to take her foot off.'

Shirley's mouth fell open. 'What? Why?'

'It's badly crushed.'

Tears left Shirley's eyes and slowly ran down her cheeks.

'That's terrible. She always wanted to be a dancer like Kay. What's Kay going to say about this?'

'I don't know, love. We've all got to help Alice as much as we can. And Joyce. And Frank.'

'What will Grandad say?'

'I don't know. I really don't know.'

'I should phone Kay later.'

'No, don't. Not till we know more.'

'She'll be worried.'

'Well just tell her Alice has had a little accident. Don't tell her everything. Not just yet.'

Ruth was shocked at how old and worn-out Joyce looked when she came downstairs.

'Dinner won't be long.'

'It smells good,' Joyce said, picking up her son and cuddling him.

'Look at all my new toys,' he said, struggling to get away.

'They're very nice,' said Joyce vaguely. 'I feel such a mess.'

'Go up and have a bath. I'll bring you in some clean clothes. Good job we're still the same size.'

'I've got some really nice bath salts you can use,' said Shirley.

'Thanks.'

They had decided not to mention the possibility of amputation to their father.

'He'll go mad,' said Ruth. 'Wait till we're a hundred per cent certain. I don't want him worrying unnecessarily.' Ruth was also worried he might lash out at Joyce as he blamed her for the accident.

Dinner was a very strained affair. Every word had to be

well thought out before it was spoken. Joyce was very tearful; Frank hardly spoke.

As soon as dinner was over Frank said he would take Joyce to the hospital. Much to Ruth's relief her sister didn't protest. Stan left, taking a reluctant Jack with him.

'Do you think they'll get together again?' asked Shirley when she was in the scullery helping her mother with the washing-up.

'I wouldn't like to say. But I hope so.'

'Does Auntie Joyce live very far away now?'

'I don't know. She's never said where she's living.'

'Bobbie was telling me about the house.'

'You mean you was pumping him to tell you about the house.'

Shirley smiled. 'Well. Yes.'

'And?'

'It sounds very grand. He had a lot of nice things for Christmas.'

'So this Pete must have a few bob then.'

'Seems like it. But Bobbie said he missed his dad and that Alice was always being naughty. She wet the bed and showed off when they had to go to school.'

'That don't sound like Alice.'

'How is she?' Ruth asked as soon as Frank and Joyce walked in.

'They still don't know about her foot. But she looks a bit better now they've cleaned her up,' said Frank.

'Can we go and see her?'

'Yes. Visiting in the children's ward is from three to four every day.'

'That all?' said Ruth.

'Afraid so. I'll try and get in, but it might not be every day,' said Frank.

'Don't worry, me and Dad can visit,' said Ruth.

'I can go on Wednesday,' said Shirley. 'Will it be all right if I take Andrew?'

'I think she'll like that. But they only allow two at a time round the bed.'

'What about you, Joyce?' asked Ruth. 'Will you be able to get there?'

All eyes turned to Joyce and waited. 'Yes. I can pick Bobbie up from school and get the bus.'

'You won't be able to take him in,' said Frank.

'I know that, don't I.' She was on the defensive.

'I'll try and get to the hospital every day so we can look after him between us,' said Ruth. 'Don't forget Dad said he'll be visiting as well.'

'At the weekend I might get Pete—'

Frank jumped to his feet and pointed his finger at his wife. 'Now you listen to me, girl. I don't want that bastard anywhere near my daughter. D'you hear?'

Joyce only nodded her reply.

'I'll go round and tell Dad tomorrow,' said Ruth, picking up the cups and saucers and taking them into the scullery.

Joyce was right behind her. She closed the door.

'Ruth, could you take me home?'

'I don't know. Where is home?'

'I'll tell you when we go.'

'When?'

'Later on. I must get me and Bobbie some clean clothes.'

'Do you want to come back here?'

'I don't know. I don't know how Pete will react to all of this.'

'Did he know you were coming to see Frank?'

'Yes. I'm worried he might think I've left him.'

'Is that such a problem?'

'Ruth, I don't honestly know. I don't know what to think at the moment. All I know is that I want my little girl well again and able to run about like everyone else. This is all my fault.' Once again her tears fell.

Ruth held her close. 'We can all make mistakes. Stay here for a few days. Just till we know how things are going. I'm sure she'll be all right.'

'How can you say that?' she sobbed. 'Look how losing his leg almost destroyed Dad!'

'He's an old man. He found it difficult to cope.'

'But she wanted so much to be a dancer like Kay.'

There was no answer to that. Ruth couldn't find any words that would comfort her sister.

Chapter 35

Ruth had waited till Frank had left before she told Alan she was taking Joyce to her new home. 'Is that wise?' he'd asked. But when she explained that Joyce needed to get clothes and tell Pete what had happened, he agreed.

'I want her to come back here, but she can't make up her mind.'

'Leave Bobbie here. That way she'll have to come back.'

'I may not be able to persuade her to do that.'

'She will if you work on her,' said Alan. 'She seems a bit bewildered.'

'That's the shock – and guilt.'

At first Joyce wanted to take Bobbie with her, but in the end Ruth managed to talk her into leaving him with Alan.

'He can put him to bed if he gets tired.'

'I don't know what Pete will say about all this,' Joyce said when she gave up the argument with her sister.

'Well, the sooner we get this sorted the better,' Ruth replied as they got into the car.

'I wish I'd learnt to drive. That way I'd be independent. I wouldn't have to rely on everybody taking me about.'

'You should learn.'

'I might have to if I've got to take a little crippled girl about.'

'Oh, Joyce. Don't say things like that.' Ruth looked at her sister. 'So where am I supposed to be going?'

'Go to Southwark, and I'll tell you from there.' Joyce sat back and closed her eyes.

Ruth was surprised when Joyce told her to stop at the top of Southwark Park Road. 'Andrew's parents live out this way.'

'Pete's is that house over there.'

'It's very big. So that's where you live.'

'I did. I'm not so sure now. Pete rents it.'

'I'll wait here.'

'No, come in. Pete's car's not here.'

Ruth looked around as Joyce opened the large front door and went in. She noted that the wide hall and staircase were nicely decorated. Her first reaction was that this must cost a few bob.

'Come in here. It's the dining room. I'll just pop upstairs for some clothes.' Joyce went to open the door, but the handle was pulled from her grasp as the door flew open.

'Where have you been? I've been worried sick about you!'

Joyce gasped in surprise. 'Pete. I didn't think you were home. I didn't see your car.'

'It's in the garage, the brakes need adjusting.'

'Pete, this is my sister, Ruth.'

'Hello,' he said sharply. 'I suppose you've come to take her away?'

Ruth looked from one to the other. 'No. No, it's not like that.'

'So what is it like then? Joyce, I've been to see Laura. She called round to your house but nobody was home. Where have you been all night?'

'At the hospital,' she said softly.

'What? Why?'

'Alice has had an accident. She was hit by a car.'

'Oh my darling. I'm so very sorry.' He went to hold her but Joyce stepped back. 'Is she badly hurt?'

Joyce nodded. 'I'm going to stay with Ruth, she lives near the hospital. I've just come back for some clothes and bits for Bobbie.'

'How bad is she?' asked Pete.

Joyce began to cry.

'It's her foot they're worried about. They may have to amputate as it was wedged under the car,' said Ruth.

'You poor darling.' Pete put his arm round Joyce's shoulder and pulled her to him. 'Do you know who did this?' he asked, stroking her hair.

Joyce nodded.

'Well I hope they string the bastard up.'

'It was Frank.'

'*Frank*,' he yelled out.

'It was an accident,' said Ruth quickly. 'He didn't stand a chance. Alice ran out after him.'

Pete guided Joyce to the beautiful dark wood polished table. In the middle stood a bowl of flowers on an off-white linen runner. Pete sat down holding Joyce's hand. Then he looked at Ruth. 'Come and sit down. You'd better tell me exactly what's happened.'

Ruth pulled a regency-striped chair out from under the table and sat opposite her sister. She filled in the details that

Joyce couldn't bring herself to describe.

'So what happens now?' asked Pete.

'I'm having them stay at my place till they know more,' said Ruth.

'Why can't you stay here, Joyce?'

'I've got to get back and forth to the hospital,' Joyce stammered.

'I can take you.'

'No, you have to go to work.'

'Well, phone me at work, any time, if you need me.'

'Joyce, I don't like to rush you, but time is getting on.'

'Yes. I'll just go up and get a few things.'

'I'll give you a hand,' said Pete, following her from the room.

Ruth sat and looked round. This was a very expensively furnished room; there wasn't any utility furniture here. Pete was a very good-looking young man. She could see how Joyce had been swept away. How would all this affect their future relationship? Poor Joyce. Ruth knew her sister didn't know which way to turn.

Joyce was very quiet all the way home. When they got to Lind Road, she went straight upstairs to be with Bobbie. Ruth told Alan what had happened. 'I don't know what she's going to do.'

'It's up to her now,' Alan said.

'Yes, I know. Let's hope she makes the right decision.'

On Wednesday, as Ruth and Joyce waited outside the ward door waiting for visiting time to start, Ruth looked at the nurses and auxiliaries dashing about. 'Now that's what I call a worthwhile job,' she mused.

'What?'

'Helping people.'

'I couldn't be a nurse.'

'No, I don't mean a nurse, but I wouldn't mind being one of those auxiliaries.'

'D'you know, I reckon that would suit you. You always want to look after people. Look at when Dad was in hospital, you used to help out then.'

'Yes, I did, and I enjoyed it.' As Ruth stood and watched, she knew she had to find out more about this: it could be a whole new world for her.

A nurse came and told Joyce the doctor wanted to see her. She gripped Ruth's arm, her face full of panic.

'Do you think they're going to tell me . . .' She looked round in terror. 'I wish Frank was here.'

Since Sunday, Joyce and Ruth had visited Alice every day, leaving Bobbie with his grandfather. Frank was always here to see his daughter; sometimes it was only for a short while, but today he wasn't to be seen.

'Where is he?' asked Joyce.

'He may have been held up. Do you want me to go in with you?'

Joyce nodded. 'Yes. Please. I can't go and see him on my own.'

'Tell them you'll see him after visiting. Christ, you only get an hour anyway.'

'You go.'

'All right.'

When Ruth returned to the ward she found Alice smiling and talking to her mother. Ruth gently kissed her bruised face. 'How are you today, poppet?'

'Look at the lovely long letter Kay has sent me. She told me to get well soon.'

'And you will. It's all right, Joyce. He'll see you after.'

'Daddy's late,' said Alice.

'What have they done to you today?' asked Joyce.

'Took a lot more pictures of my foot.'

Ruth looked down at the cage that stood over Alice's leg. *What will they tell Joyce? Please God, don't let it be something terrible.*

Frank managed to arrive in time to spend the last ten minutes of visiting time with his daughter. Ruth left him with Alice and Joyce and went to sit in her car.

She jumped out when she saw them emerge from the hospital. 'Well?' she asked.

For the first time in days Joyce gave a slight smile. 'They've decided to pin it.'

Ruth flung her arms round her sister and then Frank. Tears streamed down her face. 'Does that mean it's not so bad?'

'It's bad,' said Frank. 'But at least she'll still have a foot.'

'The doctor said it's going to take a long while to heal. She may have a limp,' sniffed Joyce. 'But she'll keep her foot.'

Ruth wanted to run and tell everybody immediately. 'We must go and tell Dad.' In the end they'd had to tell him about the awful possibility of amputation.

'You're supposed to be at work,' said Joyce, getting all practical.

'I'll drop you off at Dad's then I can go from there. I told them I may be late some days.'

'I can take Joyce to Jack's,' said Frank.

'No,' said Joyce quickly. 'You go back to work. I'll go with Ruth.'

'OK. Hope to see you tomorrow.' He kissed Ruth, then turned to Joyce, hesitating.

Joyce reached up and kissed his cheek. 'Bye, Frank.' She climbed into Ruth's car.

Ruth didn't make any comments.

Everybody was overjoyed at the news. Shirley wrote and told Kay everything. Jack was once again in tears.

At the end of the week, when they were driving back to Lind Road after visiting Alice, Joyce told Ruth that she had to go back to Pete.

'Why? You're all right at my place.'

'I know. But it's Bobbie. He should be at school.'

'So how are you going to get to see Alice every day?'

'Like I said. I'll catch the bus.'

Ruth knew Joyce had been phoning Pete and asked, 'What does Pete say?'

'He wants me back.'

'Do you want to go?'

'Course.'

Ruth wasn't sure if there was a slight hesitation in her voice. 'You're not thinking of going back to Frank then?'

Joyce didn't answer.

'He wants you back.'

'I know. We have talked about it.'

'So?'

'I can't let Pete down. He got that house for me.'

'Do you love him?'

'I don't know. I don't know anything any more.'

'What about when Alice comes out of hospital? Will Frank let her go with you?'

'He can't stop her.'

'But will she want to go with you? Remember, that's why she finished up in hospital.'

'Don't, Ruth. Don't make it any harder for me to make a decision.'

'It's only you who can do that. Think it over very carefully.'

'I have and I'm going to Pete's.'

It was coming up to Easter, and Alice was still in hospital. The doctors were very pleased with her progress, however. She was now hobbling around with her foot in plaster, using a walking stick.

Ruth was still concerned at the gap between Joyce and Frank. Although they sat and talked, and Ruth knew Frank had begged her to come back, she was still living with Pete. Ruth knew that he sometimes brought Joyce to the hospital, but never stayed around to meet Frank.

One afternoon, on her daily visit to the hospital, Ruth was playing with Bobbie, so Joyce could join Jack at Alice's bedside. When Joyce came out, Ruth would have a quick chance to go in to see Alice herself.

As Ruth stood at the window watching her father with his granddaughter, she suddenly felt certain that auxiliary nursing was the job she wanted to do. She'd had a long discussion with Alan, who had tried to point out all the pitfalls. Next week she had an appointment to see the Matron of the hospital.

'I can't get over Dad,' said Ruth when Joyce joined her. 'He's brilliant at encouraging Alice to walk – he seems to be able to make it fun for her.'

'He comes in nearly every day. He was telling Alice they could hobble about together when she goes home.'

'What are you going to do when Alice gets discharged?'

'I don't know.'

'Well, you'd better start thinking about it.'

'I will. So don't keep on.'

Ruth knew her sister was getting ruffled.

'I can't get over Dad,' Ruth repeated to Alan when she got home. 'He's got so much patience with Alice.'

'He told me he was worried things might go wrong and she'd have to lose that foot after all. By the way, there's another bag of goodies for Alice from Andrew's parents.'

Ruth looked in the bag. 'More sweets. I don't know where they get them from. We seem to be worse off since they come off ration. I looked at the queues the other day, but I didn't have time to join one.'

'Shirley said they have connections.'

'This is very kind of them. Last week it was books. I'll have to write and thank them.'

'You can do that on Sunday.'

'What? What have you done?'

Alan laughed. 'Don't look so worried. They've invited us over to tea on Easter Sunday.'

'Who said?'

'Shirley.'

Ruth smiled. 'That'll be rather nice. What on earth shall I wear?'

Shirley looked radiant when they got in the car to go to the Littles' for tea. 'I've told them all about you,' she said, straightening her skirt. 'They're really looking forward to meeting you.'

When they turned into Southwark Park Road Ruth pointed out the house that Joyce was living in. It was right at the other end of the long road.

'Do you want to call on her?' asked Alan.

'No thanks.'

Andrew was at the door to greet them. After all the usual formalities Ruth felt at home. She thanked them for the gifts they'd sent Alice and as they asked after her progress she could see they were genuinely sorry to hear about the accident. Ruth could also see they thought the world of Shirley.

'She's a very good hairdresser,' said Mrs Little.

Alan was having a deep conversation with Andrew's father about building.

When tea was finished Andrew stood up. 'Mr and Mrs Bentley, I know you think Shirley is too young to get married, but we've got the chance of a flat in September and we'd like to get married.'

Ruth sat with her mouth open.

Alan also sat speechless.

'Mum. Dad. What do you say?'

'I don't know,' said Ruth. 'I didn't expect this.'

'I'm sorry they've dropped this in your lap,' said Mr Little. 'But you see our daughter lives in the flat at the moment and she's having a baby.' He smiled. 'Our first grandchild. I've managed to get them a small but nice house, so the flat will become vacant. They can't have the house till September, so Andrew suggested that perhaps he and Shirley could have the flat then.'

'Please, Mum. Dad. Say yes.'

Alan looked at Ruth. 'Well, it does make a pleasant change to have a bit of good news. What do you say, Ruth?'

'I don't know.'

To Ruth's surprise, Alan said, 'I can't see any objection.'

Shirley threw her arms round her father's neck and hugged him. 'Thanks.'

'I promise I will look after her,' said Andrew.

'You'd better,' said Alan.

The thought that was racing through Ruth's mind was: *How much will all this cost?* These people had expensive taste, so they must have expensive friends.

'You're very quiet about it, Mum,' said Shirley.

'Will you be having a white wedding?'

Shirley held Andrew's hand. 'Yes. And we want all the trimmings.'

'Don't worry,' said Mrs Little. 'I know what they cost, and we insist that we help you out.'

Ruth smiled. 'So how long have we got?'

'Six months,' said Shirley. 'I want Kay and Alice to be my bridesmaids.'

'Alice?' said Ruth.

'I think that's a lovely idea,' said Mrs Little.

'But will she be able to walk down the aisle without a stick by then?' asked Ruth.

'I would think she'll burst to do that,' said Shirley. 'It might even help her.'

Toasts were drunk and Ruth was swept along on the wave of euphoria.

'Wait till Kay knows all about this,' said Ruth.

Shirley turned to Andrew and smiled. 'She already does.'

'What? What if we'd said no?' said Alan.

Shirley grinned and shrugged. 'Kay suggested Gretna Green.'

'Kay would,' said Alan.

'I can't wait to meet your other daughter,' said Mrs Little.

'She's really great, Mum,' said Andrew. 'You should see her on the stage, she's wonderful. If I hadn't already fallen for Shirley, I could easily fall for Kay.'

'Looks like you're going to have your work cut out keeping her under control,' laughed Mr Little.

'I gave that up when she left home,' said Alan.

'She's a good girl,' said Ruth. 'And determined to be a star.'

'But she will never outshine you,' said Andrew to Shirley.

Chapter 36

Everybody was very pleased with Shirley's news and were looking forward to a wedding in the family. But Ruth was soon distracted by the thought of the interview at the hospital.

When the morning came she dressed carefully and tried to remain calm.

A Miss Baker was sitting behind her desk looking upright and efficient. 'Mrs Bentley, you do understand what your duties will consist of, don't you?'

'I think so. I've been visiting my niece for a good number of weeks now and it was watching the auxiliaries that made me realize that this was a job I would enjoy.'

'It's not all giving out tea and arranging flowers. I do like you to help my nurses with bedpans and the like.'

'I understand.'

Miss Baker was thumbing through some papers. 'I see you would prefer part time.'

'If that's possible.'

'Just so long as you're flexible. You state you were in the Civil Defence. You must have witnessed some pretty awful things.'

'Yes, I did.'

Matron looked up and smiled. 'Well, at least I won't have you fainting at the first drop of blood.'

Ruth began to relax. 'Does that mean . . .?'

'You can start next month. I'll be in touch as to your hours. You will be in with our older ladies. They can be a bit demanding, but I'm sure you'll manage.' She stood up and held out her hand.

Ruth wanted to jump up and down with joy. But: 'Thank you,' she said politely and left.

Daisy was very upset when she heard the news that Ruth would be leaving, but wished her well.

'Are you sure you want to do this sort of work?' asked Alan. 'You know you don't have to go to work, not now.'

'I know, but with neither the girls nor Dad living here, I reckon I'd soon get fed up.'

'Just as long as you're sure.'

'It's got to be better than cleaning. And don't forget there's a wedding to pay for.'

Ruth was to go to Brown's to look at wedding dresses Shirley had picked out for her mother's comments. Everything was beginning to gather momentum and Ruth knew the time before her daughter left home would fly past.

As well as planning the big day, Shirley and Andrew talked excitedly about furniture and what they would need for the flat.

Alice had been thrilled when Shirley asked her to be a bridesmaid. But a few days later Joyce said she'd found her crying as she didn't think she would be able to walk down the aisle without her stick.

Kay wrote and told them she was going to be in a show in London, and that she was going to have time off for the wedding. It seemed that everything was falling into place.

Ruth's biggest worry was still Joyce. She was looking very sad and tired despite the fact that Alice was making such progress with her walking. Although Frank was at the hospital most days, Ruth somehow kept missing him. When she asked after him, Joyce became very jumpy, and said he seemed fine, but she didn't know what he was up to these days.

Ruth was glad to see her father spending most visiting times with Alice. It gave him a purpose and strengthened the unusual bond between the two.

A week later when Ruth hadn't been able to get to the hospital, she called in on him from work to find out how Alice was. He looked somehow different.

'Like me new glasses?' He waggled them up and down.

'When did you get those?'

'On this new National Health. I tell you, girl, it's a godsend. I'm getting me teeth done next week.'

Ruth laughed. 'So how's Alice coming along?'

His face clouded over. 'I'm a bit worried about her. I've been trying to think of a way to help her.'

'And?'

'I've tried all sorts. It's Frank she's upset about.'

'I know. I can't understand him. He don't come to see her nearly so much.'

'He told me Joyce said she was getting fed up with him hanging around.'

'That's bloody daft. She can't say that. Alice is his daughter. You wait till I see that sister of mine.'

'You know Frank wants her back?'

'I know. He thinks the world of her and those kids. What does she want out of life? What's got into her?'

'I upset her the other day. I gave her a right mouthful.'

'Oh Dad, you didn't?'

'I did. I told her she should put her kids and her husband first, instead of sodding about with this bloke. Always said she wants her arse kicked. I'd do it, but I'd fall over.' He laughed.

'You want to see if they'll give you a new leg on this National Health.'

'Now, girl, don't start on that. Just 'cos you're gonner work at the hospital. D'you know what ward you'll be on?'

'I'll be with the old ladies, just part time. I'll be doing things like the flowers and emptying bedpans.'

'That don't sound that good.'

'I think it'll be great – chatting to all the old dears.'

'I tell you, girl, I'm really worried about that little 'un. She's really down about this wedding.'

'I know. I wish there was something we could do.'

'And I wish there was something we could do about this business with Joyce. That's not helping that poor little mite either.'

Ruth had never seen her father look so angry. 'It's Frank I'm worried about,' she said. 'Whenever I see him, he seems to be in a dream. I think he has one too many sometimes.'

'That ain't gonner do him a lot of good.'

'I know. I'm going to try and talk some sense into Joyce. Someone has to.'

A week later Ruth cornered Joyce and told her just how

concerned she was about Frank.

'I don't know why. He ain't been to see Alice for two days.'

'Dad said you told him not to come.'

'I didn't say that. I told him I didn't want him hanging around outside, trying to talk to me.'

'He's still your husband, for Christ's sake. Sometimes, Joyce, I could thump you.'

'Thanks.'

'Don't you worry about him?'

'I've got enough to worry about without him.'

'There must be something wrong. He wouldn't miss seeing Alice. He loves her and Bobbie, and you.'

'Don't keep on.'

'D'you want me to go to your house and see if he's all right?'

'Please yourself.'

Ruth was angry with her sister. Why was she taking this cavalier attitude towards Frank?

The following week Ruth started at the hospital. Although she was anxious, the nurses and patients soon put her at ease. She was so happy as she drove home despite the rain coming down in torrents. The rhythm of the windscreen wipers lulled her, sending her thoughts off in all directions. She was still worried about Frank and decided to ask Alan to go with her at the weekend to see him. Suddenly a man stepped into the road. She slammed on the brakes. The car skidded to a standstill. She sat for a moment in shock, then anger took over and she jumped out of the car. The man, who was sitting on the kerb, had his back to her.

'What the bloody hell do you think you're . . .' She couldn't believe her eyes when he turned. It was Frank.

She stepped back. The rain was running down his dirty face, and it looked like he hadn't shaved for days. This wasn't the Frank she knew. He staggered to his feet and was reeling backwards and forwards.

'Frank. Frank. It's me. Ruth.'

'Hello, Ruth.' He had a silly grin on his face. The smell of whisky almost knocked her over.

'Where are you off to?' asked Ruth.

'I was gonner see my little girl, but my dear wife said I mustn't.'

'You're too late now. Come on. I'm taking you back to my place.'

'No. Don't bother. I'll be all right.'

'No, you won't. Come on, get in the car.'

'No. Joyce don't love me any more.'

'Is that what this is all about?'

'She told me I won't see my kids. She's letting that bastard take them to live in Wales.'

'What?' She let her grip go and Frank slid to the ground. 'She never told me that.'

Frank was now crying. 'I love her, Ruth. I can't live without her and me kids. What am I gonner do?'

'I don't know. Come on, let's get you back home.' With a lot of struggling and pushing she got him on to the back seat and drove him home. All the while she prayed he wouldn't be sick.

'Ruth, I'm really worried about Frank,' said Alan after he'd put him to bed.

'I know. If it's not one thing it's another with my bloody family. I've had enough. I thought Shirley's wedding would make everybody happy.' Ruth began to cry.

'It will. Come on, love. Cheer up.'

'How can I if Joyce is off to Wales and . . .'

Alan held Ruth close. 'Now come on. You've got your new job and we've got to think about Shirley. We mustn't let anyone spoil her big day.'

'My sister's the one to blame for all of this. Alice wouldn't be in hospital if it wasn't for her.'

'Calm down, Ruth. I've told Frank he can stay here for a few days.'

'What about his job?'

'I phoned the bloke he works with. He said business was very slow at the moment and he would hold the fort.'

The following day Ruth took Frank to the hospital. She was on duty till later that day; once she was off she waited outside for her sister. As soon as she saw Joyce, she leapt at her like a tiger. 'What the hell are you playing at? I found Frank in the gutter.'

Joyce looked shocked. 'What?'

'Did you tell him you're going to Wales and taking the kids?'

Joyce's eyes were wide open. 'Ruth, where's Frank now?'

'Inside, visiting Alice.'

'I'd better go in.'

'Leave it a moment. Dad's in there as well. I want to talk to you.'

Joyce looked panicky. 'Is Frank all right?'

'Do you care?'

'I still love him.'

'Well you've got a bloody funny way of showing it.'

Joyce let her tears run. 'He is still the father of my kids.'

'So why are you taking them out of his life?'

'I'm not.'

'What?'

'I'm not going to Wales. I'm leaving Pete.'

'What? Why?'

'I think the novelty wore off a while ago. Things haven't been the same since the accident. I never really understood how much Frank loves the kids. I can't keep him from them. I've told Pete.'

'So why did you say that about Wales to poor Frank?'

'I don't know. To hurt him, I suppose. I'm so mixed up.'

'Don't you think you've hurt him enough? You are a silly cow. So what happens now?'

'I'm so unhappy. Could I come and stay with you for a while?'

'My place is getting more like a hotel every day. Come on, let's go and see Alice.'

Ruth went in and Frank came out. Through the glass Ruth could see them talking.

'You should hear this one,' said her father, inclining his head towards Alice. 'She's just told her father she's not coming home till they both go back to Sutton.'

'Good for you, poppet. And d'you know something? It might even work.'

Ruth's job was all she could wish for. The ladies, despite what Matron had said, were lovely and always ready for a laugh. The camaraderie on the ward reminded her of the good times when she was in the Civil Defence. Even emptying bedpans could have its funny moments. For the first time in years she looked forward to going to work.

'What do you think, Mum?' asked Shirley when she walked round her bedroom in a beautiful wedding dress.

'I think it's lovely. Thank goodness we don't need clothing coupons now.'

'And don't forget I get staff discount. Kay's coming to the store as soon as she can, to look at some dresses. D'you know, they're even going to let me bring a couple home for Alice to try on.'

Ruth smiled. She knew Shirley was trying hard to make Alice happy, but Alice was still having trouble walking and sometimes she would just sit in the chair drawing, and not talk to anyone till her daddy came in.

In the end it was July before Alice came home and Joyce moved back in with Frank. Ruth knew it was going to be a strained relationship, but it was a start; they were together even though Joyce had told her they weren't sharing a bedroom.

Joyce also said she didn't think Pete had been overly concerned at her moving out. He'd been so busy with his work and his move that he didn't have a lot of time for her.

'It would have been like history repeating itself. Once he's in Wales his job will be taking him all over the country. I was always fed up with Frank being out; it would have been the same with Pete.'

'Things are different now, though,' said Ruth. 'What did

Pete do with all that lovely furniture?'

'It was nice, wasn't it? He took a lot with him to Wales. Cost him a few bob, but he seemed to have plenty.'

'Will you miss him?'

Joyce smiled. 'In some ways. But I always felt I had to be on my best behaviour with him.'

'Not like being with Frank then?'

'No. I can be meself with him. But it's going to take a while. I'll always be grateful to Frank for taking me back.'

'It might take time for him to forgive and forget.'

'Like a lot of things that have happened to all of us over the years, he'll never forget. And Ruth, the grass *isn't* greener on the other side of the fence.'

Ruth hugged her sister. 'Thank God for that.'

The months sped by and the plans for the great day were well in hand. The Littles had arranged and were paying half towards the wedding breakfast. It was to be held in a hotel. The invitations had been printed and sent off. Kay had been home and Shirley had bought her and Alice's dresses.

They were having a dress rehearsal in Shirley's bedroom. Their laughter could be heard all over the house. It took Ruth's breath away when she saw how lovely Kay was. The blue of the dress almost matched her eyes. 'I love that sweetheart neckline.'

'I only hope Andrew knows what a gem he's got in my sister,' said Kay.

'Just as long as you don't steal the show,' said Shirley.

Kay pranced round the room. 'I won't.'

Ruth found it hard not to cry when she saw Alice trying on her pretty blue dress.

'It's nice and long,' she said, wobbling. 'I'll try ever so hard not to fall over without my stick.'

'We know you will,' said Kay. 'You hold my hand and we'll fall over together.'

Alice giggled. 'Grandad has been helping me walk.'

'Has he now,' said Ruth.

As she walked down the stairs, leaving the girls to giggle and gossip together, Ruth was finding it hard to keep her emotions under control. Saturday was going to be her daughter's wedding day. Ruth prayed she would find happiness.

Chapter 37

The first thing Ruth had done at seven o'clock this morning was to throw back the curtains and look out of the window. She had breathed a sigh of relief when she saw the sun was shining.

Seven hours later she was standing silently in the doorway of her eldest daughter's bedroom, looking at Shirley. She looked a picture, from the garland of orange blossom in the hair that framed her lovely face, to her figure-hugging, white satin brocade gown. Tears filled Ruth's eyes.

'You all right, Mum?' Shirley asked, looking up.

She nodded. 'You look so beautiful.'

'What about me, Auntie Ruth?' Alice came hobbling towards her. Her little white ballet shoe had been cut away to fit her deformed foot.

'You look beautiful as well.'

Joyce, who had been fixing Alice's flowered headdress, beamed with pride at her daughter.

'And what about me?' asked Kay, giving a twirl.

Ruth and Joyce laughed. Kay, tall and slim, with her blonde hair in a perfect pageboy style, looked every inch the star she was destined to be – a real beauty. Ruth was a bit worried that she might steal Shirley's glory, but then Shirley wouldn't mind, she was so generous and she loved her sister.

'You all look lovely,' said Ruth.

'All brides look beautiful, and my sister far outshines them all,' said Kay.

'Your mother looks good as well,' said Joyce.

'Come on, you lot,' said Alan, peering round the door. 'When you've finished this mutual admiration society meeting, it's time to go.'

Ruth gave Shirley a quick peck on the cheek. 'See you in church.'

'That's if she don't change her mind,' said Kay, bubbling over with laughter again.

'I'll kill her if she does,' said Alan.

'No chance of that,' said Shirley, her eyes shining. She bent down to peer in the mirror, adjusting her veil over her dark bouncy curls.

At the top of the stairs, Alan took hold of Ruth's arm.

'What is it? Are you all right?' she asked anxiously.

He nodded, smiled and looked at her. 'Thank you.'

'What for?'

'For giving me two such lovely daughters.'

Ruth swallowed hard. She gently touched his face. 'Thank you. But I didn't do it on my own. See you in church.'

'She seems so young to get married,' said Joyce, taking hold of her daughter's hand and helping her down the stairs.

Kay stood behind them holding up the long skirt on her

powder-blue dress. 'They make a smashing couple,' she said softly.

'He thinks the world of her,' said Ruth. 'He's a good lad. I couldn't wish for a better son-in-law.'

'What about you, Kay? Got any boyfriends?' asked Joyce, looking over her shoulder.

'No. We don't get a lot of free time. Occasionally we go out in a crowd with some of the boys in the chorus, but we're all too busy with our careers.'

At the bottom of the stairs Alice picked up her flowers. 'I love this little basket,' she said, sniffing the blooms.

'All the flowers are lovely. You're lovely – in fact everything and everyone is lovely,' said Ruth, laughing and throwing her arms in the air.

'Blimey,' said Joyce. 'You been at that bottle?'

'Not yet. I want to keep me faculties about me.'

'You won't be able to say that when you've had a few.'

'I shan't care then!'

They opened the front door and Ruth smiled at the neighbours who had gathered outside.

'Like the hat,' one shouted out.

Both Ruth and Joyce giggled as they touched their hats. Ruth's was a pale blue picture hat to match her dress and jacket, while Joyce was wearing a navy boater that went with her suit.

'You look a right belter, young Kay,' the man who lived along the road shouted, giving her a nod.

Kay smiled. 'Thanks, Mr Jackson.'

'And don't you look a picture, young Alice,' said one of the neighbours who had helped at the accident. 'It's lovely to see you on your feet again.'

Alice smiled. 'Thank you.'

The two bridesmaids, together with Ruth and Joyce, got into the car for the short journey to the church.

'Mum, have you got the horseshoe and confetti?' asked Kay.

Ruth nodded.

'I hope Bobbie's behaving himself,' said Joyce anxiously.

'He'll be OK with Frank.' Ruth knew that since they had become a family again, Frank hardly let the children out of his sight.

'I know. That's what worries me. Those two can wrap him round their little fingers.'

'Bobbie'll be all right. He's a big boy now.'

'I'll always worry after what . . .'

Alice touched her mother's hand. 'You know Daddy didn't mean it.'

'We all know that, love,' said Ruth. But she also knew that terrible day and how it had come about would be on Joyce's conscience for many years to come.

'I only hope he don't give him sweets,' said Joyce. 'I don't want him sick in the church.'

'Don't even think about that,' said Ruth as the car came to a halt.

'Auntie Ruth, will Grandad be in the church?'

'Course, love.'

'He's been helping me to walk.'

'I know – you told me.'

Alice grinned and looked at Kay who patted her hand.

Andrew came up to them as soon as he saw them. He kissed Ruth's cheek. 'How is she? Is she nervous?'

'I don't think so,' said Ruth. 'Are you?'

'Petrified.'

'He's worried to death about the ring, the service, saying his words – you name it and he's worrying about it,' said Tom, his best man, as he put a comforting arm on Andrew's shoulder.

Kay laughed and in a loud whisper said, 'Just think about tonight, lover boy. I bet you won't be nervous then.'

'That's what I keep telling him,' said Tom.

The vicar came out and asked them if they would like to make their way inside.

Joyce gave a final tweak to her daughter's dress. 'Now, you are sure you're going to be all right?'

'Yes, Mum. I told you me and Grandad have been working hard at the hospital.'

'Well, only if you're sure, and if you get tired come and sit with me.'

'Don't worry, Auntie Joyce, I'll look after her.'

Alice looked up at Kay with loving eyes.

'You're a very brave girl,' said Kay.

As Ruth walked down the aisle she looked over the pews for all their friends.

Lucy and Charlie, who was holding Simon, grinned at her, and dear Mrs Graham who was next to Charlie held on to her grandson's hand.

Ruth gave Mrs Sharp a beaming smile. She was so pleased to see her. They had kept in touch over the years, even if sometimes it was only a Christmas card.

Dear Daisy gave Ruth a nod. She had left her headscarf at home and was wearing a truly fetching little navy hat that matched her coat. She was dabbing at her eyes, so thrilled at being invited.

Frank sat with Bobbie next to him. Bobbie gave both his mother and Ruth a shy little wave. Joyce sat next to them. Just for a second a cloud tinged Ruth's happiness. She couldn't help being concerned about her sister, who seemed to have aged since the accident. She now had a permanently worried look on her face.

But Ruth had to concentrate on Shirley and Andrew today. There were his mother and father. They looked very smart. They were such nice people, and had given their only son so much help to get them started on married life. His sister, who was very pregnant, was glowing with happiness next to them.

There were only a few staff from Brown's; most of their friends and workmates were coming that evening.

Her father was in the front row. Behind him was Stan. She took her place next to Jack and waited for her daughter.

Today was 3 September 1949. Ten years ago her daughters had been sent away and everybody's lives had been thrown into turmoil. War had been declared. Ruth reflected on all that had happened over this past decade. She had lost her mother. Her father had lost his leg and refused to wear his false one. Alan had come through the war without a scratch, physically, although she'd never really discovered what had happened to give him those horrible nightmares when he first came home. Her sister had been to hell and back with Frank and Alice's accident. Despite all the problems she and Alan thought they might have had with their youngest daughter, Kay was now beginning to make a name for herself on the stage. And at last she herself had found a job she loved. No, on the whole, things weren't too bad at all now.

The organ struck up 'Here Comes The Bride' and everybody stood up.

Ruth turned to look at her daughter walking slowly and serenely down the aisle on her father's arm. Alan was so proud; she noted that he looked repeatedly at his daughter and gently patted her hand. Shirley looked so beautiful. Ruth was having difficulty seeing through her tears.

When Shirley drew level with her mother she smiled and, leaning forward, gave her grandfather an extra big grin. Ruth quickly turned and looked at him. He was standing up without his crutches. Where were they? He was wearing his false leg. Ruth looked back at Stan, who gave her a wink.

Alice was doing her best to walk without a limp. She was smiling and holding on to Kay's hand.

The service began, and Ruth lost herself in the beautiful familiar words. Andrew and Shirley made their responses firmly, their love shining from their eyes. Yes, Ruth was sure they would find happiness together.

At the end of the service they went into the vestry to sign the register.

Ruth waited to see how her father was going to manage. She couldn't believe how well he walked.

'Dad. How long have you . . .?'

He laughed. 'We wanted it to be a surprise, didn't we, love?' he said, taking hold of Alice's hand.

Alice nodded and on her face was the widest grin ever.

'But . . . How . . .'

'When I used to visit her in the hospital, they told me it would help her if I wore my leg. They got me a new one and so, after visiting times, we learnt how to walk together.'

'Alice and Grandad told me, and we were all sworn to secrecy,' said Kay.

'Well, that was just in case I didn't quite make it. But I'd promised Alice here, and Shirley. I didn't want to let them down.'

'You all knew and didn't tell me? I can't believe you managed to keep this a secret,' said Ruth.

'We was all a bit worried when you started work at the hospital, we thought someone might spill the beans.'

'Did you know about this, Alan?' asked Ruth.

He nodded. 'Yes. Shirley told me in the car.'

Joyce was openly crying. 'I didn't know,' she sniffed.

'Are you sure you're all right, Dad?' asked Ruth.

He nodded and kissed Ruth's cheek. 'This is the best day of me life.'

'And mine,' Ruth whispered. This September day, like that one ten years ago, would live in her memory for ever, but this time it would be for far better and far happier reasons.

Hannah of Hope Street

Dee Williams

Hannah Miller is a young girl who has had to grow up fast. Since the death of her parents she has taken responsibility for her sister Alice, determined to provide her with the love and stability they've both been denied. But when a violent incident with her bullying guardian finds the girls cold and hungry on the teeming streets of East London, Hannah realises she is out of her depth. She has little option but to accept the help of the strange old woman Maudie whose ramshackle home at the end of Rotherhithe's bustling Hope Street, Hannah soon realises, is a den of young thieves.

Alice loves their new life – the companionship of the lively household and the gruff affection of the enigmatic, warm-hearted Maudie. But, despite the fact that she is growing increasingly fond of Jack, one of the most long-standing of Maudie's brood, Hannah can never be happy living outside the law. As she battles for respectability Hannah begins to see she is creating an ever-widening rift between herself and those she loves most dearly – one of whom, as the Great War approaches, might be taken from her for good . . .

0 7472 4605 X

headline

Sorrows and Smiles

Dee Williams

Pam King can't understand why her gran, Ivy, has forbidden her to see Robbie Bennetti. Robbie's a lovely lad, much less dangerous than Lu Cappa, who's always giving her the eye when he's out in his ice-cream van. Pam has to ask her best friend Jill to cover for her while she's out with Robbie.

When Ivy finds out Pam's been lying, she makes sure the relationship with Robbie is over for good. Then Jill falls in love, and it's loneliness that makes Pam accept a date with Lu Cappa. Before she knows it, they're married.

Even then, Pam knows Lu's still jealous of Robbie. And she can't help wondering what Lu's up to when he's out with his shifty brother. When Robbie comes back into their lives, it could be the last straw. One thing's for sure: until everyone starts to tell the truth, there will be as many sorrows as smiles in Pam's marriage . . .

Acclaim for Dee Williams:

'A brilliant story, full of surprises' *Woman's Realm*

'Flowers with the atmosphere of old Docklands London' *Manchester Evening News*

'A moving story full of intrigue and suspense, and peopled with a warm and appealing cast of characters . . . an excellent treat' *Bolton Evening News*

0 7472 6109 1

headline